Incendiary

IN A KILT

Other Books by Anna Durand

Dangerous in a Kilt (Hot Scots, Book One)
Wicked in a Kilt (Hot Scots, Book Two)
Scandalous in a Kilt (Hot Scots, Book Three)
The MacTaggart Brothers Trilogy (Hot Scots, Books 1-3)
Gift-Wrapped in a Kilt (Hot Scots, Book Four)
Notorious in a Kilt (Hot Scots, Book Five)
Insatiable in a Kilt (Hot Scots, Book Six)
Lethal in a Kilt (Hot Scots, Book Seven)
Irresistible in a Kilt (Hot Scots, Book Eight)
Devastating in a Kilt (Hot Scots, Book Nine)
Spellbound in a Kilt (Hot Scots, Book Ten)
Relentless in a Kilt (Hot Scots, Book Eleven)
Wild in a Kilt (Hot Scots, Book Thirteen)
Lachlan in a Kilt (The Ballachulish Trilogy, Book One)
Aidan in a Kilt (The Ballachulish Trilogy, Book Two)
Rory in a Kilt (The Ballachulish Trilogy, Book Three)
The American Wives Club (A Hot Brits/Hot Scots/Au Naturel Crossover Book)
Brit vs. Scot (A Hot Brits/Hot Scots/Au Naturel Crossover Book)
One Hot Chance (Hot Brits, Book One)
One Hot Roomie (Hot Brits, Book Two)
One Hot Crush (Hot Brits, Book Three)
The Dixon Brothers Trilogy (Hot Brits, Books 1-3)
One Hot Escape (Hot Brits, Book Four)
One Hot Rumor (Hot Brits, Book Five)
One Hot Christmas (Hot Brits, Book Six)
One Hot Scandal (Hot Brits, Book Seven)
One Hot Deal (Hot Brits, Book Eight)
One Hot Favor (Hot Brits, Book Nine)
Natural Obsession (Au Naturel Nights, Book One)
Natural Passion (Au Naturel Trilogy, Book One)
Natural Impulse (Au Naturel Trilogy, Book Two)
Natural Satisfaction (Au Naturel Trilogy, Book Three)
Fired Up (standalone romance)
Echo Power (Echo Power Trilogy, Book One)
Echo Dominion (Echo Power Trilogy, Book Two)
Echo Unbound (Echo Power Trilogy, Book Three)
The Janusite Trilogy (Undercover Elementals, Books 1-3)
Obsidian Hunger (Undercover Elementals, Book Four)
Unbidden Hunger (Undercover Elementals, Book Five)
The Thirteenth Fae (Undercover Elementals, Book Six)
Cyneric (Undercover Elementals, Book Seven)

Incendiary IN A KILT

Hot Scots, Book Twelve

ANNA DURAND

JACOBSVILLE BOOKS JB MARIETTA, OHIO

INCENDIARY IN A KILT
Copyright © 2022 by Lisa A. Shiel
All rights reserved.

ISBN: 978-1-958144-00-8 (paperback)
ISBN: 979-8-9852412-9-7 (ebook)
ISBN:978-1-958144-01-5 (audiobook)

Manufactured in the United States.

Jacobsville Books
www.JacobsvilleBooks.com

Publisher's Cataloging-in-Publication Data
provided by Five Rainbows Cataloging Services

Names: Durand, Anna, author.
Title: Incendiary in a kilt / Anna Durand.
Description: Marietta, OH : Jacobsville Books, 2022. | Series: Hot Scots, bk. 12.
Identifiers: ISBN 978-1-958144-00-8 (paperback) | ISBN 979-8-9852412-9-7 (ebook) | ISBN 978-1-958144-01-5 (audiobook)
Subjects: LCSH: Treasure troves--Fiction. | Grand Canyon (Ariz.)--Fiction. | Man-woman relationships--Fiction. | Scots--Fiction. | Americans--Fiction. | Romance fiction. | BISAC: FICTION / Romance / Contemporary. | FICTION / Romance / Romantic Comedy. | FICTION / Romance / Action & Adventure. | GSAFD: Love stories.
Classification: LCC PS3604.U724 R53 2022 (print) | LCC PS3604.U724 (ebook) | DDC 813/.6--dc23.

Chapter One

Errol

I thrust and pull back, thrust and pull back, over and over while sweat dribbles down my temples and my breathing grows heavier. Thrust, release. Thrust, release. I'm getting into the rhythm of my movements, and a long, low groan resonates in my chest as I approach that climactic moment when all the tension will evaporate. One last push… I groan and relax. There's nothing more invigorating in the world than that final thrust.

My cousin Magnus takes the dumbbells from me and sets them on the floor. "Are ye done yet? Or do ye mean to exercise until ye collapse? We both know why you're suddenly obsessed with working out, Errol."

"It has nothing to do with Ashley Hartman."

All right, maybe there is one thing more invigorating than exercise. But I will never shag that barmy woman. Donnae care how many times the lass knocks on my door and tries to seduce me into going on a pointless mission to find a treasure that doesn't exist.

Magnus locks his arms over his chest. "If you want to have a poke with Ashley, just do it. You'll feel more relaxed afterward."

"I will not touch her. The lass is off her head." I sit up, straddling the exercise bench. "She wants me to hunt for a phantom. The Grand Canyon treasure doesn't exist."

"So ye mean to go on behaving like Rory used to before he met Emery."

"No." I flash him a scowl. "I will never growl or snarl at Ashley. I willnae shag her either. So stop harassing me, Magnus. No barmy treasure hunt, no sex with an American lass, I'm done."

"But you love a good adventure."

Sighing, I push up off the bench and stretch. "Maybe I don't love adventure as much as I used to. I'm getting older, you know."

"You're thirty-seven, not eighty."

I check my watch. "Cannae haver with you anymore, Magnus. Your wife wants me."

"To help arrange the new exhibits at the Dùndubhan museum, ye *cacan*. Piper doesn't want to shag you."

"Well, she does need my body." With a wink and a smirk, I walk past Magnus. "To carry heavy artifacts for her."

Maybe I enjoy tormenting my cousin. Maybe I like to watch him squint his eyes and flatten his lips right before he calls me a *cacan* or a *bod ceann*. I don't mind anyone calling me a wee shit or a dickhead. I'm not that sensitive. It's possible I also enjoy hearing Magnus growl and snarl. Not my fault he cannae control his emotions.

I walk out of the exercise room, the one I'd installed in my house not long after the first time I met Ashley Hartman, while Magnus trails after me into the living room. The wife of my cousin Callum has set up a physical therapy clinic as well as a fitness center for people who don't have injuries, but I prefer to work out at home. In private. Not because I fantasize about Ashley Hartman while I'm doing that. No, I like privacy. That's all.

Magnus pulls the front door open but pauses there to look back at me. "Piper and I have news, but she wants to tell you herself."

"I'm going to see her right now."

"Aye. Be kind to her."

"Have I ever growled or snarled at Piper? No. You are the one who treated her like a criminal." I pat his arm. "Donnae worry. I'll give her a good firm hug and a big wet kiss for you."

Magnus shakes his head and walks out the door.

I take a shower and get dressed, then jump in my car for the half-hour drive from Loch Fairbairn to Dùndubhan. I donnae mind the drive. The country in Glencoe is bonnie, and though I've lived in this region all my life, I still love to admire the scenery. I make one stop—to buy flowers for Piper, since it sounds like she has important news to share—then I continue on my way to Dùndubhan.

My cousin Rory and his American wife, Emery, own the castle. But they moved to Ballachulish after their twin bairns were born, and Dùndubhan became part museum, part venue for family events and even corporate retreats. Today, though, I will help Piper set up a new exhibit of Scottish antiquities.

I find Piper in the long gallery, where the temporary exhibit will be on display. Wooden crates full of precious objects stand in the center of the room along with the new display cases the Dùndubhan museum had purchased for this occasion.

"*Madainn mhath*, Piper," I say as I come up beside her and kiss the lass on the cheek. "I hear you have news to share."

"Good morning, Errol." She sets down the clipboard she'd been holding and gives me a secretive smile. "I do have news. It's hush-hush, though, and only a few people know. That would be me and Magnus, of course, and also our parents."

"I'm honored to be included in that group."

She clasps her hands, raising them to her chest, and bounces on her toes while grinning. "I'm pregnant, Errol. Magnus and I will have a baby in about eight months."

"That's brilliant, Piper." I pull her in for a one-armed hug and kiss her cheek again. "Congratulations, *gràidh*. I hope the bairn is just like you and nothing like the growling bear you call a husband."

She gives my chest a light punch. "Don't tease Magnus about this. He's kind of sensitive about becoming a father."

"Oh, aye, that makes sense. The demonic bounty hunter is sensitive."

I pull out the bouquet I had hidden behind my back and thrust it at her. "For the mother-to-be."

"Aw, Errol, that's so sweet." She takes the pink roses and sniffs them. "Thank you."

"You're welcome. Now, let's get started on this exhibition. Everyone will soon get to see the fruits of all your labor, the months you spent convincing larger museums to loan us their artifacts. You should be proud, Piper. You've done an amazing thing."

Since I can tell my compliment has embarrassed her a wee bit, I get to work opening the crates with a crowbar. I insist on ringing my cousins Callum and Logan to get them to help us position all the display cases because a pregnant lass shouldn't be doing that. I also ring my cousin Iain, as well as Alex Thorne, who married my cousin Catriona. They are both archaeologists, which means they're the perfect blokes to assist Piper in placing the artifacts within the cases in a way that forms a cohesive narrative.

Alex and Iain said that rubbish about a narrative, not me.

Catriona is also an archaeologist, but she wanted to stay home with the new baby she and Alex welcomed into the world not long ago.

I donnae see myself ever getting married or having bairns.

We can't get all the exhibits up today, so Piper goes home after lunch. I decide to hang about and open the last few crates in the long gallery. Dùndubhan is quite large, and the long gallery is rather cavernous, which means the slightest sound echoes and seems louder than it actually is. That's why I can hear a visitor approaching before I see the person, before they've even finished climbing the spiral staircase and crossed the threshold onto this floor. The footfalls clap as if the visitor is wearing dress shoes rather than boots or running shoes.

I continue prying a crate open while I wait for the visitor to reach the long gallery.

"There you are," an all too familiar voice declares. "You've been avoiding me, haven't you? That's not very nice, Mr. Murdoch."

Mhac na galla. Won't she ever leave me alone?

I set the crowbar on the floor and face the lass who seems determined to drive me insane. "Good afternoon, Miss Hartman."

She stops near one of the large windows and rests her bum against the sill. "I've told you a hundred times to call me Ashley. May I call you Errol?"

"No. And I only use a person's first name if I like them." I point the crowbar at her. "Donnae like ye, Miss Hartman. Stalking is a crime, you know."

"Stalking?" She smiles and shakes her head. "This is business, not personal. Some people just can't say yes until they've gotten the hard sell."

How does she make that term sound filthy? I donnae want to shag Ashley, so I donnae care if she speaks in a sexy voice. Or if she wears a dress that hugs her sexy figure. The low neckline doesn't bother me either. And her long brown hair does not make me want to fist my hands in it while I—*Bod an Donais.* She's driving me barking mad.

Ashley rests her hands on the sill, curling her fingers over the edge. "You can make this a lot easier on yourself if you just give in."

I set the crowbar on the crate I'd been trying to open. Give in? What she wants from me is a disaster in the making. I will probably wind up in prison or worse. For months, Ashley Hartman has hounded me, showing up at random times just so she can catch me off guard. She always dresses in a way she must think will make me so randy that I'll do what she wants. I might be a treasure hunter, but I do not chase after phantoms.

Gazing at her voluptuous body, I suddenly have an idea. Can't believe I never thought of it before. Maybe chasing her away isn't that hard after all.

I amble up to her, plant my hands on the sill at either side of her hips, and bend my elbows just enough that our faces hover inches apart. I'm taller than the lass, but that's why I leaned in. I speak in a huskier voice on purpose. "I know why ye keep coming back, Ashley. Ye want me to fuck ye."

Her eyes flare wide for a split second. "This is business, Mr. Murdoch. Nothing more."

"Then why do ye keep coming back? And you always wear a sexy frock or sexy trousers. I think you're trying to seduce me, Miss Hartman."

She's breathing harder, her breasts rising and falling with her rapid breaths. "This is not about sex. You aren't that hot."

"Of course I am." Her gaze flicks to my biceps, which my short-sleeve T-shirt reveals. "If ye donnae want me to kiss you, and then fuck you, best walk away now."

"I never give up on what I want—and I want you, Mr. Murdoch." She seals my lips with one finger when I start to speak. "As a business partner, nothing else."

Standing this close to her, I feel the blood rushing into my *slat*. All right, I'm attracted to her. But we both know damn well that she uses her body to entice me to participate in her barmy scheme. Even after months of harassment, she hasn't managed to talk me into signing on.

Her eyes have darkened, and I can tell her nipples are tightening. Aye, she wants me. And aye, I want her. But it's pure lust, and I do not need this woman to satisfy my needs. I can find a girlfriend anytime I want.

I lean in a bit more, and her lips brush against mine. "Stop harassing me, Ashley."

"This job is exactly your kind of thing. You want to do it, so just say yes."

Shaking my head, I push away from her. "The Grand Canyon treasure is a myth. I might enjoy hunting for lost relics, but only ones that actually exist."

Ashley folds her arms over her chest again, and the action lifts her breasts. "You'll give in one day. If I have to spend years chasing after you, Mr. Murdoch, I will seduce you into saying yes, eventually."

My entire body has tensed in anticipation of something I know I shouldn't do. My *slat* has stiffened, and my brain is no longer in control. Walk away, that's what I should do. But Ashley drags a finger down her chest until it meets the neckline of her dress, then she drags it back up to her throat. I'm breathing harder now, and my cock jerks.

Ashley licks her lips.

Mhac na galla. I surge forward, pinning her to the windowsill with my body, my hands gripping the edge, and I crush my mouth to hers. A bolt of lust rips through me like lightning, hot and fierce and irresistible. I thrust my tongue between her lips. She moans and relaxes her jaw, pushing her tongue into my mouth, while I rub my stiff *slat* into her belly. She lashes her arms around my neck and plows her fingers into my hair, moaning again, more deeply this time. That ravenous sound spurs me to grind my cock into her like a rutting animal.

She locks one leg around my hip.

Outside, a car door slams.

I shove my hand under her dress to palm her mound.

Footfalls clap on the spiral staircase. Someone calls out, "Errol! Are you up there?"

Magnus. *Bloody hell.*

I tear my lips away from Ashley's mouth and stagger backward a few steps.

The lass stares at me wide-eyed, her swollen lips parted.

I gesture toward her body. "Fix your dress. My cousin is coming."

But if Magnus hadn't arrived when he did, I would've been the one coming—inside Ashley Hartman's body. She would've screamed my name for sure.

The lass fixes her dress and pats her hair, then she hurries down the long gallery to the stairs. She bumps into Magnus and yelps. He says something to her that I can't hear, but it causes her to race down the spiral staircase.

Magnus shakes his head and marches toward me. "What did ye do to the lass, Errol? She seems upset."

"Ashley is fine. Donnae worry about her." I meet him halfway across the room. "Why are you here, Magnus? Piper left already."

"But she forgot her purse." Magnus glances around, apparently sees what he wanted, and ducks behind a crate to pick up a small purse. "Here it is. Why donnae ye come to dinner at our house tonight?"

"No, thank you. I have, ah, things to do."

Magnus shrugs, and we walk back to the spiral staircase together. As we trudge down the steps in silence, I can't stop my mind from replaying that moment in the long gallery when I kissed Ashley. Aye, that woman is a menace—to my self-control.

I need to shag her.

Chapter Two

Ashley

As I climb into my car and yank the door shut, my mind keeps torturing me with images of Errol Murdoch—his muscular body, those gorgeous blue eyes, that silky light brown hair. Is it my imagination, or has he developed more muscles lately? He had a good body the first time I saw him, but over the past several months, he seems to have gotten more buff.

Damn, that man can kiss.

But I will never let that happen again. This is business, as I keep telling Errol, and I do not mix business with pleasure. Never. Not even if I know the pleasure would be incredible. Okay, yes, I'm attracted to him. So what? I do not seduce men into doing what I want.

So…why did I say the word seduce when I was trying to talk Errol into going on my expedition?

I start up the car and turn around too fast, which makes gravel spray up. *Get a grip, woman, he's not that hot.* Even if he is, I have willpower. As I drive out of the courtyard and through the massive wooden gateway, I can't help gawking at the castle walls and the building itself. Rory MacTaggart and his wife actually own a medieval castle.

I had never visited Scotland, or the UK, until the day I found out about Errol Murdoch and his treasure hunting skills. An article in an online magazine had mentioned him, though the story had focused on his cousin Magnus and Piper Lang, the fugitive who had evaded the Scottish bounty hunter for nearly two years. It turned out Piper was innocent, and Errol played an important role in helping to clear her of a murder charge.

But it wasn't the murder that had caught my attention. No, it was the brief mention of Errol and his vocation. He travels the world searching for things no one else can find and solves riddles no one else can solve. I need those skills if I'm ever going to prove the Grand Canyon treasure exists.

The driveway leads through the woods, and a false twilight descends as I steer the car down the gravel two-track. By the time I turn onto the main road, I've completely forgotten about that kiss. Okay, I haven't really forgotten. But I have resolved never to let that man distract me with his amazing talent for kissing, which just might outdo his puzzle-solving prowess. Ten minutes after leaving the castle, I've stopped fantasizing about Errol's lips and switched to thinking about what tactic I should try next to convince Errol to do what I want. The man loves ancient mysteries. Solving them is literally his job. Why does he keep fighting me? I've offered him a ridiculous amount of money and the chance at another adventure. As far as I can tell, he hasn't done much of anything since his escapade with Magnus and Piper. He ought to leap at the chance to dive into another mystery.

Half an hour after leaving Dùndubhan, a name I have trouble pronouncing, I arrive in the village of Loch Fairbairn. It's a lovely place. The people I've met so far have been incredibly kind and welcoming. They treat me like an old friend, even though I've only come here sporadically and always to see Errol Murdoch. Yes, I'm stubborn. But the quest for the Grand Canyon treasure means more to me than anyone could possibly understand. Maybe I should explain it to Errol, but I don't want him to accept my offer because he feels sorry for me.

Maybe I did quit my job so I could keep harassing him. Maybe I'll run out of money soon. But I will not share that information with Errol.

Don't worry, Dad, I'm keeping my eye on the ball.

By the time I walk into my room at the Loch Fairbairn Arms, my tummy is rumbling and I feel a little nauseous from not eating since breakfast. I order room service. While I wait for my meal, I change into sweats and a baggy T-shirt, my favorite outfit for relaxing after a long day. A polite young man delivers my food, and I give him a good tip. Then I dive into my food, wolfing it down a little too fast because I'm so hungry.

Once I've finished eating, I get out my laptop and reread the only piece of information I have about the Grand Canyon treasure—a newspaper article from the turn of the twentieth century. I need more clues. But only Errol can help me find them. What else can I say to convince him? With time running out, I need to do something radical.

I could sneak into his house and strip naked to lie in his bed until he comes home.

No, no, no. I will not give in to lust.

But I am getting a different idea… It's too crazy, though. I know I might be setting myself up for an even more massive failure, and potentially criminal charges for stalking Errol, but I'm just desperate enough to try it. One final push. One last chance. If this doesn't work, I'll slink home with my tail between my legs and get a job at a fast-food restaurant.

Should I do this? No. Will I do it? Well, um…

I change into my street clothes, jeans and a peasant top, then I rush out of the hotel. On my way out, I ask the desk clerk where I can find someone who can help me find a rental property. The gray-haired woman tells me there's an estate agent's office two blocks away. She offers to call a taxi for me, but I don't want to wait. Once I set my mind to something, I need to get it done right away. Besides, a brisk walk clears my head and energizes me for the task ahead.

The estate agent turns out to be a sweet man who can't be more than twenty-five. Despite his youth, he clearly knows the local market. We browse the listings on his computer until I spot one that looks right. The location is perfect, and the house itself seems fine based on the photos the agent shows me. He suggests I should view the house first, but I don't have time for that. So I tell the nice young man that I want to rent the house in question, no walk-through required.

This feels almost like fate.

Half an hour after I walked into the estate agent's office, I have a signed lease agreement and the key to my new home. Why did I choose this house? Location, location, location.

It's directly across the street from Errol Murdoch's house.

That's right. We will be neighbors. Maybe I'm taking stalking to a new level, but it's not like I'm threatening to kill him or trying to plant surveillance devices in his house. I've offered Errol a large retainer if he'll just accept my offer and accompany me on my expedition.

Now he will have no choice but to talk to me.

Never in my life have I gone to such extreme lengths to get what I want. I'm a good girl, the type who never does anything I'm not supposed to do. But I've changed lately. Circumstances have driven me to take desperate action.

Tomorrow, I will move into my new house. This village is lovely. I could picture myself living here permanently. Maybe I should take a little time to explore the area and see more of the Highlands.

No, I don't have time for that.

After a fitful night's sleep, I check out of the Loch Fairbairn Arms and head to the house I've rented. It has no furniture, or anything at all inside it. I spend the remainder of the morning hunting for furniture and kitchen stuff, though I can't afford to fully outfit the house. I'll need to settle for sparse decor and a basic kitchen. The bed isn't super comfortable, but it will do. I can get by without the creature comforts if it helps me convince Errol to go on an expedition with me.

I'm sitting in my new living room, on a used recliner, when movement outside the picture window catches my eye. A man is marching up the concrete walkway of the house across the street—Errol's house. He's home. I watch until he enters the house and shuts the door, then I race over there to ring the bell.

The door swings open, and Errol groans. His shoulders flag. He leans against the jamb, arms hanging loosely at his sides. "What are you doing here, Miss Hartman?"

"Please call me Ashley."

"Why? We aren't mates."

"But we could be." I move a little closer, and the scent of woodsy cologne wafts over me. I've never known him to use any kind of cologne, not in all the months I've pursued this man. "Why don't we sit down and talk? Then maybe you'll feel more comfortable discussing the expedition."

"Leave a body alone, would you? I have things to do."

"Such as?"

He squints at me. "None of your business, Miss Hartman."

"I realize I've made a bad first impression." I wince. "And probably many bad impressions after that. But I swear I'm not a horrible person. Give me a chance. We've never really talked about what this expedition will involve. At least give me a few minutes to explain."

"And then you'll go home to America and never bother me again. Aye?"

"Please, let me explain. That's all I'm asking." Since I don't want to lie, I instead avoided answering his question. The honest response is that no, I will not stop bothering him. I can't. "What do you say, Mr. Murdoch?"

He studies me, his gaze traveling from my face down to my toes before sliding back up to my chest. He licks his lips. "I suppose we could have a piece while you 'explain.' But when I tell you to leave, you will go. Aye?"

"Yes."

Errol stares into my eyes for a moment, then he waves for me to go inside. "Come in, lass."

I have no idea what "have a piece" means, but I'm guessing it refers to food. Errol leads me through the living room and into the kitchen, where an island occupies the center of the space. The open design accommodates a kitchen table, which stands tucked against the sill of a picture window, overlooking the backyard.

"Do ye like haggis?" he asks.

"I've never tried it."

He has the fridge door open, and he's bent over to examine the contents. He glances at me over his shoulder. "You didn't gag or run away. Most Americans have a negative reaction to the mention of haggis."

I shrug. "Can't have an opinion about something I've never eaten."

"Hmm." He focuses on the fridge again and brings out several items. "I think a sandwich will do."

"A haggis sandwich?"

"No." He holds up packages of meat and cheese. "Turkey and Gouda."

"Sounds good."

I can't help wondering why he's being so nice when he keeps telling me to leave him alone. Maybe he hopes I'll feel guilty for letting him feed me, and then I'll agree to go home and never pester him again. I can't do that. I'm in too deep to stop.

Erroll has placed all the ingredients on the island. Now he begins opening the packages.

"Want some help?" I ask.

"No, but thank you for asking." He eyes me with a touch of suspicion. "For months, you've been trying to talk me into doing what you want by mercilessly hounding me. Now you're offering to help. Must be a ploy to soften me up."

"I don't mean to be so pushy. But I need your cooperation."

"Why? What's so bloody important about a treasure that, if it exists, hasn't been seen in more than a century?"

How much should I reveal? My true motivations might make him sympathetic to my dilemma, or they might convince him I'm a conniving lunatic. I watch Errol slapping together two sandwiches, deftly tossing slices of bread onto the cutting board and smearing mayonnaise onto them like a pro. I've always enjoyed watching someone create a meal out of whatever's at hand. But observing Errol while he does that affects me in a strange way.

I'm getting so horny.

Okay, fine, he's hot. I'd love to sleep with him, but I've never done casual sex. I like to get to know a guy before we do the deed. But yesterday in that castle, I would've let Errol take me right there in the long gallery. And yes, I know that's what the room is called because I picked up a brochure in the vestibule on my way upstairs to torment Errol. Since the castle is also a museum, the place offers lots of brochures and even a map of the interior and exterior.

Yeah, I grabbed a map too. A girl needs to be prepared for anything.

But I was not prepared for how intensely attracted I am to Errol. I can keep it under control. No problem.

"Do you have a job?" Errol asks as he tears leaves off a head of lettuce. "Or are you independently wealthy?"

"I'll answer that question if you answer one for me first."

"Go on."

"Are you rich?"

He shrugs one shoulder. "Not really. I've made a decent living from treasure hunting, but I don't own a ruddy castle."

"I'm not technically rich either. But I have enough money to pay for this expedition."

"What do you mean, you aren't technically rich?"

I ignore his question and lean toward him to study our sandwiches. "Got any tomatoes?"

He stares at me for a moment, then turns around to search inside the fridge.

Yeah, I know how to be evasive. But one way or another, I will gain his cooperation. I might even kidnap him to do it. I'm that desperate.

Chapter Three

Errol

I do not understand Ashley Hartman. She stalks me for months, makes out with me in the castle, and then shows up at my doorstep asking me to listen to her proposal. I already know what the lass wants. I've already told her no, many times. She must be a bampot underneath her calm and sexy exterior. Only a lunatic would behave this way.

Maybe I wouldn't mind shagging her, but the woman clearly has problems. I donnae like getting tangled up in someone else's issues. But I did offer to feed her. And I agreed to listen to whatever she means to tell me. *Mhac na galla.*

I finish adding cherry tomatoes to our sandwiches, then lead Ashley over to the table by the window. I carefully place her plate at one end and mine at the opposite end. That way, I won't need to be too close to her. The lass is very attractive, and I seem to have lost all my common sense lately. Cannae risk being within kissing distance of Ashley.

She waits until I've sat down, then picks up her plate and takes a seat right next to me. "Thank you for making lunch, Mr. Murdoch. This looks delicious."

"My mother grew the tomatoes. She loves gardening."

"Really. Do you enjoy it too?"

"No."

She watches me while she takes a bite of her sandwich and slowly chews it.

I take a bite of mine, but her unwavering focus on me starts to make me feel uncomfortable. Why does Ashley insist on doing that? She should focus on her food, not me. "What did you want to say? I eat fast, so you best start talking."

"Please let me explain about the expedition. I need your help, Mr. Murdoch."

"Might as well call me Errol. I prefer that, anyway."

"But you didn't want to call me Ashley."

I slap my half-eaten sandwich down on my plate. "I'd rather you go home and give up. But since that seems unlikely, just say your piece. And if you must use my name, call me Errol."

"Will you call me Ashley?"

"Aye, fine. Get on with it."

She eats another bite of her sandwich first, then daintily wipes her hands and mouth with her napkin. She clears her throat. "This expedition is personal for me. I need to prove the Grand Canyon treasure is real. I don't care if archaeologists accept the find. I don't care if the media covers the expedition. All I want is proof."

"Why?"

"My reasons are personal."

I fold my arms over my chest and stare at her. "That's not an explanation."

"Maybe if we got to know each other a little better, I'd feel comfortable sharing more with you. As it stands, I don't know if I can trust you to keep my secrets."

"Ah, so ye do have secrets." I shake my head. "Donnae like that either, Ashley. If you want my help, I need facts."

"But you love solving puzzles. Don't you pride yourself on being able to figure out any mystery?"

Oh, the lass is too clever by far. That makes me want to shag her even more, but I'm not daft enough to fall for her tricks. "The puzzles I solve have clues attached to them."

"So does this one. I gave you a copy of the newspaper story that discussed the treasure."

"An article from nineteen hundred and nine is not what I call a clue. It's a rumor."

"I read every article I could find about you, Errol. And I understand you better than you think." She pushes her plate away and leans toward me to speak in a sultry tone. "You haven't gone on a treasure hunt in months, have you? I bet you're hungry for a new adventure. Your mouth must salivate every time you glance at the Grand Canyon article—and the cash I laid down on your living room table the first time we met. Why fight what we both know you want? Give in to temptation."

"Are ye trying to seduce me again? Won't work this time."

"Won't it?" She pushes her chair back and rises, only so she can rest her bonnie erse on the table inches from my plate. "We kissed yesterday. I know we would've had sex if your cousin hadn't interrupted us. Why shouldn't I leverage your attraction to me? I'll do anything to convince you to sign on to my expedition."

"Aye, I believe that." I skim my gaze over her body while a memory of kissing her yesterday unreels in my mind. "But you don't seem like the sort who uses sex to get her way. That means you'll regret it if I give in and fuck you."

"Will *you* regret it?"

I shake my head. "Not your concern, lass."

"Let me tell you about the equipment I've bought to make our expedition top-notch." She bends over even more to lay a hand on my thigh, and her shirts falls open just enough that I can glimpse her breasts. "I have ground-penetrating radar."

Never have I thought of radar as erotic. But the way Ashley spoke the words ground penetrating radar makes me picture my "radar" penetrating her "ground."

She glances at my lap and smirks. "I can tell my equipment arouses your interest."

The lass can't honestly want to have a poke just to talk me into her barmy quest. I do not sleep with women for a reason like that. But when she gives my thigh a gentle squeeze, my *slat* jumps, and I'm ready to fuck her right here on the table.

"You're breathing harder," she says. "Let's go into your bedroom."

"I don't like being manipulated, Ashley."

"But I'm genuinely attracted to you, Errol."

"Aye, but that's not the reason you've got your fingers inches away from my cock." I grasp her hand, peeling it away from my thigh, and set it on her own leg. "Hands to yourself, Ashley. Unless you can swear to me you're not doing this for any other reason than that you want my *slat* inside you."

"Your what?"

"*Slat*. It's Gaelic for 'cock.' But ye willnae be seeing that anytime soon." I give her my best hard stare, but honestly, I'm not as good at that as Magnus is. Anger isn't my strong suit. "So tell me, Ashley, is lust the only reason you want to shag me?"

The lass compresses her lips, then puckers them. All the while, her fingers tap on her thigh. "No, I can't swear that's the only reason. But it's about ninety-five percent of the reason."

"When it's one hundred percent, let me know." I rise and slide my chair under the table. "I think you should go now. We have nothing else to talk about."

"But the expedition—"

"Is not my problem." I wave my hand toward the kitchen doorway. "Let's go."

Ashley frowns briefly, then follows me out into the living room and to the front door. When I swing the door open, she compresses her lips again. But the lass walks out anyway. I admire her erse as she hurries down the walkway to the curb. She does have a bonnie bum, and aye, I'd love to shag her—but I donnae like being used.

She hops off the curb and continues across the street.

I rush outside, halting halfway to the curb. "Where are ye going, ye daft woman?"

"Home." Ashley turns around, now briskly walking backward across the roadway. She grins. "I rented the house across the street."

She spins around and sprints up to the porch of the home across the street. As she unlocks the front door, she waves at me and grins again. Then she disappears inside the house.

What the bloody hell? She rented a house just to harass me? I was starting to think she might be a semi-normal person, and that maybe I had misjudged her. But no, she is completely insane.

But I still want to shag her.

Grumbling, I hurry back into my house and spend the next hour exercising. Sweat soaks my shirt, but I donnae care. That woman drives me insane in every way, but especially with her body. Ashley knows I want her, and she uses that to manipulate me. If she means to live across the street from me, I will need to find a way to release my lust. So aye, I'll exercise until I can't do anything except collapse in bed. That ought to stop me from sneaking over to her house after dark to fuck her.

That would be giving her what she wants. So no, I will not do that. If she sneaks into my house… Even Ashley Hartman isn't that daft.

Is she?

After an hour of working out, I don't feel any less enraged and randy. I take a shower and relieve my lust for that woman on my own, but even wanking off doesn't help. I need to make that woman leave the country. How will I do that? She harasses and stalks me, so… Oh, aye. I've got a brilliant idea. I'll harass her right back.

So I march over to Ashley's house and knock on the door. When it swings open, my jaw drops. The lass is wearing a string bikini. "What in the world are ye doing?"

"It's a beautiful day, so I'm going to sunbathe on the lawn."

"What?" I can't stop staring at her body, especially her tits. "People do that in their backyards, not on the front lawn."

She shrugs. "I prefer the lawn. If I decide to sunbathe in the nude, I'll go into the backyard."

In the nude? She said that just to fash me, I'm sure. My dokey is waking up at the mention of nudity, but I will not have a poke with Ashley. She's even more insane than I thought. Who sunbathes on their front lawn?

"Did you have something else to say?" Ashley asks. "Or did you come over here just to complain about my bikini?"

All I can do is splutter. She's wearing the tiniest so-called bikini I've ever seen. It hardly qualifies as swimwear, or even lingerie. After a bit more spluttering, I manage to say, "Ye cannae go out on the lawn in that outfit."

"Why not?"

"It's—Ye just cannae."

She grabs a pair of sunglasses off the table beside the door and snags a wide-brimmed hat from a coat rack nearby. Then she sidles past me. "Mind grabbing that lawn chaise for me?"

"What lawn chaise?"

"The one behind the door."

My brain still hasn't recovered from seeing her in a bikini, so I wind up obeying her command. I get the folded-up chair and carry it onto the lawn for her. I even unfold it for the lass while she watches. Her lips tick up at the corners, and she rests her hands on her hips.

"Thank you, Errol," she says as she lies down on the chaise, wriggling to get in the right position. "Feel free to join me."

"I donnae sunbathe."

"Too bad. I've love to see you in a skimpy pair of swim briefs." She tips her head down and peers at me over the rims of her sunglasses. "Or nothing at all."

I spin around and stalk back to my house, slamming the door behind me. Why am I breathing hard? I didn't run across the street. I walked. Swiftly. When I head into the living room, movement outside draws my attention to the house across the way.

Ashley is lying there on her chaise, enjoying the sunshine.

Bod an Donais, that woman is the bonniest, sexiest lass on earth. But if she thinks her bikini will make me crack, she's in for a rude surprise. Her evil plan won't work. Aye, I'd rushed over there determined to harass her and give the woman a piece of mind. But I wound up carrying her chaise for her. That doesn't bode well for my revenge plan.

I keep standing there by the window, relishing the view of Ashley Hartman's body. My feet refuse to move. My eyes refuse to stop staring. I clench my fists while my cock stiffens. Knowing she decided to sunbathe strictly to harass me does not help me fight off the need to feel her slick, hot flesh wrapped around my *slat*.

My mobile rings.

I dig it out of my pocket and mutter a gruff hello while I keep staring at Ashley.

"Are ye all right, *gràidh*?" my mother asks. "Ye donnae sound like yourself."

"I'm fine, Ma." But my rough tone belies that statement, and my mother is not stupid.

She clucks her tongue. "You haven't come home for dinner in almost a month. Since I only live twenty minutes away, ye have no excuse for neglecting your widowed mother."

"Ma, you make it sound like Da passed away last week. It's been eighteen years, and ye have a boyfriend."

"I'm too old for boyfriends. Ailpean is my lover."

"Your what?" I whirl away from the window, too shocked by mother's statement to think about Ashley's body anymore. "I thought you two were dating."

"Aye. And adults have a poke now and then, Errol. I donnae expect you've been celibate all your life because you've never had a serious girlfriend."

"Well, that's different." I scratch my cheek, then scratch my forehead, though I have no idea why I do that. "Can we stop talking about your sex life, Ma?"

"Oh, aye." She pauses and clears her throat. "So, *gràidh*, who's your new lass? Ye haven't introduced her to me yet."

"I don't have a new lass."

"What about the bonnie brunette who visited you at Dùndubhan yesterday? I hear she was inside your house earlier today too."

"That's Ashley, and she is not my girlfriend."

"But Magnus said you kissed her."

"He—What?" Magnus wasn't there when I did that, so I have no idea how he could have told Ma I kissed the lass. Then again, MacTaggarts are nosy and sneaky. I'll need to interrogate my cousin about that later. "Ashley is not my girlfriend. End of discussion. I need to go, Ma."

"All right. But come to dinner tomorrow night. Ailpean and I would love to see you."

What choice do I have? I want Ma to be happy, so I groan and say, "I'll be there. Tomorrow night."

"And see if Ashley can come too."

No way in hell. But I don't tell my mother that. "We'll see. Goodbye, Ma."

I stuff my mobile back in my pocket and turn toward the window without thinking about it.

Ashley is still lying there on her chaise, wearing the skimpiest bikini on earth.

That lass will drive me mad. That's a dead certainty. But I might not mind so much if she does.

Chapter Four

Ashley

Okay, I sunbathed in my tiniest bikini just to get Errol worked up. I suppose that was a dirty trick. But he kicked me out of his house and didn't let me finish explaining why I need his help and what is involved. No, I can't tell him everything. Still, he could've given me the courtesy of listening to my entire spiel.

I do enjoy sunbathing, so my display wasn't entirely for his benefit. Mostly. But not only for that reason. And I told the truth when I said I'm honestly attracted to him. Subterfuge is not my style. But a girl does whatever she has to do to get things done in a desperate situation.

This evening, I've decided to give Errol a break and focus on planning my expedition. I had developed a loose framework, but it's time to double down and make a real plan. I will assume I'll gain Errol's cooperation eventually, so I leave room in my plan for that. If he doesn't cooperate… I don't know what I'll do. I can't make this happen on my own, but I can't trust anyone else to go with me. Nobody else has Errol's amazing brain coupled with his love of adventure.

I still can't understand why he hasn't done anything exciting since his escapade with Magnus and Piper. Solving that mystery might also reveal his reasons for refusing to sign on for my expedition. It couldn't possibly be as dangerous as tangling with antiquities thieves and a murderous billionaire.

Yeah, Errol did that. I read about it in newspaper stories from around the UK. What happened to that amazing, fearless man? I need him to become that hero again—right now.

Someone knocks on my door.

I toss my papers onto the coffee table and rush over to pull the door open. "Errol."

"Aye, it's me. At least you aren't so barmy that you cannae remember my name." He skims his gaze over my body and clears his throat. "What are ye wearing?"

"It's called a robe."

He rolls his eyes. "I know that. But why are you wearing it now? Do ye even have clothes on under it?"

"No. I'm naked underneath my robe."

Errol's eyes go wide. "You're what?"

"Naked underneath my robe. I prefer to sleep in the nude."

He sputters but keeps glancing at my body. "Why would you do that?"

"Because I do. What I do or don't wear when I'm alone in my bedroom is none of your business."

Unless he wants to join me in my bed. His hot body scrambles my brain, and that's my only excuse for how much I want him.

He rubs his jaw, then tears his gaze away from my body, looking me in the eye. "Your doorbell is broken."

"I know. The landlord can't come out to fix it until Friday."

"Well, I could, ah, fix it for you. If ye like."

"Really?"

"Aye."

Maybe I should let him do that, but I don't want him to think I'm accepting his offer because I hope to get something from him in return. But his suggestion makes me a touch suspicious. "Why do you want to fix my doorbell? You keep telling me to go away."

"Pardon me for being neighborly." He shakes his head. "You can't accept a hand unless you're paying me to do it. Isn't that right? You're a cynic, Ashley."

"No, I'm a realist." I step back and push the door open further. "Want to come in?"

He peers around me to see inside the house. "I don't know if that's a good idea."

"Afraid I'll tear your clothes off and have my way with you? I'm smaller and a lot less muscular, which means I can't overpower you, Errol."

"Not worried about that."

"Then come inside. We should discuss things." I turn sideways and spread an arm. "Maybe this time you'll let me finish talking. At least you can't order me to leave the premises."

Errol sighs, and his shoulders relax. "All right. I'll come in for a wee bit."

He hurries past me but halts abruptly when he notices the furniture. "All you have is a sofa and a coffee table. Not a fan of decking out your home, are ye?"

"I just moved in today." Being evasive seems like the smartest move right now. I don't care to explain that I'm strapped for cash because nearly all of my money is tied up in the expedition. "We can both fit on the sofa without getting too cozy."

Errol carefully sits down at the nearest end of the sofa. He glances around while fidgeting.

Do I make him that uncomfortable? I know I've been relentless in my attempts to talk him into helping me, but I'm not a monster. As I walk past Errol, he throws me a wary sidelong look. I'd better do something to convince him I don't want to lock him in my basement. Does this house even have one of those?

Settling onto the opposite end of the sofa, I rearrange my robe so I won't accidentally flash anything I don't want him to see. My robe only has a belt to tie it closed, after all. "I'm surprised you came to see me. Why did you do that, anyway?"

"I haven't really given you a chance to explain your proposal." He winces and scratches behind his ear. "This morning, I had the idea that I should harass you as revenge for the way you've harassed me. But I'm not the vengeful sort. I spent all afternoon trying to figure out what to do. Finally, I decided to come over here and talk to you."

"Are you going to listen this time?"

"Aye, I'll listen. But I need to ask you a question first."

"Okay."

"Why do you keep trying to seduce me?" He winces again. "I meant that you seem like a nice enough lass. Despite your harassment, I cannae believe you throw yourself at men all the time."

My knee-jerk response is to be offended, but I can tell Errol didn't mean it that way. I haven't behaved like myself lately, so I understand his confusion. "No, I don't ever do that. I can't deny that I'm insanely attracted to you, but that lust makes me feel off balance."

"Aye, that's what I thought. I've never been insanely attracted to a lass either, so we're struggling with the same problem. Aren't we?"

"Yes. It seems like we are."

I spread my hands over my thighs and stare down at them while I try to figure out how to handle this situation. An abrupt change of topic would feel weird. How can I steer the conversation in the right direction?

"Go on," Errol says. "Tell me about your expedition."

"I've already told you most of it, but I do have some information I've held back." I chew on the inside of my cheek while I study Errol, trying to gauge his reaction. But I have no idea what he hides behind those beautiful blue eyes. "Have you heard of Isaac Hartman? Everyone calls him the Artifact Bloodhound."

Errol's brows shoot up. "The amateur archaeologist who made a series of important discoveries? Aye, of course I've heard of him." He stares at me for a moment. "Are you related to the Bloodhound?"

"Yes. He's my father."

Errol's jaw goes slack. He just stares at me for so long that I think time must have stopped, but then his mouth slides into a sly smile. "That's why you're hell-bent on finding the Grand Canyon treasure. Your father put you up to it."

"No. I put myself up to it. Dad stopped going on expeditions a few years ago, and he won't even talk about the Grand Canyon treasure anymore. They broke him."

"Who broke him?"

I hug myself, suddenly feeling chilled. "My father was a respected avocational archaeologist. That means he never earned a degree in the subject, but he was an expert. Dad was a lot like you, actually. Dad traveled all over the world to hunt for relics, and he was able to do that because we had family money, inherited from my grandfather. Mom died when I was little, and I don't really remember her. Dad was my whole world, and he took me with him on his expeditions whenever he could."

"Sounds like you're very close with your father."

"Yes, I am. Or I used to be." That chill just won't go away, so I rub my arms. "Dad told me to give up on the Grand Canyon thing, but I've kept going. He was ridiculed for starting a search for the treasure, and he wound up totally demoralized, to the point where he won't even talk about archaeology or ancient history anymore."

Errol rests an arm across the sofa's back as he tips his head side to side—analyzing me, I'm sure. "Why have you kept going after your father gave up?"

"I need to vindicate him. Prove he was right."

"And show those tossers what they missed out on, eh?"

"Maybe that's part of it." I scoot over to get closer to him without invading his personal space. "But my main goal is to prove he was right. The treasure does exist."

"You're doing this because you hope your father will be grateful and become his old self again."

How does Errol know that? He's a smart man—a genius, some would say, at least when it comes to solving riddles—but I just told him about my dad a minute ago. He shouldn't have been able to figure out the truth in a heartbeat. But he did. And that proves he's the only man for the job.

It also makes me want to kiss him.

"You said your father had family money, past tense," Errol says. "Have you sunk all of it into this barmy expedition?"

Damn, he's intuitive. "Yes, that's what I did. Can you understand now why I've been hell-bent on talking you into coming on this expedition?"

"Aye, it makes sense now."

I tuck my legs under me and turn fully toward him. His eyes transfix me, and his body turns me on, but I need to focus on the mission. "Before you make your decision, I need to ask you a few questions. Okay? I've just told you my reasons for this quest. Now I need to understand you a little better."

"All right. Ask away."

"Why haven't you done any treasure hunting since your adventure with Magnus and Piper?"

Errol bows his head, not speaking for a moment. Then he looks up at me and sighs. "There are three reasons. One, my partner quit the business, and I relied on his money to finance our treasure hunting. He met a lass and fell in love, then moved to New Zealand to be with her. Without his funds, I cannae afford to go on adventures."

"I get that. But you said there are two more reasons."

"Aye." He bends his arm, the one that rests on the sofa's top, and props his chin on his fisted hand. "After the mission in Istanbul with Piper and Magnus, and the assault on Dùndubhan after that, everything else just seems…boring. Even treasure hunting, which I used to love, doesn't pique my interest anymore."

"I suppose it would be hard to top that. What's the third reason?"

"My mother. She worries about me. Always has, but ever since my last adventure, she doesnae want me to leave Loch Fairbairn."

"Well, I can understand that. You were pursuing a murderer, after all. What does your dad say about it?"

Errol's expression becomes slightly pinched. "Da died of a heart attack eighteen years ago. I was away at university when that happened, had just finished the semester, and I came home to help Ma through the worst of it. She insisted I had to finish my degree, though, and she wouldn't hear of it when I suggested I should delay that."

"I'm sorry, Errol. I know what that's like. My mom passed away, but it was a car accident."

"We have more in common than we thought, don't we?"

"Seems like we do."

He inches closer, keeping his arm on the sofa's back, and the distance between us shrinks to half of what it was. I can't help gazing into his eyes and letting their blue color mesmerize me. We've made a connection, I think, something I hadn't expected. All I wanted was to convince him to come with me to the Grand Canyon. But we've created a fragile bond that seems deeper than our mutual interest in ancient mysteries.

He roves his gaze over my body, and his tongue slips out between his lips, almost as if he's imagining something naughty. "Your robe has slipped."

For a second or two, that statement doesn't penetrate my brain. His hungry expression has made me feel warm and tingly. Then I realize what he just said. I look down and see that the belt on my robe has come undone and the halves have fallen open just enough to expose a glimpse of the hairs at the juncture of my thighs. He can see the slopes of my breasts too.

I tug my robe closed. "Sorry."

"Donnae apologize, lass. You are beautiful, and ye know I'd love to have a poke."

God, I want that too. Without even realizing it, I've wriggled even closer to Errol. He shimmies closer too, and the masculine scent of him teases my senses. I can't move, can hardly breathe, when he dips his head to brush his lips across mine. My pulse beats so fast that I feel a touch lightheaded. I've never gotten this excited by the prospect of a kiss, much less the other thing he suggested. A poke. That should sound silly to me, but instead, it makes me want to tear his clothes off.

Errol cups the back of my head with his hand, then touches his lips to my mouth. I sigh whispers out of me. My lids flutter shut, and I clutch his shirt in my hands while pressing my lips more firmly to his. He groans deep in his throat. I moan and sag against him. Errol wraps his free arm around me and pushes his tongue between my lips to tease me with it, sliding his arm down my back until he reaches my bottom. I moan again, more deeply, when he molds his hand to my ass. Our tongues glide across each other, twining and thrusting, every movement sensual and so delicious that I can't breathe anymore. My ears start to ring, but I don't care. I never want Errol to stop kissing me.

But he pulls away just enough that we can gaze into each other's eyes. "I want to shag ye, Ashley. But you need to know a few things about me first."

Chapter Five

Errol

Ashley tastes better than any woman I've ever kissed, and I want to lay her across the sofa so I can sample the flavor of her cream. It will be sweet and intoxicating, I'm dead sure of that. I hardly know this woman, yet I want to make love to her right now. But I told her she needs to know a few things about me first, and I meant that. I'm not a normal man. My hobbies often scare women away. I don't want Ashley to regret spending the night with me once she realizes the truth about me.

So I slide backward on the sofa, drawing out a distance between us. Her robe hangs open even more than before, and I need all my willpower to keep from staring at her tits and the hairs on her mound. Fuck, I can smell how much she wants me. But I will not shag her until she understands.

"What did you want to tell me?" she asks.

I force myself to look her in the eye. "The articles you've read about me don't tell the whole story. On the mission with Magnus and Piper, we did more than root out antiquities thieves. We also infiltrated the Istanbul headquarters of Sovereign World Industries, the company owned by Royce Hammond. That would be the bastard who framed Piper for the murder of Archer Caldwell."

Ashley keeps her focus on me, her expression curious, but she doesn't seem to notice my raging erection.

"I sweet-talked Hammond's right-hand woman, Dilara Terzi, into showing me their main server room," I say. "Then I, ah, sort of blew it up."

"What?"

I cannae help smirking. "Well, it's more accurate to say I shut down the fans that keep the servers cool, and then they all melted down. That's what caused a minor explosion. We were being held hostage inside the building, but I managed to copy all the data on those servers before the meltdown."

"Oh. I see. You're a computer expert as well as a treasure hunter?"

"No. But I've learned a few things from my cousin Evan. He's a tech mogul, and a billionaire."

"Really?" Ashley's eyes have gone wide. "Wow, I've never met anyone that rich."

"But you dug up information about my family. How could ye not know about Evan?"

"I researched you, not your cousins. Magnus and Piper are a part of your story, so that's how I learned about them."

"Ah, of course." I might have learned important things about Ashley tonight, but I know there's more to find out. I still haven't quite told her everything about me. Am I trying to scare her away? No, but my personality and lifestyle aren't for everyone. "I've been somewhat…subdued since I've met you. I donnae want you to be shocked by the way I behave."

"Just spit it out, Errol. I'm the daughter of a globe-trotting avocational archaeologist. I doubt you could say or do anything that would shock me."

Ohhh, she really has no idea about me. I'll need to take this slow to prevent her from fainting. She doesn't seem like the sort who would do that, though. Do women ever faint? I think that might be only in old movies.

I sit up straighter and clear my throat. "After I destroyed Sovereign's servers in the Istanbul office, we got waylaid by guards. They locked the doors, which turned out to be bulletproof or at least bullet resistant. At any rate, I had brought along a failsafe measure. And I put it to good use."

"Failsafe? I don't understand."

Suddenly, it feels like I've got ants in my hair. I scratch my scalp and grimace. "Before we drove to Sovereign's offices, I strapped C-4 to my belly."

Ashley's expression goes blank.

Maybe she doesn't know what C-4 is.

The lass crinkles her brows. "Are you saying that you strapped plastic explosives to your tummy?"

"Aye."

"Why on earth would you do that?"

I shrug. "That was my failsafe. If we got trapped in the building, I would use the C-4. So when the guards surrounded us, we managed to restrain them, and I slapped the C-4 onto the glass doors. Then I detonated it."

Ashley's jaw has fallen open.

That's the reaction I expected, though I can't say I'm not disappointed. I'd hoped a woman who would stalk me for months would be more amenable to my lifestyle. But I've clearly overtaxed her ability to accept barmy things. Aye, I'm off my head. Never denied that.

"Wow," she says. "You really are fearless, aren't you?"

"It's my trademark. That and taking insane risks."

"Okay," she says slowly, like she needs to take care in how she pronounces that word. "I understand you have a wild side, but that's exactly why I want you on this expedition."

"You aren't terrified of me?"

She snorts, apparently struggling not to laugh. "I've met much crazier people than you. Besides, no one else will even consider helping me. Turns out I need a brilliant, quirky, fearless treasure hunter who straps explosives to his tummy."

I jerk my head back, sure I must have misheard the lass. She likes that I take barmy risks? She called me brilliant and fearless too, not to mention quirky. I think I like that. Most people use less polite terms when they describe me. Well, people who aren't related to me. My extended family cuts me a lot of slack.

But I haven't finished revealing my true nature to her. "There's one more thing you should know—or rather, you should experience—before I agree to go with you on your expedition."

"Tell me."

I veer my gaze away from her and pick at the seam on the sofa's back. "You'll need to experience it in person, I think, to fully grasp the ramifications."

Her brows crinkle again, an adorable expression that makes me want to drag her into the bedroom and have that poke before I show her my most insane hobby. But I won't do that.

"I cannae show ye here," I say. "We need to go to Dùndubhan."

"Right now?"

"Aye, right now. You need to understand all of my habits before we become business partners."

"Since you're going to share everything with me, I should be completely honest with you too. This isn't just business. It's also very personal for me." She pulls her robe closed and jumps off the sofa. "Let me get dressed. Then we can go to the castle so you can show me whatever it is."

Her robe has fallen open, exposing all of her nude body. She has bonnie tits, round and just the right size for my hand, as well as wide hips and toned thighs. My mouth might actually be watering right now.

But I swallow hard and force myself to look at her face. "Aye, lass, ye best get dressed."

She glances down. Her eyes flare wide, and she quickly tugs the robe shut, holding it there with both hands. "Sorry."

"Why? Doesnae bother me at all."

I'd rather tear that robe off her body, but I'm not a *bod ceann*. Only a dickhead would seduce Ashley before she understands how "quirky" I am.

Ashley trots off to her bedroom and returns a few minutes later fully dressed. "Let's go."

She's wearing a knee-length coat, and I have to ask her about that. "Are ye cold?"

"No. But we're supposed to have a low in the fifties tonight, so I figured I'd need a light jacket. Sunset is at nine twenty-one." She ties the belt of her jacket around her waist. "I'm not sure what the difference is between civil and astronomical twilight, so I can't say for sure when it will actually get dark."

"Are you a meteorologist?"

"No. I was a librarian, but I got laid off last year. That's when I decided to find the Grand Canyon treasure."

"How does a librarian know so much about the weather?"

She brings her mobile out of her jacket pocket and turns it toward me. "The apps on my phone told me."

"Apps? How many have you got?"

The lass averts her gaze. "I have five weather apps on my phone. Each one has different features, and sometimes the radar images are slightly different in each one."

I can't help chuckling. "You are adorable, Ashley. Tell me all about your weather apps while we drive to Dùndubhan."

"You don't think I'm crazy?"

"Aye, ye are. But so am I."

We climb into my car, since I know the way and I prefer to drive. I can tell she wants to argue about that, but the lass has enough sense not to push the issue. Arguing would only encourage me to fuck her right here in the car, in the front seat, while we're rolling down the road. I've never tried that before, but this woman knows how to knock me off my head.

Just as we're pulling out onto the street, I notice a vehicle parked two houses down. A man sits inside it, and as we pass the car, I swear I recognize him. But no, it can't be Christian Frisk. My former business partner moved to New Zealand. Since I didn't get a good look at the driver, I must have been mistaken.

Ashley gets very animated while she tells me all about her weather apps. I have apps too, but for reasons she probably wouldn't understand. The lass will find out soon enough what I use my mobile for—besides making phone calls. Magnus and Piper have seen what I can do firsthand. I doubt they would approve of what

I mean to show Ashley, but I need to know she can handle me and my "quirks" before I agree to do what she wants.

The lass does have a beautiful body. But that's not a good enough reason to go on her impossible expedition.

As we approach the castle, coming up the drive but not in sight of the compound yet, Ashley has finally stopped havering about her weather apps. So I tell her, "For your information, civil twilight is when the sun has set but you can still see objects clearly. Nautical twilight means that you can make out the shapes of objects, but you can't see them clearly."

"Oh. Thank you for explaining that."

"I'm not finished." I hold the steering wheel with one hand while I lay my other palm on her thigh. "Astronomical twilight means that it's essentially dark, but you won't be able to see less obvious celestial objects like galaxies and nebulas."

She hasn't objected to my hand on her thigh, so I keep it there.

"How do you know so much about astronomy?" she asks. "I thought you were a treasure hunter."

"I am. But understanding the nuances of twilight can be important if you want to know when is the best time to measure the astronomical alignments of ancient sites."

"That makes sense." She lays her hand over mine. "You are very smart, Errol."

"So are you, Ashley. Your knowledge of weather apps is encyclopedic."

"Ha-ha."

I pick up her hand and kiss it. "Not joking. I love that you're fascinated with weather. Do you have any other secret hobbies?"

"Well, I do enjoy crossword puzzles."

"Riddles are my style."

"That's why I picked you."

We pass through the metal gate that means we're not far from the castle now. The gate is normally open, and only closed if we want to make sure no interlopers get inside the compound. The last time that happened was when Magnus, Piper, and I came back from Istanbul and Royce Hammond was waiting for us with his team of commandos, who turned out to be far less loyal than Hammond had assumed.

Ashley won't get a good look at Dùndubhan tonight, since civil twilight will end soon. But I will show her around tomorrow in the daytime. I'm sure a woman who grew up traveling to archaeological sites with her father will enjoy the history of this castle.

I park in the courtyard, near the main door. I don't see any other vehicles or lights on inside, which means we have the place to ourselves. Perfect. The demonstration I mean to give Ashley will be just between us. I open her door for her, and offer my hand to help her out of the car. Her lips curl up a touch, forming dimples in her cheeks. I can't decide if that means she appreciates my gentlemanly behavior or if she thinks I'm a moron for assuming she can't get out of a car on her own. Though I experience a strong impulse to hold her hand as we walk through the walled garden, I resist it. I don't know her well enough, do I? Not sure about dating etiquette with American lasses.

I halt us beside the concrete bench that sits near the arbor. Roses climb the trellised arbor, though it's harder to see them right now than it would be in the daytime. I point toward the bench. "Have a seat. I need to gather some, ah, supplies for my demonstration."

"What kind of demonstration is this?"

"You'll see. Just wait here."

I hurry out of the garden and turn left, aiming for the old carriage house that now serves as a garage—and a temporary home for some of my special tools. I grab a large canvas carryall and stuff the items into it. That should be plenty. I don't mean to create a huge spectacle. Only a wee one. Thus armed, I trot out another door in the castle wall, one most people don't know about, and jog out onto the green to prepare my demonstration. Once I've finished, I march back to the garden and wink at Ashley as I stop in front of her.

"I'm ready," I tell her. "Let's head out onto the green."

She follows me without questioning why I want her to do this. When we reach the wooden door on the far side of the garden, Ashley tries to open it herself. She tugs and tugs but can't make the ruddy thing budge.

"Need a hand?" I ask. "Or would ye rather keep fighting with that door?"

She makes a few more attempts, which only result in a lock of hair falling out of the stretchy thing she used to hold it back in a ponytail. She blows a breath out of the corner of her mouth. The loose lock flutters. "Okay, you can help."

I grasp the knob and give it one good yank. The door pops open. I swing it wide for her and make a sweeping gesture with my arm. "Lasses first."

"Did you make sure that door wouldn't open for me?"

"Why would I do that? I'm all for women's liberation."

She smiles and shakes her head, then we walk out onto the green. Aye, in a matter of moments, I'll know just how determined and strong Ashley Hartman is.

If she doesn't scream and run away.

Chapter Six

Ashley

Errol stops us just outside the garden door, and I can't deny I'm very curious about what he has planned. He thinks I need to "experience" more of his personality or something, but that seems like a waste of time. I know he's odd and wickedly smart. I also know he has big muscles, and he's an amazing kisser. What else do I need to experience? Something that requires a long drive to a big castle, apparently.

"I don't see anything," I say. "Where's your big surprise? There's nothing out here but grass."

"Patience, lass." He pulls an eye mask out of his pocket, the kind people wear for sleeping, and offers it to me. "Put this on."

"Why?"

"Because I told you to do it. If you're wanting to go on an adventure with me, you'll need to follow my orders. Best practice your patience right now."

"What are you up to?"

"Either trust me or don't. If ye cannae do that, I'll take you back to Loch Fairbairn, and then you should go home to America." He waggles the mask in front of my face. "Your choice."

I have no choice because I need him. I can't run an expedition all by myself. Do I trust Errol? I have a feeling we're both about to learn the answer to that question. So I strap the mask around my head. It's thick and form-fitting, which ensures that I can't see any light at all. "I'm ready."

"Good girl." He pats my rump. "Now just stand here and wait."

I shove my hands into my pants pockets…and wait.

Shuffling sounds originate from my right, but I can't quite figure out what that noise means. Then I hear a zipper being pulled down—or maybe up. He can't be undressing. No, he must be opening a duffel bag or something, though I hadn't seen him carrying anything. I want to ask him what he's doing, want to ask so badly, but I promised to just stand here and wait. *Damn.*

"All right," Errol says. "You may remove the mask now."

I peel it off, stuffing the mask in my pocket. And I freeze. But instead of feeling cold, I grow warm and tingly. Why am I reacting this way? Because Errol stands about fifteen feet away, wearing only a kilt, with a leather belt to hold it up. I barely notice the boots and black socks that cover his feet.

"What are you doing?" I ask. It's possible I sound slightly breathless. Can't help it. His muscular body, and especially that impressive chest, makes me want to rush over there and rip that kilt off. "Is this your surprise?"

"No, lass. This is."

He holds his right hand at his side with his fingers curled as if he's holding something in his palm. Then one finger twitches.

And the earth erupts.

I jump and yelp as the explosion rings in my ears. The detonation happened further behind Errol, probably thirty feet away. It's hardly the loudest sound I've ever heard, but the noise jarred my nerves for sure. I hold a hand to my chest and struggle to calm my pounding heart.

"Are ye all right, Ashley?" Errol asks. He seems genuinely concerned. "I should've warned you."

"I don't think a warning would've helped. An explosion is always a shock, even if you know it's coming." I lean sideways to peer around his body at the area where the ground had detonated. "What was that, anyway? C-4?"

"No. It was a land mine."

I jerk upright and gape at him. "Land mine? Is that legal?"

"Probably not. But I believe in being prepared, even if it means I sort of…skirt the legalities. A serious situation requires more than a bow and arrow."

"I guess so." But after another peek around his body, I have another question. "What set off the mine? Nobody stepped on it."

"These mines don't have pressure switches. They're activated by an app on my mobile." He holds up his phone. "I can set them off from the other side of the world if I want."

"Uh-huh. Was this the other thing I needed to know before you'll agree to help me?"

"Aye."

"Well, I can handle this."

He lifts his brows. "Can you?"

Errol is still holding his phone up, and he taps the screen with one finger. Another mine detonates.

I jump and yelp again. "Jeez, Errol, how many of those things do you have?"

"That was the last one."

Well, thank goodness for that. I might need a defibrillator if he sets off any more explosives. But I do get it now. He's not the type of guy who sits around talking about how tough and wild he is. Errol actually lives that way. Maybe I should worry about that, but somehow, I believe he knows what he's doing and exactly how far he can safely go. I need someone wild, someone who will do whatever it takes—and that means I need him.

My gaze wanders over his body, from that impressive chest to his bulging biceps, and further down to what I know he's hiding under that kilt. I bet he has powerful thighs too, but I can't see those. The plaid hides them.

I don't realize what I'm saying until the words tumble from my lips. "You know, it's not fair. You've seen me completely naked, but I've only seen you half-naked."

"Aye, that's not fair, is it? Well, I can fix that." He unhooks his belt and flings it away. His kilt slumps to the ground at his feet. "There. Now we're even."

My jaw drops. Errol Murdoch stands before me in the nude, every inch of his mouthwatering body on display, and I can't stop staring at his groin. At his dick. The sunset has continued to sink below the horizon, deepening the twilight, and only the floodlights inside the courtyard illuminate the green. I can see enough of Errol to know he has the kind of body that any woman would love to experience just once, to know what it feels like to have those powerful muscles flexing around her body.

My mouth is actually watering now. And slick heat pools between my thighs. God, I want him. It's crazy, and I shouldn't do it. I won't do it. But ever since our kiss earlier this evening, I keep having trouble remembering that this is a professional endeavor, not an excuse for hot sex.

I loved that kiss.

Errol saunters up to me, still completely naked except for his boots and socks. "Have I shocked you, Ashley? I thought the lass who let her robe fall open wouldn't mind seeing me starkers."

"Not shocked. But you surprised me again."

"I do that often, to everyone. Though I don't usually set off land mines to impress a woman." He tips his head to the side. "Have I impressed you?"

"Oh, yes, definitely." I try not to do it, but I can't stop my eyes from staring at his dick. "I'm impressed for sure."

He hooks a finger under my chin and lifts until our gazes meet. His voice gets deeper and rougher as he tells me, "When a woman looks at me the way you were just doing, I know exactly what she wants."

Sex with him, for hours and hours. That's what I want. But I can't let my lust interfere with the mission. On the other hand, a roll in the hay might get rid of any residual tension and make me more relaxed and ready to undertake this expedition. Sure, that's the reason I want to get naked with Errol. It has nothing to do with his rumbly voice or his gorgeous body.

He rubs his thumb over my chin. "Should we…go back into the courtyard and get in the car?"

Only if we're going to screw in the car. But I can't speak or move a muscle, not with him this close to me. Errol smells so good, looks so good, and I know he will feel so good too. Inside me. Thrusting. His body on top of mine and—

"Ye shouldnae look at me that way," he says, "unless you're wanting a good, hard shag right now."

"Maybe I do want that."

"I donnae fuck a woman who says 'maybe.' This will only happen if you convince me you're sure you want me."

"Kiss me, Errol."

His brows lift again, and his lips curve into a sly smile. "You are a bossy lass. But I've always liked women who know what they want and tell me about it."

Errol thrusts both hands into my hair and kisses me. He tilts my head back a touch, just enough to grant him deeper access to my mouth, and he begins to coil his tongue around mine over and over in a slow and sensual dance that makes my heart pound for a very different reason this time. Land mines? That's nothing. The way Errol kisses could detonate me like an atomic bomb. I moan and try to wrap my arms around him, but he tugs me into his body with my hands trapped between us. I can't stop myself from making desperate little grunting sounds.

He pulls his lips away oh-so-slowly, making me moan again. With our bodies pressed together, he brushes his lips over mine. "Tell me what you want, Ashley."

"You. Inside me. Right now. So hurry up and fuck me, Errol."

He chuckles. "If you insist."

"But first, I need to…" As my words trail off, I slither down his body until I'm on my knees with his cock waving in my face. "I need to taste you."

He sucks in a breath, exhaling it in a ragged rush.

I allow myself two seconds to simply gaze at his glorious dick and admire the smooth length of his erection. The crown is red with a drop of moisture clinging to the tip. I can't help myself. I drag my tongue across the head to lap up that bead of liquid. When I glance up at Errol, his eyes are half-closed, and his chest is heaving.

He pushes a hand into my hair, cradling my head.

I keep my gaze on him while I clasp the base of his cock, pull my lips over my teeth, and take him into my mouth as far as I can. While I lick and suck, I pump his length with my hand and watch his hooded eyes as they drift closed and his expression relaxes, making his lips curl up a touch. He groans when I massage his inner thigh with my other hand, but when I speed up the pace, he sucks in a sharp breath.

"Ah, Ashley." He grasps my shoulders and hoists me onto my feet. "Donnae want to *caith* just yet."

I've never heard the word *caith* before, but I can guess what it means. He doesn't want me to make him come. I've enjoyed oral sex with other men, but never before had I needed to do it this badly. Something about Errol makes me feel wild and free.

He unhooks the button on my jeans and yanks the zipper down.

We are about to have sex. I know this, and I want it more than I should, want it so intensely that I can't catch my breath.

Errol drags my jeans down over my hips and lets them fall to my ankles. Then he kneels at my feet, pushes my legs as far apart as they can go, and spreads his big, rough hands over my ass cheeks. With his face inches from my mound, he tips his head back to gaze at me, hunger darkening his eyes and his features. "Ahm needing to devour ye, lass. Right now."

"Oh, yes, please." Did I just beg? That's not like me, but I don't give a damn. I'll beg even more if necessary.

He shoves his head between my legs and does exactly what he said. He devours me, lapping at my flesh with rough strokes of his tongue, groaning with ravenous delight, while he tugs my hips forward to give him fuller access. When he seals his mouth over my clit and torments it with his teeth and lips, I cry out and my knees threaten to buckle. He pulls one hand away from my bottom to thrust two fingers inside me, pumping hard and fast, grunting as he suckles my nub so fiercely that I know I'll come any second.

Then he thrusts two more fingers inside me, and I scream as my body convulses around his fingers. I grip his head, my nails digging into his scalp, and hold on while he keeps fucking me with his fingers and his mouth. By the time the last wave ebbs, I'm gasping for breath.

I wobble on my shaky legs, but he holds me up with his body—and with his face still buried between my thighs. "Errol, holy shit. You—Oh God, you're incredible."

He lifts his head to look at me, half his face glistening with my cream. Then he pulls his fingers out of me and raises them to his lips. He slides one finger into his mouth, sucking it clean, and repeats the process three more times, once for each finger.

That's the weirdest and hottest thing I've ever seen.

"Ye taste so fucking good," he growls. "I could spend all night feasting on ye."

I can't speak. Can't move. What he just did… I've never experienced a climax that intense in my entire life.

Errol rises and grips my ass again to lift me onto my tiptoes. "Get ready to come even harder—several times."

Several more explosive orgasms? I might die of a heart attack, but I don't care.

Chapter Seven

Errol

I pull her snugly into my body, loving the warmth and softness of her skin, and my erection rubs against her belly. My brain has essentially shut down, had done the moment I yanked her jeans down, but it still manages to remind me of one vital issue. "Do ye have a condom, lass?"

Ashley bites her lip, releasing it so slowly that my *slat* throbs. "In my purse. I dropped it over there."

She points over her shoulder, toward the garden doorway. In the waning light, I can see an object slumped on the ground there. That must be her purse. I keep hold of her erse as I stride over there, then set her down only long enough to grab her purse and tear the zipper open so I can excavate a condom packet from its depths.

I toss the purse away and grin as I hold up my prize. "Now we're ready to fuck."

Ashley traces her tongue over her bottom lip. "Hurry up, Errol, please. I need you inside me."

"I love it when a woman tells me that, but especially when you say it. Ye have the sexiest voice."

"So do you. Every time you speak, I want to rip your clothes off."

Cannae help chuckling. "Donnae need to do that now."

I clamp my hands over her erse and lift her off her feet as I rush toward the castle wall until her back smacks into it. She flings her arms around my neck, tunneling her fingers into my hair while she mashes her mouth to mine and dives her tongue between my lips. *Bod an Donais*, the lass kisses like a wild woman, and I love it.

When I try to pull my mouth away, she clasps the back of my head with both hands to stop me from doing that.

I need to get the condom on, but Ashley is too far gone to give a toss about anything. So I work around her ravenous kisses. Rocking my hips back, I gain enough leverage to rip open the packet and roll the condom onto my *slat*. All the while, Ashley keeps ravaging my mouth and making the sweetest little grunting sounds. I never would've guessed she had so much passion hiding underneath her all-business exterior.

She tries to wrap her legs around me, but her jeans get in the way, and she relinquishes my mouth so she can give me a look of such intense frustration that I cannae resist smirking.

"Are ye wanting something, lass?" I ask. "We could go into the house and have a piece first."

"Don't you dare do that. Fuck me, Errol. Right now."

I thrust into her body, and her cream dribbles down my cock. *Mhac na galla*, the scent drives me mad. Ashley lashes her arms around me and squeezes her eyes shut while I pump into her over and over, trying to start slow, but I cannae do that, not when she's so fucking wet and the heat of her penetrates the condom. She keeps gasping and crying out too. Faster, faster, I thrust into her. She bends her knees and clings to me tighter while I pound into her body, and the sound of our bodies slamming into each other echoes off the castle walls.

Ashley throws her head back and shouts, "Errol, yes, don't stop!"

Does she think I could even if I tried? No chance of that.

The tension inside me mounts, like I'm climbing a sheer cliff without any ropes, using only my hands and feet to ascend. I drive into Ashley even harder, even faster, her body bouncing on my cock while I keep climbing up that imaginary cliff. Cannae breath. Cannea stop. Donnae want to even if I could. Since I've lost complete control of my body and my senses, I stagger backward with no idea of why I'm doing that. Then my knees buckle, and I spin around to drop us both on the grass while still fucking her.

Ashley rolls us over and pushes up with her arms straight—and *she* starts fucking *me*. "I need to be naked with you, Errol, please, please, please."

She pauses in rocking her hips into me just long enough to fling her jacket and shirt away. Then the lass fumbles with her bra.

I grasp the middle of her flimsy lace garment and wrench it apart.

Ashley slaps her hands on my chest and starts rocking her hips again with abandon, while I lunge up to latch on to her nipple. She cries out and quickens her movements, her breaths accelerating too. I squeeze her tits, lunge up again to suckle one, and flick my thumb over her nipple until she starts to come.

Her body grips my length, spasm after spasm, squeezing and releasing, while a strangled scream erupts from her. I flip us over and raise onto my straight arms for better leverage, pumping into her while she digs her nails into my back, and her entire body curls in on itself. Her orgasm pushes me over the edge. I've reached the summit, and now I'm tumbling backward in free-fall, letting out a long, hoarse cry while I pump into her a few more times until I'm finished.

We're both struggling to breathe and sheathed in sweat. I just lie here held up by my arms, gazing down at Ashley while my pulse gradually slows, and finally, I can breathe somewhat normally again.

Her mouth slides into the sexiest smile I've ever seen. "You are more explosive than your land mines."

"Thank you, lass. And you are the most passionate woman I've ever met." I catch her lip with my teeth and release it slowly. "Not an uptight stalker after all."

She slaps my chest with the back of her hand. "I was never uptight."

I still have my cock inside her, but I don't want to move yet. Besides, I need to tell her something. So I look into her eyes and say it. "All right. I'll be your partner on your barmy expedition."

"Are you saying that because we just had sex? I didn't do that so you'd help me."

"I know. And I'm not saying yes for that reason." I reluctantly pull out of her body and sit back on my heels. "What we just did reminded me of how much I love being reckless. My mission with Magnus and Piper made me think I'd never find another adventure that could live up to that one. But I was wrong."

She climbs onto her knees and waddles closer to me. "The Grand Canyon treasure could be the greatest adventure either of us has ever undertaken."

I didn't mean that, but I won't explain the truth to her just yet. We have an expedition to prepare for, and besides, it would be madness to tell her I've never felt more alive than when I was fucking her. We hardly know each other. So for now, I'll let her believe I meant that the treasure excites me. It does, just not as much as the lass herself.

She picks up her ruined bra. "Thanks for destroying this."

"You're thanking me?" I say with a laugh. "You are a bampot, for sure."

"That means I'm crazy, right? Well, I can't deny that. Only a lunatic would search for a treasure everyone thinks is a myth."

"Not everyone. And yes, a bampot is a lunatic." I hand Ashley her shirt. "I'm assuming this expedition isn't entirely legal."

"Do you care if it isn't? I mean, your land mines can't be legal either."

"Not strictly speaking." I crawl on my knees until I find my kilt and belt, then I hop to my feet to get them on again. "Sometimes a bloke needs to skirt the law to get things done. I'm not a criminal, though. I've never stolen anything or hurt anyone, not even Royce Hammond."

Ashley has her clothes on again, but her hair is a tangled mess and has bits of grass in it. She glances at my backside. "You have grass stains on your ass. I saw that before you got your kilt back on."

"You must have some grass on your erse too." I point toward her head. "You have it in your hair, for dead sure."

"I guess we'd better take a shower."

"Aye. Dùndubhan has a large bathroom on the ground floor."

"Sounds perfect." She sets her hands on her hips. "But we're showering together strictly to save water."

"Ah, of course. It's the environmentally friendly way to get clean." I wink. "You're not just desperate to get your hands on me again."

Though she tries not to do it, her lips twitch into a slight smile. "This is business, Errol. The sex was fun, but from now on, we are strictly partners in the expedition. Agreed?"

"Aye, we're partners." We didn't explicitly state what the term partners means, so I can interpret it however I like.

We make our way into the house and share the large shower, though Ashley keeps her back to me and stays on the opposite side of the stall. I imagine she has never done anything as wicked as what we did on the green, so she can't reconcile her all-business attitude with the way she rolled about in the grass with me and begged me to make her come. Do I want to get involved with her? In a personal capacity? Not sure. I've never had a serious girlfriend, and Ashley Hartman is very serious—most of the time. Well, I'll get to know her much better during the expedition.

Cannae believe I'm doing this.

The drive home is quiet since we're both too jeeked to talk, and Ashley falls asleep. Luckily, I'm driving. I'd have to back out of this cockeyed adventure if she turned out to be a narcoleptic.

Once I've pulled into the driveway of her house, I give her shoulder a gentle shake. "Time to wake up, lass."

She opens her eyes partway, but still seems very sleepy. "Mm, what?"

"Never mind." I get out and go around to her side to open the door, but her eyes are closed again. So I unhook her seatbelt and pick her up, about to carry her into the house, but I hesitate. "Ashley, is the door locked?"

"Hmm?" She doesn't even open her eyes.

I hold her with one arm while I grab her purse off the floor and root about inside it until I find what must be her house key. When I carry her to the door,

I discover the key does open it. She stirs faintly as I enter the house, kicking the door shut behind me, and flick a light switch on as I wander down the hallway that must lead to her bedroom. I see the bathroom, and I peek inside another small space that seems empty. The last room is the right one. It has a bed, and a floor lamp beside it. But I don't see any other furniture. Her living room isn't well-furnished either. A woman who wants to embark on a crazy quest for a mythical treasure must have shedloads of money, aye? How else would she pay for all the equipment we'll need? Yet she barely has anything inside her house. I'd better ask her about that tomorrow.

For now, I pull back the covers on her bed and lay her down on the mattress with a pillow tucked under her head. She moans again, faintly, and stirs a wee bit. I remove her shoes and socks, then I manage to get her jacket off without jostling her overmuch. She licks her lips and wriggles but doesn't open her eyes. Should I remove the rest of her clothes? She cannae sleep in jeans. Can she? No, I should not undress her. I might have seen her naked, and we might've shagged like maniacs, but that doesn't give me leave to strip her while she's asleep.

Instead, I pull the covers over her and tiptoe out of the room. I switch the hall light off on my way out of the house.

As I drive my car to the other side of the street, I start to wonder about this expedition. Ashley hasn't provided any details. I've assumed that's because she wanted to be sure I'd go along with her plan before she explained all of it to me. But in the morning, we will need to have a long conversation about everything involved in this mission. No more sidestepping questions. She told me about her father, but I need to be fully briefed now.

I toss my kilt into the laundry room on my way through the house. I'll need to wash it tomorrow, and possibly ask one of my female cousins how best to remove grass stains from a plaid. Isla might know about that. Or maybe Catriona. Magnus would have no bloody clue, I'm sure.

Ten minutes after I left Ashley's house, I crawl into bed and try to forget about what happened on the green. If we're to be business partners, Ashley and I cannot ever again have a poke. No, never. I got that out of my system tonight, which means I'll have no trouble controlling myself around her. Now, if she cannae stand not to fuck me, well, that's her problem. I will say no.

Absolutely, I will.

Unless she goes down on me again. What? I cannae be blamed for a lass's actions.

Chapter Eight

Ashley

I wake up in the morning with cotton in my mouth and grit in my eyes, not to mention a rat's nest for hair. Do I have to get up this morning? Maybe I could just sleep in for another hour or two…or eight. What happened last night? Did I dream that I had sex with Errol up against a castle wall, and on the grass too? Yeah, I must've dreamed it. I never do anything as irresponsible as that.

Sitting up, I stretch and instinctively slide my hands into my hair.

And a blade of grass falls onto my lap.

Oh, shit. I actually did all of that, didn't I? Maybe Errol gave me the most incredible sexual experience of my life, but that changes nothing. I will not let intense pleasure get in the way of my mission. Vindicating my father matters more to me than anything I might possibly feel toward Errol Murdoch. Not that I feel anything…feely. It was just a "shag," as the explosive Scot likes to say.

I definitely did not hallucinate Errol setting off land mines. Weirdly, watching him do that triggered a hot bolt of lust inside me that led to the unfortunate but mind-blowingly amazing incident on the green. *Don't think about that anymore.*

At least I kept my cool in the shower—and kept my distance.

But damn, Errol has an incredible body.

No, no, do not think about that. Right, I will focus on the tasks ahead of me this morning. Shower, dress, eat breakfast, go across the street to make sure Errol hasn't backed out. I can handle those tasks, no problem.

Twenty-two minutes later, I step onto the porch of Errol's house and ring the bell. I'm carrying my portfolio, which holds all the pertinent information for our search.

When the door swings open, Errol is wearing workout clothes. Sweat glistens on his exposed arms and darkens the color of his sleeveless gray T-shirt. His shorts reveal most of his powerful legs too. I remember what it felt like to have all his muscles plastered to my body and his hips pumping into me.

Ugh. I told myself I wouldn't think about that anymore.

"Good morning, Ashley," Errol says, as he raises a small towel to wipe sweat off his forehead. "You look as bonnie as ever. Here for another poke?"

"No. I'm here to discuss the expedition."

"Of course you are." He opens the door wider. "Come in, lass. Let's discuss the expedition."

I don't know how he does it, but he turns those simple words into a naughty come-on. I ignore that and walk into the living room, then take a seat on a modestly padded wooden chair.

Errol stops beside me and shakes his head. "Why don't you sit in the recliner? It's more comfortable, and the chair you're sitting on is just for show. Nobody actually wants to rest their erse on it. My cousin Isla picked it for me, and even she said 'donnae rest your erse on it, Errol, it's a show piece.' So go on, Ashley, move to a comfortable seat."

"Why would you have furniture that nobody uses?"

"You're a woman. Don't you know the answer? I never question a lass's ideas about home decor."

He just stands there staring at me with his hands on his hips and his brows raised.

I give up and move to the recliner, though I have no intention of reclining the chair. This does have a lot more padding. Why had I chosen an uncomfortable seat? Maybe I'm slightly flustered being around Errol after what we did last night. I need to get over that right now.

So I set my portfolio on my lap and clasp my hands atop it. "Rule number one. We will never have sex again."

Errol drops onto the sofa, in the exact center of it, and spreads his arms across the back. Then he grins. "Won't we? Ye donnae seem able to control yourself around me."

"Last night was…temporary insanity. Now that we're business partners, our relationship must remain professional. No flirting. No kissing. No 'pokes.' Understand?"

"Aye. But we'll see if you stick to your own rules."

Of course I will. But I refuse to respond to his insinuation. "Now, we need to discuss the logistics of the expedition."

Errol sighs with no small measure of sarcasm. "If you insist, Miss Hartman. I assume you'll want to be businesslike and have me use your surname."

"That won't be necessary. Business partners can be on a first-name basis."

"Glad to hear it, Ashley." He hooks one ankle over the other knee, still seeming far too pleased with himself. "Since you told me rule number one, I assume you have more rules to share with me."

"Yes, I do." I wriggle a little in my seat, though I have no idea why. It's a stupid impulse. "Rule number two. I'm in charge of this expedition."

"Afraid I can't agree to that. You brought me in on this barmy mission because I'm the expert on treasure hunting. Either trust me to be in charge, or find someone else."

I want to balk at his demand, but I stop myself just shy of doing that. As much as I dislike the idea, I know he's right. I spent months trying to convince him to do this with me because he's the only man on earth who might actually find the Grand Canyon hoard. That means I need to relinquish a bit of control—to him.

Well, this will hardly be the first time. I surrendered my body and my self-control to him last night.

"Fine," I say. "You will be the boss, but I reserve the right to argue with you if I think you're doing something wrong."

"Argue all ye like, lass. Passionate disagreement can lead to other sorts of passion."

"Stop trying to turn everything into a come-on. This is strictly—"

"Business. Aye, you already told me that."

I take a breath to calm myself, then open up my portfolio. "I've collected quite a bit of information about the Grand Canyon treasure, and I'd like to show you the most interesting items."

Errol sits forward, hands on his knees, as if he's waiting for me to provide the information.

I shouldn't assume that means he'll believe any of it. The first time we met, he told me the Grand Canyon treasure was "bollocks" and a myth. But some legends turn out to be real, and I need to convince Errol this one has both merit and enough excitement to trigger his swashbuckling nature. From my research, I know he loves a good adventure. Now I need to convince him once and for all that my plan is worthy of his skills and commitment.

"You must remember the *Phoenix Gazette* article," I say. "You've probably read the whole article, so you know it mentions two specific people—G.E. Kincaid, who supposedly found the 'great underground citadel,' and S.A. Jordon who was allegedly an archaeologist with the Smithsonian Institution. The story also alleges that the Smithsonian funded multiple expeditions to the 'mysterious cavern.' The discoveries were said to include hieroglyphic inscriptions which might have been Egyptian in origin and might date back to the Nineteenth Dynasty."

"Why do you assume it's the Nineteenth Dynasty?" Errol asks. "There were several pharaohs called Ramses, and the article doesn't specify which one."

"I know. But Ramses the Second is the most famous, and the one referred to as the Great. It seems reasonable to assume the article refers to him."

He rests his elbows on his knees and links his hands. "Go on. Tell me more things I already know."

My first instinct is to say something smart to him, but his lips have a slight curl at the corners that suggests he's teasing me. I'll assume that's the case and keep going. "I acknowledge the fact that ninety-nine percent of the information about the Grand Canyon treasure comes from conspiracy websites, and I acknowledge that the *Phoenix Gazette* article isn't a completely reliable source."

"Good. Then we can forget about this barmy quest and have a poke on the sofa instead."

"No sex, Errol." I clutch my open portfolio to my chest and struggle to get up so I can sit down on the coffee table in front of Errol. My knee sideswipes his, but he just keeps watching me with a neutral expression. I lay the portfolio down and fan its contents across the table. "Look at all the evidence I've collected. It took me two years, but I found some things that no one else has ever mentioned."

He tilts his head to the side a touch, and I swear I see a glint of curiosity in his eyes. "I'm listening."

"First, a brief recap of what is publicly said about this treasure." I pluck up the printout of the newspaper article. "I think it's important to remind ourselves of the details. The man calling himself G.E. Kincaid claimed to have found a massive network of caves in the Grand Canyon, and he described numerous passageways and chambers that contained various kinds of artifacts—weapons, copper implements, idols, pottery, a gray metal that resembles platinum, cat's eye stones littering the floor, stone tablets, urns made of copper and gold, and even prehistoric items."

"Aye, and there were allegedly granaries, a storehouse, and even mummies. Kincaid believed fifty thousand people could have occupied those caves. If Kincaid himself ever existed."

"That's right. He did exist, and I can prove it."

He sits up straighter, his gaze nailed to mine. "You found proof? Did you verify the existence of S.A. Jordan too?"

"Yes. But before we get into that, I'd like to remind you of the details Kincaid recorded about where he found the cave complex." I set the article on the table. "He said he traveled approximately forty-two miles from El

Tovar when he noticed interesting colorations in the rock formations along the canyon and decided to investigate. He had to climb about two thousand feet up. A rock shelf hid the cave from view from ground level."

"Aye, but he magically found a way up the sheer cliff so he could stumble onto the hidden shelf."

"Not magically. But let's put that information aside for now. You wanted to know how I found proof that Kincaid and Jordan really did exist."

Errol lays a hand on my knee. "Yes, Ashley, I want to know."

The feel of his hand on my knee triggers a ridiculous flutter in my tummy. But I ignore it. "The Smithsonian insists no such person as S.A. Jordan ever existed, but they've got archives galore that include tons of data that hasn't been digitized yet. I scoured those documents for months, and I scoured the Library of Congress too, until I finally found proof that Professor Jordan did exist. His excavation reports were hidden deep inside the archives, and I don't think anybody had looked at them since shortly after the turn of the twentieth century. Then I also dug through genealogical records, on websites and in the National Archives, to find someone with that name. I found multiple men with the initials S.A., but only one who identified himself as an archaeologist affiliated with the Smithsonian. His name was Samuel Arthur Jordan."

Errol stares at me as if I've baffled him. What's confounding about the evidence I unearthed? I thought he'd be excited to hear what I've learned.

"You spent months hunting for that information?" he says. Then he pats my knee and gives me a patient smile. "Ye didnae need to do that. If you'd found me sooner, I could've tracked down Professor Jordan in a few hours, a day at most."

"I hadn't heard about you yet. Only when you and your cousin showed up in newspapers did I realize someone like you existed."

He straightens and spreads his arms wide, smiling with genuine sweetness. "Well, now you've got me. You will never again need to scour archives or websites. I tracked down the cryptocurrency trail of an evil *bod ceann*, after all. And I deduced from those transactions and from his movements that Royce Hammond was involved in antiquities smuggling. I can find the Grand Canyon treasure. That's a dead certainty."

"But you kept saying it's a myth, and it's a 'barmy' expedition."

And part of me still can't believe I've gained his cooperation. I'm waiting for that other shoe to drop—and expecting that shoe to come in the form of a pair of concrete galoshes.

Chapter Nine

Errol

You've convinced me that I need to do this." I lower my arms and sigh, resigned to explaining myself to Ashley. The truth is not the most exciting story, and it doesn't make me look that good. But I tell her anyway. "Honestly, I didn't think I'd ever want to go treasure hunting again. After my adventure with Piper and Magnus, nothing else could live up to the thrill of hunting down a murderer. I felt burned out on dangerous missions. That's why I resisted so much when you tried to talk me into this expedition. But I realize now that even if the Grand Canyon treasure turns out to be bollocks, I need to see this mission through to the end."

"Because it will be exciting."

"Aye. But also because I've lost my mojo, and I need to get it back."

She bites her lip, releasing it slowly while she admires my body from head to toe. "Seemed to me like you had all your mojo last night. And then some."

"You didn't know me before the Istanbul escapade and the assault on Dùndubhan."

Ashley crinkles her brows, an expression that always makes me want to kiss the adorable lass. "You've mentioned the assault on the castle before, but you didn't tell me what happened."

"Royce Hammond brought a small army of hired men to breach the castle compound and kill Piper and Magnus, probably me too. But Hammond did not take into account the size of the MacTaggart clan or how dedicated we are to helping each other, no matter how dangerous doing that might be."

"Was your mother a MacTaggart? Your last name is Murdoch, so I assumed that was the case."

"Aye, Ma is a MacTaggart. She married my father, Jock Murdoch, and they named me after Ma's favorite actor, Errol Flynn. And that's how I became the amazing Errol Murdoch."

She tries not to smile, but her lips twitch just enough that I know she wants to let that expression come to life. "Well, I can't deny you are amazing. Any man who blows up a corporate server and blasts his way out of a building with C-4 deserves that title."

"Ye havenae seen my most amazing feats yet."

A half-suppressed laugh splutters out of her. "Maybe not, but I'm getting a good look at your supreme self-confidence. Are you always like this? I've never seen this side of you, but I guess that's because you've been off your game since before we met."

"You need a self-assured man for this mission. Only someone as crackbrained and confident as I am will have any chance of finding the treasure for you."

"I guess I like crackbrained men, considering that I had sex with you last night."

"Sex?" I chuckle. "Oh no, lass, that wasn't just a shag. We set off a different kind of explosives on the green, so I think it would be more appropriate to say we fucked the living daylights out of each other."

"That's a mouthful. I think I'll stick with 'unbelievably hot sex.' But remember, that was a one-time deal."

"Oh, aye, one time." I wink. "Until the next 'one time' you take my cock in your mouth and beg me to shag you. I know how women think. 'Only once' means that it will only be once each day—or for you, once an hour. You are the most passionate lass I've ever been with."

She bows her head and shuffles the papers on the table as if she's hunting for something. Then she plucks up a photographic print, raises her head, and clears her throat. "Here's another piece of evidence I found. I had to take a photograph of it because the item is enclosed in glass and held in the private collection of a wealthy man who loves to collect rare antiques."

I accept the sheet when she offers it to me and study the picture it contains. "Is this a map?"

"Yes. A treasure map, to be precise." She points to a spot on the left quarter of the photograph. "I think this is a map to the location of the Grand Canyon treasure, or more precisely, to the location of the entrance to the network of caverns that contain the treasure."

"Have you authenticated this?"

"No, I can't. The owner wouldn't let me borrow the map so I could have it checked by an expert."

"I see." As I turn the map this way and that, I begin to sense a pattern in the lines drawn on it. "I think you might be reading this the wrong way round."

"What do you mean?"

"The map is upside down." I flip it around and tap the photograph. "I'll need to examine this more closely to be sure, and it would be best if I could see the original, not just a picture of it. Where does the owner live?"

"Manchester, England. I have his address, obviously, since I went to his house."

"Can you arrange a meeting? You and I need to study the map in person."

"I can try." She digs her mobile out of her purse. "I'll give him a call right now."

While she dials a number, I pick up the map and squint at the lines. Something about them makes me curious, but I can't quite put my finger on what it is, not just yet. I'm hoping that if I see the original map, I'll have an epiphany. A trip to England might be fun, anyway, and even if we don't learn anything of value from the map, we'll have started our adventure in earnest. That means there's no going back now.

A sort of excitement I haven't experienced in months raises the hairs on my arms. Ashley was right. I've got my mojo back.

I ignore whatever she's saying to the bloke who owns the map and focus on decoding the lines and shaded areas that seem like topographic elements. Well, the Grand Canyon is a canyon, after all. There would be deep valleys and mountains on a map of the area, but this isn't a traditional type of map. It reminds me of medieval renderings of the world rather than the modern version, and the quality of the photograph, taken through a glass case, doesn't clarify the matter.

Ashley finishes her call. "We can see the map, but only if we can be there tomorrow at ten o'clock in the morning. I said we could do that."

"We can." I gather up her papers and hand them to her. "Marilyn will get us there."

"Marilyn? I thought this was strictly a job for you and me, not your girlfriend too."

"Do ye think I'd have shagged you if I had a girlfriend? No, I wouldn't."

"So, Marilyn is another cousin?"

I try not to smile, because I want this to be a surprise for her. But she is adorable when she tries to wheedle information out of me. Ashley is adorable, full stop. Of course I'd love to have another poke with her, but I doubt we'll have time since we need to begin preparations for our trip to America, and we have our quick jaunt to Manchester too.

"You'll meet Marilyn tomorrow," I say. "Now, let's talk about how you're paying for this expedition and what equipment you already have."

She screws up her mouth and gazes at the wall. "I don't have equipment as such."

"What does that mean?"

"I have the money to buy equipment, but I haven't actually purchased anything yet." She fiddles with the papers in her portfolio. "I, um, kind of assumed you would take care of that. That's what I'm paying you for, after all. To be my expert partner."

"And you would be the financial partner."

"Exactly."

I slump against the sofa and let my mind digest everything I've learned this morning. That leads to another question. "Yesterday, you told me you're not technically rich. I want to know what that means."

"Don't worry. I have enough money to fund this expedition."

"That's not good enough. I want to know where you got the money. Librarians don't earn that much. Are you sure you're not a billionaire superhero? Or a bank robber?"

She rolls her eyes. "Yes, I'm sure. I quit my job so I could focus on this expedition exclusively, and I sold my house to pay for it."

"You're homeless?"

"No. I've been living with my dad. He doesn't know that I quit my job. I told him I was laid off."

"Lying to your own father?" I shake my head slowly and cluck my tongue. "That's not a nice thing to do."

"He wouldn't understand if I told him the truth. He thinks I've been working as a freelance editor for a UK publisher."

"More lies? You are a naughty lass, aren't you?"

She hugs her portfolio to her chest. "Haven't you ever lied to your family for their own good? Dad will thank me once we prove he was right all along about the Grand Canyon treasure."

"You do understand this expedition will be illegal. Unless you've magically acquired a permit. I donnae think the US government likes to let people who have no official qualifications root about on their land."

She stares down at her portfolio, still hugging it to her chest. "I know it will be illegal. We might even get arrested. We'll have to pretend that we're just going on vacation in the Grand Canyon and that we accidentally stumbled onto a major find."

"You really are keen on lying, aren't you? Fortunately, I think that's the sexiest plan I've ever agreed to participate in."

Her brows squish together over her sweet little nose. "You think breaking the law and lying to everyone is sexy? You are completely insane."

"I think you're finally catching on." I move onto the coffee table right beside her and catch the lass's chin with my fingers. "There's a reason my cousins call me the fire starter, and it's not only because I have land mines and C-4. I'm also famous for my scorched-earth method of getting things done. So the question you need to ask yourself is this. Are you prepared to go to any lengths, even commit crimes, to vindicate your father?"

"Yes, I am." She leans toward me until our mouths hover millimeters apart. Our gazes lock. She lowers her voice to a huskier register as she says, "I can handle anything you can, Mr. Murdoch. Anything. And I won't back out, not now, not ever. You're stuck me with."

"We'll be living in close quarters for as long as this mission takes. No house to go home to every night. The best we might get is a tent."

"Separate tents."

"Hmm." I rub my thumb over her lips. "You want to crawl into my tent and seduce me, aye? That's even sexier than your proclivity for lying."

"No 'shagging,' Errol."

"The more you say that, the more I know we'll be fucking again very soon."

She stands up, and some of her papers fall out of the portfolio.

I grab them and hand the lot to her. "Relax, Ashley. Having sex doesn't mean we're getting married. Now, if you shag me twelve times, that would qualify for automatic marriage according to Scots law."

"Oh please. Do you think I'm that naive?"

"No. I think you're that uptight." I slap her erse. "But you loosened up last night, and you'll do it again."

"Can we please focus on the expedition?"

I rise and stretch. "Aye, we can do that. Have you at least made a list of the equipment we'll need?"

She makes a slightly sheepish face. "Afraid not."

"Then we have work to do. Keep in mind that we can only take with us what we can carry into the Grand Canyon. No vehicles, just our muscles."

Ashley lifts her chin. "I can handle whatever you can."

I flex my biceps. "Have ye been lifting weights often lately? Donnae look all that buff to me. But I like a woman with plenty of soft curves."

She marches toward the door. "We should go to a restaurant for breakfast and start compiling a list of what we'll need."

"Loch Fairbairn has only one restaurant."

"Then we'll go there, obviously. I'll drive."

I slap my hand on the door when she tries to open it. "Do ye even know where the café is?"

"No," she says slowly. "But I can look it up on Google Maps."

"Donnae need that." I tap my temple. "I'm your map of Scotland. That means I will drive."

She drums the toe of one shoe on the wood floor in a rapid rhythm ,while she puckers her lips a wee bit. Then she huffs and throws her arms up. "Fine. You can drive."

"Thank you, Ashley. As a consolation prize, I'll let you pick the location for our next shag."

She rolls her eyes again. "Ugh. Do ever think about anything else?"

"Not since we kissed in the castle, and especially not since last night." I peck a quick kiss on her lips. "Here's your lesson in Scottish etiquette for today. Donnae swallow a Highlander's cock unless you want him to keep trying to seduce you forever after."

"A little late to share that nugget of wisdom."

I remove my hand from the door.

She yanks it open and stalks outside.

Oh aye, we'll be shagging again for certain.

Chapter Ten

Ashley

Once we've climbed into Errol's car, he announces that I'd better "buckle up good and tight because this will be a wild ride." He's trying to unnerve me, but it won't work. His implication that he will drive too fast and terrify me is, I'm sure, just payback for the fact I refuse to have sex with him again. Errol doesn't seem like the vengeful type, though. Still, he must be teasing me again. Wild ride? The term applied that night at the castle when we, um, did things I never imagined I would do. Not outdoors. Well, probably not indoors either.

Okay, I've never been the adventurous type. I can admit to that. But Errol makes me feel…things that kind of terrify me, but also excite me at the same time.

Errol starts up the engine and pulls out onto the street.

Well, this doesn't seem terrifying. Wild ride? Yeah, right.

Then he floors the accelerator, and the car rockets forward, pinning me to my seat.

"Why are you driving so fast?" I ask. My voice might have risen an octave or two.

"Ahmno driving fast." He grins at me. "Would ye like to see me really go fast?"

"No, I would not."

He veers around a corner. I'm thrown into the door, and the portfolio flies off my lap, scattering the papers on the floor between my feet.

Errol holds the wheel with one hand while looking directly at me. "Relax, lass, I'm an expert driver. Never had an accident or got a point on my driving license."

"A what on your what?" Now I might be screeching. Can't help it.

"On my license. Bad driving will get you points, and if you accrue too many, they won't let you drive anymore."

How can he not have gotten the maximum number of points if he drives like this?

"Look at that," he says while continuing to drive with one hand. But now he's looking out my window. "That's Mungo Gunn's house. He used to have a diary that belonged to my ancestor, Efrica MacTaggart, but he gave it to my cousin Kirsty. It's a fascinating story. You see, Mungo thought his family was cursed—"

"Watch where you're going, Errol. Please."

"I am watching." He stops looking out the window, and though he faces forward, he keeps glancing at me sideways. "Land mines donnae scare you, but my driving does. Is that right?"

"Yes."

Errol swerves around another corner, then mercifully slows down to a normal speed. When we reach the café, he veers his car into a parallel parking space. It winds up perfectly placed in the slot. How can he do that? The man is nuts, but I can't help admiring his driving skills.

Not that I will ever get in a car with him again. I'd rather walk back to my house.

When I move to open my door, Errol swings an arm out to block my body. "Allow me, *gràidh*. A gentleman doesn't let a lass climb out of the car without giving her a hand."

"But a gentleman does scare the holy living shit out of a woman with his reckless driving."

"Stay where you are, please."

He gets out and trots to my side, then pulls the door open and offers me his hand. I hesitate briefly, then accept it. We've parked on the opposite side of the street from the café, so we jog across both lanes to reach the entrance to the outdoor section of the restaurant. Errol holds my hand while we cross the street. This man confuses the heck out of me. Gentleman or lunatic? He's both, but that doesn't seem possible.

Errol Murdoch is an enigma.

We find a table in the outdoor portion of the café, and Errol pulls my chair out for me. I glance at him with what must seem like shock on my face, but he just smiles a touch and pats my shoulder. Then he sits in the chair across from me while we both browse our menus.

"Look at that," a male voice behind me says, his tone full of humor. "Errol Murdoch finally got a girlfriend."

"Donnae be rude," Errol says. "Come out from hiding behind the lass."

A man almost as muscular as Errol comes up alongside our table, where we can both see him. The man thrusts his hand out to me. "I'm Callum Mac-Taggart, Errol's much more fun cousin. I ride a Harley, after all. My cousin just has that wretched Marilyn."

"Who is Marilyn?" I ask. "Errol won't tell me."

"Then I'd better not ruin the surprise."

"Aye, ye best not," Errol says, sounding a touch grumpy. "Why don't you tell Ashley what your wife calls your Harley?"

Callum chuckles. "Kate wants to call it 'Brad.' Donnae ask me why. No one will be calling my bike by a man's name."

"I'm Ashley Hartman, by the way," I tell Callum. "And I am not Errol's girlfriend."

"Too bad. I've never seen my cousin with a woman before, unless he was hanging out with Piper or one of our cousins who are lasses." Callum rubs his chin as if he's thinking hard, but it seems like sarcasm. "Of course, Errol spends most of his time out of the country. Maybe he has a harem hidden somewhere."

"I donnae have a harem," Errol says. "But Ashley and I came here to discuss business. That means we don't want to hear about your Harley anymore."

Callum rolls his eyes in the direction of the street. "I saw the way you drove up to the café. I'm surprised Ashley didn't run for the hills the second the car stopped. Sticking with the scorched-earth method, eh, mate?"

"Haud yer wheesht, Callum. Donnae see your wife here, so she must've gotten tired of you too."

"Touchy, aren't you? Kate sent me to get breakfast and take it home. But I'll leave you and Ashley to discuss your *business*."

Callum winks at me, then walks away.

"Is your entire family weird and sarcastic?" I ask.

"Aye, the entire family. I could tell you stories about my cousins and their bizarre behavior. Might make me seem like the normal one."

"Hmm. Not sure I believe that. But I would love to hear stories about your family."

"Later. Right now, we need to talk about the expedition."

We order delicious food and enjoy it while we hash out the details of our mission, mostly what equipment we'll need once we get to the Grand Canyon. Earlier, Errol had pointed out that this will be an illegal expedition, though I prefer to think of it as unsanctioned. After all, the national parks belong to the whole country. I don't intend to destroy anything in my quest to vindicate my father. No, I want to preserve whatever we find.

After breakfast, we head back to Errol's car. He opens the door for me, and as I climb inside, he gazes at me with a strange expression. "You shouldn't have sold your house for this, Ashley. Will you have anything left when it's over?"

"Maybe not. I don't care."

"You should care. If you wind up destitute and still can't prove the treasure exists, what will you do?"

"I'll worry about that when and if it happens."

He flattens his lips and studies me for a moment. "Even if you don't care what happens to you, I do."

Errol shuts the door.

I watch him walk around to the driver's side. He cares what happens to me? I can't understand why. We don't know each other well. But he sounded completely sincere when he told me that.

During our meal, we agreed that we need to go to a bigger town to shop for equipment. Errol suggested Inverness. It's three hours away from Loch Fairbairn, and I expect we will endure the trip in silence or maybe listen to the radio. Instead, Errol tells me about his huge extended family. The Mac-Taggarts really are a wild bunch, though I still think Errol is the wildest by far. He loves to blow things up, for heaven's sake. But he swears his cousin Munro is even crazier.

"He's known as the Wild Man," Errol says. "He earned that nickname, and he's very proud of it. But let me tell you more about Logan…"

Every story he shares makes me laugh. His cousins are strange, for sure, but I can tell he has genuine affection for every single one of them. I don't have cousins. All my grandparents passed away years ago, and my mom is gone too, which leaves just me and my dad. I can't comprehend having a huge pool of cousins, aunts, and uncles.

Our shopping excursion is successful, netting us nearly all the supplies we'd hoped to find. Errol tells me he will need to "acquire" a few more "specialty items," but that I don't need to worry about that. Since the last "specialty item" he showed me turned out to be a land mine, I do worry. What crazy thing will he "acquire" this time?

Despite his weirdness and his cavalier attitude toward explosives, I do trust Errol. I believe he would never knowingly hurt me or lie to me.

On the drive back to Loch Fairbairn, Errol tells me even more stories about his family. I feel like I need to reciprocate, so I relate some stories from my adventures in the field with my dad. My experiences aren't anywhere near as wacky and entertaining as his tales of the MacTaggart clan, but he seems to enjoy listening to them anyway.

"Have you ever been married?" Errol asks after I've finished my last story.

"I was engaged once, but it didn't work out."

"What happened?"

"He screwed my maid of honor in the cloakroom of the venue where we held the rehearsal dinner—during the rehearsal dinner. Everyone heard them. They didn't even try to be sneaky about it."

"That's horrible. I hope you gave the *cacan* a right skelping."

I glance at him sideways. "Not sure if I did that, since I have no idea what you just said."

"A *cacan* is a wee shit. I said I hope you smacked him about."

"No, I didn't do that. I threw a glass of champagne in his face, and the next day, I pawned the damn engagement ring."

"Good for you, *gràidh.*"

"Don't congratulate me. I also cried for the better part of two days. A strong woman would've walked away and never looked back."

"That's rubbish." Errol holds the wheel with one hand so he can clasp mine. "Even strong women cry. Strong men can too. Real strength comes from picking yourself up again after a devastating blow. You've done that."

"How do you know?"

"Because you're here, fighting to prove your father was right about the Grand Canyon treasure." He squeezes my hand. "You are a force to be reckoned with, Ashley."

My eyes sting, like I might cry. But it's not shame causing that reaction. I want to cry because Errol just gave me the best compliment, and for the first time in my adult life, I feel like I have someone besides my dad on my side, someone who will never betray me or ridicule me. "Thank you, Errol. That's the nicest thing anyone has ever said to me."

"It's the truth, that's all."

"You honestly are a gentleman. And a sweetheart too. Not crazy at all, just quirky."

"Donnae spread that rumor. Can't have my image as the fire starter tarnished."

I lay my hand over his on my thigh. "You like for everyone to think you're a lunatic?"

"Aye. It serves my purpose." He flashes me a wicked grin. "But I am wild and barmy, just not as much of a bampot as some people think."

"I see." Oddly, I'm experiencing a powerful urge to climb onto his lap and unzip his pants. "Maybe I'm a bampot too. I got turned on by your land mine display."

"The mines did it? Here I thought it was my kilt that got you fired up."

"It was. But your wildness pushes me over the edge." I slide his hand up my thigh until his fingers brush my groin. "For example, right now I'd love to fuck you while you're driving down the road."

He chuckles. "As much as I want to do that, I think we should wait until we get home. I won't do anything to knowingly put you in danger."

"Oh, come on. Give it a try."

"Not this time." He pulls his hand away but wags his eyebrows at me. "But if you want to shag me while I'm flying Marilyn, feel free."

"Flying Marilyn?"

"Aye, that's my plane. We'll be traveling the retro way to reach England tomorrow."

"Your cousin called Marilyn wretched."

Errol makes a rude noise. "Callum likes to ride a motorcycle. That's far more dangerous than taking a trip in a World War II era DC-3."

"Is your plane really that old?"

"Aye. She's an antique." He glances at me and smiles. "Trust me, lass, Marilyn will get us there safely. Just ask Magnus and Piper. They've traveled the old-fashioned way on my private airline."

Taking a trip on an antique plane doesn't sound terribly appealing. So I have to ask a question. "Why don't we just buy airline tickets?"

"Airline?" He huffs. "No, lass, we'll travel in style and get there without going through security. This is a clandestine expedition, after all."

He won't give up on the idea of traveling on his decrepit plane, and I have to trust he knows what he's doing. Because he's right, this is a clandestine mission.

The man who has an app for setting off mines is going to fly me to England. What have I gotten myself into?

Chapter Eleven

Errol

I think Ashley has finally realized just how barmy I am and just how dangerous this mission will be. Not because of Marilyn. Not because of my land mines, either. I think my preferred mode of travel has convinced her that we will not be embarking on a holiday in the Grand Canyon. This is serious, and we will need to fly under the radar, literally and figuratively, on this adventure.

When we arrive in Loch Fairbairn, heading for our homes, I invite Ashley to have dinner at my place. She declines, politely. I think the lass is exhausted from our supply mission in Inverness, but I also think she hasn't quite digested everything we talked about today. Our unsanctioned expedition will put us in a perilous position. I can't help that. But I suspect Ashley engaged in a wee bit of self-delusion to convince herself this mission wouldn't be dangerous. Now she realizes it will be. The lass needs time to get used to the idea.

I've had years to get used to it. She has days, at most.

Once I've gone into my house and started making some food for myself, I wonder about Ashley. Will she remember to eat? She did seem off kilter when I walked her to her door earlier. Maybe I should cook something for both of us and take a meal to her. I won't insist on eating with her. She can have her privacy and quiet time, but I need to make sure she's well-nourished.

When I knock on her door, holding a plate of food, she opens the door and stares at the plate. I hold it out to her. "Not here to fash you. Just wanted to give you a good meal."

"You made me dinner?"

"Aye." I thrust the plate even closer to her. "There are no strings attached to this food, if that's what you're worried about. I only meant to ensure you ate enough."

She cautiously accepts the plate. "Thank you, Errol. That was very thoughtful."

I shrug. "Just taking care of my business partner. Get plenty of rest tonight. Tomorrow, we leave at eight thirty for our trip to Manchester."

"Okay. I'll be ready."

"Good." I clasp her free hand and kiss it. "Sleep well, *gràidh*."

Then I walk away.

In the morning, I get dressed and consider whether I should make breakfast for just myself or for Ashley too. She'll need a full stomach for our journey. But she might have eaten already. So I decide to gather some snacks for us instead, then I eat a quick breakfast and head over to Ashley's house.

At eight fifteen, I knock on her door.

The lass swings it open and raises her brows. "What's that? More food? I do know how to feed myself, you know."

I hold up the insulated bag. "These are snacks for the trip. I assumed you would have eaten breakfast already."

"Yes, I did. Snacks were a good idea, though."

"Glad you approve." I offer her my arm. "May I escort you to the car?"

She gives me an exasperated look, then accepts my arm. "Let's get going. I don't want to be late."

"We will get there on time, you have my word."

"If you fly like you drive, we'll probably get there an hour early and with our hair standing on end."

"Marilyn can't go that fast." I lead her toward my car. "A DC-3 has a maximum cruising speed of about two hundred miles an hour. An average airliner goes about six hundred miles an hour."

"We're traveling the slow way?"

"Speed isn't always the best option." I open the car door for her. "Several of my cousins have private jets that go even faster than an airliner. But Marilyn is less obvious."

Ashley doesn't seem convinced, but she climbs into the car. "Could you please drive a little slower?"

"You wouldn't want that. My insanity makes you randy."

"Maybe it does, but I'd rather not arrive at the airport looking like I just stepped off a roller coaster."

I laugh. "Airport? No, we're not going there."

"But we're flying to Manchester. In your decrepit plane, but still, we're flying."

"Aye. But Marilyn isn't parked at an airport. She's waiting for us…elsewhere." I think I'll make it a surprise for Ashley. She might leap out of the car while we're racing down the road if I tell her where I've left my plane. She's a fiery lass with a wild heart, but she can be a wee bit squeamish.

When I veer around a corner, Ashley grips the arm rest on her door as well as the one between our seats. She grimaces faintly.

"All right over there?" I ask. "Not much farther to go."

"Thank God for that." She begins to look a touch green around the gills. "Just get us there."

"Feeling queasy?"

"Not until you said that word."

I swerve off the highway into the car park of a petrol station. We don't need petrol, but I think Ashley needs a different sort of service. "Stay here. I'll be right back."

Ashley slouches in her seat and exhales a big breath.

My quick trip into the petrol station's shop gets me what I'm sure Ashley needs. I jump into the car again and hand her the wee bag. "This is for you. Look like you need it."

She eyes me with suspicion but takes the bag. When she pulls out the single item inside it, she holds up the small bottle. "Motion sickness pills?"

"Aye. The less drowsy sort, according to the information on the bottle."

"Um, thank you. It was very sweet of you to stop and get me this."

I brush the back of my hand over her cheek. "Whatever you need, I'll get it for you."

While Ashley opens the bottle and swallows a pill, I get back on the road—and do it more gently this time. I suppose my way of driving would make a lot of lasses nauseous, though none of the girls I've dated complained about that. But maybe that explains why so many of them don't want to go out with me for more than a few dates. They can't handle me.

Ashley can. Despite her need for motion sickness pills, she hasn't backed out of our expedition.

We've just turned onto a gravel road when I glance sideways at her. "Feeling better?"

"Yes, much better."

"Good. At least you're already drugged for the next leg of our journey."

She leans toward me. "You're not scaring me off."

"Donnae want to."

The trees open up to reveal an oblong clearing. At one end lies a small house. Just in front of that, my favorite girl waits for us. Well, my second favorite girl. Aye, Ashley has taken the top spot away from Marilyn. Not that Ashley *is* my girl. I haven't asked if she wants to be, but she has insisted this is business only.

I stop the car near the house. "Here we are."

She leans forward to peer out the windscreen. "Where's the runway? All I see is the plane and lots of grass."

"That's right. It's a grass strip. Only I have permission to use it."

"Do you own this property?"

"No. You'll meet the owner any minute now." I exit the car and shut the door, then take a deep breath of woodland air. The Highlands smell better than anyplace else on earth.

Ashley gets out too and yawns. "They lied about the less-drowsy part."

"You can have a wee nap once we're in the air."

The front door of the house bursts open, and a gray-haired man with unkempt hair and a bushy beard stalks up to us. He drags me into a bear hug—briefly, thank goodness.

"Good to see ye, laddie," he says. "Come to give Marilyn some exercise?"

"Aye, sort of." I wave for Ashley to come closer and slip an arm around her shoulders. "This is my Great Uncle Torcall Murdoch, who's the uncle of my father. He's lived out here for so long that we've all decided he wants to become a bear and repopulate the species in Scotland."

"Tosh," Torcall says. "Are ye taking your lass on an aerial tour of Loch Fairbairn to scare the tourists? Last time you did that, we had UFO reports filed at the police station."

"A DC-3 looks nothing like a UFO. Besides, I only flew low over the village twice, and that was ages ago."

"So now 'ages' means 'last week'?"

"No. It was…at least a month ago."

Ashley's lips tighten into a closed-mouth smile. "I missed all the fun, huh?"

"Not at all. I've got plenty more excitement for you, donnae worry about that." I turn to Torcall. "Would you mind if I leave my car here? We'll only be gone for the day, back before nightfall, I'm sure."

"I'll guard your car, Errol. Not that it looks like anything a thief might want. Why donnae ye buy a nice, shiny new Land Rover?"

"I like the classics."

Torcall snorts. "Not everything old is a classic."

"Come on, Ashley," I say. "We'd best get on our way, or else we'll miss our appointment."

"I hope ye brought earplugs, lass," Torcall tells Ashley.

She looks at me. "Is your plane really loud?"

"Of course not. Torcall likes to exaggerate, and he's never even taken a ride in Marilyn. So he doesnae have a clue what he's on about."

Torcall snorts again. "I have ears, Errol. Your plane makes a bloody awful racket every time ye take off. It's no wonder they wouldn't let you park your monstrosity at the Glencoe Airfield."

No, that's not why I was, ah, sort of banned. They didn't like it when I buzzed the airfield and scared a school group who were having a tour of the facility. I thought they would appreciate it, and the children did. The adults… Well, they lacked the sense of humor required to appreciate a low fly-over. They thought I was going to crash, but I've never missed a landing.

Don't think I'll tell Ashley about that. Not yet. Maybe once we're in the air, and she's recovered from takeoff.

Torcall folds his arms over his chest. "Did ye ever tell anyone at the Glencoe Airfield about your security system? They would've had you arrested if you did, so you must not have."

"Haud yer wheesht, Torcall." I take hold of Ashley's hand. "Let's go."

We stride a third of the way down the clearing to where I'd parked Marilyn after my last flight. I haven't flown much lately. Ever since Istanbul, I just can't muster any excitement for anything.

"Didn't you say you flew this thing to Istanbul?" Ashley asks. "That means you must've flown it all the way back to Scotland, huh?"

"Aye. It took about sixteen hours, with three stops along the way to refuel—Marilyn and me. She's easier to feed."

"Were you flying alone?"

"That's right." I release her hand as we reach the aircraft. "Stay here. I need to open the door."

"What did Torcall mean about your security system?"

"It's nothing. I don't even use it anymore."

No, I will not explain that. Well, maybe once we're in the air and she can't escape.

I open one side of the large cargo door and grab the ladder, leaning it against the plane. Then I wave to Ashley. "Come on. I'll help you up."

She approaches the plane and stops at the ladder, chewing on the inside of her lip. "You're sure this is safe."

"Aye. If you trust me, then trust Marilyn too."

"Might help if you stopped referring to it by a woman's name. Why Marilyn, anyway?"

"Because I like Marilyn Monroe movies. Would you rather I rename this thing Magnus?"

"No. Can't you just call it 'the plane'?"

I shake my head and sigh, then offer her my hand. "Time to get in, lass. You can criticize the name I gave my aircraft later."

She accepts my hand, climbing up the ladder. I give her erse a wee push to help her make the last step into the plane. Maybe I do that because I enjoy touching her erse, but I also have a legitimate reason for doing it.

She glances back at me. "Do I get to put my hands on your ass too?"

"Anytime ye like. But I don't need help getting into the plane." I reach up to grasp the top of the rail on the ladder and hoist myself up and into the plane. Then I pull the ladder inside and sigh with satisfaction. "See? No problem at all."

Her jaw has fallen open a touch. "I can't believe you did that. The door must be six feet off the ground."

"Not quite. But I'll accept your compliment anyway."

"I didn't give you a compliment."

"Of course you did." I pat her erse. "Your gaping jaw told me so."

"Can we get going now?"

"Aye. Follow me."

I start walking toward the cockpit, but since the aircraft is on the ground, the rear section is angled downward with the tail wheel resting on the ground. This creates a rather steep grade. Ashley trips over one of the floor rails. I catch her before she falls.

"What are these rails for?" she asks. "Seems dangerous to have them there."

"The rails are for securing the cargo with the belts you see." I pick her up and carry her toward the open doorway to the cockpit. "Time to get strapped in, Ashley. We're about to take off."

Chapter Twelve

Ashley

Is this plane actually air-worthy?" I ask, as he carries me into the cramped, somewhat dilapidated cockpit and sets me down on a seat that has no arms. "I see wires hanging out of the doohickeys on the dashboard or whatever you call it. Is it even legal to fly a rickety old plane? Do you have a pilot's license? Maybe we should drive to Inverness and catch the next commercial flight to Manchester."

Errol straps me in with a lap belt and gives me a patient smile. "Relax, lass. I know what I'm doing, I haven't killed anyone yet."

Not yet? Oh, yeah, that's very comforting. I might be panicking. My pulse is racing, my breaths come fast and shallow, and my face has started to tingle. *Breathe, idiot, slow and easy.* My self-administered advice helps a little. I swear I'm not a coward. But after experiencing how Errol drives a car, I can't help worrying about the way he plans on flying this plane.

Errol lays a palm on my cheek and urges me to look at him. "Would it help if I kissed you? That seems to make you very relaxed and mindless."

"Not sure if—"

He seals his mouth over mine and pushes his hand into my hair to cradle my nape. His breaths warm my face, and the feel of his lips does have the desired effect. I can't stop my body from softening or a slight moan from flowing out of me. This shouldn't work. A kiss to make me less anxious? But every time Errol touches his lips to mine I melt and suddenly can't remember anything except how much I want to thrust my tongue into his mouth.

When he pulls his head back, he smirks at me. "That did the trick, aye? Let me know when you need another kiss to boost your morale."

It's not my morale that got slick and hot from a simple lip-lock.

Errol climbs into the other seat and buckles up, then he starts fiddling with controls. "We'll take off shortly."

"You never answered my question about the wires and stuff that stick out of the dashboard."

"It's the instrument panel, not the dashboard."

Knowing the correct term for it also doesn't make me feel any better. Maybe I do need another "morale boost" from Errol, but I'll never tell him that. He must think I'm a moron, but I know he's insane, so we're even.

In front of me, I see a steering wheel. But the thing seems to have something wrong with it. When I glance at Errol's side of the cockpit, I notice his wheel looks the same. "The steering wheels are broken. The top third is completely missing. How can you fly that way?"

He gives me another patient smile. "They're called control wheels, and they are not broken. This is what the wheels are meant to look like. Would you feel better if I explained the purpose of every instrument? Rudder pedals, aileron trim, azimuth indicator…"

"You can stop. We need to get going, so I'll just live with not understanding how this plane works. But I am worried about those wires."

"They're fine, Ashley. You said you trust me, so trust me."

"Okay. I'm sorry to be such an annoying pain in the ass."

He leans over to pat my cheek. "You are not a pain, and I'm not annoyed. But I do love your erse."

"You're very patient, Errol. After your pyrotechnic display, I wasn't expecting that." I glance up at an instrument I do recognize. "You have a compass."

"Aye."

"No GPS?"

He sighs. "No, lass, I prefer the old-school ways."

"Do you have a radio? In case of emergency?"

Errol starts fiddling with controls on the instrument panel. "Yes, Ashley, I do have a radio. It was broken, but I bought a new one in preparation for this flight. No need to panic. But if the radio should stop working, I have an alternate means of communication." He wrestles an object out of his pants pocket and holds up his phone. "Right here."

"Oh. Good."

He messes around with more instruments. "No more talking. I need to focus on getting us off the ground."

I keep my mouth shut and grip the edges of my armless seat. I have motion sickness pills, but I think I should've asked Errol to get me some

Xanax. I've traveled to remote locations with my dad, and we experienced some scary moments now and then, so I can't explain why the idea of going for a ride in a World War II era plane makes me freak out.

Maybe it's not the plane or the man flying it. Maybe I'm panicking because the expedition I've spent years planning for is finally about to happen. What if we fail? What if the treasure is a myth after all? I'll have let my dad down and burned through my savings, leaving me penniless.

A loud sputtering noise erupts outside and quickly ramps up, mutating into the loud growling of an engine.

Oh God, we're about to lift off.

I want to squeeze my eyes shut, but I feel like I need to see what's happening—at the very least, to prove to myself I'm not a coward.

"Hold on," Errol says, flashing me a grin. "It's takeoff time."

The plane begins to roll forward, faster and faster every moment as we race toward the end of the clearing—the end of the grass airstrip. We won't crash into the trees. Will we? Errol must know what he's doing, right? Magnus and Piper flew in this plane with him, and they're still alive.

"Here we go," Errol says.

The front of the plane rises, and the ground vanishes from my view as the aircraft levels off.

"All done," Errol says, patting my shoulder. "Ye didnae die, did ye? I'd call that a successful takeoff."

Well, I can't argue with that.

He holds the wheel in one hand while we soar across Scotland from high above. The houses and trees look tiny from up here.

"Lookie there," Errol says, using his free hand to point out my window. "That's Dùndubhan. Seems like a child's toy from this vantage point, aye?"

"Yes, it does. But honestly, I think I'll avoid looking out the window. Not used to flying this way."

"With no flight attendant or drinks service?"

"Uh-huh."

"Did you fly first class from America?"

"First class?" I shake my head. "How do you think I could afford that? You know every penny I have is sunk into this expedition."

"I've never flown first class either." He executes a slight turn to the right. "Not being rich isn't a crime. I'm not rolling in money either, though several of my cousins are. I donnae feel bad about myself because of that, and you shouldn't either. You're a clever, determined, strong woman. Money didn't make you that way. It came from deep inside you."

His words trigger a warm glow in my chest. I have no idea why. Hearing Errol sing my praises shouldn't have this kind of effect on me, but then, I've endured ridicule for years because I refused to declare that my father is a crackpot. Errol believes in me. He wants to help me. Sure, I'm paying him to do that, but he could've told me to buzz off. Maybe he did say that a few times. But he didn't tell me that every time I showed up at his home to pester him to go on this mission with me.

"How are you doing over there?" Errol asks. "If you need a sick bag, I've got a few under my seat."

"If you mean a barf bag, no, I don't need one. I feel fine."

"So, only my driving makes you ill."

"Well, I did take a motion sickness pill earlier. Maybe that's why I'm okay now."

He flicks some switches or whatever the proper term is for them. Then he takes his hands off the wheel and relaxes in his seat.

"Why aren't you flying the plane?" I ask, trying so hard not to screech.

"Take it easy, *gràidh*. I turned on the autopilot."

"Oh. Sorry I freaked out again."

He stretches an arm out to lay his hand on my shoulder. "You didn't do that."

"Most men would've gotten fed up with me way before we reached the airstrip. Thank you for putting up with me."

"No need to thank me. We're partners now, which means it's my job to help you in whatever way you need."

Is that the only reason he puts up with my behavior? We had sex the other night, and though I insisted we're still only business partners, my heart has other ideas. It insists that incident meant a lot more. But I can't think about that right now. Too much is at stake.

"How should we while away the time until we reach Manchester?" Errol asks. "We could haver about the expedition. Or we could play card games."

"I doubt I could concentrate on a card game. And there isn't much to talk about until after we study the map."

"Well, then. It's option three." He unhooks his lap belt. "Let's have a shag."

"What? You need to fly the plane."

"It's on autopilot. And besides, we donnae need to leave the cockpit to have a shag. Just climb onto my lap, *gràidh*."

Sex in a dilapidated airplane? Oh, I can't do that. Can I? I've never been adventurous, when it comes to sex, but Errol showed me I have a lot of pent-up wildness inside me. What we did on the green at Dùndubhan would be nothing compared to getting it on inside the cockpit of an airplane.

"Have you ever joined the mile-high club?" Errol asks.

"No. Have you?"

He shakes his head, then cups his groin with one hand. "But I'd love to reach that milestone with you."

Errol is one hundred percent serious. I can tell that much. He wants to have sex right now, and suddenly, I realize I want that too. It's insane. We shouldn't do this. But I'm already wet just from thinking about it, and my nipples have started to ache, their tips growing sensitive. My own breathing makes my bra rasp over my nipples, heightening my desire.

For Errol Murdoch. No other man has ever wanted me the way he does, and I've never wanted any other man this way.

"Okay," I almost whisper. "Let's do it."

A slow, wicked smile stretches his lips. His voice shifts into a deeper, hotter register. "Remove your trousers and knickers, Ashley, then climb onto my lap."

My breaths have quickened. I want this more than I should, more than common sense allows, but I don't care if it's crazy and wrong and might result in a fiery crash if we bump into the autopilot controls. All I can think about is that soon I'll have Errol inside me again. What happened to business partners only? I don't give a damn. My hormones have taken control, and I intend to ignore my brain.

I unhook my lap belt, kick my shoes off, and shimmy out of my pants and underwear. Naked from the waist down, I stand up on my seat and jump over to Errol's side, then lower myself onto my knees. He sets his hands on my hips as I wriggle to get in a good position. While he whisks his palms up and down my thighs, I unzip his pants and pull his dick out. It's already firming up.

"Need my purse," I say. "It's on the floor behind my seat. Can you reach it?"

"No need. I've got a condom in my pocket." He shoves a hand into that pocket, bringing out a foil packet. "Here it is."

I snatch the packet away and tear it open with my teeth.

He lunges his head forward to push his face between my thighs. He licks my flesh with such vigor, such intense hunger, that I gasp and grip the back of the seat with one hand. Errol keeps going, devouring me like he hasn't eaten a crumb of food in weeks and he'll die without the nourishment my body gives him. I gasp and moan and grunt while the need to come builds inside me, and my sex throbs.

"Oh God, Errol, yes." I thrust my hips forward, silently begging him to hurtle me over the edge.

He plunges two fingers inside me.

And I plummet off the cliff. My inner muscles clench his fingers while he latches on to my clit and suckles it so fiercely that I scream. He doesn't stop, though. He keeps pumping his fingers and consuming my nub, wringing every last spasm from my body. The pleasure becomes so intense that I can't scream anymore, can't even gasp. I can only clutch the seat back and ride out the orgasm.

I glance down. His dick is rock-hard now.

Errol leans back and snatches the condom packet from my fingers. His face glistens with my cream, the way it had on that night at Dùndubhan. He's always ravenous for me, and that fact makes my clit throb again.

Errol rolls the condom over his length. "Mount me, lass. Do it right now."

Chapter Thirteen

Errol

I love to do wild things, but even I have never shagged a lass in my DC-3 while we're in the air. Why haven't I done that? It's exactly the sort of thing I would do. Most women never get past my method of driving, so they never get to meet Marilyn or take a ride with me in my World War II era plane. Ashley was terrified, but she wanted to come with me anyway. She initiated the explosive sex we had at Dùndubhan the other night. And as soon as I suggested fucking in flight, she agreed immediately.

I could fall in love with this woman.

Ashley bends her knees and slowly lowers her body onto my *slat.* My pulse accelerates from the feel of her heat surrounding me and the knowledge that this lass is about to ride me like the naughtiest cowgirl on earth. I groan when she finally has sunk herself all the way onto me. I can still taste the flavor of her on my tongue, and the scent of her lust for me surrounds us like the most intoxicating perfume. I've never craved any other woman like this, but ever since we shagged for the first time, I couldnae stop thinking about doing it again.

She begins to rock her hips, and the friction of our bodies merging makes me breathe harder and grasp her hips to encourage the lass to move faster. But she doesn't. She sets her hands on my shoulders and keeps rocking in a leisurely rhythm with her gaze locked on mine and her lips parted.

Bod an Donais, I need to kiss her.

The lass sinks deeper into my lap and slows her movements even more, as if she means to relish every moment to the fullest. I want that too, but I donnae have the willpower. It takes all my self-control to stop myself from thrusting up to fuck her harder and faster. Since I've tasked myself with not doing that, I grit my teeth and push my hands up under her shirt until I feel the edge of her bra, then I reach behind her back to unhook the clasps. A wee gasp escapes her lips. I slide my hands inside the cups of her bra to push them out of the way, and her tits spill into my palms. Cannae resist flicking my thumbs across her nipples.

"Oh," she gasps. "Don't stop, Errol."

Does she think I could stop even if I wanted to? I couldnae, and I donnae want to. So I palm her tits and massage them gently. "Faster, *gràidh*, faster. Willnae last much longer. Let go and be the wild woman who fucked me on the green."

"I loved that."

She digs her fingers into my shoulders and bounces on my cock, her breathing hectic and her sharp cries growing louder every moment. Then she suddenly shifts to rocking wildly back and forth, and I pinch her nipples to make her cry out again. She shouts my name, riding me with abandon, throwing her head back so her hair lashes my face. Donnae care. I shove a hand between her folds to pinch her clit.

A strangled scream bursts out of her, and her body grips my *slat* over and over, the spasms powerful enough to make me shout. I grasp her hips and punch into her twice more until I come inside her, shouting as the rapid-fire spasms in my cock force me to spend myself deep inside her hot sheath. *Mhac na galla*, that was incredible.

The lass falls into a heap on top of me, her head on my shoulder. "Wow, Errol, I didn't think anything could be as good as the first time. I was wrong."

"Aye, it was just as good. Next time, we'll do even better."

For a few minutes, we just sit here recovering from the intensity of that bloody incredible poke. I hadn't intended to take her again, but Ashley is the sexiest woman I've ever met. I can't control myself when I'm with her. Does that mean something? No, it only means that I enjoy her body and her passion.

"Best climb off me, lass," I say. "Need to turn off the autopilot and prepare for landing."

She raises her head to look at me. "I told you we would never have sex again, that this was strictly business. But I just ripped that idea to shreds and threw the pieces out the window."

"It's all right." I smile and palm her erse. "I don't mind if you want to use my body for your own pleasure."

"You're giving me an out. Why?"

"Because I like you, Ashley. Let's not overanalyze a fantastic poke."

"Okay." She crawls onto her own seat and struggles to get back into her clothes. As she ties her shoelaces, she glances at me sideways. "Will we be landing on another grass strip?"

"No. We will land on an actual runway." I switch off the autopilot and take hold of the wheel. "The Manchester airport hasn't heard about my unique style of flying."

"It's more like your unique style of living."

"Aye, that's an accurate assessment."

"How long until we land?"

I check the clock on my mobile. "Forty-five minutes, give or take. Depends on whether they've had delays for other flights. Donnae worry. We will get there on time."

"What if our landing is delayed?"

I give her my best naughty smile. "Then once we do land, I'll drive extremely fast. You'll be screaming, though not in ecstasy this time, and we will arrive at our destination by ten o'clock."

"Good. I believe you will do that."

"And you aren't going to complain about my driving?"

"No, that's your domain." She grabs her purse from the floor and pulls out a pill bottle. "Besides, I've got my motion sickness remedy. That means you can go nuts on the streets of Manchester."

Oh, aye. I could fall in love with this woman for certain.

Not that I plan to do that.

As we get closer to the airport, I need to focus on our approach and keeping in contact with the air traffic controller via radio. Ashley stays quiet and watches out the side window as we gradually make our descent toward the runway. She must be anxious, but the lass is hiding it well. When I reach over to give her hand a quick squeeze, she aims a tight smile at me.

"Almost there," I say. "Now it's time to make our final approach."

I've done this many times at many different airports, air strips, and even in the desert with no runway. I could tell Ashley that, but I think she understands now that I will not crash us into anything. We touch down without incident, and we're directed to our assigned slot where we will leave the plane. I help Ashley climb down the ladder and follow her onto the tarmac.

"See?" I say. "No explosions or fiery crashes. We survived."

Ashley throws her arms around my neck and kisses my cheek. "Thank you for being so patient with me, Errol. And thank you for the amazing orgasm too."

"Orgasms, plural. I made ye come twice."

"That you did." She steps back and straightens her clothes, then pats her hair as if she's checking that it still looks all right. "Where's our car?"

"It will be here any moment." I sling an arm around her waist and tug the lass into me. "How about a kiss while we wait?"

She opens her mouth as if to speak, but something past my shoulder grabs her attention. "What is that?"

I turn sideways while keeping her tucked against me. "Ah, that would be Roger. He lets me borrow his car whenever I fly into Manchester."

"But that is a hearse."

"Roger also owns a funeral home."

Her eyes go wide. "Please don't tell me there's a dead body in that car."

I chuckle. "No, lass. Only you and I will ride in that vehicle."

Her shoulders sag. "Oh, thank goodness."

My mate meets us near the plane and hands me the car keys. Then Ashley and I take our seats and begin the last leg of our journey to the home of Wilfrid Ellsworth, the bloke who owns the original version of the map Ashley had shown me. As we pull into the driveway, I can't help smirking.

I point at the dashboard clock. "Look at that. I got us here two minutes ahead of schedule. Now, I seem to recall someone was worried we would never get here on time."

"Yes, okay, I admit it. You were right. I was wrong. Never again will I question your ability to get me somewhere on time."

"Thank you. I always appreciate validation from a bonnie, sexy lass."

I park alongside the car I assume belongs to Ellsworth. His driveway is quite wide, so there's plenty of room. Our hearse is an older model, while Ellsworth's car looks like a brand-new red Aston Martin. Well, if he's rich, that would explain how he could buy a rare artifact like the map we've come to see.

Ashley and I walk up the steps onto the porch, and I ring the bell.

The door opens a moment later, and a gray-haired gent with a deeply wrinkled face scans us as if he means to determine whether we're friend or foe. "Who are you?"

No pleasantries, then.

I offer my hand. "Errol Murdoch. And this lovely lass is Ashley Hartman, the one who called you yesterday to arrange a viewing of the map."

"Do you have identification?"

So he's that sort. This man reminds me of Mungo Gunn, but without the smell of marijuana wafting off him. I get out my driving license and hand it to him.

He seems satisfied, but he also seems to be waiting for Ashley to produce her ID too. She digs her license out of her purse and offers it to our host.

"All right, you can come in," Ellsworth announces. "But don't touch anything. I have many valuable and delicate artifacts on display."

Ellsworth leads us down the entryway, but he veers away from the living room to head down a long, gloomy hallway. All the doors down this hall are closed. At the second to last door, Ellsworth pulls a key out of his pocket and inserts it into the lock. Then he swings the door inward.

"You may enter," he says. "But do not touch anything without my express permission."

This gentleman might not be as barmy as Mungo Gunn, but he does seem to be a wee bit paranoid.

Ellsworth leads us into what looks like an office, with a large mahogany desk and a globe on a stand in the corner. I also notice a massive unabridged dictionary on another stand, as well as an entire encyclopedia sitting upright on a long table in the corner.

"Where's the map?" I ask.

Our host waves for us to follow him to the desk, then gestures for us to sit down. He rolls the leather chair behind the desk backward to make room and settles onto the seat, leaning forward to unlock a drawer and pull it open. Gingerly, Ellsworth slides out a rectangular sheet of paper protected by a clear plastic cover. He lays it down flat on the desk.

"This map was discovered by my great grandfather, Aldis Ellsworth, in nineteen hundred and twenty-three." He spreads his palms over the plastic-shielded treasure. "He was hiking in the Grand Canyon, hoping to retrace the steps of John Wesley Powell's expedition. He befriended the Havasupai tribe that lives deep inside the canyon, and they shared a story with him about ancient oriental treasures found some distance away from the Havasupai encampment. They provided him with this map, as a gift, since they had no use for a treasure."

"And it's been in your family for all this time?" Ashley asks.

"Yes. We've kept it as a family heirloom, and we assumed it was a hoax. No one has ever found oriental treasures from the distant past in Arizona."

"Are you familiar with the newspaper story from nineteen oh nine? The one that claims to relate the story of an expedition mounted by the Smithsonian."

"I have heard of that. Honestly, I don't care about the myths that surround the map. I care only for its intrinsic value as an artifact."

Ashley is wriggling in her chair and wringing her hands while she stares at the map on Ellsworth's desk. Aye, the lass is a wee bit excited. I am too, but not visibly. Her impatience makes me want to kiss her again, but then, essentially everything she does makes me want to do that.

The lass shimmies forward in her chair. "May we examine the map? I brought white gloves. We won't damage the artifact in any way."

White gloves? Not sure what that's about, but then, I'm not a museum archivist like Piper. Ashley isn't an archivist either, as far as I know, but she seems to have studied up on how to handle precious artifacts. Why else would she mention white gloves?

Ellsworth rises from his chair. "You may examine it for thirty minutes at most. Keep the map inside its plastic sheath as much as possible. If you need to remove the sheath, please wear your gloves and handle it with care. I will be in the solarium. Come find me when you are finished."

Well, maybe he's not as paranoid as I thought after all. The bloke means to leave us alone with his priceless artifact.

Ashley looks and sounds quite serious and sincere when she says, "We will treat this like the treasure it is."

Ellsworth nods and leaves the room.

And at last, we get to examine the map.

Chapter Fourteen

Ashley

I approach the desk while tiptoeing, which seems like a silly thing to do, but I've never handled an antique document before. When I'd learned this map existed, I read several books on how to preserve and handle old documents, so I'd be prepared if I ever got the chance to view the Ellsworth map. I should probably call it the Havasupai map, though. They created it, after all.

Leaning forward, I peer at the upside-down illustration.

Errol comes up behind me, leans around my body, and sets his hand on the plastic-shielded map. Then he twists his hand to spin the thing so it faces us. "Easier to read this way, eh?"

"But you said the map is upside down."

"Aye, and this is the right way. Ellsworth had it flipped the wrong way in the drawer."

"I see. Well, let's take a good hard look at this."

Errol and I pull our chairs up to the desk. I bring out my magnifying glass, but he insists we'll get better, clearer magnification by using his phone's camera to zoom in on the images. He's right. That method provides clearer images than if we used the magnifying glass. I can see details that weren't visible in the photographs I'd taken the first time Ellsworth let me view the map. Then, he wouldn't let me remove it from the plastic cover, but today, he did. I wonder what changed. Finding out will have to wait.

I bring out two sets of white gloves and hand one pair to Errol. "We need to wear these."

"Whatever you say, *gràidh*." He slips on the gloves. "I'll follow your lead."

"But you're the riddle-solving expert. You should take the lead."

"All right, I will." He plants one hand on the desk, tilting forward slightly, and stares down at the map. "You should study it too. Four eyes are better than two, especially when I have such a clever partner with me."

We both pore over the lines and shaded areas on the drawing, which has an off-white background as if it's made of parchment. Maybe it's animal skin. Vellum was popular in medieval Europe, and it was fashioned from sheepskin. Would the Havasupai use that sort of paper? The type of material hardly matters. I need to focus on the imagery. I see nothing that resembles words, in any language I know of, so I assume the map is strictly an image. Like any good treasure map, it contains symbols that seem to represent natural features.

"Doesn't this look like the Colorado River?" I ask. "But there's another river-like feature that might be an offshoot."

"Aye, that must be the Colorado." He traces another line with his fingertip. "This looks like the Little Colorado River, and that might be the Pariah River. There are also smaller waterways, like Knob Creek and Havasu Creek."

His list of Grand Canyon waterways makes me stop and look at him. "How do you know so much about the Grand Canyon? Have you been there before?"

"No, I haven't. But my cousin Munro used to be a river guide in the canyon, so he told me all about the various rivers and streams."

"He used to be a river guide? What does he do now?"

Errol shrugs. "Not sure. He's kept himself to himself ever since he gave up his job. He loved being a guide, so I donnae understand why he quit."

"Does he live in Scotland?"

"No, not for years. He went on holiday in America, visiting all sorts of places. But when he saw the Grand Canyon and went on a river excursion, he fell in love with that place. Never wanted to leave, apparently."

Though I'd love to hear more about his cousin—all his cousins, actually, and any other family members he wants to tell me about—we have more pressing issues. Figuring out this map might take days, but we have half an hour. Less, in fact. We've already spent eleven minutes examining the map and chatting about his cousin. Only nineteen more to go.

"What about these faint lines here?" I ask. "Do you think that could be a route to a specific place in the canyon?"

"You're hoping it marks the way to the secret system of caverns."

"Of course I am. That's what we're looking for."

"Aye, but the lines aren't clear. I'd need to study this for hours, not minutes, to decipher what meaning, if any, those faint streaks hold."

I bow my head and sigh. "We have seventeen minutes left."

"Donnae worry. I have a backup plan."

"You don't need to pretend for my sake. There's no way Ellsworth will let us take the map with us, or give us more time to study it. He seems very protective of the map, like it's his sacred family legacy."

"To him, it is. The Havasupai made this map for his great grandfather and gifted it to him. That must've meant a great deal to the elder Mr. Ellsworth."

"Yeah, I'm sure it is important to the family." I stare down at the beautifully rendered map, with its mysterious symbols and enigmatic lines. And I suddenly get a naughty idea. So I sidle closer to Errol and whisper in his ear, "Let's take high-resolution pictures of the map. Lots of them. Close-ups and full views, everything in between. We have enough time for that."

"Breaking the rules our host set? Ashley, I'm shocked." He palms my ass. "And randy too. Your bad-girl side arouses me."

"I'm desperate. That's the only reason I'm willing to break the rules."

"All right. We'll use the camera on my mobile. It has higher resolution than yours, and a better quality lens."

"How do you know that?"

Errol's lips form a mischievous smile. "Because I took a peek at your mobile while you were staring out the window during our flight to Manchester. I had the same idea as you, to snap high-res pictures of the map. Didnae expect you to suggest that, though. I assumed I'd need to talk you into it."

"Shush. We need to take those pictures now."

For the next fifteen minutes, we take as many photos as we can from as many angles as possible, and we also use different types of lighting. The desk lamp casts a golden light on the map, while the sunshine coming through the window provides natural tones. We've just finished, and Errol has just stashed his phone in his pocket, when Ellsworth walks into the room.

"Are you finished?" he asks. "I have errands to run."

"Yes," I say. "We're finished. Thank you so much for letting us view the map."

"If you ever prove my great grandfather's tale is true, please let me know."

"Of course. Thank you again, Mr. Ellsworth. You have no idea how much this map has helped or what deciphering it means to me." Since I feel a tad guilty about sneakily photographing the map, I decide to share a sliver of my story with him. "My father was an avocational archaeologist, and he believed in the Grand Canyon treasure. His colleagues ridiculed him for that, and he eventually gave up the quest. I want to prove he was right—which would also prove your great grandfather was right."

"I wish you well, Ms. Hartman. Many men and women have gone through what our families have, and it's time someone proved they've been right all along."

Ellsworth walks us to the front door and waves as we climb into the hearse. Then he retreats into his house. Errol insists on driving, naturally, but he keeps to the speed limit. That seems odd, considering the way he's driven every other time I've been in a vehicle with him.

"Are you feeling okay?" I ask.

"Me? Aye, fine."

"I only ask because you're driving, um, like a sane person. That doesn't seem like your style, so I assumed you were distracted or upset about something."

Errol eyes me sideways. "Donnae worry about me, lass. I was thinking, that's all. Deep thoughts require less adventurous driving."

"Oh, sure. Maybe I should drive so you can keep thinking."

"We're almost to the airport. Once we're wheels up, I'll set the autopilot and let Marilyn take over for a wee while so I can concentrate on solving the puzzle of the Havasupai map. Sound good?"

"Yes." I relax in my seat and gaze out the window. "Do you think you really can decipher the map?"

"Aye. I've never failed yet. Puzzles and riddles are my forte."

I believe him, and I trust him. Usually, I need considerable time to get to know someone before I lay all my hopes and dreams in that person's hands. Not this time. I know Errol will figure out the mystery.

Errol's friend meets us at the airport. Apparently, Errol had texted the man while he was driving down the road. I've always believed multitasking was a myth, but Errol proves me wrong at every turn. While his friend drives off in the hearse, we climb the ladder to board Marilyn. Yes, I've decided to go along with the anthropomorphizing of an airplane because, honestly, I've met men who gave women's names to much weirder mechanical devices. Okay, maybe I assign male names to certain devices that I own, the kind that vibrate and never call me "babe," which I've always hated. But I don't need those inanimate stand-ins anymore. I've got Errol.

Why did I think that? It's not like we're dating.

At least he doesn't call me "babe." Or maybe he does. I think he's been speaking Gaelic, which means I have no clue what he's saying sometimes.

Errol plants both hands on my ass to "help" me get into the plane. Oh yeah, I've figured out he's doing that to feel me up, but I don't care. Maybe I'll feel him up too. I get a sliver of revenge when he jumps into the plane and walks past me. Yeah, I slap his ass.

He glances over his shoulder and winks. "Wanting another shag in the cockpit, eh?"

"No. You're supposed to study the map while we're flying back to Scotland."

"Aye, but I'd feel even more motivated to do that if you go down on me while I rack my brain for the solution to the map riddle."

I assume he's joking, though maybe I shouldn't. Errol can be an even bigger enigma than the map.

He scoops me up in his arms and carries me into the cockpit. Then he sets me down on my seat. I watch him hop onto his seat and can't help admiring his ass again while he does that. The man has a fantastic bottom. I'd love to nibble on it. But more than anything, because Errol mentioned it, I desperately want to take his dick in my mouth again. He didn't let me finish last time, and I want to taste him so badly that my mouth waters every time I think about it.

I've never been like this with any other man. Either I'm losing my mind, or I'm finally releasing the wild woman who had hidden inside me for so long.

Errol starts up the engines and contacts the control tower for clearance to take off. Within minutes, we're in the air, flying over northern England on our way back to the Highlands. Errol engages the autopilot and pulls a computer bag out from under his seat.

"Where did that come from?" I ask. "Didn't see it when we left Scotland."

"I keep a spare laptop in the cockpit under my seat." He unzips the bag and brings out his computer. "That way, I've always got computing power on hand."

"That's a smart idea. Do you have another laptop at home?"

"Aye. And both computers are linked via the cloud, so I can access all my files at any time." He flips up the laptop's lid. "Of course, we're well away from the cloud at this altitude. I'll need to let the computer upload everything once we land."

"But we're in the clouds right now."

"Very funny, ye cheeky lass. Cumulus clouds can't transmit data."

I watch as he starts up the computer and digs a cable out of the bag, then uses that to connect his phone to the laptop. Soon, he's downloading all the high-resolution images we took of the map. He flips through the pictures too fast for me to keep up, and he repeatedly zooms in and out at high speed too. I think Errol's brain works differently than anybody else's, which helps him process information much faster.

Since I can't follow what he's doing, I resort to gazing out the window. Pretty clouds can't hold my attention for long, though, not when I desperately want to know if Errol has found anything. Pestering him won't help. I know that, and I bite my tongue for as long as I can, vowing to myself that I will not harass him until at least an hour has passed.

The wait drives me crazy.

I try to take a nap, but I don't feel tired enough for that. So I get out my phone and play games on it, but I've never had any interest in that sort of thing. I lean over to study the instruments on the dashboard—the instrument panel, Errol said—but I have no idea what an altimeter is, and the only thing I recognize on the panel is the magnetic compass.

My phone tells me thirty-five minutes have elapsed. Is that close enough to an hour? Probably not. I count clouds for a while and try to see shapes in them. That gets boring too.

"Eureka!" Errol shouts.

I jump and squeak. "What happened?"

"My eureka moment, that's what." He turns his computer screen toward me and grins. "I've broken the code."

Chapter Fifteen

Errol

I have actually done it. I solved the riddle of the map in less than an hour. Ashley stares at me like I've sprouted green grass on my head, but I think she just doesn't realize what I've done. I need to explain it to her, but first, I want to celebrate. So I stand up and set my computer on the seat, then I lean over to plant a solid kiss on her lips.

Now she's staring at me with wide eyes.

"Are ye having a stroke?" I ask. "Didn't ye hear what I just said? I solved the riddle."

"I heard you. But I—I can't believe you did that so fast. Are you sure you got it right?"

"Aye, I'm positive. Let me show you." I pick up my laptop and sit down again. After bringing up the right series of images, I rotate the computer screen toward Ashley. "Here's the proof."

Her brows knit together as she looks at the screen. "Proof of what? I still don't see anything other than squiggles and funny symbols."

"It's not a map. It's the legend for the map, which means it's a list of symbols used on the actual drawing." I point toward one of the squiggles she had mentioned. "This is the symbol for a river or stream. Some squiggles are narrower than others, and that seems like a notation for a creek."

"Okay. That makes sense."

"And here…" I point to an upside-down L-shaped symbol. "This clearly represents a canyon."

"But the whole map would be one long canyon, right? The Grand Canyon."

"Aye, but there are smaller offshoots throughout the length of the Colorado River and its tributaries."

"I didn't think about that. But you're right. There are numerous smaller canyons." Ashley slants closer to the screen and squints. "What do you think that symbol is?"

She points at an arching line.

"Ah, yes, that." I can't resist smirking. "I figured out what that represents too. It's a cave."

The lass gives me a skeptical look. "How could you possibly figure that out? It's a curved line. I was willing to accept that an L-shaped thingy is a canyon, but I see no way you could determine that a curved line is a cave."

"Allow me to elaborate." I gesture with my finger as I point out various shaded areas. "These areas represent the cliffs along the rivers, and darker shading shows anomalies in the vertical surfaces—fissures, mostly, I would guess. But also caves."

"That makes sense. But again, how can you tell which symbol signifies a cave? A curved line could be an arch."

"Aren't many of those a thousand feet up on a sheer cliff face."

"But you still haven't proved—"

"Let me finish, *gràidh*."

She gets the most adorably confused look on her face. "What is that thing you keep calling me?"

"Thing?"

"I can't pronounce it. But you said 'let me finish,' followed by a bizarre word you've said before."

"Ah, that." I scratch my cheek and focus on the computer screen. "It's not a bizarre word. It's Gaelic."

"What does it mean?"

I hadn't realized I keep calling her "darling" in Gaelic until she told me that a moment ago. But now that I think about it, aye, I have been saying that word lately. It means I like her, I suppose. And I do like Ashley, but not enough to call her "darling." Or maybe I do like her enough to say that. Donnae have time to think about that right now.

"Getting back to the legend," I say. "Those curved lines are much more likely to be a notation of caves. The section of the Grand Canyon where the treasure is supposed to be hidden doesn't have any arches that I know of. I could call my cousin Munro for confirmation once we get back to Loch Fairbairn."

"Let's put a pin in the curved-line issue for now." Ashley squints at the screen. "Did you find anything else?"

"Oh, not much. Only the actual map which, accompanied by the legend, will tell us where to find the treasure."

Her head pops up. "What? How did you do that? You said this document isn't really a map, just a legend."

"That's true. But the real map is on the opposite side." I use my finger to navigate the touch screen and bring up the backside of the sheet on which the legend was drawn. "This is it."

She squints even harder, then shakes her head and rubs her eyes. "It's a blank sheet on the backside. I'm getting a headache from staring at it, trying to see things that aren't there."

"Exactly. The map isn't there."

She throws her hands up and huffs. "You just told me it's on the back of the sheet."

"Aye, and it is. But it also isn't."

The lass narrows her gaze on me and flattens her lips. Then she growls. "You are driving me insane, Errol. It can't be there, but also not there."

"Of course it can. Have ye never heard of invisible ink?"

"Was that around more than a century ago?"

The lass might know about ancient history, but only in the context of her father's expeditions, I think. She clearly knows nothing about the very long history of invisible ink. The Greeks had it, the Romans had it, and many other cultures had it too. Why shouldn't the Havasupai tribe have discovered the same thing? Invisible ink is quite useful. We don't have time for me to explain how invisible ink works, though, since we'll need to land fairly soon. Instead, I'll show her what I mean.

"Watch this," I say. Then I fiddle with the settings in the photo app on my computer until I've revealed the hidden lines and shapes on the backside of the sheet. "See? All is revealed."

Ashley stares at the black-and-white map now visible on the screen. Her eyes have grown large, and her lips have fallen open, creating the most charming expression of surprise and delight. "Now that looks like a map."

"Because it is. The only problem is that I don't know where the map starts. What I mean is, I can't tell what section of the canyon this map represents, and so I have no idea where we should start our exploration."

"But you said you had solved the riddle."

"I have. But..." I sigh and sink back in my seat. "Solving the riddle of the map legend is only the beginning. The starting point for the journey is the missing link. And we still need to find that."

While I slump deeper into my seat, gazing out the window, Ashley picks up the computer and sets it on her lap so she can study the screen. She nibbles on one side of her bottom lip as if she's focusing all her mental energy on the image in front of her.

I love it when she concentrates on a task like that. It makes me want to pull her into my arms and kiss her senseless. She's adorable and sweet, and I liked her even when she was harassing me for months on end. I couldn't help admiring her determination even back then.

She hums softly, tunelessly, while her gaze remains fixed on the computer screen.

I shut my eyes and try to relax. Solving a riddle takes a lot out of a bloke. I have a little time before I need to start preparing for landing, so I can take a few moments to rest.

"Errol," Ashley snaps. "Wake up."

"Not asleep. I was resting my eyes and my brain."

"Resting your brain means you're asleep." She smacks my arm. "Isn't it about time to land the plane?"

I open my eyes, then stretch and groan. "Aye, it is. And I was about to open my eyes and do that. You worry too much, Ashley."

"Not wanting to die in a plane crash isn't worrying too much."

"Don't you trust me?"

"Yes, of course I do." She focuses on the computer screen again. "Sorry. I shouldn't have pestered you."

"Donnae mind at all if *you* pester me. It's all my cousins who drive me off my head with their meddling." I begin my preparations for landing, but I don't need to contact a control tower this time. Torcall doesn't care if I warn him or not. He'll hear Marilyn coming. "Buckle up your seat belt."

Ashley shuts the laptop and buckles up. Then she grips the computer with both hands while she stares out the windscreen as if she thinks we're about to crash. Well, she's only flown with me twice. I can't blame the lass for feeling uncomfortable. But she seems to worry about a lot of things, not just my ability to fly and drive a car.

"I've never crashed yet," I tell her. "Marilyn and I flew over the Swiss Alps, so I think we can handle the Scottish Highlands."

"Not worried about your pilot skills. It's what we might find when we reach the Grand Canyon that makes me anxious."

I glance at her. "Really? I assumed it was my vigorous driving method you couldn't tolerate."

She shakes her head. "I trust you, Errol. That means I know you won't get me killed, not on purpose. I believe in your skills—as a pilot, a driver, and a treasure hunter."

What can I say? She keeps giving me compliments and proclaiming that she trusts me. I should give her a compliment in return, shouldn't I? But I cannae think of a thing to say.

So I concentrate on landing the plane instead.

We touch down without incident, and Ashley doesn't even hold the laptop in a death grip. As soon as I've shut down the engines, she jumps out of her seat. "Let's get moving. I have an idea about how to find the starting point for the treasure map, but I need to see a topographic map of the Grand Canyon to be sure."

"We can find one of those at Dùndubhan. My cousin Rory's office, which used to be the library, has quite a few maps. Mostly of Scotland, but other places too."

Before Ashley can step around her seat, I sweep her up in my arms and carry her out of the cockpit, through the cargo area, to the doors. She doesn't seem to mind that I like to carry her. I think she might even enjoy it, based on her sweet smile. I need to put her down, though, so I can open one side of the cargo doors and lower the ladder. Then I climb out first. She throws me a sassy smile when I place my hands on her erse—for support, that's all. Aye, it's the gentlemanly thing to do.

Ashley reaches the ground and taps a finger on my nose. "You'll take any excuse to feel me up, won't you?"

"I was only making sure ye didnae fall."

"Uh-huh." As she walks past me, she pauses to grasp my erse. "Mm-mm-mm. Delicious."

Then she sashays toward my car, swiveling her hips in a blatant attempt to get me hard again. Sex in the car? We haven't done that yet. In fact, I've never had a poke in any sort of vehicle, not until Ashley and I had our fun in the DC-3 earlier. I'll never again be able to look at my plane without thinking of Ashley Hartman riding my cock in the pilot's seat.

And aye, the term cockpit now has a completely different connotation.

We say goodbye to Torcall, but as we're climbing into the car, he shouts to us, "Kirsty wants your help, Errol. Give the lass a ring, will you?"

I nod and wave to him. Whatever Kirsty wants, it will have to wait a bit.

Once Ashley and I are in the car, she opens up my laptop again and resumes scrutinizing whatever she thinks she sees on the screen. Since I'd left the computer I normally use for everyday work at home, we brought the one from the plane with us. She excavates a piece of paper from inside her purse and goes about squinting at that too, alternately studying the map and the sheet with words and numbers scrawled on it. I'm driving, so I can't take a good look at what she's doing. I drive more sedately than usual too, since Ashley wants to stare down at her lap instead of gazing out the windscreen. I don't want her to get motion sickness again.

When I try to turn onto a side street to head for home, Ashley insists we should go to Dùndubhan instead. It's only lunchtime, so I agree to her plan. I try to convince her we need to eat something first, but she refuses to do that. "Feed me later," she says. I persist, though, and she eventually agrees to eat first. I do love a bonnie, bossy lass, even if I don't always agree with her ideas. Well, I love *this* bonnie, bossy lass. I'm amazed I got to shag her once, much less twice, considering how obsessed she is with finding the Grand Canyon treasure.

We found clues. We know where to look.

Mhac na galla. We just might find the mythical treasure after all.

Chapter Sixteen

Ashley

We stop at a pizzeria in Fort William for lunch, one that Errol claims has the best pizza in the world "despite what those Italians think" because "Scots do everything better, including pizza." I don't bother arguing with him. That would take time, and I need to get to Dùndubhan soon, before my brain explodes from the pressure of thinking about what I might find when I view a topographic map of the Grand Canyon. I feel like we're so close, right on the edge of a major breakthrough, and I can't stand waiting to find out if I'm right. For so long, I've worked myself to exhaustion trying to find a clue, any clue, that might point me in the right direction.

After a few days with Errol, I've got more than a clue. I have a map, a legend, and a brilliant Scot to guide me.

The fact that Errol is the hottest man alive… Well, that's a bonus.

He was right about the restaurant. It does have the best pizza I've ever tasted, and I wind up eating four big slices. A girl needs nourishment before she can solve a mystery that has confounded people for more than a hundred years. Errol insists on ordering dessert too—New York cheesecake. I can't resist making a sarcastic comment about a Scottish pizzeria serving New York style cheesecake. Errol doesn't mind. He calls me a "cheeky lass" and proclaims that I could beat his cousin Callum in a pizza-eating contest.

The more time I spend with Errol, the more I like him. He makes me feel so good. And he believes in me like no one else ever has, except for my dad. But my father lost his faith in everything after his colleagues humiliated him. I feel like I'm so close to vindicating him that I could almost touch the proof. With Errol's help, I know I can succeed.

We will succeed.

Now that I'm stuffed, and Errol must be too, we climb into the car again and head for the castle. I don't even try to talk Errol out of taking the wheel. His gonzo manner of driving upset me during our first trip together, but I must've gotten used to it by now because I no longer need to take motion sickness pills while in the car with him. Since I needed that this morning, maybe my lack of nausea has nothing to do with his driving skills. Maybe I just feel safe with Errol now, and I trust him not to kill me by crashing his car or his plane.

This time, he turns on the radio so we can listen to music. Whatever this station is, it plays what sounds like a cross between sea shanties and bagpipe music with a dash of modern pop thrown in there too. I actually kind of like the music. When Errol starts singing along, I can't help laughing and clapping to the rhythm of the songs. He has a surprisingly good singing voice. By the time we reach Dùndubhan, a name I still have trouble pronouncing, I feel like I'm floating on a cloud with the sun beaming down on me.

Errol parks in the courtyard, near the main door of the castle. He orders me not to move a muscle, then hurries over to my side to open my door for me. He holds out his hand too. I lay my palm in his and let the Scot help me out of the car, though I don't really need the assistance. He seems to like taking care of me, and his chivalry makes me feel even warmer and floatier, like I'm still sunbathing on that imaginary cloud.

He holds my hand while we enter the castle, and we make our way to the first floor, which is not the ground floor. His cousin Rory's office, aka the former library, lies at the far end of the great hall. I had never set foot inside a building like this in my entire life until the day I cornered him in the long gallery a few days ago. I knew castles existed, obviously, but I hadn't visited one, not even as a landmark for tourists only. But Dùndubhan is a living castle, populated by a bevy of MacTaggarts and their friends who take turns hosting events here, maintaining a museum, and I'm sure even more things that no one has mentioned to me yet.

These people are unbelievably industrious.

We walk into the office, bypassing a large wooden desk, and approach the far corner to the left of the large windows and the bench beneath them. The object we're seeking hangs on the wall, in a niche between the windows and the corner beside them, and a wooden frame and a pane of glass protect it.

"Is this an antique map?" I ask. "Doesn't look old, but it's very well protected."

"You're right. It's not old, but Rory wanted to display it in a professional way. That's just the way he is."

"Well, the map does look amazing inside that case. But why does a Scotsman have a huge map of the Grand Canyon?"

"Weren't you listening?" Errol feigns disappointment. "No, ye weren't. Aye? Well, I already explained that my cousin Munro used to be a river guide in the canyon. He gave Rory this map as a birthday present last year."

"Oh, I see." I inch closer to the framed map, squinting to see through the glare cast on it by the sun shining into the room. "I wish the windows had curtains. It might blunt the glare."

"Donnae need curtains." Errol snatches the framed map off the wall and carries it over to the desk, where he lays it on the flat surface. "We can take it out to look at it."

"Are you sure Rory won't mind?"

"Nah. He's nowhere near as uptight as he used to be. Emery ironed that out of him."

"Did he want to be ironed out?"

Errol chuckles as he removes the metal tabs that hold the frame in place. "Ask him yourself sometime. But believe me, Rory is much happier now."

I watch while he takes the frame apart, exposing the large topographic map. He sets the elements of the frame on the big executive chair behind the desk, then lays the map out on the desktop.

Errol steps back. "It's all yours, lass."

"Wow, this is a beautiful map. It shows every little geological feature." I skate my fingertips over the map's surface. "It's textured too. I can feel the bumps of mountains and the depressions of valleys."

"This ought to give you all the information you need."

I still have my purse hanging over my shoulder, but now I drop it on the padded wooden chair behind me and hunt through the bag until I find the slip of paper on which I'd written down the pertinent facts about where the mysterious G.E. Kincaid claimed to have begun his trek down the Colorado River and where he'd found the cavern. I lay that paper on the desk beside the topographic masterpiece.

"Could you bring up the Ellsworth map on the computer for me?" I ask. "I need to compare it to the directions provided by Kincaid, and compare both of those sources to this topographic map."

Errol lays a hand on my lower back, sliding it up to my nape. "When you start talking in technical terms, it makes me very randy."

"Cool down, cowboy. I've got work to do."

He steps back. "I'll leave you to it. Let me know if I can help."

"You don't need to stand back and wait. We should work on this together."

Errol grabs the laptop and moves to stand alongside me, though he doesn't caress my back this time. Now we need to figure out this mystery. Errol brings up the images of the Ellsworth map and sets the computer on the desktop beside the topographic map.

"Can you show me the legend and the invisible ink drawing side by side?" I ask.

"Of course." Errol does what I asked. "There. Is that good enough? I can get out the projector that's in the file room. It's behind the door in the far corner."

"No, this is great. I can see everything. Besides, you can rotate the invisible map or zoom in for me if necessary."

"I am your servant, *gràidh*."

While Errol waits patiently beside me, peering down at the map but saying nothing, I search for points on the topographic rendering that match the Ellsworth map and its legend. This is much more complicated than I'd expected. The two drawings have different layouts, and the topographic one doesn't have a legend. We can figure this out, I know we can.

"In the *Phoenix Gazette* article, Kincaid describes his route through the Grand Canyon," I say. "He claims he started at El Tovar Crystal Canyon, but I've never had any luck finding those locations. Not on a traditional map, anyway."

"Maybe they don't exist, not the way Kincaid supposedly described them." Errol gets his phone and flicks his finger multiples times as if he's searching for something. "Ah! Here it is. There is a Crystal Creek in Grand Canyon National Park. And there's an El Tovar Hotel in the Grand Canyon Village, located along the South Rim."

"How far is it from El Tovar to Crystal Creek?"

"About twenty-two miles."

I rest one hand on the table beside the map. "That's about half as long as the journey Kincaid claimed he took. He said the cavern was forty-two miles from El Tovar Crystal Canyon. But those are two different places, separated by twenty-two miles."

"Since Kincaid seems to have conflated El Tovar and Crystal Creek, maybe we need to look twenty miles past Crystal Creek."

"Okay." I lean over the map to find Crystal Creek, then I study the surrounding area. "Kincaid said the cavern was on the east wall. If we follow the creek for another twenty miles..." I let my head drop. "I don't see anything in that area that matches the description."

"Maybe we need to look east of El Tovar. You're assuming the endpoint is Crystal Creek, but it might be the opposite."

"Good idea." I trace Kincaid's path past El Tovar until I estimate I've tracked twenty more miles. "Let's take the cues from the legend and the invisible map and see what we can find in the area past El Tovar."

Errol and I both lean in to study the computer screen, our shoulders nudging each other. I glance at him just as he glances at me, and we both smile. Then we focus on the screen again.

"I don't think we need the legend anymore," I say. "Can you remove that so we can just see the map?"

"Of course." Errol taps a few keys, and now the map fills the screen. "You said you had an idea for the starting point."

"Yes. El Tovar or Crystal Creek. Now I think you're right, and Kincaid's journey probably started twenty miles before El Tovar, then continued past it to Crystal Creek, for a total of about forty-two miles."

Errol uses his finger on the touch screen to rotate the map, glancing at the topographic version now and then as if he's trying to align the Ellsworth map to the Grand Canyon version. Finally, he stops messing with the screen. "This looks like the best alignment. Your starting point, the path that goes through El Tovar, fits with the way I've rotated the map."

"Yeah, it does. That's perfect, Errol." I slant closer to the screen and scrutinize every line, squiggle, L-shape, arching figure, and shaded area. Then I groan and sag my shoulders. "We need to be there, in the Grand Canyon, to see anything useful."

"Aye. That was always the plan, wasn't it?"

"Yes. But I'd hoped we would be able to pinpoint the location before we went there."

Errol lays a hand on my upper back, rubbing in slow circles. "Relax, Ashley. We'll get better clues once we're in the canyon. I've gone on more treasure hunts than you can imagine, and I've never found a hoard strictly with computers. The human eye is still the best tool."

"Yeah, I know you're right. The topographic map did help, though."

"Aye, ye found the starting point." He kisses my cheek. "You are the cleverest lass I've ever met. Cleverest person, full stop."

"I'm not as smart as you."

"Rubbish. We're equally clever." He claps the computer's lid shut. "Now, let's get moving on our expedition to the Grand Canyon. We'll travel in style—on a Gulfstream jet loaned to us by my cousin Evan."

"How do you know he'll let us borrow it?"

Errol smirks. "Because I asked him yesterday."

"But you hadn't agreed to participate yet at that point."

"I knew I'd say yes. But being a stubborn *bod ceann*, I had to delay for a wee bit."

"*Bod ceann?*"

"It's Gaelic for dickhead."

"Oh, I see. But you aren't like that."

He smiles. "Thank you, Ashley."

I get a warm sensation in my chest, but I have to ignore it. Too much to do now. Equipment to load onto the plane. More supplies to buy. Wow, this is really happening.

Our expedition is about to begin.

Chapter Seventeen

Errol

I can't believe I'm going on a barmy expedition to find a mythical treasure. That's how I viewed this hunt yesterday. But now, I don't think of it as barmy or mythical anymore. Ashley has convinced me, and we found evidence that strongly suggests the treasure might actually exist. I haven't agreed to this escapade solely because I want to discover a lost treasure. No, I've done this for Ashley and her father too. Well, mostly for her.

When I ring Evan to inform him we want to leave as soon as possible, he assures me he'll arrange everything. The jet will be waiting for us at the Inverness airport. Next, I ring another of my cousins—someone I haven't seen in several years. No one has seen him because he prefers to keep to himself. No matter how many times my cousins try to coax him into rejoining the family life, he refuses.

Aye, I'm ringing Munro.

I get his answering machine, which doesn't surprise me. My other cousins have told me that Munro uses an old-fashioned answering machine since he does not own a mobile phone and uses only a landline. He screens his calls and rarely picks up. I have a feeling what I mean to suggest to him will convince Munro to answer the bloody phone this time.

After his curt recorded message, I hear the beep. "Munro, it's Errol Murdoch. Your cousin. Remember me? I've heard you hide out in a remote cabin in the woods, like a serial killer. But I could really use your help now. I'm going on a hunt for a mythical treasure, and anyone who comes along will probably die in a cliff collapse or drown in the rapids. It's the Grand Canyon treasure, and I've teamed with a bonnie lass to find it."

I hear a click, then Munro's rough voice. "What do ye want, Errol?"

"You know what I want. You are the best river guide who ever worked in the Grand Canyon."

He grunts. "I donnae do that anymore."

"But you're still the best. This will be a small, secret expedition that will probably get us all arrested. Just me, you, and Ashley Hartman."

"Who the bloody hell is Ashley Hartman?"

"A bonnie, sweet lass who's also very clever. This is her expedition, but we could use your expertise."

"Cannae do it. The salmon are running."

"This will be more exciting than that."

Silence follows.

I can hear Munro breathing, but he says nothing for long enough that I can't take it anymore. "You know ye want to come. So just say yes and get it over with. Then you can start griping about it."

"Donnae gripe." He sighs heavily. "Taking a woman into the Grand Canyon is not a clever idea."

"You're a sexist, eh? Ashley is clever and strong, not a silly wee lassie."

More silence. More faint breathing sounds. "All right."

"You'll do it?"

"That's what I said, isn't it? Don't annoy me, or I'll change my mind."

I'm grinning, but he can't see that. Munro would probably snarl at me if he could see my expression. "That's brilliant. Ashley and I will leave for America in a few hours. You can meet us at the Flagstaff airport."

"No, I won't do that."

"But Munro, ye just said—"

"Haud yer wheesht, Errol." The sound of shuffling papers follows. "Tell me where your expedition will begin."

"Well, we'd like to start about forty-two miles upstream from Crystal Canyon."

"Hmm. Let me check my maps." I hear more paper-shuffling, and soft grunts too. "I know a suitable place where you can start, but we'll need to travel by helicopter for the first leg. Then we'll land on a little spot I know of, just north of Vasey's Paradise. That will give us a starting point that's a good ways upriver from where you want to start searching."

"You know the Grand Canyon better than I do. I trust your judgment."

He grunts again. "We'll see about that."

Then he hangs up on me.

Munro used to be more fun and less rude. I suppose he has his reasons for behaving like a *bod ceann*. As long as he can assist us in our expedition, I donnae care if he shows up wearing a kilt made of grizzly bear fur.

Why did Munro say "we'll see about that" when I told him I trust his judgment?

Ashley and I dump all our gear into my car and head for the airport. I let Ashley take the wheel this time. The lass deserves a break from my style of driving. We arrive in Inverness just as civil twilight has begun. The pilots offer to help us carry our things into the jet, then we take off. Aye, Evan's jet has a much quieter and smoother ride than Marilyn could ever provide. But Evan hasn't given the jet a name. If he did, he would probably call it Keely after his wife, or maybe Joy after his daughter. I don't think billionaires generally give their jets a name, though.

Maybe I should invent one for Evan's jet, strictly to fash him. But that wouldn't work. My cousin doesn't get upset that easily. If I gave Magnus's car a name, he would definitely go apoplectic.

Now we are in the air, flying toward America.

Since we have about seven hours to kill, I suggest to Ashley that we should go into the bedroom and shag. She shakes her head, giving me a tolerant smile, and suggests we should eat dinner instead. The jet does come with a gourmet chef, after all. By the time we've finished our meal, we're both ready for bed. I offer to sleep on the sofa, but Ashley assures me we can share the bedroom.

She sits at the foot of the bed to remove her shoes and socks.

I kick my shoes off and start to unbutton my trousers.

She gives me a strange look but goes back to removing her socks. Then she stands up to shed her trousers. Instead of taking off her shirt, she reaches inside it to unhook her bra and pull it out through the arms of her shirt. Ashley then pulls the covers back and climbs onto the bed while wearing only her knickers and T-shirt.

I get rid of my trousers and shirt, then slip my fingers inside the waistband of my shorts, intending to push them down.

"What are you doing?" Ashley asks, bolting upright.

"Taking my clothes off. That's what I'm doing."

"At least keep your undies on. Your shirt too would be best."

I raise my brows. "Best for what? I always sleep in the nude. And you told me you prefer to sleep that way too."

"Well, yeah, but—" She tugs the covers up to conceal her chest, though she's still wearing her shirt. "I'd rather we kept at least some of our clothes on."

"Ah, of course. I know what's going on here." I snap the waistband of my shorts. "You're afraid ye cannae resist me if I'm naked."

"Honestly, I can't resist you even when you're wearing all your clothes." She flops backward onto the bed and moans. "Fine, get naked. It won't make any difference."

"If it makes you feel any better, I'm too jeeked to seduce you right now."

"Really? Yes, that does make me feel better."

A chuckle rumbles out of me. "You are a strange lass, but I like that. One minute, you're ravishing me on the green. The next, you're too shy to let me see you naked. And you're suddenly afraid you can't restrain your lust if I sleep in the nude."

"Thank you for the recap, but I remember all of that without you telling me."

Her lips have taken on a teasing slant, so I know she isn't fashed. The lass did seem genuinely surprised when I stripped. I imagine that's because she still hasn't quite reconciled her all-business attitude with her lust for me. I can wait until she's ready. Besides, I told the truth when I said I'm too tired for sex right now.

We arrive in Flagstaff in the early morning, local time, though for me it's more like afternoon. I'd wager Ashley will suffer more jet lag than I will since she flew from America to Scotland, then back again. As we step out of the jet, heading down the stairs, I spot an SUV parked aways off. A man gets out of the vehicle just as Ashley and I step onto the tarmac. He saunters toward us, and we meet halfway.

My cousin dresses like a hermit who lives alone in the woods, and that's because he is a hermit. His bushy beard and bushy hair must chase away a lot of lasses, but I don't know if he cares about that. Today, he seems to have put on his Sunday best, because his khaki trousers and olive green T-shirt seem almost new, not like he's worn them for two months straight.

"Munro," I say, smiling as I grab his hand to shake it. "Haven't seen you in ages. Glad you're coming with us on this expedition."

"You're a bampot, Errol. We'll be lucky to get out of this alive." Munro clamps his hand around my wrist, pulling me toward him. His voice drops to a harsh whisper. "If ye get me killed, I'm coming back from the grave to skelp ye myself."

"No one will die. That's why we've got you." I slap his arm. "You're the world's greatest river guide."

"Still spouting rubbish, I see." Munro releases me and looks at Ashley. His mouth curves into a smile that I do not appreciate at all. "Who is this bonnie lass?"

"Ashley Hartman. I told you about her."

"Oh, aye. But you didn't mention she's a Renaissance painting come to life." Munro moves toward Ashley and sandwiches her hand between both of his. "It's a pleasure to meet ye, lass. How much are you paying Errol to go on this hunt for a myth?"

"Our business arrangement is private. Wouldn't you rather know how much I'll pay *you*?"

"My rates are nonnegotiable. Ten thousand dollars upfront, then forty percent of whatever hoard we find. If there is no hoard, you pay me an extra ten thousand dollars."

"That's outrageous," I say, as I insert myself between Munro and Ashley. My proximity forces him to release her hand. "When did you become a con artist? Twenty thousand dollars for a trip through the Grand Canyon? It's bollocks."

"It's what I'm worth."

Ashley pushes me aside. "Now-now, boys. This is my expedition, and you both work for me. That means I set the rates. If you can't handle that, Munro, then I say thank you and please go on your way."

"What do you think I'm worth?" Munro asks.

Ashley waves for him to follow her as she walks away. When I try to follow, she shakes her head at me. I stand here on the tarmac, alone, wondering what the bloody hell those two are discussing. Rates? Rubbish. Munro is trying it on with Ashley, and she's too naive to notice.

But Ashley isn't naive. She's clever. So she must realize Munro is trying to fleece her with his mountain-man charm. He looks like a ruddy grizzly bear to me, but women seem to like that. Magnus never had trouble finding women to bed. I suppose I should stop shaving and let my hair grow out, then start growling at women. Apparently, lasses like that more than big muscles.

I am not jealous.

Ashley strides back to me. "Let's go. Munro has arranged for transportation for us, though he won't say exactly what it is. We'll begin our journey just north of Vasey's Paradise."

"How much are you paying Munro?"

"Your cousin doesn't want you to know. Since I won't tell him how much I'm paying you, I see no reason why he must share with you the details of my agreement with him."

She's right, and I'm an erse. But I can't help feeling a wee bit...left out. Munro and Ashley got on immediately, but she and I needed months before we could speak to each other without one of us getting angry. All right, it was me who kept doing that. I've grown as a person since then.

I follow Ashley and Munro across the tarmac to a large hangar that houses a private jet. Just in front of the hangar, I note several small planes and a helicopter. "Munro, are we flying to the canyon?"

"Aye." He veers away from the planes. "By helicopter."

"What?" Ashley says, almost shrieking. "No, I can't do that. No, no, no. All that swerving and all those sharp turns. What if we crash? Do you even know how to fly a helicopter, Munro?"

"No, and Errol can't fly one of these beauties either. So I've hired a pilot." He halts a short distance from the helicopter and squints at her. "Do you have a fear of flying?"

"No, I came here on an airplane. But helicopters are…different. What if one of us falls out?"

My cousin groans, with a hint of growling too. "No one will fall out. Errol didnae warn me his partner is afraid of flying."

"That's not what Ashley said," I point out. "She doesn't like helicopters, but she's fine with airplanes."

Ashley hugs herself. "Not small planes. Helicopters are worse, though. I'll probably wind up vomiting."

"We have air sickness bags," says a man who approaches us from behind. He speaks with an American accent. The bloke shakes hands with my cousin. "Good to see you again, Munro."

"Aye, it's been a while." Munro looks at me. "Last chance to back out. If your lass can't handle a helicopter ride—"

"I can handle it," Ashley says. Then she pokes around in her purse, retrieving the bottle of motion sickness pills. "I'll take one of these."

"Take two or three," I say. "Just to be sure."

Ashley shakes her head. "The maximum dose is two pills."

"So take that. Maybe it'll make you sleepy so you won't mind the ride."

Munro claps a hand on his mate's shoulder. "I forgot to introduce our pilot. This is Peter Heymans, the best helicopter pilot you could hope to have on your side. He'll get us to the landing spot without crashing."

"Oh, great," Ashley all but moans. "That's so comforting."

My cousin glances up at the sky as if he thinks the sun will give him the strength to endure this expedition. "Errol, you should sit in the backseat with Ashley. Maybe you can distract her so she won't vomit all over Peter's new helicopter."

Peter and Munro climb into the front seats while I help Ashley into the back. We get headsets that let us talk to each other, as well as to Peter and Munro, and the headsets even come with advanced noise cancellation to make the journey less stressful. Munro and Ashley talk during the whole half-hour trip to wherever we're landing, and she smiles and laughs while essentially ignoring me for the whole time. I'm glad Munro can distract her so she won't be anxious, and I'm glad Ashley is having a good time. But I wonder why she doesn't behave that way when I take her somewhere. Oh aye, it's a mystery. The fact that I drive and fly like a lunatic has nothing to do with it.

Of course she likes Munro. He acts like a normal person with her, but with the rest of our family, he makes Magnus seem like a cuddly teddy bear. He's not as threatening as the bounty hunter can be, but Munro does not even try to temper his grumpiness.

And none of us know why he's so grumpy.

Suddenly, Munro bursts into song. He's belting out "Scotland the Brave" while Ashley laughs and claps in time with his song. When he finishes, the lass claps even more and shouts, "Woo-hoo! That was amazing."

I donnae think his singing was *that* wonderful.

"Almost there," Peter announces. "We'll set down on the little patch of flat, sandy shore."

We have no permits for this expedition, and many obstacles to survive before we find the treasure—if we find it. And I mean "obstacles" literally. No, I haven't told Ashley about the whitewater rapids. But we are about to face some of the toughest stretches on the Colorado River.

Maybe I should tell her to take two more pills.

Chapter Eighteen

Ashley

I can't believe it. We're here. At the Grand Canyon. Ready to search for the treasure. Well, okay, we haven't landed yet, so technically we aren't there. But I can see the winding green waters of the river, and also the steep, narrow walls of the Grand Canyon. Part of me wants to jump and shout and dance around like a moron. Another part of me knows I need to stay focused and level-headed. But when Munro tells us that we will reach our destination in a few minutes, a feeling of unreality descends on me. A tingle sweeps over my entire body. I've never felt this excited before, not in all my life. None of the expeditions I'd gone on with my dad can compare to this.

We will find the treasure. I know we will.

Since we can't take anything with us that we can't carry on our backs, I had to keep the equipment to a minimum. Luckily, modern technology helps us out. I was able to buy miniaturized versions of almost everything, giving us plenty of tools to aid our search. I even found a miniature device for performing ground-penetrating radar scans. Technology is amazing. I also bought us MREs, those freeze-dried meals that military personnel eat. I had taste-tested one at home yesterday—"home" meaning the house I rented in Loch Fairbairn—and the food tasted okay. We need nourishment for our trek, not a gourmet meal.

Munro and Errol both have huge backpacks that seem like they must be twice as big as mine. Well, probably not quite that. But they are much larger. Big men, big packs. I'm lucky to have these two guys with me because they not only understand how to search for treasure, but they also can carry heavier weights than I can. I'm not ashamed to admit that. I'm no wimp, but I don't have the bodily strength of a full-grown, well-muscled Scot. Both Errol and Munro clearly have trained for this kind of athletic challenge, and they also clearly assume I'm unprepared.

But I have prepared. Did they seriously think I'd go into this blind and ignorant? I knew that reaching the Colorado River, so we can follow Kincaid's journey, would require an arduous effort. I've trained for months, following the routine advised by an experienced Grand Canyon hiking guide whose book I had read. When I tell all of this to Errol and Munro, they seem suitably impressed.

"That's my girl," Errol says with a smile. "Sometimes it pays to be uptight, aye?"

He winks, letting me know he's joking. I could've figured that out on my own. Errol Murdoch is not a jerk who thinks women can't handle outdoorsy stuff. I'm also not so arrogant that I think I can do everything my heavily muscled companions can. We need to rely on each other's strengths and admit to our weaknesses if we're going to survive this expedition without getting hurt.

"Make sure your seat belts are buckled up," Peter declares. "We're about to land."

I suddenly realize I've stopped breathing and force myself to do that.

Errol clasps my hand, smiling at me with his lips sealed, the expression sweet and encouraging at the same time. Just the feel of his hand holding mine reduces my anxiety. How does he always know what to do to keep me calm? I'm not normally a bundle of nerves, but we are about to descend into a canyon that has high, steep walls.

"Take slow, deep breaths," Errol tells me. "Munro swears Peter is an expert pilot. Trust his skills and try not to look out the windows."

Munro glances back at us and gives me a tight smile. Then he makes the thumbs-up sign. "You're doing fine, lass."

The helicopter descends gradually, sinking below the rim of the canyon, following the serpentine track of the Colorado River. I grip Errol's hand tightly. I'm probably causing him pain, but he just keeps smiling at me.

"Final descent," Munro says. "If you look out the windscreen, you'll see the sandy area where we'll set down."

"Errol said I shouldn't look out the windows."

The man still holding my hand gives it a light squeeze. "If you want to have a peek, go on. We aren't racing across the sky anymore."

"Okay, I want to look. But don't let go of my hand." When he nods, I crane my neck to peer out the windshield. "Oh, I see the sandy spot."

"Best sit back now," Munro says.

I lean back in my seat and bite my lip. Then I shut my eyes because I can't watch if we're going to crash. Logically, I know we won't. The odds are infinitesimal. But my emotional side can't stop worrying.

The noise of the rotors begins to slow down, and soon it fades away.

Errol removes my headset. "Open your eyes, *gràidh*. We're on the ground."

I peel my lids apart and cautiously glance out the windows. We are indeed on solid ground, on a sandbar, with the Colorado River rushing past. We made it. None of us died.

Errol unhooks my seat belt and his too, while Peter and Munro climb out of the helicopter. Peter opens my door and helps me out. Errol and Munro meet us on this side of the chopper.

I can't resist taking in the surroundings, turning in a circle to get the full experience. I have finally reached the Grand Canyon. Without thinking about what I'm doing, I throw my head back, spread my arms wide, and whoop. I do that three times before I realize the men are all staring at me like I'm a lunatic who just escaped from an asylum for the criminally insane.

"What?" I say. "This is a big moment for me, and I needed to celebrate it."

Errol kisses my cheek. "Celebrate all you want. You've earned it."

I try to help the guys unload our gear, but they insist on doing it themselves. Errol orders me to enjoy my first experience in the Grand Canyon. But I end up watching them instead, because they're hauling a flat, rectangular cardboard box out of the backseat area. I'd noticed that box when we boarded the helicopter, but I'd assumed it had nothing to do with our expedition. I purchased all our equipment, and I know I didn't order anything that isn't already in my backpack or Errol's. My partner also brought another bag that isn't a backpack, but he wouldn't tell me what's in it. Errol just winked and smirked when I asked.

"What is that big box?" I ask, inching toward the men while trying not to get in their way.

"You'll see," Errol says. "It's a surprise."

"Uh-huh. Tell me what it is anyway."

Munro lifts a single brow. "Demanding, isn't she? I suppose you need a lass like that, Errol, so she can stop you from blowing up the entire United Kingdom."

Errol rolls his eyes.

The men set the box on the sand. Munro and Errol say goodbye to Peter, and the pilot jogs back to his helicopter. Before getting in, though, he pulls two long objects out from under the backseats. Peter tosses the paddles toward us, though they slap down on the sand several yards away. Then he climbs into his big machine. Just before he shuts the door, Peter shouts, "Good luck! I hope you find whatever it is you're looking for."

Munro tosses the cardboard box about thirty feet away from us, where it splats down on the sand, and waves for me and Errol to follow him as he jogs away from the helicopter. He snags the paddles along the way. We carry our backpacks, but drop them on the sand once we've reached a safe distance.

The helicopter starts up. Within a few minutes, Peter has taken off, and the chopper is rising toward the canyon's rim. Not long after that, the machine has flown out of sight.

"I'm confused," I say. "Are we going to walk up these steep cliffs?"

"No," Errol says with a chuckle. "We're going on a rafting adventure. Ye want to see what Kincaid saw, aye? Well, that means rafting."

"But we don't have a raft."

Munro nudges the cardboard box with his boot. "Actually, we do. It's in here."

Eying the box, I feel my brows crinkling. "That doesn't look big enough to hold one person, much less three."

"It's an inflatable raft."

"Oh. Are you sure that's sturdy enough for river rafting?"

Munro narrows his eyes and clenches his jaw.

Before he can speak, though, Errol steps in. "It's very safe, Ashley. I wouldn't have agreed to using an inflatable raft if it weren't tough enough to handle whatever we run into down the river. Munro recommended this particular model, and he knows what he's doing."

"Right." I hunch my shoulders as I tell Munro, "Sorry. Didn't mean to insult your skills. You must've gone on a lot of rafting vacations, huh?"

I swear Munro's nostrils are flaring, just like an angry bull.

"Calm down," Errol tells his cousin. "I forgot to tell Ashley that you were the co-owner of a rafting company. I only mentioned that you used to be a river guide. We couldn't have a better leader for our expedition because Munro is an expert, not just on rafting but also on wilderness survival."

Since I hadn't understood what a river guide does, I hadn't realized what kind of skills Munro brought to the table. Now at least I know we're in good hands with an expert to guide us on our journey. Errol trusts his cousin, and that's all the endorsement I need.

Munro insists on inflating the raft himself, so Errol and I sit on the sand to watch the river flowing past us.

"Have you ever gone on a river expedition before?" I ask Errol.

"Aye, I've taken some river-rafting trips. Not in the Grand Canyon, though. Munro will get us where we need to be, so donnae worry about that. But if you get tired or nauseous, don't downplay how bad you feel, all right? If you're too jeeked to go on, speak up. We can find a spot to camp for the night."

"I'm not too 'jeeked' yet. But I know you're trying to watch out for me, and I appreciate it."

Munro saunters over to us and kneels between me and Errol. "We all need to watch out for each other. The Grand Canyon is beautiful, but it's also treacherous."

"I understand," I say. "And I'll be extra careful."

"Of course you will," Errol says. "You're a clever lass."

Munro lifts his brows, and his lips tick up a touch. He glances from Errol to me and back to Errol. Then he rises, stretches his entire body, and exhales a satisfied sigh. "Time to get moving. The raft is ready. Let's grab the paddles, toss our packs in, and go."

We had already gotten out our life jackets, which had been inside the box with the deflated raft. So now Errol tosses the paddles into the raft, and the three of us work together to drag the thing across the sand, partway into the water. Munro keeps hold of the raft as Errol and I climb aboard, then he gives it a final shove just as he leaps inside. The current picks us up, and our journey begins.

Munro and Errol sit in the front, side by side, while I take the seat in back. Our backpacks lie between me and the men, tied down securely, along with Errol's secret bag. We all have paddles, which means I can help keep our raft moving smoothly down the river. Maybe it's mostly the boys doing the work, and maybe I wish I could be in front instead of stuck in back, but Errol and Munro have experience with river rafting. I'm a newbie, and I have enough sense to listen to the expert seated in front of me.

As I paddle gently, my sense of awe grows. The emerald green river snakes out ahead of us, between the red cliffs that shift to a lighter shade nearer to the canyon floor, leading us toward a destination we haven't yet identified. The clear blue sky above us contrasts with the earthy landscape, and I can't wait to see the stars tonight.

Munro tells me to stop paddling and focus on searching the cliffs for any sign of Kincaid's cavern. I retrieve my binoculars from my pack so I can get a closer look at any features that catch my eye. Before we left Scotland, I had printed out a high-resolution copy of the Ellsworth map and laminated it to protect the document. Now, I hold that laminated sheet on my lap while I study the landscape, searching for anything that resembles what Kincaid described.

If my hunch is right concerning where the mysterious explorer began his trek, we should find some clue to the cavern's location along this stretch of the canyon, between the spot where we entered the river and Crystal Canyon. Every time I think about how close we might be to finding the lost treasure, a shiver of excitement rushes through me.

Kincaid described seeing a "stain" on the cliffs about two thousand feet above the canyon floor, so I keep that in mind as I scan the surroundings. The word stain could mean virtually anything. That clue doesn't add much to my knowledge of where the hoard might be hidden.

We hadn't shared with our pilot the exact nature of our expedition. The fewer people who know, the better. Munro trusts Peter, but we all realize most people will think we're nuts for doing this. Better to keep the details to ourselves until we prove the treasure exists. Of course, we're also engaging in a not-quite-sanctioned expedition inside a national park. I'm sure we'll be breaking at least a few laws. Maybe I should care about that, but all I can think about is vindicating my father. Yes, okay, I'm obsessed with doing that. But I know Errol sometimes skirts the line between legal and not quite aboveboard, so I doubt he thinks less of me for trying to do the same thing. What about Munro? I get the feeling he doesn't mind straying outside the lines either if it's for a good cause.

Since we're traveling down a relatively calm stretch of the river, I have the chance to ask a few questions. "Munro, are you sure you're okay with going on an unsanctioned, kind of illegal expedition?"

"I told ye already. Yes, I understand the stakes."

"Sorry to be annoying. I've never done anything like this before, so I'm a little nervous about it."

"Take a breath, Ashley, and try not to worry so much." Munro glances at Errol. "Though maybe what you really need to ease your anxiety is a good, hard kiss. I'm sure my cousin can handle that."

"I'm fine, really. No need for anybody to kiss me." I gaze at the river ahead of us. "How far do you think we've gone? According to Kincaid's comments and the stuff Errol and I figured out, we should see something anytime now."

"We should get out the GPS." Munro turns to his cousin. "Can you find the unit I brought? It's in my pack, in the lower pocket on the outside."

"Aye, I can get it."

Errol carefully crawls to the rear of the raft, where I sit beside our backpacks. Both men had insisted I should remain back here in case we run into unexpected rough water or a rockfall. I have no idea what kind of dangers we might face. Despite the uncertainty looming over this expedition, I've never felt as invigorated as I do right now. Well, maybe I have felt more invigorated—when Errol and I were having sex. But I won't tell either of my companions about that. Munro doesn't need to know, and I'd feel weird about admitting the truth to Errol. I don't know anymore what we are to each other. Business partners doesn't quite fit.

I gaze down at the laminated map, and another shiver tingles through me. No matter how this expedition turns out, my quest to prove my father was right will end here in the Grand Canyon.

Chapter Nineteen

Errol

I sit back on my heels to locate Munro's pack and find the pocket my cousin had mentioned. I dig out a device that looks similar to a smartphone, but it's not for making calls. The GPS unit has a wee antenna sticking up from the top corner that taps into the signal from satellites in geosynchronous orbit around the earth. Now that I have the device, I zip up the pocket on Munro's pack and waddle back to my cousin, taking a seat beside him once again.

"You know how to use GPS, don't you, Errol?" Munro says.

"I do."

"Good. Check how far we've come."

Why does he want me to do that? I can tell we haven't gone far, maybe a mile at most. But I gather he wants to reassure Ashley that our journey has only just begun and she doesn't need to worry that we've missed a vital clue in the landscape.

I dutifully turn on the GPS unit and check our progress. "Not quite one mile. Still plenty of territory to search." I glance back at the lass. "All right, Ashley? Keep watching the cliffs."

"Thank you for checking, Errol."

Munro grumbles, "It was my idea."

I pat Munro's shoulder. "But I did the actual work to get your GPS and check it. Donnae worry, Ashley will thank you for something sooner or later."

Up ahead, I can see a bend in the river that looks like a ninety-degree turn. We pass by a smaller canyon on the right, then it's time to navigate the left-hand turn.

"Watch out," Munro says, loud enough that Ashley can hear too. "Around that bend, we'll find some rough water and rocks. Best hold on, Ashley, and stay in the middle of the raft at the back. I don't expect trouble, but it always pays to be vigilant."

I glance up at the red cliffs, feeling a strong sense of awe at the beauty of this landscape. But then it's time to navigate the turn, and I have no time to sightsee. We come around the bend and slide between a sandbar and a rocky patch with only a wee bit of jostling, then ease to the left to avoid another obstacle. Now we're clear, heading down a winding stretch of the river.

"We're approaching Redwall Cavern," Munro says. "Expect to see some tourist rafts there. It's a popular destination."

As we pass by the cavern, we do see a couple of rafts, clearly from professional river guide companies. When I glance back at Ashley, she's craning her neck to try to peer inside the cavern, but I doubt she can see much. I wish we could stop to let her have a sightseeing experience. We have a mission, though, so we steer clear of the tourists and continue on our way.

"We're approaching a rapid," Munro announces. "Class four, so hold on. It shouldn't be too difficult to navigate, though we will need to squeeze through a tight spot. Ashley, stay at the back of the raft. Errol, follow my lead."

"How many classes are there?" Ashley asks.

"Ten. This one might be lower on the scale, but any sort of rapid requires vigilance. Make sure your helmet is on good and snug, Ashley. Errol, best put yours on too."

"What about you, Munro?" I ask. "Where's your helmet?"

"Donnae use one." He thumps his palm on his head. "Plenty hard enough as-is."

I glance over my shoulder and relax a wee bit when I see Ashley has her helmet firmly strapped under her chin.

Munro already holds one paddle, but he instructs me to grab the other one and start paddling in a digging motion to keep the raft moving relatively straight. But we've only reached the beginning of this obstacle, and we need to move to the right side to avoid a sandbar and some rocks. The raft jostles and bounces while we paddle through the rough water and come out the other side unscathed.

When I look at Ashley, she's grinning.

"No motion sickness?" I ask.

She shakes her head. "This is fun."

Well, at least she isn't terrified or about to vomit.

Munro leads us through several more rapids, none of which are too difficult, and none higher than a class four. Ashley loves it. I'd love to just watch the look on her face every time we hit a rough patch, but I need to focus on the river ahead of us. I hear her laugh or whoop whenever the raft bounces.

"I know you're interested in history, Ashley," Munro says. "Up ahead, we will enter President Harding Rapid, which was renamed in that bloke's honor when he died. It's class four, but a large boulder sits right in the middle of our path. Errol and I will need to push our raft to the left to avoid that obstacle."

We get through it fine, but Ashley loves the rough ride. She even gets splashed once, which makes her whoop even louder than before.

Since we've traveled for more than four hours, we decide to take a break for lunch near Eminence Break, a popular hiking trail that starts on the rim and ends at the bottom of the canyon. This area also features a wide sandy area along the river that serves as a fine spot for a picnic. We haul the raft onto the shore to enjoy a meal and rest, since we have a long journey still ahead of us. MREs aren't the tastiest meals, but they keep us fueled up.

Then we board the raft and get moving again.

Eventually, we come to more rapids, though most of them aren't rough enough to count in my book. But then we reach a longer stretch of turbulent water that Munro tells us is known as the Nankoweep Rapid. It might be longer than the previous ones, but it doesn't seem much rougher than the others. I'm glad for that, for Ashley's sake, but I think she had hoped for a wilder trip.

That lass really does love danger. Aye, I think she might be the perfect woman for me.

After a few more stops to rest and recharge, we finally reach the confluence of the Little Colorado River, where it empties into the big kahuna, the Colorado River itself. We take a break there so Ashley can "find a girl bush," then we're on our way again, though we only go for another few miles. After a long day of rafting, and with sunset looming, we all agree to stop on the western side of the canyon for the night and make camp there. We didn't bring tents, but we do have sleeping bags.

Ashley and I gather dry brush and twigs, then start a fire. Munro wanted to "cook dinner" for us, but he sneaked away behind the brush to do that, which makes me slightly suspicious about his intentions. If he brings us a bowl full of insects, I'll toss him into the river. Though I would eat that rot if I were starving, I'm not that famished yet. Besides, we have those MREs. They're slightly better than insects.

By the time we've gotten the fire going good, Munro saunters out from behind the bushes—carrying three fish.

"How did you get those?" I ask. "We didnae bring fishing poles. Or hooks, come to think of it. No bait either."

"Donnae need that," Munro says as he kneels by the fire. "I found a stick, sharpened the end, and stabbed the fish with it. Had to wade out into the river a bit, but that just makes it more fun."

"You might've drowned out there."

"No, I wouldn't. Other people would." He holds the fish out to me. "Since I caught these, you can gut them. I'd rather cook them whole, but you two are sensitive city folk."

"I live in Loch Fairbairn, not London."

Munro sighs as if I'm a hopeless fool. "Just gut the bloody fish."

"All right." I accept the fish and excavate my switchblade from my pocket. "I had no idea you could do that, Munro. I finally understand why everyone calls you the Wild Man. You're like Bigfoot, but slightly better looking."

He grunts. "Rather be Bigfoot than a pasty erse who works in an office cave all day, like those creatures in that H.G. Wells book."

"*The Time Machine*," Ashley says. "I love that book. The nineteen sixties movie was good too. But the Morlocks didn't work in offices."

"They weren't very friendly either," I say. "Eating humans isn't a nice thing to do."

Our conversation goes on after that, and I manage to make Ashley smile more often than Munro does. Not that I'm counting. She also laughs more at my jokes than at Munro's, but I swear I am not keeping track. I just happen to notice that.

In the midst of astronomical twilight, Munro rises and stretches, groaning the way I've realized he always does when he stands up. "Think I'll go wash off in the river."

"Right now? It's almost dark."

"Aye, but I can see in the dark." He gives me a deadpan look for so long that I almost start to believe he's being serious. But then he smirks and says, "That was a joke. I don't have night vision, but I do have this."

He bends over to pull an item out of his backpack. He holds up the small flashlight.

"Is that waterproof?" I ask.

"Aye. So donnae worry, Errol. I can find my way back to camp without you holding my hand." He starts to turn away, then pauses to glance back. "Think I'll take a nice long bath in the river. You and Ashley should have some alone time, anyway."

Munro winks. Then he ambles off into the bushes again.

Alone time? I have no idea what he's insinuating.

Well, all right, maybe I have an idea. But I can't be sure that's what Munro meant.

Ashley stretches her arms above her head and sighs. "Getting clean does sound good. I've gotten so dirty."

Is it my imagination, or did she say that in a husky tone?

Ashley stands up and unzips her sweatshirt. Aye, she has a T-shirt on under that, but still, she seems to be undressing right here on the shores of the Colorado River.

"What are ye doing, lass?" I ask, and now my voice has grown huskier too.

She turns toward me and drops her sweatshirt on the ground, then kicks off her shoes. Her socks go next.

I cannae move. My erse has become glued to the ground.

Ashley strips off her shirt and trousers. "Does this answer your question?"

The lass gets rid of her bra and knickers too.

Oh, aye, now even my muddled brain could crack the code of what she means to do. So I jump up and shed my clothes slightly faster than she stripped. We both leap into the water, wading in up to our chests. Her tits float in the water, and I cannae stop my eyes from veering down to admire those bonnie breasts. I've seen her naked before, but somehow this feels like the first time again.

Ashley links her arms around my neck. "I've never gone skinny dipping in the dark. Actually, I've never gone skinny dipping, period."

"I have."

"Why does that not surprise me? The man who blows things up isn't shy about swimming naked."

"Not shy, full stop. I went to a nudist resort once, when my cousin Catriona married Alex Thorne. They wore clothes during the ceremony, but as soon as it ended, Alex whipped his kit off."

Ashley laughs. "A nudist wedding? You know a lot of crazy people, don't you?"

"Yes, I do. So donnae assume I'm the craziest, because I absolutely am not."

"I believe you." She pastes her body to mine. "Let's make love in the Colorado River, under the same stars that have lit this spot since the beginning of time."

"You read my mind, *mo chridhe*."

I push inside her body slowly, relishing the sensation of her silky wet flesh conforming to my cock. She exhales a satisfied sigh and wraps her legs around my hips, rocking them just enough to sink my length even deeper inside her. A soft wee moan spills from her lips. I begin to thrust gently, while I take possession of her mouth and spread my palms on her back, tugging her more firmly against me. Her breasts are mashed to my chest, their rigid tips scraping against my skin.

She feels so fucking wonderful.

Ashley moans in the sweetest way when I tease the roof of her mouth with my tongue, even while I keep thrusting at a leisurely pace. The river flows around us, but our movements create wavelets that lap against our bodies.

I tear my mouth away from hers and gaze up at the starry sky. Even while I keep shagging her, I find myself saying, "Look up, *gràidh*. Look at the sky."

She glances up, and a smile curves her lips. The moonlight glows on her bonnie face, and I cannae stop myself. I rush out of the water while still holding her to me, and I pause in my thrusting only long enough to lie her down on the grass. Then I start moving again, rolling my hips in a circular motion, pushing even deeper inside her, bracing myself with my elbows on the ground. Her face lies just below my chin, and her hair tickles my lips.

Then my brain finally reminds me of something vital.

"*Mhac na galla*," I hiss. "Forgot a condom."

The lass rolls us over and disentangles herself from me so she can crawl on all fours toward her backpack. I hear a zipping sound, then she returns to me—with a foil packet held between her teeth, glistening in the moonlight. I take the packet from her and cover myself.

"Still raring to go?" she asks.

"Oh, aye, donnae worry about that." I flip us over and lie down on top of her as I plunge inside her body, groaning deeply. "Love the way you feel, *gràidh*."

Ashley grips me with her entire body, from her arms and legs lashed around me to the silky recesses of her body. Her mouth grazes my throat with every thrust. She alternately gasps and moans, while her breaths grow ragged and quicker, a sure sign she'll come soon.

When she drags her nails down my back, I suck in a breath, and my *slat* throbs. Then she sinks her nails into my erse while tightening her inner muscles around me.

"*Bod an Donais*," I hiss. "Donnae do that, unless yer wanting me to explode like one of my mines."

"Oh God, yes, I want that."

"You come first, *mo chridhe*."

I hoist myself up with both arms straight, giving me better leverage for thrusting into her. Then I clasp her hand and guide it down to her folds, where the tip of her index finger grazes her wetness. "Rub yerself, lass. Make yerself come."

She slips her fingers between those slick, hot folds and begins to massage her clit. "Errol, please, don't stop fucking me."

"Cannae stop." The pressure in my *slat* grows every second, and I feel an electrical surge ramping up inside me, like a transformer about to explode. So I fuck her harder and faster, grunting and gritting my teeth while I struggle not to come before she does. "Rub harder, lass. Come *now*."

She rubs herself furiously. Even when her body tenses up, frozen in the moment before climax, her finger keeps moving at a frenzied pace.

Then a strangled cry bursts out of her.

All the muscles inside her clamp around my cock in a pulsating rhythm that shatters my self-control. I throw my head back and roar like a wild animal, coming inside her so hard and fast that I cannae move a muscle. When it finally subsides, I drop onto the ground beside her, sprawled on my back and breathing hard.

I can't do anything except gaze up at the sky.

Until a stupid thing comes out of my mouth. "These aren't actually the same stars that shined at the beginning of time. Precession makes all the stars shift gradually over the eons."

Ashley sits up and slaps my chest.

Oh aye, I deserve that.

Chapter Twenty

Ashley

That's the first thing Errol says after we just had fantastically hot and romantic sex on the shores of the Colorado River on a beautiful, starry night? He needed to point out that I was wrong because precession moves the stars. I knew that. But come on, when I said we could make love under the same stars that have shined since the beginning of time, that wasn't meant as a literal statement. It was supposed to be romantic.

Why did I slap his chest? I'm not angry. Well, okay, maybe a little. But mostly, I feel disappointed because the moment is ruined.

Errol sits up and turns toward me. "I'm sorry, Ashley. Donnae know why I said that."

"You must have some idea why."

He rubs his neck, wincing slightly. "I suppose I might have, ah, gotten anxious."

"Aren't people supposed to do that before they get naked? Post-sex anxiety isn't a thing as far as I know."

"Can't a man get anxious whenever he bloody well feels like it?"

I wriggle to get cross-legged, facing him. "You're right, sorry. I guess I'm a little anxious because you got anxious. Sex is usually relaxing, right?"

"Aye. And I did feel very relaxed."

"So why did you feel the need to correct me on what the stars do?"

He shrugs one shoulder. "Maybe I'm, ah, not entirely sure you want to be with me and not Munro or some other bloke who might come along."

"You think I would have sex with you when I really want Munro? If I were hot for him, I'd have dragged him into the river instead of you."

"Aye, of course ye would." Errol sighs, and his shoulders flag. "I've never had a serious girlfriend, so I guess I don't know how to handle that. Of course, we haven't talked about whether we want a relationship with each other. I shouldn't assume—"

"I want to be with you, Errol. You don't need to worry about that." I wriggle to get even closer to him and sling my arms around his neck. "You are the only man I want to get naked with. I like Munro, but as a friend."

"Oh. That's...good." He makes a pained face. "You must think I'm a bloody moron."

"Not at all." I grasp his face and kiss him. "You're just a typical man who doesn't understand his own feelings."

"Aye, I'm a bloody stupid erse, like all my cousins."

I kiss him again, holding my lips to his for longer than before. "We'd better get dressed. Munro must want to come back to the camp."

"Aye, you're right. Though I think Munro likes hanging about in the wilderness by himself."

I consider that statement while we get dressed and return to where we'd laid out our sleeping bags. I've just crawled inside mine when Munro ambles out of the bushes. In the waning light of our fire, I can tell his hair is wet—and his clothes too, though they aren't dripping. He looks like he took a dip in the river with his clothes on, then waited a while before returning to camp.

The Wild Man has manners.

While I zip up my sleeping bag, the boys crawl into theirs. I hear Munro start snoring softly, and when I look at Errol, he has his eyes closed and soft breaths whisper out of him, sort of like mini snores. It's adorable. Fortunately, neither man snores loudly, so I fall asleep without any trouble.

In the morning, I wake to find Errol stoking the campfire.

"Aren't we leaving this morning?" I ask.

"We are. But we need to eat first. Munro volunteered to catch us some fish." He gives me a deviously sexy smile. "Someone needs protein after what she did last night."

"What *we* did last night. You kind of participated too."

He smirks. "Aye, a wee bit."

I unzip my sleeping bag and rise to stretch my whole body. I yawn too.

"Ready for another day of searching?" Errol asks. "Or maybe I should ask if you're ready for more whitewater rafting."

"I do love that. If you'd asked me beforehand whether I wanted to ride the rapids, I probably would've said no. Turns out, I'm an adventure seeker." I find my shoes and a fresh pair of socks, then sit down to put them on. I'd slept in my clothes I wanted to wear today, to make sure I wouldn't slow down our progress. "I searched both sides of the canyon yesterday, using binoculars and my naked eyes. But I didn't see anything that might be the cavern Kincaid described."

"We'll keep searching. Still plenty of cliffs to examine."

Errol always makes me feel better every time I start to get bummed out and worry we've undertaken a pointless mission.

Munro returns a few minutes later, and after enjoying a nice breakfast, we douse the fire and load our gear onto the raft again. Errol and I climb in, then Munro gives our raft a push to get it into the river. He jumps in just in time.

And we're on our way again.

Twice, I get excited when I glimpse dark spaces on the cliffs that might be hidden caverns. But both times, when I look through the binoculars, I realize it's nothing but an overhang that casts a shadow. *Damn.*

The river had turned muddy just past where we'd slept last night. A few miles after that, Munro points out a canyon up ahead, on the right. "That's Lava Canyon. We're about to hit the rapid named after that feature. Ashley, I know you love whitewater, though this will be brown water rapids. Would you like to ride in front to get the full experience? Errol and I can move to the back to paddle us through the rough water."

"What?" Errol says. "No, she shouldn't do that. It's dangerous."

"I can handle it," I tell him. "Please, let me ride in front just this once. Munro wouldn't suggest that if he thought I'd be in danger."

"There's an alternative," Munro says. "Errol could stay up here with you. I can paddle by myself. I've done it before."

Errol glances back at me, seeming worried.

I smile and wave at him. Then I blow him a kiss.

His entire demeanor softens, and his lips relax into a smile. "All right, lass. Ride up here with me."

Munro carefully moves to the back, and I half crawl to the front at the same time. The raft only rocks a little. Now I sit beside Errol. He hands his paddle to Munro, who begins paddling with both hands, one on each side of the raft. He can't make that digging motion in the water like he and Errol usually do, but given his massive biceps, I have no doubts that he can maneuver us through the rapids with no problems.

"Hold on to your trousers, lass," Munro shouts as we enter the rapid. "The real fun is about to begin."

"This is a class four rapid," Errol tells me. "Yesterday, we went through some class fours and a class five. Lava Canyon will be no problem for you, since you're a seasoned veteran now."

He winks when he says that.

Errol always knows how to make me feel like I can do anything. But I have to ask, "Will we go through any rapids that are higher than class five?"

"Oh, aye, we will." He pats my thigh. "Trust me and Munro to get you through it."

I do trust them—with my life.

"Luckily, we shouldn't need to go far enough to reach Lava Falls," Errol says. "That rapid is a class ten."

"Yeah, let's not visit that one. I love whitewater rafting, but a ten sounds like suicide."

Errol hooks a thumb over his shoulder. "You're rafting with a man who has paddled through class ten rapids many times here in the canyon."

As we enter the rapid, the current doesn't seem super turbulent. Even when the water grows rougher, and powerful waves lift the raft up a bit, I feel only a normal amount of anxiety that's overwhelmed by my excitement. I whoop as a wave crashes over the side of the raft, drenching me. Errol grins and holds my hand. The next time a wave breaks over us, we both whoop and Errol thrusts his free hand into the air. We're both grinning like idiots. I'm kind of disappointed when we emerge from the rapid and the river calms down again. I loved experiencing rapids from the backseat, but I loved it even more when I sat here at the front with Errol beside me.

Munro and I switch places, and I go back to searching the cliffs for any sign of Kincaid's cavern.

I'd never gone whitewater rafting, or done any kind of rafting at all, before yesterday. It had always sounded scary and likely to make me vomit. I survived Errol's driving, though I needed motion sickness pills for that experience. Yet I've traversed class four rapids without getting sick. Maybe I'm getting used to wild rides.

We continue down the river in relative peace for a while. Errol and I both take time now and then to admire our surroundings, though Munro stays focused on the river ahead of us. The Grand Canyon is beyond breathtaking, majestic, and so ancient that it's impossible to put into words how I feel while gliding through this landscape. Still, I hope we make another pit stop soon because I could use a break from sitting in this raft—and I need to pee. When I mention that, Munro suggests I should hang my "erse" over the side to relieve myself. Uh, no, I don't think I'll do that. My bladder can wait.

A few minutes later, Munro announces, "We're approaching Tanner Rapid. It's a class six, but donnae let that bother you. I've shot this rapid many times before, and you'll do just fine, Ashley."

"She'll love it," Errol says, and he turns his head to give me a playful smile. "Won't ye, *gràidh*?"

"Absolutely. Let's shoot that rapid, boys."

I'm glad Errol finally stopped fretting over my safety and can enjoy the trip along with me. Errol seems like his old self again.

We make our way around a ninety-degree bend in the river, followed swiftly by another, identical turn. Now I see the rapid ahead of us. I barely have time to brace myself before we run straight into the turbulent water, which seems to be littered with rocks on the right side. Errol and Munro guide the raft to the left to avoid those obstacles. Though our raft bounces a bit, and we get splashed once, we make it through the rapid without incident. I whooped a couple of times, and Errol shouted, "Yeah!" Even Munro got into it, whooping in his own gruff way.

After crossing through another rapid, our journey takes us around more ninety-degree bends until we reach yet another rapid. Wow, I had no idea the Grand Canyon was full of these kinds of obstacles. The river narrows as we approach the next rapid, a class six that curves to the right, which I imagine makes it more treacherous to navigate than the previous class six we'd gone through earlier. But with Errol and Munro in control of the raft, we pass through the rapid without incident. I get to whoop some more, which always makes me feel exhilarated. After that, I realize I need to focus on searching the cliffs rather than having a good time. Since we apparently have many rapids ahead of us, I've decided to ignore most of them. Well, I can't completely ignore them, but after a few class sixes, the thrill has worn off just enough that I no longer whoop every time. I actually study the cliffs while in the midst of a roiling rapid.

"Time to hold on to your trousers again," Munro shouts to me. "See that up there? It's a class eight rapid."

Holy cow. Class eight?

Despite the higher number giving me a twinge of anxiety, we rush through the rapid without any of us falling out of the raft. We get doused a couple of times, that's all. But Munro tells me we can expect even stronger rapids as we approach the Kaibab Trail. But we won't get there for hours yet, and I really need to stop this wavy train for a while.

Errol laughs when I say that phrase—"wavy train." Munro just gives me an annoyed look. I guess he doesn't appreciate silly humor. Errol calls my description of the rapids "clever and adorable."

"Have you spotted something?" Munro asks in his grumpy tone. "Or do ye need to use another 'girl bush'?"

"Both. I did see something up on the cliff we just passed. Can we go back? Or is that not possible?"

"Can we do it?" Munro says in a scoffing tone. "We're MacTaggarts, Ashley. We can do anything."

"But Errol's a Murdoch. That means we can't paddle upstream, huh?"

"He's a Murdoch and a MacTaggart."

Errol rolls his eyes at his cousin. "She's having you on, Munro. Ashley knows I'm also a MacTaggart."

"I know she was joking, ye *cacan*. Now, let's get paddling to show the lass what Scots can do."

I watch as the men easily swivel the raft around to face upstream, then paddle hard to reach the spot I point out to them. It's just this side of the worst part of the rapids we just traveled through, which means the boys need to paddle even harder to reach the shore. They're both breathing hard by the time they push our raft onto the short sandy stretch hemmed in by cliffs. I chose this area because it has what could be called a "stain" on the cliffs as well as a dark overhang that might hide a cave. I couldn't tell for sure while floating down the river.

After going behind some rocks to relieve myself in private, I return to the sandy spot and bring out the laminated map.

Time to prove I can do this.

Chapter Twenty-One

Errol

I stay a discreet distance away while Ashley pores over the Ellsworth map. This is her moment, and I won't interfere unless she wants my help. The lass knows what she thinks she saw, and it might take time for her to figure out how it relates to the map. I am not good at waiting, though.

Munro took off a few minutes after we landed on the shore, but he didn't explain where he was going or why. He just leaped into the river and disappeared around an outcropping. If the bampot drowns, I will need to explain to Ashley why I let him go off on his own. So I give up watching her from a distance and climb up the steep slope on the downriver side of the wee valley to do a visual search of the water below.

Ah, there he is. Munro is sitting on a small boulder, drenched from head to toe, apparently doing nothing more important than sunning himself. I doubt I will ever understand Munro. But then, most of the family says that about me.

I return to Ashley and can't hold back my curiosity any longer. I kneel beside her. "How is it going? Any breakthroughs?"

"Well, I've decided that overhang up there probably isn't the right place." She cranes her neck to see past my head. "Nope. It doesn't match the symbols on the map legend."

"You'll figure it out, eventually. You are the cleverest person I've ever met."

"I'm not the one who deciphered the map."

"We're a good team."

She smiles. "Yes, we are."

"May I see the map?"

Ashley nods and hands it to me.

I flip it over to the legend side and study the notations there. "Maybe I was wrong about what these symbols represent. Squiggles might not indicate rivers or streams."

She wriggles closer and stares down at the drawing. "What do you think it does mean?"

"Ah, well… Ahmno sure. Maybe a different kind of water." I exhale a sharp sigh. "But that's a bloody useless thing to say, isn't it? Another kind of water."

The lass bites her lip, which I realized a while ago means she's ruminating on the matter. Then her mouth curls into a sly smile, and she rolls her gaze up to mine.

"I can tell you've got something," I say. "Tell me."

"Might be wrong again, but…" She runs her finger along the squiggly line. "Doesn't this remind you of rapids?"

Now my lips form a sly smile. "Oh, you are dead clever, Ashley. I think you're right. Those lines represent rapids." I flip the map over to the cartographic side. "Look at the lines. They start with one squiggle, then it becomes two, and finally three. Those notations appear in the same order every time. Let's see if we can connect the lines to specific rapids."

She glances around as if she's looking for something.

"What is it?" I ask.

Ashley cranes her neck again. "Where's Munro?"

"He went down the river, remember? I saw him sitting on a boulder a few yards from the shore."

She stands up. "Let's go get him."

I chuckle, rising too. "We don't need to go anywhere."

"But how—"

"Munro!" I shout so loudly that it echoes off the canyon walls and Ashley winces. "Get your erse back here now! Munro!"

She claps her hands over her ears.

I peel them away. "I'm done, lass. You don't need earplugs."

Ashley glances around and pretends to be confused. "I don't see Munro yet. Are you sure you hollered loud enough? Maybe he needs hearing aids."

"Munro does everything in his own time. No point in trying to hurry him—or slow him down."

A figure appears along the shore, wading through the water's edge. Munro takes his time heading for us, and he has his damp shirt draped over one shoulder.

Ashley admires my cousin's chest. And I don't care. She can look at his body all she wants because I'm the only one she wants to shag. I prefer to admire her body, rather than Munro's. Unfortunately, the lass is wearing clothes that cover almost all of her sexy body, except for her arms.

"Did ye solve the mystery?" Munro asks, as he stops near us to wring out his wet shirt.

"Not quite," I say. "But Ashley is a genius. She deciphered the real meaning of the squiggly lines on the map."

"Squiggly?" His lip curls a wee bit, and he speaks the word as if he's just swallowed a rotten egg and wishes he could spit it out.

"Aye, squiggly. That's a word, Munro. It's even in the dictionary."

"Which one?"

"Oxford, of course."

Before Munro can complain about that, Ashley speaks up. "It's in the Merriam-Webster dictionary too."

My cousin rolls his eyes. "Well, if Americans say it's a real word, it must be true."

I give up on trying to convince him. Let the grumpy sod think what he likes.

"The point is," I say, "that Ashley and I understand what we're looking for now. The map will be of much more use to us."

"Good. Where is the treasure?"

"Slow down, Munro. This is a quest, which means it will take time."

He grunts.

Aye, Munro makes Magnus the Pig-Bear seem like a cheerful chatterbox. I still think his wife's nickname for him is bizarre, but then, they are a strange couple. Not as strange as I am, though. And I will fight to maintain my title as the most bizarre member of the MacTaggart clan.

Ashley holds the map with both hands while staring down at it. "I know we can figure this out. Maybe if I just squint my eyes, I'll be able to see…" Her eyes go wide, and she jerks her head up. "We're heading toward another rapid, right?"

Munro moves closer to us, peering down at the map. "Aye, that's right. We'll go through Sockdolager Rapid next. It's a class seven. Then, about three miles later, we'll hit the Grapevine Rapid, also a class seven. The Grand Canyon is riddled with stretches of rough water."

"Errol, can you bring up satellite images of the canyon?" Ashley asks. "I need to compare those to the map."

"No problem." I bring out my mobile and go to a map site. "Would it be easier to use my laptop? It has a much bigger screen."

"Oh, sure. Let's get that out."

I shove my mobile back into my pocket and hunt inside my pack for my laptop computer. The three of us sit down on the sandy ground and huddle together so we can all look at the images on my computer screen. I've zoomed in on the location where we are now, as well as the immediate area around it.

Ashley stares at the screen without blinking, though her eyes repeatedly flick back and forth between the satellite image and the map in her hand. She uses her fingertips to zoom in and out on the screen while continuing to flick her gaze back and forth. I cannae see how she won't get motion sickness from doing that. But she seems fine, and I don't want to interrupt a clever lass at work.

Finally, she raises her head to look at me. "I think I've found something, but I need a genius's input."

"You're wanting to ask yourself a question?"

"Ha-ha. You are the genius, Errol."

"No, you are."

She shakes her head. "You deciphered the map and—"

"Enough!" Munro snarls. "You're both ruddy geniuses. Can we skip the annual meeting of the Mutual Admiration Society? Or would you two like to have a poke right here in front of me?" His irritation melts into a devilish smirk. "Though I might not mind watching Ashley take her kit off to enjoy some solo—"

"Haud yer wheesht," I say. "Or I'll leave you here while we take the raft downriver."

Ashley sighs. "Are you two done harassing each other? I really do need your input, Errol."

"I'm always ready to assist you, *gràidh*. How can I help?"

"Look at this." She points to the Ellsworth map and several squiggles on it. "If I'm right and these lines represent rapids, then we should expect four sets of rapids, with the last one situated alongside a pyramid-shaped cliff. There's a canyon beside the pyramid formation, which also coincides with the map. So does the rapid just after the canyon. But I don't think the pyramid is the location of the cavern. It's just a landmark."

"I didn't notice a pyramid on the map."

"Neither did I at first. But when I compared the map to the satellite images, there was a definite similarity between this section of cliffs on the map and the pyramid formation in the satellite data."

"I do see what you mean now. The map shows that bit of the cliffs as having a sharper peak and what seems like squared off sides." I slant in for a closer look. "According to the map, we should look out for a dark blob near the base of the cliffs, about a mile past Zoroaster Canyon."

"A blob?" Munro says with a chuckle. "Aye, that's exactly the sort of directions we needed—look for the blob."

"I bet it's a boulder," Ashley says. "It's not attached to the cliffs. It looks like it's in the water."

"You know there are mountains with Egyptian names in the Grand Canyon," I say. "Shouldn't we look there?"

"Those are too far from the river. I still believe we need to search here. And it's too on-the-nose for the map to direct us to the Egyptian-themed landmarks. Everybody would look there." She tucks the map into her backpack. "We're going to Cremation Creek."

"Zoroaster Canyon was named after an Iranian prophet, so we still have the 'oriental' connection. Victorian explorers used the word oriental to mean anything in the Middle East or Far East."

"Good point." She picks up her pack. "Come on, boys, let's not dawdle anymore. Get your asses moving."

Munro lifts one brow. "If you weren't so bonnie, I'd complain about a woman ordering me to move my erse."

"I wouldn't," I tell him, while wagging my eyebrows at the lass. "Ashley can order me to do anything she wants."

Munro groans and grabs his pack, then leads us back to the raft. Soon, we're on our way again, with Ashley in the back and Munro and me in front. We have about two miles until the next rapid. Ashley spends that time surveying the cliffs and even taking some photographs. She snaps a picture of me when I turn halfway toward her to check on the lass. Then she blows me a kiss.

No, I am not worried anymore that she prefers Munro.

Though the next two rapids are both class seven, we get through Sockdolager without any serious problems. Munro and I need to paddle harder and take care not to let the wild currents sweep us away. But Ashley loves the ride, especially when a wave crashes onto us. She falls off her seat but remains inside the raft, and she laughs with so much joy that I want to kiss her.

I always want to kiss Ashley, though. She is very kissable.

Despite knowing a trip down the Colorado River would involve some danger, I hadn't anticipated how that risk would affect me. I don't fear for my own safety, though. I worry about Ashley. I'd gone on a few river rafting trips before this, as part of my job, but she's a novice. The thought of anything happening to her makes my throat thicken and my heart pound. My mouth has gone dry too. It's done that every time we crossed into a section of rapid, but more so when we're navigating rapids with a higher class rating. I'd enjoyed the lesser rapids with her, but class seven has me on edge.

My adventure with Magnus and Piper had involved plenty of danger, but I hadn't worried this much about either of them. Piper had managed to evade the authorities for almost two years, and she evaded Magnus too. The three of us put ourselves in mortal danger, more than once, but still I didn't get anxious about that. Yet with Ashley, I can't stop worrying. But I need to concentrate on the rapids ahead of us. That means I must forget about the lass, at least for a while. Just long enough to get us through the rough water and back to safety. Well, relative safety. With Munro taking the lead, all I need to do is follow his orders and stay calm.

Shortly after Sockdolager Rapid, the river turns muddy and we enter the next challenge, Grapevine Rapid. Our raft gets slammed by big waves that crash over the three of us. Munro and I struggle to keep the raft heading in the right direction, but I can't stop myself from glancing back at Ashley repeatedly to make sure she's all right. She did fall off her seat in the midst of the previous rapid. This one seems more turbulent.

"Let's shoot the rapid," Munro hollers. "Ashley, move into the middle of the raft at the rear. We need to keep this thing balanced."

"Shouldn't I paddle too?" she asks. "Since this is a more difficult rapid."

"Normally, yes," I say. "But with only three of us, you might destabilize the raft. That almost happened at Sockdolager. So just hold on and let us do the work."

"These rapids don't seem deep," Munro says. He looks back at Ashley. "Donnae worry. We've both done this before."

Aye, I have done this before—three times. And none of those occasions happened on the Colorado River. I'd navigated easy rapids on smaller rivers. But I give Ashley an encouraging smile.

Then we dive into the maelstrom.

We paddle hard, fighting against the churning water, in a motion reminiscent of digging. We hit a rough patch, and the raft bounces. Ashley yelps, but when I risk a glance backward, I see she's grinning. The lass enjoys a ride through Grapevine Rapid, despite the muddy brown water that smacks into the raft.

But we've gotten through it. The river has returned to its normal state.

"That was fun," Ashley says. "When will we hit more rapids?"

"Easy, lass," Munro says. "That was a class seven, but we will run into worse rapids."

"Whitewater rapids?"

"Please don't wish for whitewater," I say. "You're a novice, and I donnae want anything to happen to you."

Munro throws me a smirk, but only for a second because he knows we need to focus on what might lie ahead for us. The Colorado is known for its rapids, after all. Munro is the expert, the one who knows where all the toughest sections are, so Ashley and I both need to listen to him and do what he says. Staying alert is key.

Why Munro smirked at me, I have no idea. He might often be grumpy, but he seems entertained by my interactions with Ashley. The man is strange.

As we float down a calm stretch of the river, I let myself experience the scenery. The steep cliffs almost make me feel like I've landed on Mars, thanks to the starkness of the landscape with very little vegetation and seemingly none anywhere except along the river. The Colorado doesn't offer any beaches, either, just the occasional patch of rocky shoreline or grassy beach. Nothing anyone would want to sunbathe on, though it wouldn't surprise me if Ashley tried that. I don't see any obvious caves, certainly nothing large enough to qualify as Kincaid's cavern. But we haven't gone forty-two miles from where that bloke said he started his journey, which means we might yet find the mysterious network of caverns.

Birds fly past high overhead, but I can't tell what species they are. When I glance back, I see Ashley has moved back to the side of the raft so she can lean over a wee bit to get a better view. The sun on her face makes the lass look even bonnier, and her sweet smile triggers a pang in my chest.

But I don't have time to think about what that means. Another gauntlet lies ahead of us.

Chapter Twenty-Two

Ashley

As we float down the river, Errol suggests I should switch places with him so I can get a better view of the cliffs. Munro can paddle by himself since we're on a calm stretch. I crawl to the front and slide onto the seat beside Munro. Yeah, I can see things a little better from up here. I get out my binoculars and start searching for any sign of…anything. But I don't notice any unusual features. After a few minutes, my eyes need a break from staring through the binoculars. What can I do to pass the time?

Harass Munro, of course. It's called conversation, but I suspect he won't agree with my definition. "Munro, mind if I ask you a personal question?"

The Scot grunts. "Does it matter if I mind? Lasses always do what they want no matter what I say."

Okay, I'll take that as permission. "Why did you stop being a river guide?"

"Because I died."

His bald statement stuns me for a moment. He obviously isn't dead, so he must've meant something else. Right? "But you're still alive."

"Aye. But I was clinically dead for three minutes and five seconds."

"My God. I had no idea."

He throws me a scowl. "Of course ye didn't, because I never told anyone."

"Donnae be a grump," Errol says. "Tell us what happened. This is the first I've heard of you dying."

Munro shuts his eyes briefly, then tells us, "I took newlyweds on a white-water rafting trip through the roughest part of the Grand Canyon. When we hit Lava Falls Rapid, something went wrong. Still donnae know what it was. But the raft nearly flipped. I managed to stop it just in time, and the couple were fine. But then another wave slammed us, and I got thrown out of the raft. The last thing I remember hearing was the wife screaming. I passed out. When I woke up on the shore, I found out a mate of mine who was also shooting the rapid that day saw what happened and fished me out of the river. He performed CPR."

"Wow, that's an incredible story," I say. "Will we be going through Lava Falls Rapid?"

"No." He glares at the river ahead of us. "Under no circumstances will we go that far down the river."

I open my mouth to ask another question.

"Time to switch places," Munro says. "Get your erse up here, Errol."

He doesn't want to talk about his near-death experience anymore. I can understand that. So I climb to the back of the raft and take my seat like a good girl.

We go through two more rapids, and the last one takes us past Zoroaster Canyon to a spot about a mile further down the river where that "blob" we had discussed earlier lies. It's a boulder, like I thought. Munro and Errol manage to maneuver our raft onto a flat rocky area near the boulder so we can consider our next move. The boys want to hike up the creek bed to check out the area, but I have a hunch we don't need to go that far.

"A hunch?" Errol says. "About what?"

"The boulder. I told you that." I approach the rim of our rocky ledge and lean forward a touch to study the big rock. "The map has given us clues and even two landmarks—the pyramid cliff, and now this boulder. It has to mean something."

Munro sets his hands on his hips and squints at me. "A boulder has to mean something, eh? I've seen lots of large rocks that have no significance whatsoever, other than being in my way."

"You think my idea is silly, but you were quite willing to hike up that steep hill based on zero evidence. I want to examine the boulder, and I do have evidence to support that decision."

Munro stares at me for a moment, then sighs and throws his hands up. "I surrender. But how do you suggest we examine that rock? It's in the river."

"We have ropes, don't we?"

"Aye." He studies me with his eyes narrowed even more. Then his face goes blank. After a moment, he shuts his eyes and groans. "I am not letting you jump into the water to 'examine' a boulder. The current is too swift. You'd get swept away. I cannae guarantee even ropes could keep you from getting dragged under."

"I'm willing to take that risk."

Errol approaches me and glances down at the big rock. "I'll do it."

"But this was my idea."

"I know. But I have experience with rock climbing and swimming in rough waters, not to mention free diving. I should be the one to do it."

He does make a good point. I haven't gone swimming in a pool very many times. As much as I want to be the one who inspects the boulder, I know Errol is right.

"Okay," I tell him. "You've got the job."

Munro grunts. "Aye, he's the only one barmy enough to try it."

Errol gets his life jacket, and Munro ties a rope around his waist. That should protect him, but he's still in danger. And he's doing this for me. I could kiss him for that, even while I wish he wouldn't do it. Errol jumps into the water, and thanks to his life jacket, he stays afloat as he paddles across the thirty feet or so to the boulder. The slab of rock must measure about thirty feet in diameter too, so Errol climbs onto it while Munro unreels just enough rope to let his cousin do that. He hunts around, searching for any sign of a clue.

Yeah, that's such a specific mission I gave him. Find me a clue. But Errol has spent years working as a treasure hunter, and I have complete faith in his ability to discover signs that might aid our expedition. But the more he crawls around on the boulder, the more I worry he won't find anything and we'll need to start over, deciphering the map again in hopes of spotting what we'd missed before.

Then Errol springs to his knees. "I see some sort of carving, I think. Part of it pokes up out of the water, but it seems like there's more under the surface. I need to dive in to check it out."

"Dive in?" I say, sounding anxious because I am. The river rushes around the boulder, so naturally, I'm afraid he might get swept away. And I don't feel like a wuss for feeling that way. "Are you sure that's necessary? Can't we use the ground-penetrating radar to look under the surface?"

"Not sure that would work. I know how to free dive, Ashley. Let me give it a go. Munro can always drag me out if I get caught in the current or stuck on an obstacle underwater."

"Well, if you're sure…"

"I am, *gràidh*." He points toward my feet. "But you are too close to the edge for my comfort. Take a few steps back, would you, love?"

"Sure." I back away from the edge. "Be careful, Errol."

He sheds his life jacket. "I've blown up corporate computer servers, remember? I can handle a wee dive in muddy water."

Before I can say anything else, he rises to his full height, raises his arms, and dives into the river.

He called me "love," and something else that I suspect is Gaelic. Was "*gràidh*" an endearment too? I haven't used any endearments when speaking to him, but mostly because I don't know how he might react to that. Men sometimes get weird about those things.

Errol has completely submerged himself, and I can't see him through the brown water. I know he's down there only because his rope floats on the water and disappears beneath the surface. I count the seconds until he emerges. One, two, three, four, five, six, seven, eight, nine, ten. Still no Errol. I inch a teeny bit closer to the edge. Eleven, twelve, thirteen, fourteen, fifteen.

"Shouldn't he have come out by now?" I ask Munro. "It's taking an awfully long time."

"He can hold his breath for a few minutes, at least."

"Minutes? How do you know that? I thought you guys hadn't seen each other in a long time."

"Aye, but I knew him before…I withdrew from the family." Munro keeps his gaze on the water where Errol had dived in, not even glancing sideways at me when I spoke. He gives the rope a light tug. "Ah, there. He tugged in response. That means the laddie is fine."

Laddie? Errol isn't a child. Munro's use of that word spurs me to ask a question. "Are you older than Errol? He told me he's thirty-seven."

"I know that. And since I can tell you're dying to know, I'm forty-three. Satisfied?"

"Yes. Thank you. I'm thirty-two, by the way." My foot has a mind of its own and decides to tap furiously on the rock ledge beneath me. My hands want to wring themselves too. I keep staring down at the muddy river, but I still can't see a thing. "Maybe you should pull him out. It's been too long."

"Relax, Ashley."

"No, I can't do that. Pull him out, please."

Munro gives me an exasperated look.

I point down at the water. "Get him out of there."

"You're being overly—"

Errol springs up out of the water. He lets out a triumphant shout, then swims over to the ledge to climb onto it a few feet from me. Errol grins. "Success!"

I throw my arms around him. "Oh, thank goodness. I thought you were drowning."

"No, lass, I was never in any danger." He grasps my face and kisses me deeply. "But I like knowing you care enough to panic."

I glance at Munro. "What were you going to say? Something about me being overly…what?"

Munro actually seems sheepish, though only for a moment. Then he reverts to his usual grumpiness. "I was going to say you're being overly lenient in letting Errol free dive like that."

"Oh, sure, that's what you wanted to tell me. Afraid I'm not buying that 'overly lenient' bullshit. I think you were about to say something sexist."

Munro urges Errol to step aside. Then he clasps my hand and kisses it. "My deepest apologies to you, Ashley, for any affront I may have caused you."

"I accept your apology, even if it is partially sarcastic."

"Thank you, lass. You have unburdened my heart."

"Quit while you're ahead."

Munro bows and kisses my hand again. Then he moves away to let Errol come closer to me.

"What did you find?" I ask. "Seemed like you stumbled onto something."

"I did. Do you have a piece of paper and a pencil? I'll draw it for you."

Munro retrieves a pad of paper and a pen from his pack and gives them both to Errol. I watch while Errol sketches something on the sheet, his pen moving so swiftly that I have trouble keeping track of his strokes. When he's finished, he hands me the pad of paper.

I study what he drew. "This looks a lot like the map we have."

"Aye, that's what I thought too."

"But this must be a continuation of the original drawing. Whoever created the cavern Kincaid found must have wanted to keep it a secret. Why else would somebody hide the next part of the map underwater?"

"Ye read my mind, Ashley." Errol slaps the back of his hand on Munro's chest. "See? I told ye she's a clever lass."

Munro rubs his forehead. "So now we're following another map that will lead to yet another one, and on and on and on."

"I'm paying you to be our guide," I tell him. "So shut up and be happy. You'll get piles of money when this is over."

He rubs his chin. "Aye, that is the silver lining."

Errol slaps his palms together. "Back in the raft. Our journey hasn't ended yet."

I help the boys push the raft halfway into the water, but Munro insists that Errol and I should climb in while he gives us the final push into the river. Then we're off again. Munro and Errol immediately begin paddling to avoid the boulder and the rapid that flows around it.

Since Errol and I have already proved that Kincaid's meager instructions didn't provide all the details, we should continue following our instincts and the maps. I doubt Kincaid created the boulder map, but he knew it existed.

We draw closer and closer to our goal every minute. I know it. I can feel it. But Errol needed to risk his life to dive into the river just so we could find the next clue, and that makes me wonder. How many times will we need to risk our lives for my quest?

And will we survive it?

Chapter Twenty-Three

Errol

The new map we found suggests we haven't overshot the mark and missed the cavern. A few miles down the river, we cross under the Kaibab Bridge, a suspension bridge that takes foot traffic across the river. We need to stop to discuss the new map, but we bypass the Phantom Ranch Boat Beach, the first landing spot we see, because tourist boats like to stop there. We don't want to explain to anyone why we don't have a permit.

Instead, we stop just past the Boat Beach, on the opposite bank, and haul our raft onto the rocky shore. Here, we have time to consider our next move with a measure of privacy.

Munro lies down on the ground, clasps his hands under his head, and seems to go to sleep. No, I donnae believe he's sleeping. He wants us to leave him alone, that's all. Or maybe he prefers to listen in on our conversation without having to participate in it.

Ashley and I pore over the map together, our heads almost touching while we discuss what I found under the water. The new map doesn't include anything that resembles a suspension bridge, but I imagine it hadn't been built yet at the time the Havasupai gave Ellsworth their map. But we do see two blobs that lie near us.

"Must be those boulders," she says, pointing across the river.

I glance in that direction. There are indeed two large rocks. "Aye, those could be the ones shown on the map."

"Someone's coming," Munro says, while keeping his eyes closed.

"How can you tell?" I ask.

"Listen."

I close my eyes and listen. At first I hear nothing, then I notice the faint rumble of a boat engine. I stand up and look around. "Could be a tourist boat."

"Tourists don't stop on this side of the river."

I don't know how he could possibly tell which side of the river that boat is traveling along, but Munro is an expert on the Grand Canyon. Maybe he can tell that just from the sound of the boat approaching.

A white raft comes into view, motoring toward our little rest stop, piloted by one man alone. A wide-brimmed hat conceals his face. Even as he shuts off the motor and jumps out to pull his raft partway onto the shore, I still can't see his features. He walks toward us, removing his hat, and at last I can see he has dark hair and a weathered face that suggests he spends a lot of time outdoors. He might also be older than I am, if his wrinkles provide an accurate gauge.

"Who's the new guy?" Ashley whispers to me. She just stood up and now studies our visitor. "Why is he alone? And why did he want to come over here?"

"No idea."

As the bloke reaches our wee expedition party, he smiles at Munro. "Wake up, lazy head."

My cousin stands up, then yawns and stretches. "About bloody time ye got here. Should I have shot off a flare gun?"

The stranger, who Munro seems to know, strides over to my cousin and grasps his forearm. "It's been a long time. Where have you been hiding? The best river guide in the Grand Canyon vanished without a trace."

Munro grasps the bloke's forearm, which seems like some sort of handshake. "I didn't vanish. I retired."

"Who's your mate, Munro?" I ask.

"This is Joseph Butler. We both used to be river guides, and technically we were rivals since we worked for different companies. But I decided to let Joey have a chance without my brilliant skills overshadowing him." Munro slaps his friend's arm. "You can thank me later."

"Same old goat, eh? You even brought your girlfriend with you."

Munro chuckles. "That's my cousin's girlfriend. Joey, meet Errol Murdoch and Ashley Hartman."

Joseph approaches us to shake hands. Then the bloke turns toward Munro. "What are you guys doing out here?"

"How did you know we were here?" I ask.

Joseph smiles and taps his temple. "Magic powers."

I can't figure out if he's having me on, or if he honestly claims to have special powers.

He chuckles. "I was pulling your leg. My brother works at the Marble Canyon Airport, and he alerted me when you chartered a private helicopter ride. Tyler had never seen a Scotsman before, much less two of you. He was kind of excited."

"Donnae understand," I say. "Have you been tracking us ever since the helicopter dropped us off?"

"No. I was curious whether Munro was one of the Scots that Tyler saw. So I leveraged my contacts to find out if there had been any sightings of a beastly Scotsman on the river. Your pilot buddy was seen loading the inflatable raft into the chopper."

"It was in a cardboard box. How could anyone know what it was?"

Joseph grins. "It said 'inflatable raft' on the side of the box."

I hadn't noticed that. Am I losing my touch? I'm the man who solves puzzles, but I failed to notice the large words on a large box.

"You didn't come here just to have a riverside chat," Munro says.

"No. I thought I should warn you. Somebody else knows you're in the canyon, and they've been tracking you." Joseph shoves his hands into his trouser pockets. "I don't know who it is, but this man might've planted a GPS chip on your raft or maybe in your backpack."

"Who told you that?"

"It's a secondhand rumor, but my brother heard from one of the guys who works for Peter Heymans that Peter happened to see a stranger milling around by the chopper right before you guys turned up."

Munro crosses his arms over his chest and stares out at the river. "Donnae suppose you brought a bug detector."

"What do you think?" He pulls a device out of his back pocket. It looks like a small black box with an antenna sticking up from it. He hands the device to Munro. "This will detect any tracking devices, including GPS trackers."

Munro takes the device. "Thank you, Joey."

"Gotta go. I'm giving some tourists a joy ride down the river starting at the Phantom Ranch Boat Beach." Joseph and Munro shake hands. "Be careful, hey? And give me a call on your satellite phone if you need any backup."

The bloke ambles back to his raft and starts up the motor, heading toward the opposite shore.

"You have a satellite phone?" I ask Munro.

"Aye. Mobiles don't work in the canyon." He turns toward me. "Someone is watching us. Who have ye rubbed the wrong way this time, Errol?"

"No one. I haven't done anything lately except try to chase Ashley away."

My cousin arches one brow. "I see that worked out well."

"She finally brought me round to her way of thinking." I sling an arm around Ashley's waist to pull her close. "Now we're partners, in every way."

"I see." Munro turns toward our raft. "Best check for tracking devices."

"Can I help?"

"One-man job, laddie. You and the lass should go on contemplating where we ought to search next."

Ashley and I go back to studying the new map, and we agree that the sandbar shown on satellite images must be the brownish, oblong feature represented on the drawing. We also agree we should stop there to search.

Munro finds a miniature GPS tracker hidden on the raft, tucked under one of the seats. He tosses it onto the ground and stomps on the thing until it shatters. We might've noticed that tracker if we had bent over to look, but we had no reason to do that. I could never have guessed that someone would try to track me—or Ashley. Maybe she's the target, though I suspect it's me.

"What about your satellite phone?" I ask Munro. "Could that have a tracker on it too?"

"Joey said the person who planted the tracker was seen doing that before we stowed our gear in the helicopter. My satellite phone hasn't been out of my control since I left my house." He glances down at the destroyed tracker. "But I did scan the entire raft and our packs. No other trackers were detected."

Just to be safe, Munro scans me and Ashley for trackers. We're clean. He had already scanned himself while searching the raft, so we climb in and continue our journey down the river. We stop at the sandbar Ashley thought might be clue on the map, beaching our raft at the eastern end so we can get out and look around. Ashley suggests the sandbar is an arrow pointing us in the right direction. After searching through the binoculars, though, we agree that the sandbar is probably on the map solely to tell whoever possessed the map that they're on the right track. The Ellsworth map had included notations for caves, but those must have, ah, caved in a long time ago. We hadn't found any of those on our journey. The second map has been harder to interpret.

We get back out on the river.

Munro suggests I should move into the rear of the raft as we approach a class eight rapid, just to make sure Ashley doesn't get swept overboard. Apparently, the rapid ahead of us can be quite powerful at lower water levels. Though Munro assures us it doesn't look low right, he wants us to take every precaution. Ashley did almost fall out in a previous rapid. Even the lass herself doesn't object to Munro's plan.

As we enter the rapid, Ashley grins and holds on to the seat.

I love how excited she gets about these things, but I can't stop worrying about who might be following us and why. Only my family knows anything about our expedition. No MacTaggart would ever divulge private information, certainly not to a stranger. How did our unwanted guest learn about our plans? Or is that person simply trying to learn my tactics? Not that I have a set of tactics for anyone to puzzle out. I'm more of a "by the seat of my trousers" type of man.

Suddenly, I'm glad I brought my secret weapons on this expedition. Not sure Ashley will appreciate that. Then again, she seemed fine with it when I gave her my wee demonstration.

Munro veers our raft to the right, then swerves it back to the left to avoid a rock ledge.

A wave sideswipes the raft, making it bounce, and Ashley whoops. She is adorable when she does that.

The lass keeps searching the canyon for anything that matches our new map, but I can tell she's growing disappointed with our lack of discovering a definitive clue. Maybe I had misread the map, since I practically had to rub my nose against that mostly submerged boulder to see the carvings on it. The muddy water made my task more difficult. If I cocked this up, and we don't find the treasure because of that, I'll never forgive myself. Ashley needs to find the cavern. She'll be devastated if she cannae go home to her father with brilliant news.

While we float down a calm section of the river, I close my eyes and try to relax and let all my thoughts and worries blow away on a wisp of wind. I focus on one thing—the carvings on that boulder. But I don't force the images to come back to me. I stay relaxed and calm, letting my mind give me those clues when it's time. The carvings are blurry at first, but gradually, they resolve into sharp lines etched onto the stone.

"Oh, bollocks!" I open my eyes and wince. "It's my fault, Ashley."

"What is?" She climbs onto the backseat where I am. "What just happened?"

"I used a meditation technique my cousin Iain taught me, and I took my mind back to the moment when I saw the carvings on that boulder." I groan and drop my head into my hands. "I drew the last few symbols wrong. I'm sorry, *gràidh*."

She lays her hand on my thigh. "It's okay, Errol. Everybody makes mistakes, and you were deciphering that map in the river surrounded by muddy water."

Munro glances over his shoulder at us. "Care to share with the class, Errol?"

"I drew the bloody symbols wrong."

"So what? You'll figure it out. You and Ashley together are twice as clever, so donnae worry about anything. Just reconfigure your assumptions."

"Thanks for the suggestion, Munro." Not that I have one ruddy clue what he meant by reconfiguring my assumptions. Well, maybe I do. Sort of. "Ashley, can you get out the second map?"

We had hidden it inside her pack to protect it from getting wet. Unlike the Ellsworth map, this one is not laminated.

Ashley hands me the paper.

I spread it over my lap, and we both scrutinize it. Something catches my attention, but I need a moment to compare what I drew on this paper with what my mind suggested is the real version of the symbol on the boulder. Then I point at the symbol. "Here. That's not quite right. Can you get me another sheet of paper, please?"

The lass doesn't hesitate. She roots inside her pack until she finds her pad of paper.

I take it and ask her to keep the original illustration on her lap while I redraw it on the pad of paper, comparing the two so I don't cock things up any more than I already have. At least I can fix it. A good treasure hunter always knows when to give up—and when to keep going.

And it's nowhere near time to stop.

Chapter Twenty-Four

Ashley

Errol makes several more adjustments to the boulder map—hey, I have to call it something—and draws them on the paper. By the time he's done, we have a new version that's about fifty percent based on the original boulder map, but the rest is different. I know Errol blames himself for screwing up his first drawing, but I don't. Jeez, he created that drawing from memory after observing it in muddy water that I couldn't see into at all. I'm amazed he got as much right as he did. Now we're pretty sure we have the correct landmarks that we can search for as we continue down the river.

"Pretty sure" is as close as anyone can get while searching for lost treasure.

When Errol hands me the corrected map, I kiss him. "You're amazing."

He gives me a baffled look. "I cocked it up and had to fix my mistakes. That's not amazing."

"You didn't get upset about it. You just saw what needed to be fixed, and you did it." I kiss him again, harder this time. "That's what makes you amazing."

"Couldn't have done it without my muse and partner." He pulls me into his arms and ravishes my mouth so thoroughly that I feel a touch lightheaded afterward. Only Errol could kiss me that way.

"Time to stop snogging," Munro declares in his grumpy tone. "Errol, get up here."

Errol climbs onto the front seat with Munro, who pauses in his paddling, which he's been doing for a while now at a relaxed pace. He leans over to have a hushed conversation with Errol. Munro's expression has turned rather serious, but he'd been grumpy when I first met him, so I have no reason to believe something has gone wrong. He might just have gotten tired and cranky again.

I want to ask what they're talking about, but I don't want to be the annoying newbie who questions everything. I can wait until they decide to tell me about whatever it is.

Errol swallows hard enough that I can see his Adam's apple jumping. Then he wipes a hand over his mouth and glances back at me.

Yeah, that's not concerning at all.

Munro thumps Errol's arm, then returns to paddling.

Errol turns halfway toward me, still seeming disconcertingly worried. "It's nothing to panic about, Ashley, but you need to prepare for what's coming."

Way to ease my anxiety, Errol. But I maintain a relaxed expression when I ask, "What's going on?"

"We're coming up on Hermit Rapid," Munro says. "Class eight, with the biggest, roughest waves anywhere in the canyon. Ashley, make sure you have your helmet and life jacket on tight."

"Donnae worry, love," Errol tells me. "Ahmno letting anything happen to you. But maybe you should crouch behind the seat and hold on to it with both arms."

"Okay. You be careful too, hey?"

He smirks. "You know me."

Does that mean he'll be extra careful? Or that he'll turn back into the lunatic who sets off land mines and possibly get himself killed? If Hermit Rapid is the worst one of all, rougher than the rapid that nearly knocked me out of the raft… *Holy shit.* But I trust Errol completely, which means I need to stop worrying about him and pay attention to my surroundings.

Errol and Munro start paddling harder than ever.

I'm about to test my newfound bravery.

"We will handle the raft," Errol says, glancing over his shoulder at me. "You just hang on and try not to fall out. If you should feel yourself about to go over the edge, scream."

Oh yeah, I can handle this. No problem. If I'm about to die, I'll just scream.

We head straight into the rapid.

The water reminds me of storms at sea, the way it roils and shifts directions. I hang on and brace myself for a wild ride.

The boys paddle even harder, gritting their teeth and fighting with the monster currents roiling around us. The deeper we go into the gauntlet, the more the raft bounces. A constant barrage of insanely big waves crash over the raft, swamping it again and again. A whirling dervish of colliding breakers slam into us as one, and the front of the raft lifts up and to one side—Errol's side. I scream his name, but through the swells I can make out the shapes of both men still inside the raft.

I cling to my seat, suddenly getting nauseous though none of the previous rapids had affected me this way. Munro did not exaggerate. Hermit Rapid is the scariest maelstrom yet, and every time I shriek, it's not from the joy of an awesome ride. My heart thuds whenever I lose sight of Munro and Errol, their figures lost in the muddy madness that sprays up and over us.

The gnarliest cluster of waves I've ever seen rushes toward our tiny raft. The front end is hoisted up, almost vertical, just as another monster wave collides with the side. The raft tips sideways high enough that I can't keep hold of my seat. I slide down toward the foaming, thrashing breakers beneath me, unable to stop myself from going down, down, down. I claw at the raft as my legs go over the edge, and I know any second I'll fall into the maelstrom and get sucked into hell.

I scream as loud as I can, my throat scorched by the ferocity of my cry.

"Ashley!" Errol hollers. "She's about to go under, Munro!"

"Get her! I'll take your paddle too."

I cling to the raft, but my fingers are starting to slip. The raft has settled down again, but the waves keep pounding against it, pounding against me.

Errol crawls toward me, rises to his knees, and grips my life jacket to haul me out of the thrashing waves. Then he hugs me so tightly that I can't breathe. After a couple of seconds, he loosens his grip just enough that I won't pass out from oxygen deprivation.

"Almost out," Munro shouts.

Errol drags me to the center of the raft and keeps his arms locked around me until we've exited the rapid.

"Clear," Munro announces. "You can start snogging again if ye like."

Errol grasps my face in both hands. We're both struggling to breathe, and my heart still pounds like crazy. He leans in as if to kiss me.

I lurch toward the side of the raft to vomit into the river.

The man who saved my life watches me with a pinched expression. He lays a hand on my back and holds my hair out of the way while I throw up again. Then I raise a hand to let him know I'm done. Nothing left in my stomach, I'm sure. I turn around and slump against the side of the raft.

Errol brushes wet hair away from my face. "All right now? Should we call for help?"

"Not necessary. I'm okay now that I've emptied my stomach." I manage a weak smile. "Guess I'm not totally over my motion sickness."

"I got nauseous too, so donnae feel bad." He kisses my forehead, then says loudly, "I'm sure Munro got a wee bit nauseous too."

"Never happens to me," Munro says. "My stomach is made of iron."

"You were meant to commiserate with Ashley, not brag about how tough you are."

Munro casts me a sheepish look that seems less than sincere. "Aye, lass, the waves got me too."

"You don't need to lie," I tell him. "Doesn't bother me at all that you have an indestructible stomach."

"One of us has to stay in command, aye?"

"Absolutely." I pat Errol's cheek. "You're still my hero. I would've drowned without you."

"I hope I never need to do that again. Nearly gave me a heart attack."

"Me too."

Luckily, we seem to have smoother waters ahead for quite aways, which means I'll have time to recover from that harrowing episode. Well, I'd wanted excitement. Ask and you shall receive, right? This was a bit more than I bargained for, and I don't care to repeat the experience.

Errol and I study the map again and compare it to the surrounding landscape. The map seems to include Hermit Rapid as well as a few other rapids further up the river, but then it seems to suggest we should stop just before the next rapid. That one begins at Crystal Creek. I would've expected the map to point us toward Crystal Creek, or maybe even past it, but Errol and Munro both agree we should stop before that. The symbols on the map match what I see in the satellite images on Errol's computer too. We plan to stop where there's a small section of rocky beach right beside a big ledge of black stone. What looks like a dry creek bed or maybe just a stripe of lighter rock winds up the cliff there.

We survive the next batch of rapids and reach our destination. The big black cliffs dwarf the scrap of rocky beach where we land, and I can't resist tipping my head back to take in the stark beauty of the geology in this region of the canyon. But I give up my awe of the landscape and help the boys unload our gear, then find a place to hide our raft while we explore the cliffs above us. They feature forbidding overhangs that seem like places where, long ago in the distant past, molten sandy rock had oozed down the cliffs and somehow gotten frozen partway down, like cloaks dropped there by ancient giants. I'm no geologist, so I have no idea how those formations came to exist. But they are startlingly beautiful.

Below those overhangs lie darker rocks, separated from the lighter formations just past them by a stripe of light-colored sediment. Well, I assume it's sedimentary rock. Don't really know for sure, and as much as I'd love to learn all about the geology here, we need to get moving.

Besides our backpacks, we also have the extra bag Errol brought along, the one he didn't want to talk about at the time. Now I wonder how he plans to carry two packs. When I ask him, he just smiles and says, "Let me worry about that."

"Are you going to tell me what's in your mystery pack?"

"When the time comes. Trust me, *gràidh*."

Errol helps me get my pack onto my shoulders, though I could've done that on my own. I like that he's sweet enough to give me help even when he knows I could do the task myself. He also knows I would help him too, if he wanted it.

"What is that word you keep calling me?" I ask. "All you told me last time I asked was that it's Gaelic."

Errol pulls on his pack and uses adjusting the straps as an excuse not to speak, though it's not really an excuse. He can still talk while doing that.

I clear my throat, hoping to snare his attention. "I asked what that word—"

"He's calling you 'darling' in Gaelic," Munro says. "Errol is embarrassed to admit to that."

Errol flashes his cousin a dirty look. "I am not embarrassed, ye *cacan*. And that means he's a wee shit, Ashley."

"He doesn't look small to me," I say. "But I'm wondering why you've been hesitant to tell me you've been calling me 'darling.' It's a sweet thing to say, not something to be ashamed of."

"Can we discuss this later?" He sidles closer to me and whispers, "When you-know-who isn't listening and interfering?"

"I can still hear ye," Munro says.

Errol sticks his tongue out at his cousin.

"Very mature, laddie. Will ye thumb your nose at me next?"

"Maybe. If you don't stop interfering."

"It's not interference." Munro has just finished adjusting his backpack. "What are ye meaning to do with your other pack?"

"Ashley already asked me that."

"You didn't answer her question."

Errol unzips the mystery bag and carefully pulls out a rolled-up rope without letting us see what's inside. Then he unfurls the rope and ties it onto the bag. "This is how I'm going to carry it."

He starts walking, dragging the bag behind him.

"Ye cannae climb a steep cliff," Munro says, "with that thing dragging behind you."

"I've done it before." Errol slings the rope around his shoulders. "Now haud yer wheesht, unless you've got something mission-related to say."

We climb up the steep path single file, with me between the two men. They probably need a little space from each other after their argument about how Errol chooses to carry his mystery pack. I think tensions are running higher now because we all feel like we're so close to finding the prize we've hunted for and nearly died to track down. Well, maybe I didn't almost die. But I came too close to that for my comfort. It won't be in vain, though. I swear I can almost taste victory.

I need to bend over and almost crawl up the path. Even Errol and Munro hunch over more and more the higher up we travel. Though I keep going for as long as I can, sweat begins to pour down my temples and I'm breathing hard.

Errol turns to glance back and notices me struggling. He's clearly winded too. "Time for a break. Even Munro seems to be struggling."

I expect Munro to balk at that assessment, but he doesn't say anything about it. We all sit down and drink some water while we recharge our energy. I close my eyes and lean back against a boulder, listening to the occasional cries of birds and the distant sounds of voices down on the river, probably tourists excited about riding the next rapid. The voices gradually fade away, and I let the warmth of the sun penetrate my skin, lulling me into a state of deep relaxation.

"The lass is exhausted," Munro says. "We should go down the river a little further to find a place where we can camp. We all need to recover from our trip through Hermit Rapid."

"Just let me take a wee look around before we leave," Errol says. "I have an intuition."

"About what? I donnae see anything of interest up here."

"You aren't looking at it the right way. Solving riddles is my forte, not yours. Let me do what I need to do."

Munro grunts. "Go on, then. Impress me."

I open my eyes and sit up. "Stop arguing, you guys. You're like a couple of little old men complaining about whose hemorrhoids hurt the most."

Errol stands up. "You two stay here. I want to check out my hunch."

"On your own?" I say. "No, we should go together."

"You can come with me, Ashley. But Mr. Grumpy should stay here to guard our gear."

Munro puckers his lips but doesn't complain about Errol's command, not even when Errol steals the GPS unit from his cousin's pack. He takes the mini GPR out of my pack and grabs a head-mounted flashlight from his own bag.

I follow Errol a little further up the path to a spot where the earth has gouged out little canyons in the reddish brown cliffs. But Errol seems uninterested in those features. He heads straight for an overhang that drapes down so low that we would need to lie on our bellies to peer into it.

Errol turns on the GPS unit so he can mark this position on its map. Then he hands the unit to me so he can turn on the ground-penetrating radar and scan the area.

He freezes, staring at the small screen on the GPR device. "My intuition was right. There's some sort of cavern behind this overhang. I need to crawl in there to check it out."

I lean against him while I study the GPR data on the screen. "I'm not an expert on this technology. Are you?"

"Not an expert, no. But I've picked up a thing or two on other expeditions."

"That's not comforting. You want to crawl under an overhang without having any idea whether the space behind it is even stable. What if you get trapped in there?"

He sets the GPR on the rocky ground and clasps my hands. "Trust me, love. I've done much more dangerous things and survived. I wouldn't do this if I weren't sure I could handle it."

"Okay. But you have to keep talking the whole time."

"Agreed." He kisses my knuckles one by one. "Try not to wring your hands too much while I'm gone."

Then he crawls under the overhang.

Chapter Twenty-Five

Errol

Maybe this wasn't the best idea I've ever had, but I wouldn't have become known as the greatest treasure hunter in the world if I refused to take big risks. I'm surprised Ashley didn't demand to come with me into this unknown cavern, but I suspect her near-calamity in Hermit Rapid has affected her more deeply than she wants to admit. It affected me, for sure. When I'd turned around and watched Ashley struggling not to tumble into the writhing waves, I swear my heart stopped for a second or two—right before I rushed toward Ashley to pull her back into the raft. I'd been terrified of losing her.

No, I donnae ever want to feel that way again.

I lie on my belly as I shimmy under the overhang, then turn on my headlamp so I can see where the bloody hell I'm going. I can't explain why I believe I'll find something important in here, but I learned long ago to trust my gut instincts. Besides, the map directed us here. This place must hold a clue or another map.

Just as I'm starting to think this foot-high space holds nothing more interesting than clammy rocks, I emerge into a small cavern. Once I've slid my legs out and my feet touch the floor, I rotate in a circle to get a three-sixty view of my surroundings. The cavern probably measures about fifteen feet in length and width. I walk the perimeter while running my hands along the walls to feel for anomalies, while I also scrutinize the space with my eyes too.

My fingers fall into a hole in the wall.

I stop and bend over to peer into the narrow slot in the solid rock surface, but even with my headlamp, I can't see anything inside there. So I do something that would probably make Ashley panic, or at least chastise me for being reckless. I push my hand into the slot.

"You're supposed to be talking, Errol," the lass shouts.

"Sorry. I forgot. Found something, though."

"What is it?"

"Not sure yet."

In movies, whenever a bloke sticks his hand into a mysterious hole in the wall of an underground cavern, he winds up losing that hand. But so far, mine has remained attached to my wrist. I push my hand deeper into the slot, exploring with my fingers until I find what feels like paper. I carefully slide it out and cradle the paper in both hands. It's clearly old, more than a hundred years, I'd wager. The sheet contains handwritten words—in English.

Oh aye, Ashley will want to see this. The lass will probably jump up and down when I show it to her.

"Coming out now," I shout to her. "You're going to like what I found."

Cautiously, I roll the paper up and hold it in one hand. Then I climb into the foot-high space under the overhang to belly-crawl through it again. As I draw closer to the exit, the sunlight almost blinds me. I didn't think I'd been inside the cavern long enough for my eyes to have adjusted to the gloom this much, but it hardly matters. I shove my hand out, proffering the rolled-up paper.

"Take this," I say. "Cannae crawl out while I'm holding it."

Someone takes the paper, and I assume it's Ashley.

I climb out and manage to land on my feet. As I brush damp dirt off myself, I blink rapidly until my eyes readjust to the sunshine.

"Mind if I unroll this?" Ashley asks. "I'm dying to see what you found."

"I think crawling through there squeezed some weight out of me and probably flattened all my muscles."

She skims her gaze over my body and rubs her lips together. "You look as good as ever to me."

Her sultry tone woke up my *slat*, but I don't have time to obey my cock's commands. We have earth-shattering discoveries to make. Since Ashley seems to have gone semi-catatonic, with her focus on my groin, I snatch the paper from her hand, unrolling it so I can finally read the words written on it.

Ashley tears her gaze away from my *slat* and moves closer to examine the paper. "Holy cow. Is this really a letter written by G.E. Kincaid?"

"It appears to be." I read through the text again to make sure I understood it correctly. "And he seems to be saying the treasure is not here."

"But he also says he retreated into the cavern here because S.A. Jordan, the archaeologist from the Smithsonian, wanted to steal the treasure and sell it on the black market." Ashley rests her chin on my arm as she reads more of the letter. "Kincaid claims Jordan tried to kill him, and he was forced to defend himself with lethal force."

She's paraphrasing. But aye, that's the gist of it. Kincaid goes on to explain that Jordan wounded him before he killed the archaeologist in self-defense, and Kincaid hid his note here because he knew he was dying.

"I think I understand," Ashley says. "No wonder it was so hard to find any information about Jordan. He died on the expedition."

"The *Phoenix Gazette* article stated there had been a large expedition to the Grand Canyon to find the hoard." I stare down at the stained and wrinkled paper. "Of course, the article might've been exaggerated. Back then, newspapers often embellished their stories or outright lied to increase circulation."

"Maybe Kincaid lied to the newspaper because he wanted to keep the location of the hoard a secret. He might've worried someone would steal it."

I read the letter again, trying to ferret out clues that Kincaid might've hidden between the lines. But then I have what my American mates would call a "duh" moment. I suddenly realize I haven't examined both sides of the paper. I flip it over—and see nothing. I'm about to flip the paper over again when Ashley lays a hand on it.

"Wait," she says. "There's something odd about the paper."

She picks at the top left corner of the sheet.

"Ah, what are ye doing there?" I ask.

"Hush." She peels the corner apart, revealing another sheet that had been glued to the first, though not literally glued. "Look at this. It's another page."

She separates the pages and hands me the one she just freed.

I read the handwritten text, which matches the writing on the first page, suggesting the same person composed both. "Kincaid says that someone should find the treasure, and he's made a crude map to show where it can be found. He hopes whoever discovers this letter will use the information wisely."

Ashley curls an arm around my waist. "That's exactly what we will do. The world should know the truth."

"They will know." I roll up the papers, gripping them in one hand. "We'll make certain of that."

I give the papers to Ashley so I can carry the GPS and GPR devices. Going down the path proves much easier than trudging up it, naturally. We arrive at the spot where we'd left Munro without dying from dehydration caused by too much sweating. My cousin is lying on the ground with his hands linked under his head, but instead of closing his eyes, he seems to be studying the rock formations.

"We found something," I announce. "There was a cavern, but it was hard to access. I crawled in there and found a letter apparently written by Kincaid."

Munro sits up as if he wants to hear what we found.

Ashley and I explain about the letter, and we show Munro the new map. He seems interested, and dare I say, rather excited by this new information. Munro MacTaggart excited? I never thought I'd see the day.

We drag our packs back down to the rocky shore and get back out on the river, following the new map created by the man who claimed to have discovered the greatest treasure in history. If Kincaid really did die in the canyon, his remains must have been washed away a long time ago. Will we find Jordan's remains inside the cavern? Or did Kincaid bury the body? Maybe he just left the bloke who tried to kill him lying out in the open. I guess that would depend on where Jordan died and whether Kincaid could haul the man's body out of the cavern on his own.

If he was alone. That's another mystery.

Map number three points us to a spot just past Crystal Creek. To reach our destination, we'll need to traverse the Crystal Rapid. When Munro informs us of that fact, Ashley's face goes a bit grey, and she straps her arms across her belly, probably because she's feeling nauseous just thinking about what lies ahead for us. The trauma of Hermit Rapid is still too fresh in the lass's mind, so naturally, she must worry about what might happen when we hit another class eight rapid, one Munro says can be very dangerous. We'll need to take care to avoid large holes and a feature he calls a "rock garden," which he assures us is an official term for the big rocks that stick up out of the middle of the river. Why anybody wants to call a treacherous rapid a "rock garden," I cannae understand. That term sounds innocuous, like a playground for bairns rather than a death trap.

"It's not a death trap," Munro tells me when I voice my confusion. "I'll get us through the rough parts, so donnae let it fash either of you."

I turn partway toward Ashley, where she sits at the rear of the raft, and give her a reassuring smile. "Munro is an expert at riding the rapids. You know that. We got through Hermit Rapid, and we'll come out of the next one unscathed."

"Errol, maybe you should ride in back with Ashley," Munro suggests. "The company might ease her anxiety."

"Sure you can handle the raft on your own?"

"Aye." My cousin aims an irritated look at me. "First, ye tell the lass I'm an expert. Then two seconds later, you imply I cannae guide the raft on my own."

"I meant no offense."

"Never said I was offended."

But he looked it. Well, if he prefers to pretend he didn't get touchy about how well he can steer the raft, I'll pretend it didn't happen.

I climb back to the rear seat and settle onto it beside Ashley. Her anxiety does lessen then, with her shoulders no longer bunched up and her arms relaxing too. She slips her fingers between mine, and I give her hand a quick squeeze.

Then we dive into the rapid.

Munro paddles hard, steering the raft left and right to stay on track and avoid the obstacles he'd mentioned. We hit a few big waves that swamp us, but nothing like what we'd experienced back in Hermit Rapid. Ashley keeps hold of my hand the entire time, and only when we've left the rapid behind does she loosen her grip on me.

I pull Kincaid's map out of Ashley's pack, where we'd stowed it for safe keeping, and begin to scan the canyon for signposts that match what's on the paper.

"There," Ashley says, pointing toward the cliffs on the left side of the river. "That looks like the squiggles on the map."

"I thought squiggles meant rapids."

"Not on this map." She taps her finger on the snaking line of the river as depicted on the paper. "These little wave shapes are the rapids. They have sharper peaks than the squiggles that are clearly the lighter-colored rock embedded in the cliffs."

Though I had studied the map earlier with Ashley, we didn't want to waste too much time on it then. We need to reach our destination before nightfall. Traveling down the river in the dark would be too risky, and we might miss the landmark that will take us to the place where we need to be.

"Watch on the left, Munro," Ashley says. "We need to land on the flat area at the base of that gorge."

"Aye-aye, captain. Any other orders?"

"Do I need to come up there and skelp you, Munro?" I ask. "Donnae be harassing our fearless leader."

Ashley laughs. "Fearless? I freaked out in Hermit Rapid."

"No, you didn't." I throw an arm around her. "You showed a reasonable amount of panic under the circumstances."

She eyes me sideways. "You're full of shit, but it's endearing. I'm not the leader, though. We're a team."

"Landing spot coming up on the left," Munro informs us. "Doesn't look too difficult."

I keep my arm around Ashley until the raft bumps into the rocky shore. Then Munro and I jump out to push it fully out of the water, far enough away that it won't slide off and float away, leaving us stranded. We also resort to a tactic we haven't felt was necessary until now. We cover the raft with a camouflage tarpaulin. That won't stop someone who seriously wants to steal our raft, but it should deter the casual thieves. I also plant a device from the stash in my "mystery bag," as Ashley calls it, and hide that under the tarpaulin. If someone should attempt to nick our raft, their movements will trigger my security device.

"What is it, exactly?" Ashley asks me. "Your anti-theft whatsit, I mean."

"Donnae fret the details."

Munro grunts. "That usually means it involves explosives."

"Ahmno blowing anybody up." Well, not right here, right now. But I won't share what else is in my stash, not quite yet.

"I know that look," Ashley says, leaning toward me and squinting with obvious sarcasm. "I can practically see little land mines going off in your eyes."

"Only when you rub yourself against me like you're doing right now."

"My body is at least six inches from yours."

I take hold of her upper arms and tug her into me. "No, it's not."

"That's cheating."

Munro snarls, "Are you two done flirting?"

"Jealous, are ye?" I say with a smirk. "When was the last time you had a girlfriend? I used to have one for every day of the week."

Munro snatches up his pack and stalks toward the gorge.

"I think you hit a nerve," Ashley murmurs. "Maybe you should apologize."

"He would batter me for sure if I tried that. Munro isn't the sort who cares if anyone insults him, which is why I'm confused by his reaction a minute ago."

"Grill him later. Let's find the cavern first."

Chapter Twenty-Six

Ashley

Trudging up the gorge proves a bit less strenuous than when Errol and I climbed up the path that brought us to Kincaid's mini cavern. Now we're searching for the real thing—the "big kahuna" as Errol likes to say—where we should find the most incredible hoard ever. A mishmash of eastern cultures in one cavern? Nobody has found anything like this before. I don't care about the glory. I only want to see the smile on my father's face when he learns he was right all along, and those jackasses who belittled him were wrong, wrong, wrong.

About three hundred feet up the gorge, Errol stops us. He's been dragging his mystery bag, but this time it doesn't seem to bother him as much, possibly because we're scaling a more gradual grade. We've halted here because Errol wants to compare the Kincaid map to the surrounding terrain.

He points to the left side of the gorge. "We need to go there. A narrow path will take us through to the other side, where we can access the cavern."

A tingle of excitement sweeps over me as I realize the import of his statement. We are actually going to do this. Find the hoard. Prove my dad was right. Maybe I should stay circumspect about all of this, but I can't do that, not anymore. Knowing I'm so close to the truth…I want to jump up and down while shrieking like a crazy person.

I'll save that for when we step into the cavern.

Errol guides us out of the gorge, down a very narrow opening in the cliff. It's so narrow, in fact, that we need to remove our backpacks and carry them in our hands, by the straps, to fit through the space. I feel a teeny bit claustrophobic, but then I glance up at the sliver of sky visible overhead, and my anxiety lessens. It completely vanishes, though, when Errol winks and smiles at me.

Munro sidles through the crevice behind me. Both he and Errol have more trouble shimmying through it than I do, a side effect of having way bigger muscles. Errol exits the crevice first, and by the time Munro and I have wriggled out, Errol is already surveying the box canyon we've wound up in. Unlike some box canyons I've seen, this one has no way out on the other side. The vertical walls rise high above our heads. Our only entrance or exit is the narrow crevice we shimmied through to get here.

Errol drops his bags and trots toward the far side of the canyon. Since it's a hundred feet in width and length, at most, he doesn't need to run far. He stops where a very low overhang almost touches the ground.

"Underground spring," he says. "I think that's what it is, anyway. Get over here, you two."

Munro and I dump our packs and race over to Errol, who hands me the Kincaid map.

"What am I supposed to be looking at?" I ask. "The map doesn't show any underground spring, and I don't see how that relates to the cavern we need to find."

"Look more closely." Errol moves beside me to tap his finger on the map. "It shows that we come out of the narrow trail—Kincaid's words—and step into an amphitheater with the entrance to the cavern in the northeast corner."

"But that would place the entrance…" My words trail off as I realize what he's telling me and what he intends to do. "No, Errol, we can't do that. It's too dangerous."

Munro glances between me and Errol. "Do you two have your own secret language now that only dolphins can hear? Because I have no bloody clue what you're havering about."

"The cavern is in there," Errol says, pointing at the overhang. "And it's underwater. Ashley thinks it's too dangerous to try to get inside because it would require swimming through an unknown length of underwater caves."

"You're just barmy enough to try it."

"Not without having a clue what I'm getting myself into." Errol leans over my shoulder to study the map. "Kincaid described the flooded section of the cavern as 'a brief interlude' with 'breathing space.' I can handle that."

I slug his arm. "This map is a hundred and twenty years old, Errol. The conditions in there might've changed drastically. Did you bring any scuba gear?"

"No."

"Then it's too dangerous. You can't go in there."

He lodges his hands on his hips and bows his head. "Ashley, I've done things like this before. You have no idea how many risky situations I've walked or swum into voluntarily. It doesn't fash me."

"But it 'fashes' me, Errol."

He lifts his head, gazing at me with surprise in his eyes.

"No way am I letting you go in there alone," I say. "If you get into trouble, nobody will be there to save you."

"What are you suggesting? That we give up on finding the hoard? It's the reason we came here."

"I know that, and I'm not saying we should give up." I lift my chin and swallow hard. "I'm going in there with you."

"Oh no, you are not."

I bar my arms over my chest. "Yes, I am, Errol. Either we go in together, or nobody goes in there."

"Munro can—"

"Uh-uh." I step up to him, so close that my arms brush against his chest. "Munro should stay here in case we need help."

Errol stares at me with a stern expression that I'm sure matches mine. I feel sternly determined, and he will not talk me out of this. Why do I want to go with him? Maybe I can't explain why I need to do this, but all I know is that I cannot stand out here waiting for his drowned body to float back to the surface. I'd rather die with him than live without him.

Finally, Errol sighs and gives in. "You're coming with me. But I won't be able to give you pointers once we're under the water. It will be dark in there, and you'll need to hold my hand at all times. Understood?"

"Yes."

He marches past me and Munro, heading for his mystery bag. Errol grabs the rope he'd attached to it and unties the end knotted to the bag. Then he retrieves another rope and brings all of that over here, offering the ropes to Munro.

"We'll tie ourselves to the ropes," Errol says. "We need you to keep hold of the other ends. If we're in trouble, we'll tug on the ropes. If they go slack, we're probably dead."

Gee, that makes me feel so much better. But I volunteered for this, and I will see it through to the end.

"How will you take the map with you?" Munro asks. "It will wash off the paper."

"The map only goes as far as the main cavern."

"Once you're in there, you won't have any landmarks."

"Aye. But we can handle it."

Munro grabs his cousin and gives Errol a quick, firm hug. Then he backs away and clears his throat. "Donnae get yourself killed. I don't want to explain to your mother why you drowned in the Grand Canyon." Munro glances at me. "And if you get Ashley killed, I'll batter you with the sharpest, largest rock I can find."

The rough tone of his voice convinces me he's not exaggerating. Munro will avenge my death if Errol causes it. But that won't happen. I trust Errol with my life and so much more.

We tie the ropes around our waists, and Munro grips the other end of each one. I ask if we should remove our shoes, but Errol suggests we shouldn't. We have no idea what the cave floor will look like, and we don't want to end up walking on sharp shards of rock. Now that we're ready, we climb under the overhang, take a big, deep breath, and jump into the water. Errol grasps my hand as we swim toward our destination.

As we swim further and further into the flooded cavern, I begin to see glimmers of light up ahead. Am I hallucinating? I hope not, because I don't think I can hold my breath for much longer. We hadn't anticipated under-water exploration as part of our mission.

The glow enlarges and grows brighter.

Um, wait. How can there be light in an underground cavern? I can't ask Errol. But I'm about to learn the answer because we've just reached a ledge, and the sun-like light streams down on us. Errol plants both hands on my bottom and pushes me up and out of the water. I slap my palms down on the ledge to give myself an extra boost, landing sprawled on the wet rock.

Errol surges out of the water to flop onto the ledge beside me. Once we've both caught our breath, he sits up and gives both our ropes a swift tug. That's the signal to let Munro know we've arrived safely. Errol then unties our ropes. He pulls some kind of metal clip out of his pants pocket, then uses his fist to hammer the clip's screw-like end into the rock. He tugs twice on the ropes.

"What's that for?" I ask.

"Munro and I came up with a plan while you were behind your 'girl bush.' I just gave him the signal to send my bag."

"How can he do that?"

"I had a hunch the cavern would have a slight downward slope, so I tested that by using my pocket level. It showed exactly what I expected—a downward slope, as evidenced by the water level."

"That's very clever."

He shrugs. "Not really. It's common sense."

Not sure I would've thought of that. Errol's mind works differently than most people's do.

A metal clip thingy races up the line to Errol. He unhooks it, hoisting his mystery bag onto the ledge.

"I know your bags are waterproof, but can that really protect the contents when the whole thing is submerged?"

"Probably not. That's why I put everything inside it into tightly sealed plastic bags."

"I see. You think of everything, don't you?" I tip my head back to gaze up at the natural skylight that casts its golden light into the cavern. "We haven't even found the treasure yet, and already I'm in awe of this place."

"Aye, it's inspiring." He gazes up at the skylight too, for a long moment, his lips curled in the faintest of smiles. "Cannae believe we're here."

"Neither can I."

Errol rises and begins to strip off his clothes.

"What are you doing now?" I ask. "Please don't tell me we need to be naked to enter the rest of the cavern."

He chuckles. "No, lass. I'm going to wring out my clothes. You might want to do the same."

"Oh, sure, I will."

After we both do that, Errol and I explore the cavern. But soon, we realize the ledge must not be the cavern itself. It's more like an entryway. How do we access the main area? I can't see any doorways or holes in the walls. Errol insists there must be a way. If Kincaid's map ended here, then we just need to look harder.

"I think you were right," he says. "The cavern must have changed over the past hundred and twenty years. The original entrance has probably caved in. "Let's keep looking around for a bit longer." He waves toward one side of the cavern. "You look over there, while I search on the other side."

"Okay."

I explore the cavern with my hands and my eyes, using a small flashlight Errol had retrieved from his bag to enhance my vision. He took an identical flashlight. But I still can't see anything that resembles a crack, much less an opening into a secret world of forgotten treasures.

"Ah-ha!" Errol shouts, the sound echoing inside the chamber.

I rush over to him. "What did you find?"

He slaps a palm on the wall beside the pool. "I used your GPR device to see how much rock lies between us and the canyon outside. Turns out, I can blast a hole in this wall quite easily."

"Blast a hole? Why on earth would you do that?"

"To create a tunnel to the outside."

"Yeah, but—" I can't figure out what to say. I'd known before we undertook this expedition that Errol loves to blow things up, but this seems like an inappropriate time to suggest doing that. "What if the whole cavern caves in?"

He clasps my hand and kisses the palm. "Trust me, *gràidh*. I've done this before. No one has ever died while working with me."

"I trust you, but not the composition of this cavern."

"Do you think I'd ever do anything that might hurt you? The GPR gave me enough data to convince me I can open up a doorway here."

Well, either I trust him or I don't. There's no middle ground. So I nod and say, "Do it, Errol."

Chapter Twenty-Seven

Errol

I extract a block of C-4 from my bag and cut off two small portions, then tape them to the wall at strategic points. Ashley has started to wring her hands, but she'll feel better once the blast is over. I urge her to move to the other side of the cavern, and I join her over there once I've set the timer. She huddles against me with her eyes tightly squeezed shut and her fingers curled like talons.

"Plug your ears, lass," I say. "The big boom is coming."

She shoves her fingers into her ears, and I do the same as I turn us both so my body shields her.

The explosion rocks the entire cavern, but only powdery bits shower down onto the floor and into the water. I push Ashley away and grasp her upper arms. "All right, love?"

She nods. "But the wall is still there."

"Not for long."

I stride over there and kick at the wall. A cloud of debris is still settling around the hole excavated by the explosion, but I keep kicking until the last remnants fall away, revealing the canyon beyond. Sunlight filters through the debris cloud.

Ashley hurries over to me. "That's unbelievable. The wall was only six inches thick there? But we swam through more than that."

"That's right. But the canyon wall is thinner over here."

"Honestly, I don't care how you did this. I'm just glad we have another way out besides holding our breath to swim back to Munro."

I lean out the opening and shout, "Surprise, Munro! Come and see what I've done."

The crunching of Munro's shoes tells us he is indeed coming over here to see what I've accomplished. When my cousin halts a few yards from the new doorway, he affects an air of disinterest. Maybe it's not affectation. Maybe he genuinely is unimpressed, but I rather doubt that. Everyone expresses awe, and occasionally a wee bit of fear, when they see my handiwork.

"Congratulations," Munro says. "Ye managed to blow up a wall without killing yourself or Ashley."

"I made it easier to access the cavern. You could try being slightly impressed."

Munro grunts, as he often does. "I'll be impressed if the roof doesn't cave in before we leave."

He's in a sour mood, isn't he? I wonder why, but we shouldn't waste any time. If someone really is following us, we need to find the treasure as quickly as possible. The longer we stay in here, where we can't see who might be coming after us, the worse things could get for us. But I'll keep that to myself. I suspect Munro has realized the same thing, so that might be the cause of his bad mood.

We retrieve our packs from outside and bring them into the cavern, but we still have no bloody idea how to access the hoard. Kincaid claimed to have done that. I'd told Ashley earlier that the entrance might have caved in, but I don't see anything that looks like a demolished section of the wall.

Ashley curls her arm around mine. "Something's wrong. What is it?"

"How do you know something's wrong?"

"Because I've gotten to know your moods and your expressions over the past few days. Well, I started to learn that long before now. But spending every day and night with you has accelerated my learning curve."

Aye, she is a clever lass. Of course she understands me. I think she probably knew that before this expedition.

"I can't see anything that looks like a collapsed section of the wall," I say. "Maybe this isn't the right place after all, or maybe the treasure never existed."

"Oh no, you don't get to give up on me now." She presses her body into me. "We've come too far to call it quits. Now, let's hash out the problem together."

"While we're naked? That's when I do my best thinking."

She glances at Munro, who's kneeling several yards away and seems to be playing with rocks. "I don't get naked in front of company. But I'd be happy to whisper dirty things in your ear if that would help jump-start your brain."

"Best not. If you do that, I'll be shagging you on the rock floor in thirty seconds flat."

"Plan B, then." She folds her arms over those bonnie tits and surveys the wall. "I wonder if there's a secret latch or something that will open a hidden door. Or is that too Indiana Jones-ish?"

"My whole professional life has been like an Indiana Jones movie, except without the Nazis and the women salivating over me."

"You wouldn't want women to do that." She goes back to studying the wall. "What might a secret doorway look like?"

I consider the section of rock wall in front of us. "We should look for a seam. It wouldn't be obvious, which means we need to examine every inch of the wall with a fine-tooth comb. Well, not literally. I don't think an actual comb would help."

"Thanks for the clarification. I was about to get out my comb."

"You've gotten much more sarcastic lately. I love it."

She bumps her shoulder into me. "It's your fault I'm more sarcastic. But I'm glad you like it, because I like the new me too."

"It's not new. I think you were hiding your true self because you were afraid other people might think you're barmy. Now you're free to be yourself."

Ashley waves a finger toward the wall. "Guess we better get up close and personal with a big slab of rock."

We approach the wall and, without even discussing our strategy, Ashley kneels to explore the lower portion while I examine the higher sections. I can honestly say I have never felt up a wall before, and neither have I hunted for a secret panel in a cavern. So aye, I've never experienced the sort of thrill I'm getting right now, though that might have more to do with the bonnie lass kneeling beneath me with her erse raised.

Peripherally, I notice Munro watching us with his forehead wrinkled and his head tipped slightly to the side. But I ignore him, and Ashley's erse, to focus on the wall. Must be a seam here somewhere. If I were an ancient person from an unknown culture who wanted to hide a collection of mismatched artifacts, where would I put the seam in my secret door?

"What are you doing over there?" Munro asks. "Did ye get hypoxia swimming through the flooded passageway?"

"No, ye *cacan*," I say. "We're looking for a hidden doorway."

"Sure you're not using that as an excuse to stare at Ashley's erse?"

The lass glances up at me, and one corner of her mouth ticks upward. "Maybe I'm using it as an excuse to ogle Errol's ass."

But she seems to be looking at my *slat*, not my erse.

Munro approaches the wall on the other side of the cavern and begins to search for something—a sign of a hidden doorway, I assume. "Don't go blowing up any more walls, laddie. Might not be so lucky this time."

He has no idea how many things I've blown up in my life.

Ashley runs her fingers up and down a spot on the wall, her gaze narrowed and her lips puckered. She's adorable when she focuses hard. The lass spreads both hands on the wall and slowly rises while swinging her hips, like a sexy cobra emerging from a wicker basket. I don't think she realizes she's doing that, but I lose focus for a moment, mesmerized by her movements. I can also glimpse her cleavage. So aye, I'm a bit distracted from my mission.

She notices me admiring her body and kicks my foot. "Eyes up, Errol."

"Ah, yes. Sorry." I go back to searching the wall and resist my every impulse to glance down at Ashley.

"Oh!" she exclaims.

I freeze and look down at her. "What is it? Did you hurt yourself?"

"No, silly. I think I found a seam."

Bending my knees, I level my head with hers. "Where is it?"

"Here." She takes my hand, guiding my index finger toward a very thin line of darker rock that seems to form a vertical seam. "What do you think?"

"Do you have a hairpin or a needle or something like that?"

"No, sorry."

I move her fingertip onto the thin line. "Keep your finger there. I need to get a few things from my bags."

"Sure. I won't move a muscle—in my finger."

Cannae resist. I pat her erse. "Good girl."

Ashley does not move even one millimeter as far as I can tell. Munro comes up beside her to scrutinize the line, but he seems confused rather than impressed by what we've found. I understand his response. We haven't proved that thin, darker line on the wall means anything.

But I'm about to do that.

After gathering what I need, I return to the wall. Munro is leaning against it with one hand in his trouser pocket, while Ashley still has not moved at all. I use a roll of duct tape to sketch out the line we'd found, then get out my pocket knife to carefully remove the dirt to make sure the line isn't just mud that got stuck in there. The more I excavate, the deeper my knife sinks into the tiny crevice. But my enthusiasm remains tempered, until I feel a faint draft teasing my fingers.

I hold perfectly still, to make sure my breaths or my movements hadn't caused the draft.

"Are you okay?" Ashley asks. "You look like… I don't know. Like you're afraid to move, I guess."

"Needed to be still for a moment to make sure."

I dive my knife into the crevice as deep as it will go and forget about taking care. No, I carve as much dirt out of the wee crevice as I can, feeling more and more of a draft with every bit I excavate.

"Tell me what's going on," Ashley says. "Have you found the doorway or not?"

"No, I haven't." I lay my hand on her cheek, realizing too late that it's covered in dirt. "You found it, *gràidh*."

I raise her hand to place it over the crevice.

Her eyes widen. Her mouth falls open. Then she grins.

"What's so bloody amazing?" Munro says, in his usual grumpy tone.

Ashley removes her hand, and I grab Munro's wrist to slap his palm over the crevice.

My cousin's brows lift. "A draft. That's interesting, but you still don't know—"

"Haud her wheesht. Ahmno done yet." I pick up another item I'd gotten out of my bag and raise it. "Step two."

Munro eyes the tool with suspicion. "You think that will help."

"Aye, I do." Raising the crowbar, I insert the tapered end into the crevice. It's a tight fit, but I already cleared out the dirt, so I think I can make this work. "Move away, Ashley. Donnae want to hit you by mistake."

She backs away.

"You too, Munro," I say.

He grunts and moves to stand beside Ashley.

I jam the crowbar into the crevice and try to lever the doorway open. Maybe it moves on hinges. I try to pry it open like a stuck door, but that doesn't work either. I go back to using the crowbar as a lever, employing all my strength, my muscles burning and sweat dribbling down my face and temples.

With a disgusted shout, I drop the crowbar.

"That doorway," Munro says, "has been there for a long, long time. It won't be easy to get it open."

"Really, Munro? I hadn't noticed."

"Now-now, boys," Ashley says. "Let's not fight. Why don't you try to blow it open, Errol?"

I love that lass.

"Brilliant," Munro declares. "Why don't you see if you can blast the entire Grand Canyon to smithereens while you're at it?"

"You should try optimism, Munro," I respond. "Not all bears are grumpy. Yogi was very cheerful."

"I don't do yoga."

"Yogi Bear is a cartoon character."

Munro grunts again.

"Go into the far corner with Ashley," I tell my cousin. "I'll get ready with the C-4. A smaller amount this time, just enough to rattle the door open, hopefully."

"Hopefully?" Munro shakes his head and looks upward, as if he's hoping to see an angel hovering near the ceiling.

Ashley smiles and gives me the thumbs-up sign with both hands.

I carefully cut some thin slices of the explosive and stick them to the crevice I'd excavated. Then I attach the detonator and set the timer. By the time I jog over to Ashley and Munro, the timer has a few seconds left on it. I shield Ashley's body with my own.

Boom.

The relatively low-key explosion rumbles through the floor. But when I turn to look at the suspected doorway, nothing has changed. The wall still stands. Did I cock it up somehow? I trot over to the doorway and stand here staring at it with my hands on my hips. I did make a mistake, didn't I?

"Bloody hell," I snarl.

Then I kick the ruddy door with the flat of my foot—which stabs a sharp pain through my foot. Perfect. I've probably broken my toe but accomplished nothing of value. Ashley approaches behind me, accompanied by Munro. We all stare at the damn door that clearly isn't a door after all.

A grinding noise starts up, and bits of the wall crumble to the floor.

"Back away now!" I shout, as I try to herd Ashley and Munro away with my arms spread wide.

The door that wasn't a door tips away from us while stone grinds against stone and bits of dirt and pulverized rock shower down on the floor. The slab falls backward to whump down inside a passageway. Once the dust settles, we inch toward the now-open doorway and gawp at the foot-thick slab that has fallen away from the wall.

Bod an Donais. I did it.

Chapter Twenty-Eight

Ashley

A cloud of dust has plumed up around the fallen slab of rock, obscuring our view of whatever lies beyond the opening. We wait until we can see what's in there, then we climb over the slab and find ourselves inside a passageway that has smooth walls and a ceiling taller than either Errol or Munro. I don't see any carvings on the walls or artifacts lying around on the floor. In both directions, beyond the vanishing point for the sunshine coming in through the opening high above the entrance, I see nothing but darkness.

Errol pulls out his pocket flashlight to illuminate the area, but it can't penetrate the deeper recesses of this man-made cavern. "We need more light. Let's get our packs, bring out our battery-powered lanterns, and start exploring."

I follow the boys back into the entryway cavern so we can grab our stuff. I remember a device I had bought, though I wasn't sure I would ever use it. Errol had encouraged me to buy the laser-mapping device, if I had enough money in my budget for it, because it might come in handy considering that we're searching for a hidden cave. But the device doesn't detect caves. It can create a map of them.

Now I realize he was right. The laser-mapping device will help us. Not only can we create an accurate picture of the cave system, but we will have a map to guide us out of what might turn out to be a labyrinth if Kincaid's description matches what we find here.

After we've geared up, we climb over the slab again and consider which way to go in the passage. We toss a coin to settle the issue. Left it is.

We walk for about fifty feet, then stop. A doorway on the right opens into a large chamber, though we can't see any artifacts inside it. Errol leads the way as we cautiously enter the room, glancing around for any sign of something interesting. I'm just about to get depressed, thanks to the lack of any artifacts, when my boot crunches on something under my foot. I kneel and pick up the object, which measures about the size of my thumbnail, and run my finger over the dirty surface. When I turn the green stone between my fingers, the light flashes across its center like a cat's eye.

I jump up. "I found it!"

Errol and Munro stare at me.

"Proof," I say, not caring if I sound like a little kid who just found a silver dollar lying on the ground. "The cat's eye stones."

The boys amble over to me.

I kneel again to search for more stones, and I find many more of them scattered around the floor, stones of various sizes and colors but all with the signature cat's eye flare.

Errol crouches beside me and picks up a stone. "This is incredible, Ashley. You proved at least one part of Kincaid's story is true." He kisses my cheek. "Congratulations, *gràidh*."

"We haven't found the big stuff yet."

"Over here," Munro hollers. "This might be something."

Errol and I trot over to the far wall, where Munro seems to be peeking behind a length of canvas that hangs from nails driven into the wall.

Munro lifts the canvas. "You might be interested in this."

I shine my lantern into the space behind the canvas—and freeze. The fabric hides a long niche that holds a collection of small statuettes that span the ancient civilizations of Egypt, Babylon, Tibet, South America, and more. I can't move or speak. The realization of what this means sinks into me ever-so-slowly, and goosebumps raise up and down my arms. The goal I had struggled to achieve for so long has finally come to fruition. I can prove my father was right, finally.

"This is it," I say, almost whispering the word. "We found the hoard. But where's the rest of it?"

"We haven't searched the entire complex yet," Errol says. "Let's map this room and keep going."

Errol seems to know more than I do about how the laser-mapping device works, so I let him handle that. Since he had scanned the passageway before we started our exploration, we already have good data under our collective belt. An exhaustive search of this chamber yields nothing else. We take pictures of the statuettes in the niche, first with the dust and cobwebs, then we clean them off and take another round of pictures. Before we did anything else, though, we had photographed the entire chamber.

When I ask Errol if we could use his satellite phone to get the exact coordinates of this network of caverns, he tells me that doesn't work underground. *Rats.* We'll need to rely on an old-fashioned compass to keep track of the cardinal directions. I don't know if that's necessary, but I want to have as much information as possible.

Since this chamber doesn't seem to have any hidden doorways, we head back into the passageway and continue our search. We reach the end shortly, but another passageway leads to the right, where we can see another doorway. Our footfalls echo in the corridor as we increase our pace to reach the mysterious opening. Errol steps into the room first and sweeps his lantern back and forth.

The beam flashes on metal in several places.

We enter the chamber and set our lantern flashlights on the floor with their beams aimed straight up, creating a glow that fills the space.

I see statues. Everywhere. Gold. Bronze. Partially concealed by cobwebs.

My feet refuse to move even one more inch. My eyes don't want to blink either. I just stand here gaping at the genuine hoard in front of us. Besides the statues, I take note of wooden boxes on the floor that seem to hold more treasures inside them, though I won't know for sure until we examine the boxes.

Errol stops beside me and gives me a light shove. "Wake up, Ashley. Cannae catalog the artifacts while standing over here."

I blink rapidly, then look at Errol. "Guess I just can't believe we're actually here. We found the Grant Canyon treasure."

"Aye, we did." He claims my hand. "Because of you, *gràidh.* Your determination to harass me endlessly until I gave in, that's what got us here."

I let Errol guide me around the chamber and gaze at the treasures before us while in a state of shock. Sure, I'd spent so much time and money to get to this moment that I should be shrieking and jumping up and down. But the reality still hasn't sunk in, not completely. When Errol brushes dust and cobwebs off a lifesize statue of an Egyptian pharaoh, I think I stop breathing. I've seen statues like this one in museums. But to stand here gazing into the jewel eyes of a pharaoh's golden likeness… No words can describe how I feel right now.

Errol comes up behind me and grasps my shoulders, rotating me to the left. "Have a look. We've got more than pharaohs in this room."

He stretches out one finger to indicate a statue several yards away. Munro has just removed the grime from it with his shirt, which he stripped off, and normally I would enjoy the chance to admire a sexy man's chest. But my focus is locked on the statue.

"The Buddha," I murmur. "Wow. I've never seen anything like this, not in person. Pictures can't do justice to a piece this beautiful. It's a lot like the famous Golden Buddha, but this one seems bigger, at least from what photos show."

"I think it is bigger," Errol tells me. "But I've never seen the Golden Buddha either."

Right in front of the Buddha statue, I see a long table that holds much smaller artifacts, including a square bronze vessel that has a ram's head at each corner, a style I remember from reading about the ancient history of China. I can't resist moving toward the table so I can examine the jade suit laid out along its length, beside the bronze vessel. Nobles during the Han Dynasty sometimes opted to be buried in suits like this. I remember seeing pictures of one in a magazine ages ago.

I trail my fingers along the table's edge as I walk its length to study the many artifacts. Egyptian scarab amulets. A Hittite vessel shaped like a bull. A prehistoric stone figurine from the Arabian Peninsula. A Moche vessel shaped like a human head, from Peru. God, the variety of cultures displayed here truly boggles the mind, so much so that I feel a touch light-headed. Kincaid was right. My dad was right. One vital question remains unanswered.

Who brought these treasures here? Why? And when?

Okay, that's three questions. But they're all related.

Errol wraps his arms around me from behind, resting his chin on my shoulder. "Hard to believe this is real, aye? Feels like a dream."

"Maybe you should pinch me just to make sure.

He kisses my neck, then pinches my nipple, making me gasp.

I twist my head around to raise my brows at him.

"You wanted me to pinch you," he says, while smirking. "Didn't specify where on your body."

"My mistake. I should be more careful with what I ask you to do." I glance around. "Where's Munro?"

"Donnae know." Errol steps away from me, cups his hands around his mouth, and shouts, "Munro! Where the bloody hell are ye?"

His cousin appears in the doorway. "I was having a look around in the other rooms. Might want to take a peek yourselves. This room is only the beginning."

Errol and I follow Munro, hand in hand, as he takes us to the next chamber. It lies about thirty feet past the one we just left, but on the opposite side of the passageway. Inside, we find even more treasures. So many, in fact, that cataloging them all might take months or even years. The smaller artifacts housed in this chamber represent a multitude of cultures and time periods, from prehistory through ancient Greece and Japan, and so much more.

But this room doesn't hold statues or jewelry. It stores written history.

I drop my backpack on the floor and get out a pair of white fabric gloves, pulling them on. Then I gently pick up a papyrus scroll and unroll it with great care. The scroll is Egyptian. The beautifully rendered hieroglyphs tell me as much, though I can't translate the words. The scroll also has illustrations of a pharaoh and his queen. I set down the scroll and take a look at a series of clay tablets that have what looks like chicken scratches on them, but I know this is the cuneiform script used by the people who lived in the ancient Middle East. I don't know much of the cuneiform script, only that several cultures employed it, including the Sumerians and the Akkadians. I pick up a tablet, strictly to appreciate the fact that I hold an ancient document in my hands. Then I carefully set it down.

"Ah, found something else," Munro shouts from across the room. "It's not an artifact, and I donnae know what to do with it."

Errol and I hustle over to the far corner, where Munro stands there staring down at the floor with a puzzled expression. I understand why when we come up beside Munro.

On the floor lies the skeleton of a human being.

The ragged remnants of clothing still cling to the bones, and the skull appears to have been caved in, as if by a powerful blow. Kincaid had mentioned in his letter that he was forced to kill Jordan in self-defense. Kincaid would've had a lot of trouble trying to transport Jordan's body out of the cave system inside this mountain, thanks to the submerged entrance. I assume it was submerged then too, but who knows. Either way, one of the men who found this ancient stash of artifacts died in this room.

Errol grabs a blanket from his backpack and drapes it over the remains. "Rest in peace, mate."

We remain in this spot for a few minutes, our heads bowed, each honoring the dead man in whatever way we choose. Even if Jordan tried to murder Kincaid, he was still a human being and deserving of a modicum of respect in death.

What happened to Kincaid? We might never know the answer to that question.

Munro clears his throat and turns away from the remains. "What now? We found the treasure, but I'm not clear on what happens next."

"We document the discovery," I say. "Then we make our way back to civilization and report it to the proper authorities."

"Aye, but we'll need to be careful," Errol says. "I don't think the US government looks favorably on treasure hunters."

I smile. "We are not treasure hunters. We're a couple on vacation who stumbled onto the greatest hoard in history, with the help of our river guide."

Chapter Twenty-Nine

Errol

Maybe we should contact a lawyer," I say. "Chance Dixon is a mate and a lawyer, living in New Hampshire these days. He used to live in New York City, so he's been in America for quite some time. He could advise us on which laws we might've broken."

"Ashley's idea is better," Munro says. "Pretend we're ignorant. Just a guide and his barmy clients who insisted on exploring a hidden canyon. Then we stumbled onto a place where the rock had collapsed, opening up a passage into the secret hoard."

"I suppose this plan also involves claiming the slab door had already fallen over long before we found the cavern."

"Aye. And we haven't taken any artifacts. We're documenting them with the intention of reporting the find to the authorities."

"Let's forget about the legal issues for the moment," Ashley says. "We need to document everything, meticulously."

"Aye, you're right."

I take the laser-mapping device and scan every room and corridor we've seen so far. I go beyond the already explored region too, uncovering more artifacts in caverns we hadn't discovered yet. Ashley and Munro photograph everything. The three of us make a better team than I would've expected when I first signed on for this expedition. Munro seems like a grumpy sod who has no interest in anyone else, and Ashley had harassed me mercilessly. But once we came together, our individual strengths and skills merged into a strong team.

We've just finished searching for additional chambers, and have decided no more exist, when I feel a draft tickling my arm. I turn toward the wall, but I don't notice any sort of seam, like the one I blew open to get us inside the cavern complex. Still, I feel the draft.

"Ashley," I say, "come here for a moment. I need your opinion."

She doesn't ask why. The sweet lass just hurries over here to help me. "What is it?"

I take her hand, pressing it to the wall. "Do you feel a draft here?"

She holds still for a few seconds. "Yeah, I do feel that."

"But where is it coming from? There's no seam that I can detect."

Ashley runs her palm up and down the wall.

"Try the floor," Munro says. "Maybe it's coming from below."

Cannae hurt to try his idea. I lie down on the floor and press my cheek to the cold stone. The draft tickles my lips. "Aye, it's down here. The seam must go all the way across the passage."

"A seam for what?" Ashley asks.

"Not sure."

Munro offers me his hands to help me up. Though I don't really need his help, I appreciate that my cousin is making an effort to participate. Actually, he started doing that not long after we reached the Grand Canyon.

I plant my hands on my hips, gazing down at the floor. "The draft is coming from the floor, so we need to try to pry up the slab so we can see what's beneath it."

"Maybe it's not movable," Ashley says.

"Haven't you learned anything from me? Where there's a Scot, there's a way."

She shakes her head, smiling. "I don't think that's the correct formation of that colloquial expression."

"For me, it is."

She waves toward the floor. "Let's do it your way."

"No explosives," Munro barks. "It's too bloody dangerous."

"No explosives," I tell Munro. "But we will need crowbars. I have two of them."

"What can I do?" Ashley asks.

"Stand over there and look bonnie." I point toward the juncture with another passageway. "Please, Ashley. Not sure what will happen if we manage to pop this cork. I need to know you're well away from it."

"Okay. But next time, I get to help you pry open the mysterious floor slab. Or any mystery slab we come across."

"It's a deal."

Munro and I get the crowbars and try to push their tapered ends into the crack in the floor. It's hard to see that crack, but it's even harder to drive the crowbars into it. With a lot of maneuvering and grunting and cursing, we finally get some leverage. The slab grinds against the surrounding rock, and we manage to lift it a wee bit, no more than a few millimeters.

"Would lubrication help?" Ashley asks.

I pause to catch my breath before responding. "Might be useful. But I don't have any grease on hand."

"What about baby oil? I have a big bottle of it in my backpack."

Munro's lips twitch upward the slightest bit. "Do I want to know why you've got an industrial supply of mineral oil?"

"A lady never tells."

I hold my hand up like a baseball player about to catch the ball. "Toss it to me."

She finds the bottle and pitches it like a pro. Everything I know about baseball came from movies about the sport, so I don't know for certain if I'm using those terms correctly. But I do catch the ball, so maybe I should take up the game.

I think I'll stick to shinty.

Munro and I pour the mineral oil into the seam along its entire length. Then we shove our crowbars into the sliver of a gap and start pushing again. Will this work? Donnae know. It's worth a try.

I lose control of my crowbar, and it flies up out of my hand, clattering onto the floor.

We try again to lift the slab.

It moves a bit more than before, and my hands don't slip this time, so we keep trying. I'm fair certain we're straining every muscle in our bodies in the effort. I can feel my crowbar has slid into position, right where I want it to be, but I can't get enough leverage in a kneeling position. So I stand up and press my foot down on the crowbar, where it's nearest to the floor, and I slam my other foot down on the highest end. The slab lifts a little more.

Munro sees what I'm doing and tries the same thing.

Now we've both lifted the slab a bit, but I realize we need another tool. "Find something we can wedge in here, Ashley."

She nods and sets about searching our bags, but after a moment, she gives up. "I can't find anything."

"No worries." My strained voice probably doesn't convince her it's no problem.

She chews on her bottom lip while watching us fight with the crowbars and the slab. Then she starts crawling around on the floor on her hands and knees.

Munro and I have taken a break so we won't die of heart attacks. I have time to ask her a question. "Ashley, what are you doing over there?"

"I suddenly wondered if there's a latch or something that pushes the slab out of the way. I mean, whoever created this place might have wanted to get back inside the chamber below us. It could be a storage room for the most important artifacts."

"Aye, that seems logical." It's as good as any idea I've got, so we might as well test her theory. "Have ye seen any latches?"

"Not yet." She keeps crawling around while exploring the floor seam with her fingers. "Sorry I didn't think of checking this first, before you guys broke your backs."

"Our backs are fine." I walk over to her and kneel beside the lass. "Can I help?"

"Yes—by resting. You and Munro need a break, so let me do this part. It might be a wild goose chase, anyway."

I take her advice and rest, leaning against the wall while I watch her crawling about with her erse wriggling every time she moves forward. At least I get a bonnie view while I recover from wrestling with a monolith.

Since she started in the middle of the slab, when she reaches the wall she turns around, while still on all fours, and crawls toward me. Three-fourths of the way to me, she freezes. "Get me the baby oil, Errol."

I jump up to retrieve the bottle.

Ashley scurries in the other direction, retracing the path she'd already taken across the floor. This time, however, she stops three-fourths of the way to the wall.

I hand her the bottle.

She pours some of the oil into the minute gap created by the seam. Then she hurries toward the other wall, halting three-fourths of the way there again. I watch while she pours more oil into the seam there.

Ashley sits back on her heels. "Try again, boys."

Munro and I grab the crowbars and head for Ashley's side of the seam.

She holds up a hand. "Stay over there. I think the slab has hinges on this side."

Hinges? Munro and I exchange curious looks, and I expect he's as surprised as I am by what Ashley said. We grab our crowbars and try again to lift the slab. This time, it slides up much more easily. We still need to exert a great effort to lift it, and the mechanism makes a loud noise, but the hinges Ashley had lubricated for us make the job less backbreaking. I don't think we'll need spinal surgery, after all.

The slab now stands upright, leaning back a wee bit so the whole thing doesn't fall back down.

I leap around the three-foot-high slab to grab Ashley and kiss her. Behind me, I hear Munro groan. After a moment, a good long one, I release Ashley and face my cousin. "Jealous, Munro?"

"Can we get back to work?" He peers down into the dark space revealed by the slab. "Or are ye no longer interested in this hole?"

I pick up Ashley and jump over the slab, landing near Munro. "Aye, we're still interested."

We retrieve our lanterns and shine them down into the abyss we've discovered. The light shows us a set of stone steps that lead down into the unknown. I lead the way as we cautiously go down the steps one by one, but my light can't reveal much since the steps are enclosed on both sides. When I reach the bottom step, I need to make a sharp left turn to provide room for Ashley and Munro to follow me. When I see what this chamber holds, I fight the instinct to freeze and stare at what fills the space. But I need to move so Ashley and Munro can join me. Once we're all inside, we shine our lights around the chamber.

What do we see? Mummies. Dozens of them. Wrapped in various types of cloth and in various positions. An Inca mummy of what most likely was a young girl sacrificed atop a mountain. An Egyptian wrapped tightly and accompanied by canopic jars, which should contain the deceased's organs. I don't recognize what cultures many of these mummies come from, but it's clear they have all lain here for a very long time.

Ashley shakes her head slowly. "Why on earth would anyone want to bring mummies from all over the world to this underground storage site in the Grand Canyon?"

"No idea," I say. "It must have taken a long time to find and transport these remains. Whoever did it was either obsessed with death or obsessed with preserving ancient remains. To what purpose, I have no bloody idea."

We photograph all the mummies, without disturbing them, and employ the laser-mapping device to create a 3-D replica of the chamber.

After that, we return to the main doorway, the one I'd blown open, and stand inside the entrance while we discuss what to do next. Report our discovery, yes. But how to do that without getting arrested? Not sure we can accomplish that feat. But in the beginning, Ashley had told me she didn't care if anyone else ever knew about the Grand Canyon treasure. She only wanted to prove her father had been right, to alleviate his shame.

But to abandon all these historical treasures…

It feels wrong.

"We need to consult with an archaeologist," I say. "I know several, but they all live in Scotland."

"I know some," Ashley says. "Or I used to know them. They won't talk to me anymore, not since Dad announced that he believes the Grand Canyon treasure is real—and I backed him up."

I slide an arm around her shoulders and give her a squeeze. "You've sacrificed a lot to get here, and it was all for your da."

A shadow falls over the hole I'd blasted in the canyon wall.

We all look in that direction, but the person hovering there is concealed by the shadows and the sun blinding us. Something about that figure seems familiar, though, and I step away from Ashley to take a few cautious steps closer. I cock my head, squinting at the figure.

"Do you know that person?" Ashley asks.

"Not sure." I shuffle closer to the man, who moves minutely sideways. And suddenly, a shaft of light spills across one side of his cheek. "Christian? Is that you?"

"Yeah, it's me." That American voice convinces me I have correctly identified the man, despite not seeing his whole face. The stubble on his jaw threw me off for a moment, but hearing his voice confirmed his identity for me. "Errol, you really shouldn't have come here."

Christian Frisk raises a gun.

Chapter Thirty

Ashley

I shouldn't have come?" Errol says. "Why the bloody hell are you here? Last I heard, you'd moved to New Zealand to be with your sweetheart. How did you even know where I was? Or where the treasure was?"

The stranger chuckles. "You might be the best at solving riddles and finding lost treasures, but you have no aptitude for covert missions. It was depressingly easy to keep track of you. I'd hoped for a little more resistance."

"We haven't even started to resist, ye *cacan*."

"Aren't you going to introduce me?" the man asks. He saunters into the cavern, now lit by the sun shining down through the skylight. "All right, I'll do it myself."

He approaches me.

Errol places himself between me and the new guy. "Ye donnae need to know her name. Tell me what you're doing here."

The man ignores Errol and leans sideways to give me a smile I can only describe as creepy. "Allow me to introduce myself. I'm Christian Frisk, Errol's partner in crime."

"My former partner," Errol says. "You quit, remember?"

Frisk shrugs one shoulder. "I've reinstated our professional relationship. That means half of everything you've found here belongs to me."

"It belongs to the world," I say. "The relics we found shouldn't go into a private collection. They should be available to everyone. Or no one at all."

"No one?" Frisk raises his brows. "Are you honestly that stupid? The greatest hoard in history is not public property. It belongs to me, because Errol and I have a contract."

"You're off your head," Errol says. "We never signed a contract, and you quit, anyway."

Errol had mentioned his partner to me, but like he just said, he believed the man had moved to the other side of the world. What does Christian Frisk want now? To plunder the Grand Canyon hoard, apparently. But I can't help wondering if Frisk has an ulterior motive, beyond wanting to claim the treasure for his own.

Frisk taps his gun on his thigh, as if he's considering what to do now. "If you have any weapons, give them up now. I won't ask again."

"There's one of you," Munro says, his gruff voice no longer grumpy, but now tinged with menace. "And there are three of us. Unless you want to die, best turn around and leave."

Frisk's lips twitch in an almost smile. "Scots always are arrogant, eh? Errol never seemed that way, and he never seemed particularly smart either. He's more of an idiot savant, well-versed in solving puzzles, but clueless in every other way."

"Insults won't get you what you want," I say. "So let's cut the crap and be upfront with each other."

"Are you in charge here?" Frisk smirks, glancing at Errol and Munro. "I should've guessed Scots are like neutered puppies. You need a woman to take the lead. Fine. Let's chat, Ashley."

He must've thought speaking my name, when I hadn't told him that, would knock me off balance. It didn't. Munro's friend and fellow river guide had warned us that someone might've bugged our raft, which turned out to be true, but a GPS tracker means that person wanted to follow us. We had no choice but to keep going. Destroying the tracker clearly didn't stop Frisk from finding us. I wonder if he might've planted a tracker somewhere else too, like on Errol's backpack or his clothes.

"How did you find us?" I ask.

"We can discuss that later." Frisk backs up to the doorway Errol had blasted out of the rock. He tips his head backward and to the side, then hollers, "Come in, gentlemen."

Frisk moves to the side.

And more men file through the opening, each carrying at least one weapon—handguns, rifles, machetes, and even brass knuckles. Every man has a physique that rivals that of Errol and Munro, and every single one of them wears a hard expression. Most have tattoos and scars, as if they've fought in many rough battles. Frisk's companions look like men accustomed to doing whatever it takes to accomplish their task, whatever that might be. We're about to learn the answer, I suspect.

I count five men.

Then a straggler clomps into the cavern, hauling a plastic sled that's loaded with tough-looking boxes. The last man sets the sled down and straps his arms over his chest. He seems just as rough-and-tumble as the others. Frisk is the odd man out in his gang, since he lacks visible evidence of down-and-dirty fights. I suspect Christian Frisk never gets his hands dirty. He has other people do that work for him.

"Now that you understand the situation," Frisk says. "Let's have a real conversation about what will happen here."

Errol's eyes flick to the side as he glances at his bag of explosives.

"Uh-uh-uh," Frisk says, wagging his finger at Errol. "You won't blow up my treasure. Do you have any idea how much the hoard will be worth on the black market? It's beyond calculation." He flaps a hand toward one of his lackeys. "Confiscate their bags, please. And be careful with the big one. Getting blown to smithereens will annoy me."

I bet he went to an Ivy League university. He probably came from a wealthy family too. Christian Frisk has the attitude of a spoiled rich boy who never had to work for anything and expects to get whatever he wants whenever he wants it. Not all rich people are like that, but Frisk could be the poster boy for the stuck-up elites.

"Harvard or Yale?" I ask.

Frisk stares at me, his brows cinching up. "What?"

"Did you go to Harvard or Yale? I'm guessing Harvard. You seem like the kind of guy who loves the colors crimson and black. Those are the Harvard colors, right?"

"Yes, but—Stop talking. The only one whose voice I want to hear is Errol." Frisk turns to his men. "Tie up Ashley and Munro."

Errol starts to move toward me.

But Frisk holds up a hand. "I wouldn't do that. These two are of little interest to me, which means I won't be upset if my men accidentally kill them. Do you want to see Ashley's guts sprayed across the floor?"

Errol grits his teeth, making a muscle pulse in his jaw. "When did you become such an evil *bod ceann*?"

"Call me whatever you want. I'm in control now. Step back, or I'll order my men to… What would be the worst thing I could force you to see?" Frisk grins with feral glee. "Oh, yes. I've got it. How would you like to watch my men having fun with your girl? We've been working so hard lately that they haven't gotten the chance to fuck a woman, and I can't promise they'll control their passions."

I glance at Errol exactly when he glances at me. Though he still wears an angry expression, something in his eyes tells me that he's forming a plan. Whatever happens next, I know Errol will do whatever it takes to stop these men from ravaging me. I'll fight them with everything I have, but a gang of big, strong cretins could easily overpower me.

"What do you want me to do?" Errol asks, his lips peeling back from his teeth with every syllable.

"Show me the hoard. I'll explain the rest once I'm satisfied you haven't taken anything from these caverns or tried to hide something inside these walls."

"And you won't hurt Ashley or Munro if I do what you want."

"No harm will come to them while you take me on a tour, unless your girl or your cousin try something. My men will defend themselves with deadly force."

Errol turns his gaze to me. I know, though I can't explain how, that he has some kind of plan, or at least is on the cusp of forming one. I've learned enough about Errol Murdoch to realize the man never goes into any situation without understanding what might lie ahead. I want to demand that Frisk let me go with him and Errol, but I can't risk angering the man.

Instead, I gaze into his eyes and pray he understands what I want him to know. *Don't die on me, Errol, please. I need you.*

He faces the doorway that leads into the cavern complex. "Follow me, Christian. And grab a lantern. It's dark in there."

Frisk grabs a lantern and hands it to Errol. Frisk keeps hold of his gun, with his finger poised over the trigger guard. The bastard will shoot Errol if he doesn't get what he wants. I know this with a conviction borne of intuition. Maybe I never used to believe in that, but I do now. And I pray we all come out of this alive.

Errol and Frisk climb over the fallen slab and enter the passageway.

Frisk calls out over his shoulder, "Tanner, come with me. Rendon, stand guard in this passageway."

Soon, the light of their lantern fades into darkness.

I curl my fingers into loose fists, but then force myself to relax them.

Frisk's men herd me and Munro into the corner of the cavern, directly in front of the doorway Errol had created with C-4, and order us to sit down. Maybe we could make a run for it, but I will never leave this place without Errol. I can't discuss our situation with Munro, which means I need to work out a plan on my own. I'm sure Errol is doing the same thing. Waiting for him to return seems like a bad idea, though. We need a backup plan in case these thugs decide to try something while we're waiting for their leader to come back.

All the research I'd done can't help me now.

One of the men rubs his belly and groans. "Damn, I'm hungry. Did we bring any food?"

"Left it on the beach, in the raft," one of his buddies tells the guy. "Be a man. Your sensitive little tummy can wait until the boss comes back."

"I have granola bars in my backpack," I say. "Feel free to eat them."

Giving up my food seems better than letting a brute go hungry. He might decide to gnaw on me to satisfy himself. Besides, I don't feel like eating. I'm too anxious.

"I'm hungry too," a third man announces. "Let's get those granola bars."

The two starved men trot across the cavern to where we'd left our backpacks.

"Mine is the one with the star logo on the front," I tell them. "The granola bars are in the smaller zipper pocket on the front."

One man rips open the zipper pocket and grabs a handful of foil-wrapped bars. "Chocolate chip. Oh, yeah, this'll do."

The two men start chowing down, paying no attention to me, Munro, or their comrades. The guard in the passageway has moved just past the big slab, and only his shadow tells me he's still there. The two guys left in here with us, the ones who aren't stuffing their faces, watch their comrades instead of us. That makes me wonder... Since Frisk had taken one of his men with him and Errol, and he ordered a second man to guard the passageway, leaving four men here in the entrance cavern with me and Munro...could we effect some kind of escape? Not to leave without Errol. Just to get away from these men. They don't know the layout of the underground cavern network.

Since the thugs have congregated on the opposite side of the cavern, I decide to risk whispering to Munro. "Got any ideas? We need to overpower those men somehow. Don't trust Frisk not to kill us all once he gets what he wants."

"I agree. If we could get to Errol's bag of explosives, I think I saw some flash bangs in there. Those are grenades that don't explode. They create a blinding flash of light and a bang so loud it will disorient your enemy."

Yeah, I've heard of those. But could Munro and I pull that off? We need to try.

Because I don't trust Frisk not to kill Errol.

"I have an idea," I tell Munro. "Just follow my lead, okay?"

He eyes me sideways, then sighs and nods.

I stand up and cross my legs. "Um, guys, I have a small problem."

The two creeps who are standing up rotate toward me, while their buddies remain hunched over my backpack. One of the upright creeps rakes his gaze over me. "What is it, babe? Did you get tired of Scottish losers and want to try some red-blooded American fun?"

"I need to pee. Like, really bad. If I wet my pants, you guys will have to smell it until your boss comes back."

The man curls his lip. Then he glances at his buddy. "What do you think, Unger? Should we take her outside to, ya know, relieve herself?"

"No, Milliken. You're such an idiot. Dump the girl in the pool. She can do it there."

"What if she drowns? Boss won't be happy."

Unger makes an irritated noise. "Fine. But if you lose her, Frisk will have your head."

One of the men kneeling beside my pack pauses in wolfing down a granola bar. "Boss told us never to leave one of these jerks alone. Two escorts, at least."

"Fine," Unger snarls. "I'll schlep out into the hot sun to make sure one measly little girl doesn't overpower poor Milliken."

Unger and Milliken march over to me, each seizing one of my arms, and half drag me out the doorway into the sunlight.

A scuffle erupts inside the cavern. Men shout. The whump of a powerful gut punch echoes in the space.

"What the fuck?" Unger says.

Then a gunshot detonates.

Chapter Thirty-One

Errol

What the bloody hell was that?" I whirl around, but I can't see the entrance cavern. We've traveled too far into the network of chambers. But I know that was a gunshot, and every cell in my body has turned to ice. "We need to get back there and—"

"No, Errol. My men have shot your cousin, I imagine. He seems like exactly the type who would try something stupid." Frisk jams his gun into my back. "Keep moving."

Like hell I will.

We've just reached the hinged slab that had concealed the mummy chamber. That means I have one chance to get this bastard off my back. He made me hold the lantern, so I shut it off.

Then I spin around and punch Frisk in the gut. He grunts. Shuffling sounds follow. I switch the light on again to see the *bod ceann* doubled over, struggling to catch his breath. He won't get the chance. I punch him in the jaw and kick him in the shin. Frisk shouts and stumbles sideways. The gun pops out of his grasp, and I snatch it up.

Before he can recover, I sprint down the corridor with the lantern in my hand. Frisk will find himself in the pitch dark soon, once I turn the corner and start running faster.

A howl of pain echoes down the passageway behind me.

I donnae care what happened to Christian Frisk. All I want to know is who fired that shot and why. If those bastards have hurt Ashley or Munro,

I'll empty this gun into them. No, I never wanted to kill anyone, but I will not stand by while the people I love are in danger.

When I turn the corner into the main passageway, I slow to a quick walk and sidle up to the wall. Then I shut off the lantern. Donnae want the villains to see me coming or know which way I might go when I reach the doorway. The sunlight from the entryway skylight leaks into this passage, so I'm not completely blind.

Someone moans and whimpers.

Ashley? No, it sounded like a man. But I can't picture Munro rolling about on the floor while whimpering, no matter what the cretins have done to him.

I slow down even more as I approach the slab. The man Frisk had left to guard this corridor is facing away from me. I whack him on the head with my lantern. As he crumples to the floor, I realize I have one chance to surprise the rest of Frisk's men. I raise the gun, take a breath, and leap over the slab, landing on my feet. "Freeze! I won't hesitate to shoot ye if ye make any moves."

Ashley and Munro stand in the center of the cavern. The four men who had held them hostage now lie on the floor with their wrists and ankles bound with zip ties.

I study the scene but can't make sense of it. "Ah, would anyone care to tell me what happened?"

"Ashley lured two of these blokes outside," Munro says. "She kneed one in the groin and hit the other with a rock, then she ran back in here. I had already subdued the other two blokes. When the pair she'd left outside stumbled back into this cavern, it was easy to tie them up. They weren't thinking too clearly. Concussion, most likely."

"Well, I…" Have no bloody idea how to respond to that. "Good job, you two."

Ashley rushes over to hug me. "Are you okay? What happened to Frisk?"

"I'm fine. He's probably lost in the caverns. I left him in the dark, literally." I hold up my lantern. "We should go check on him. Just to make sure he doesn't have another weapon."

She kisses me, and though she flicks her tongue as if to deepen the kiss, she pulls away instead. "I was so worried about you, but I shouldn't have been. You know how to handle yourself."

"And so do you." I whisper into her ear, "You have no idea how much I want to shag you right now."

She struggles not to smile.

I look at Munro. "Can you handle these five eejits while we find Frisk?"

"Aye. This lot aren't the sharpest tools in the shed."

I give Ashley the lantern and hold her hand while we make our way back to where I'd left Frisk. We haven't seen any sign of him between the main entrance and the mummy chamber, so he must be here someplace. We peeked into all the chambers along the way, but there was no evidence Frisk had hidden in those places. Where did the *cacan* go?

A strange moaning noise reverberates below us, down in the mummy chamber. The way it echoes makes it hard to tell if that's a human sound or some type of bizarre draft. When the moaning starts up again, though, it sounds distinctly human.

I lean over the hinged slab and wave for Ashley to shine the lantern into the pitch-dark chamber below.

Frisk lies prone at the bottom of the steps.

"Have ye broken any bones?" I shout down to him.

"As if you care."

Oh, aye, now is the right time to be petulant. What a bloody stupid *cacan*. "Do ye want to be rescued? Or should we leave and lock the door behind us?"

"Yes, fine, help me."

"Say 'please' first."

He grumbles, "Please."

Ashley gives me a disapproving look, then shakes her head.

Maybe that was a wee bit childish, but he threatened to kill the people I love. Demanding he genuflect in some small way seems appropriate.

"All right," I say. "I'm coming to get you, though you don't deserve to be rescued. You should be grateful that I'm the good Samaritan sort."

I hand Ashley the gun and carefully descend the steps. After a brief examination of the *bod ceann*, I decide he isn't badly injured. A few cuts and scrapes. He'll probably have some bruises later. I sling an arm around his midsection and move toward the steps. When the eejit cries out, then whines like the most annoying baby on earth, I resort to virtually carrying him up the steps.

Once we reach the top, I pull out a pair of zip ties and secure Frisk's hands in front of his body. I'd grabbed those restraints on our way out of the entrance cavern because I do not trust my former partner anymore. But I have questions for him, ones he will answer as soon as we've reached the entrance again. These catacombs give me the chills.

"You won't win, Errol," Frisk hisses. "My men—"

"Are incapacitated. Ashley and Munro took care of them."

He shuts his mouth and settles for silently fuming.

The longer we walk, the less he insists on making me hold up his useless body. He hasn't said a word since he informed me I would never win, whatever he meant by that. As he shuffles into the entrance cavern, I shove the *cacan* toward his men, who lie huddled on the floor.

I crouch beside Frisk. "Time for answers, Christian."

"Go to hell."

"You first." I sit back on my haunches. "I want to know what in the world this was all about. You disappeared for months, then sent me an email saying you'd quit the game and were moving to New Zealand with your fiancée."

"I did move to New Zealand. But Amelie left me two weeks later."

With mock sympathy, I pat his shoulder and shake my head. "That's just awful, Christian. But donnae worry, you'll find your soul mate one day. I hear prison is a great place to meet someone. After all, no one can leave."

"Come off it, Errol. You never liked me any more than I liked you."

That's not true, but I won't admit that to him. Maybe I hadn't thought of Christian Frisk as a close mate, but we went on seven expeditions together over the course of three years. We relied on each other to get the job done safely. I trusted the bastard, and now he's shown his true face.

"I thought we understood each other," I say. "But now it turns out I knew nothing about you. Why did you deceive me?"

He glowers at me for a moment, then blows out a breath that makes his shoulders slump. "What the hell? No point in lying now. I invited you to become my partner because I'd heard about your special skills. And I realized that one day you would lead me to an incredible hoard. Didn't know what form that hoard would take or how long I'd need to wait. But I'm a very patient man."

Aye, I know that. Christian never seemed to be in a hurry to make any discovery. Taking it slow, he'd once told me, would bring greater rewards than rushing. Aye, he taught me that. I'm grateful for what I learned from this man, but he only shared his knowledge because he wanted something from me.

Frisk steeples his fingers, then begins tapping them against each other. His gaze narrows. "Tell me, Errol, did you enjoy the time you spent in my Basel apartment?"

Why is the *cacan* bringing up his flat in Switzerland? Aye, he let me stay there whenever I wanted. So what? I remain silent and wait for him to get antsy and volunteer the information.

It takes about thirty seconds.

"You thought the apartment was a safe place," Frisk says. "But I had bugged every inch of it, even the bathroom. I heard every sound and saw every video recorded in that apartment."

Oh, he really doesn't know me as well as he thinks.

My lips gradually slide into a knowing smile. "The last time I was in Basel, did you overhear what happened in the bedroom?"

"I heard everything."

"Who was in the bedroom?"

Frisk makes an irritated noise. "You, of course."

"And what did you see in the video?"

"It was too dark to see, but it was you. No one else goes there."

"Afraid not, mate." I reach over to slap his back. "You were enjoying a pornographic film. I turned down the exposure on the video so anyone spying wouldn't know it was a ruse. I never imagined you would be the one bugging the apartment, but I didnae want to assume no one could break through the security measures. So I reconfigured the system."

His face goes blank for a moment. Then his features twist into an expression of sheer rage. "You lying, cheating piece of shit!"

I chuckle. "So, it's all right when you try to spy on me having a poke with a lass, but how dare I upgrade the security system. If I'd known you wanted to spy on me, maybe I wouldn't have made those changes." I rub my chin, pretending to think hard. Then I grin. "No, I still would've done it. But I also would have hunted you down and skelped you good."

"Let me go, Errol. I'll give you twenty percent of the treasure."

"Twenty percent of stolen property? Donnae think so, Christian."

The lass kneels beside me. She has the gun tucked inside her waistband, nestled against her spine. "What should we do with these guys? They're criminals. But we can't risk exposing our illegal expedition."

"Oh, I have an idea about that. But I'll need to pop outside to make a call on Munro's satellite phone."

"I'll stay here with Munro and the bad guys."

"Back in a moment."

I grab the phone and duck outside, but I can't get a signal right in front of the doorway. Even satellite signals aren't available everywhere, though they have a much bigger range than mobile phones. I slowly move away from the cavern entrance until I get a good signal, then I dial a number I know well.

When the man I need to speak to answers, he sounds a wee bit sleepy. Well, it is several hours later over there.

"Hello, Alex," I say. "It's Errol."

"Errol who?"

"Murdoch. Your wife's cousin." I hold the phone away from my face and shout, "Wake up, Alex Thorne!"

"Bloody hell, Errol," Alex says when I return the phone to my ear. "What do you want? It's very late."

"Not here in the Grand Canyon."

"I repeat, what do you want?"

"Ashley, Munro, and I need your special expertise."

He yawns loudly. "I don't understand."

"We need the only man in the world who is both an expert archaeologist and a con artist. Feel like visiting Arizona to stop a thieving bastard from getting away with it? Or aren't you interested in adventures anymore?"

Silence follows for several seconds.

When Alex speaks again, he's wide awake. "Tell me exactly what you want me to do, Errol."

I quickly outline my plan for him. "What do you think?"

"You don't need me, that's what I think. You can do this on your own."

"But I'm not a con artist. My skills—"

"Are up to the task. It would take at least nine hours for me to get to Arizona, then I'd need to find a helicopter to get me close to your location. Do you really want to wait that long inside an ancient cave with a man who wants to destroy you?"

Well, when he phrases it that way… "No, I don't. But I have no other options."

"Of course you do." Rustling in the background of the call suggests Alex is getting out of bed. "Everyone knows about your adventure with Magnus and Piper. And Magnus loves to tell the rest of us what a consummate actor you are, and how you talked your way out of being captured by the villains."

"It wasn't my acting that did that. It was my explosives."

"But you also convinced a murderer to confess. That takes top-notch conning skills. You can do this, Errol. And you don't need me."

I've never told anyone how I talked Dilara Terzi into confessing, and I won't explain that to Alex now. Maybe I should tell Ashley. Nobody else needs to know.

"All right, Alex," I say. "Thank you for the advice. I think I know what I need to do."

"Good luck, Errol. Sounds like you're going to need it."

Chapter Thirty-Two

Ashley

When Errol comes back after making his call, he seems more confident. A phone call did that? He's normally self-assured, but he'd lost some of that during our trip through the canyon, when he grew slightly jealous of his wild-man cousin. Then he'd regained that self-assurance after we found the treasure trove, only to let it slip away shortly after we learned his partner had betrayed him.

But he seems relaxed and confident once again.

Christian Frisk might have been Errol's partner once upon a time, but Errol doesn't need that jerk anymore. He has me—and Munro. We would never use Errol in a scheme to plunder an ancient treasure.

Errol crouches beside Frisk. "You are a thief, Christian. We're not friends anymore, and I will never let you steal the treasures in this hoard. I helped stop an antiquities theft ring, and I convinced a murderer to confess. Your skills donnae matter to me at all." He glances at me, then his cousin. "I've got the best partners in the world."

"My men will break free," Frisk says. "You can't stop us. By the time the police get here, we will be long gone."

"I don't think so." Errol rises. "You see, I have a plan. You don't."

Errol leads me toward the entrance. As we pass by Munro, Errol asks, "Can you keep these men contained while Ashley and I discuss the plan?"

"Aye." Munro aims his flinty stare at Frisk and his men. "They willnae go anywhere, except to hell."

Errol and I walk out into the sunshine, though the canyon walls around us mute the light. It still feels good to have the sun warming my skin, after spending so much time deep inside the caverns. He takes me well away from the entrance he had blasted out, then turns to me.

"What's the plan?" I ask.

"This might sound barmy."

I can't help laughing softly. "Am I supposed to be shocked? Your best ideas are completely insane. That's one of the things I love about you."

"Really? I love a lot of things about you, especially the way you go along with whatever insane plans I cook up." He grows more serious as he studies me. "Christian is more dangerous than I ever knew. He fooled me once, and I cannot let that happen again. We have one chance to make sure Christian and his men go to prison and the hoard falls into the right hands."

"I agree. Whatever you've got up your sleeve, I'm in."

"You haven't heard my plan yet."

"Don't need to. Tell me what to do, and I'll do it."

Errol searches my face as if he can't quite believe I would do anything for him. But I would. He has proved to me time and again that I can trust him with my life and everything else that matters.

He nods once. "All right. Here's the plan. First, I'm going to disable Frisk's raft."

"His raft? How do you know he has one?"

"Nobody swims up the Colorado River. I suppose he and his men could have hiked through the canyon to get here, but I doubt that. The terrain in this sector is rough and difficult to navigate, particularly for novices."

I glance at the cavern entrance. "You think Frisk brought novices with him? Is he that dumb?"

"No, he's that arrogant. I always knew he was up himself, but I didn't realize how far that went until today." Errol jerks his head toward the cavern entrance. "Do those eejits seem like river guides? Or wilderness experts? They probably don't even realize their mobiles won't work here. One of them is wearing a designer T-shirt, for pity's sake."

"Yeah, I did notice that. Hard to miss the logo plastered across that guy's back."

"They are dangerous, though. Donnae forget that."

My gaze wanders to the cavern again, and I wonder what Munro is doing in there with those goons. But I need to focus on what Errol wants to tell me, so I swerve my attention back to him. "How will you disable Frisk's raft?"

"I'm going to slash it."

"I don't understand."

He whips a large switchblade out of his pocket and flips it open. Then he makes a slashing motion. "Understand now? I'm going to slice a hole or two in their raft. No getting away then, aye?"

"Guess not. Does this plan have anything to do with whatever you did to our raft?"

"Not directly. I installed a security system to prevent anyone from stealing it."

Whenever Errol gets cagey, I get suspicious. "What exactly did you do?"

He jams his hands in his pants pockets and screws up his mouth. "Probably best if you don't know."

"Uh-uh. We're partners, in every way. That means you need to share your whole plan with me."

He pats my arm. "Trust me, lass. You're better off staying in the dark, for now. Plausible deniability."

"You said you'd tell me your plan."

"For dealing with Frisk and his men, aye. But my raft security measures are best left unexplained, for the time being."

Though we'd moved far enough away from the cavern entrance that I see no way Frisk or his goons could hear us talking, I still feel a little weird about discussing our plans here. Where else could we go? I don't want to get too far away either, not when we've left Munro alone with those men.

Errol grasps my arm and guides me behind a boulder that stands slightly taller than the Scotsman in front of me. He keeps his voice hushed. "I rang a mate of mine, Alex Thorne. He has, ah, unique skills. I needed his advice on how to handle our current situation."

"Is he a cop?"

"No."

"A spy?"

Errol shakes his head.

"What, then?" I ask. "Just spit it out."

"Alex used to be a con artist. A grifter, if you prefer that term. He only did that when he was a laddie, and his parents forced him into it. Now, he uses those skills to help his friends and family."

"Uh-huh. A noble con man." I'm feeling rather confused, but I get that we don't have time for the unabridged version of his friend's life story. "How does that help us?"

"Alex gave me pointers on how to convince people to believe what they're told instead of what they see and experience."

"Sounds tricky. But I'm still confused."

"We need to contact the authorities to report the discovery of the Grand Canyon treasure. But we can't risk getting tied up in legal rubbish since we don't have a permit to be in the canyon, much less one for conducting field work."

"Right. I know that." But I still don't get what he's trying to tell me.

"We need to make it seem like we stumbled onto the cavern by accident. And we wandered inside to see what was in there, strictly out of curiosity."

"I'm with you so far. But how does this involve Frisk and his men?"

Errol stares at me intently for a moment. Then he takes hold of my upper arms and bends his knees to level our gazes. "Did you mean it when you said you don't care who gets credit for discovering the Grand Canyon treasure?"

"Yes, of course I did. I only care that my dad is vindicated, and that I can bring him proof of the find. That's why I'm taking pictures, and we're laser-mapping the whole thing."

"All right." He straightens. "Because we're going to let those tossers take credit for it."

"Huh?" I gape at him, and I think a mosquito just flew into my mouth. I accidentally swallowed it. "Errol, you'll need to explain that to me. I don't get it. Letting those bastards take the glory? No, we can't do that."

"Not the glory." He gives me a smug smile. "They'll take the fall."

"For what?"

"Antiquities theft. Looting. Violating federal law. Take your pick, love."

For a moment, I can do nothing but stare at him. The full implications of what he suggested sink into my brain gradually, leaving me dumbfounded until I finally comprehend his plan. "Let me see if I've got this right. We're going to pretend to stumble onto the caverns and stumble onto those men attempting to loot the priceless treasures contained in the complex of chambers."

"Exactly."

"They won't get any accolades for discovering the treasure. Instead, we will report the theft, and they will go to prison."

He taps the tip of his nose. "Now you're catching on."

"You must have a plan for how to contact the authorities."

"Of course I do."

"And your friend Alex gave you pointers on how to convince those authorities that we're just innocent tourists, not people who tried to illegally excavate in the Grand Canyon."

Errol spreads his arms, palms out, and adopts the most convincing look of fake innocence I've ever seen. "We haven't excavated anything. Those caverns are exactly how we found them."

"But you, um, blasted a hole in the entrance cavern. And you blasted the doorway open."

"Did I? Seems to me those blokes in there must have done the blasting. Why would tourists like us want to do that?"

He sounds damn convincing too. Wow, I never knew Errol had such good acting chops. Of course, convincing me is easy. Will the authorities buy his story? I guess we'll find out soon enough. We don't have much of a choice, not with Frisk and his men in our custody.

"Do you want to hear the rest of the plan?" Errol asks.

"No, I trust you to handle this. Just tell me what I need to do to help you."

He pulls me close with one arm, and I tip my head back to meet his gaze. Those blue eyes glimmer in the sunlight, like polished gemstones with a thousand facets, as complex as the man himself. He brushes a lock of hair away from my eyes. "Be careful, *mo chridhe*. The scheme I've come up with could be fun, but it's also risky. Frisk and his men are not nice people."

"I know. I'll keep my eyes peeled at all times."

He wraps both arms around me and lifts me onto my tiptoes. Then he presses his lips to mine, holding them like that without even trying to deepen the kiss, and my heartbeat accelerates. I love the feel of his lips on mine, even though they're slightly dry, and I can't stop my body from relaxing into him.

"I need you to make me a promise," he says, with his lips still touching mine. "If this plan goes sideways, you will run as far and as fast as you can."

"No, I won't leave you—"

"Please, Ashley. I need to know you're safe."

While I understand why he wants me to promise I'll run, I won't lie to him. Where would I go, anyway? I have no idea how to navigate the Colorado River and its many rapids. I don't have a map to guide me either. But mostly, I refuse to leave Errol because I'm not the kind of person who flees while someone I love is in danger.

"I will try to stay out of the fray," I tell him. "But I can't promise to run away. I won't do that. I can't do it. As long as you're here, this is where I'll be too."

His lips curl into the smallest of smiles. "I knew I couldn't talk you into leaving, but I had to try. Your safety matters more to me than my own."

"Ditto. So, what can two stubborn people do when neither of us gets our way?"

His smile curves into a sly slant. "We take the wild and crazy approach, naturally."

Errol kisses me, deeply this time, teasing me with light flicks of his tongue and driving me wild with powerful thrusts. I dissolve into him, curling my tongue around his, desperate to taste him and explore every inch of his mouth. Kissing has never been as good with anyone else. I can never go back to dating regular men who have regular jobs and who give me regular kisses. Errol is extraordinary in every way.

He pulls away and pecks a kiss on my forehead. "Be careful, Ashley."

"You too."

Errol nods, then saunters away toward the opening of the box canyon.

I keep watching until he disappears. As much as I long to follow him, I know he needs me to stay here. Slashing Frisk's raft couldn't take that long, could it? Errol should be back soon. I head back inside the entrance cavern, where Munro leans against the wall, watching Frisk and his men with his gaze narrowed and his demeanor relaxed but alert.

"How's it going?" I ask Munro.

"They've been good wee laddies."

None of those men qualify as "wee," but I don't care what Munro wants to calls them. I sidle up to him and whisper into his ear, "Errol had an errand to run."

Munro still doesn't react in a way that our guests would notice. But he does whisper out of the corner of his mouth, "Watch out for these laddies. They're plotting something."

Yeah, I get that feeling too. The men seem too calm, too accepting of their status as captives. These guys might not seem like geniuses, but even half-wits can sometimes come up with decent schemes. They did manage to track us here, after all.

I sneak the gun out of my waistband and hand it to Munro.

Errol marches into the cavern. "How are our guests doing? Should we serve lunch now? Crab cakes and champagne are on the menu, with a dessert of crème brûlée."

"Shut up, you insufferable moron," Frisk snarls through clenched teeth. "I've had enough of you."

Two of his henchmen swing their arms out, revealing their lack of zip ties, and surge to their feet. One rushes at Errol, while the other slugs Munro in the gut. As Munro struggles to catch his breath, the man who'd punched him races to his buddies and brings out a knife to snap their ties.

I grab a crowbar off the floor and whack it into the man's back.

He whirls around and kicks me in the stomach.

And I fly backward into the deep, dark flooded hole.

Chapter Thirty-Three

Errol

I watch as Ashley falls backward into the pool, but I cannae help her because the bastard who tackled me has pinned me to the wall beside the cavern entrance. I try to knee him in the groin, but I can't move my leg enough to do that. I snarl a slew of Gaelic curses while I bite the tosser's nose and grab his wrist to yank it backward. He shouts and loses his grip on me. I seize the opportunity to ram my knee into his groin, making him wail and stumble backward. With my hands tightly clasped, I slam my joined fists down on the back of his neck.

The bastard crumples to the floor.

I leap over him and dive into the pool.

The murky water makes finding her more difficult. *Mhac na galla.* If she drowns, I will snap the necks of every one of Frisk's men—then strangle him with my bare hands. My heart pounds so hard and fast that I have trouble focusing, but a dark shape below snares my attention. That must be her. The shape sinks deeper into the water, and I know I might have seconds to catch her before she vanishes into the murk, too deep for me to find her.

Donnae care if I drown. I must save Ashley.

Kicking my feet furiously, I follow the dark shape and draw closer to it with every second. Her body floats limply, her hair fanning out around her head. I stretch an arm out to snag her shirt, but my fingers just miss her. So I kick even harder, knowing I can't hold my breath forever but not giving a damn. I draw closer, closer, and thrust my hand out again. My fingers grasp her upper arm. I tighten my grip and drag her toward me. Once I've got the lass in my arms, I flip over and start paddling madly toward the surface of the pool.

I bob up out of the water with Ashley's head on my shoulder and suck in a deep breath. Munro leans over the pool to help me get the lass onto the floor of the cavern. While I clamber out of the water, my cousin checks Ashley's pulse.

"She's alive," he says.

Then he turns her onto her side and thumps her back. She bursts into a hacking fit, coughing up water at first, and after a moment, she stops hacking. Munro lies her down on her back and moves aside.

I kneel beside Ashley, peeling wet hair away from her eyes.

She gazes at me through half-closed lids and tries to smile, though the expression falters. "Hi."

The single syllable, half-whispered, rushes relief through me so thoroughly that my knees would buckle if I weren't already kneeling. "Welcome back, *gràidh*. Donnae ever scare me that way again."

"I'll try." She raises a hand to touch my cheek. "Sorry. I should've known better than to try to attack that guy."

"You were very brave. But I'd rather you not try that again."

"Did they escape?"

"No, lass, donnae worry about those bastards." I help her sit up, and fold my arms around her gently. "Just rest, love."

Maybe I shouldn't have told her not to worry about Frisk's men, because I haven't bothered to look at them and find out if they're free. Two of them had cut their bindings right before Ashley went into the water, though I don't know how they did that. When my attention lands on the ersehole who had thrown Ashley into the water, I clench my hands into fists and clench my jaw too, nearly overpowered by the need to leap on the bastard and hurl him into the pool—after I batter him senseless.

But I cannae do that.

He's holding a gun. So are his three mates. That leaves two of them who have gone somewhere. Since I don't see Frisk either, I suspect he and two of his men sneaked into the catacombs while Munro and I dragged Ashley out of the pool. Frisk must want to catalog his booty before he tries to ship it out of here. They couldn't have left the cavern, not with Munro and me fighting his men. Sure, we had forgotten all about them once we saw Ashley go into the water. But I would've noticed those bastards if they'd skulked past me. Wouldn't I?

We cannae risk it. We need to know where they went. And that means we need to regain control of the situation. Three of us against four armed enemies, not to mention their two missing mates and Christian Frisk.

Aye, this should be a piece of cake.

"Get away from the girl," the bloke who had thrown her into the water snarls at me. He wields his gun in a negligent gesture, as if he knows nothing about gun safety or simply doesn't care. Either option is dangerous. "I said get away from her. Right now."

I rise gradually, holding my hands up, palms out. "Relax, mate. We're moving."

Munro follows my lead, standing to raise his hands too.

"Back away," the man who seems to be in charge commands. "Get to the corner over there."

Munro and I walk over to the corner, where we had corralled these men earlier. We keep our hands raised. But this situation won't go on for much longer. We need to find an opening, that's all.

"What should we do with them, Unger?" another man asks, directing his question to the bastard I'm going to murder soon.

The bloke who nearly killed Ashley grunts. "I don't give a shit. Shoot them if you want."

"Frisk won't like that."

"Screw that dickhead, Milliken. He's not here. I am. That means I'm in charge."

"When did I put you in charge?" Frisk asks, having just crossed the threshold of the doorway to the main passage. He hops off the slab and marches straight to Unger, raising his gun in the other man's face. "I think you've forgotten who pays you."

"Sorry, boss. I was just—"

"Acting like a useless asshole. Correct?"

Unger swallows hard, making his Adam's apple jump. "Yes, sir."

"Now that we've cleared that up, take Milliken and go get our duffel bags from the raft."

"Sure thing, boss."

Though Unger speaks the words of a dutiful servant, the tightness around his eyes and the slight curl of his lip belies that. He doesn't like his employer, not at all.

Frisk approaches Ashley. "You are going to take me through the rooms full of treasures and show me which items are of the most value."

"I'm not an archaeologist."

"But you spent most of your life trailing after your father like a good little puppy, learning from him. You wouldn't be here now if you hadn't picked up enough information to know whether the treasures in these caverns are real or counterfeit."

"I can't do that. You need an expert."

"Aye, she's right," I say. "You need me. Take me into the caverns with you, not Ashley. That's what you did earlier."

Frisk grasps Ashley's upper arm as he turns partway toward me. "Yes, but now I don't trust you, Errol. You tried to get away from me."

"Aye. And I'm so awfully sorry about that, Christian. You've been the perfect host."

"Do you really think sarcasm is appropriate right now?"

"It's always appropriate with you." I hold my wrists out, held together as if they're shackled. "You can zip tie me. I donnae mind."

"That won't suffice. I'd need to shackle your hands and feet."

"Cannae walk that way."

"Yes, I know. That's why Ashley is coming with me." He drags her toward the slab. "I'll be nice, though, and not tie her up."

No, I don't think I'll thank him for that. The last thing I want to do is watch Ashley head back into the catacombs with Christian Frisk. I'm holding back only because I'm waiting for the signal.

"Christian," I call out as he steps onto the slab that had once been a doorway. When he pauses to glance at me, I say, "How long have you been a thief?"

"I don't steal. I liberate items that would've languished in a museum basement somewhere without me to save them from that fate."

"Ah, I see. You're a savior of orphaned artifacts."

Frisk rolls his eyes. "I have never liked your sarcasm, Errol. So shut your fucking mouth."

He takes half a step across the slab.

Screams echo through the box canyon from further away.

Aye, that's the signal.

The pounding of boots grows louder, along with the panicked cries of two individuals. I cannae see them yet, but I know those noises belong to Unger and Milliken, the two lackeys Frisk had sent to retrieve duffel bags from their raft.

Frisk releases Ashley and hurries to the cavern entrance, peering out as the men's thumping boots and less-than-manly cries draw closer. Frisk makes a disgusted noise. "What are you idiots doing? You don't have the duffel bags. That was literally your only task."

The men push past Frisk and fall to their knees. Unger cradles his left arm, while Milliken scratches his cheek.

Their employer turns to look at them and shakes his head. "I should toss you both into the cavern pool—with large rocks tied to your ankles."

"It-it's not our fault," Milliken stutters. "W-we went to the raft, but it was trashed. Some-somebody slashed it to ribbons."

"Yeah," Unger agrees. "The duffel bags weren't there either. We thought maybe that damn Scot hid your bags in his raft, so we pulled the tarp off it."

Milliken whimpers. "That's when it happened."

Unger's face goes pale, as if the memory terrifies him. "The damn raft electrocuted us."

Frisk aims his gun at Unger. "Stop lying. You two screwed the pooch, and you're trying to cover up that blunder with a ridiculous lie."

I resist the urge to chuckle. Christian Frisk might think he knows me, but I never told him about my security system. I'd only used it on Marilyn, until this week, and I only ever used it to stop evil bastards like Frisk from stealing from me.

"We aren't lying," Unger says. His fear seems to have waned, and anger is clearly taking its place. "Don't believe us? I dare you to go out there and touch that damn raft."

"It was a wee shock," I say. "Not even enough to knock you out."

Frisk grabs Ashley. "Someone toss me two zip ties."

Another of his men, whose name I don't know, gives his boss a pair of zip ties. Frisk uses one to restrain Ashley. Then he orders one of his minions to drag me over there so he can zip tie me too.

Frisk jabs a finger toward Unger. "You and Milliken are coming with us. The rest of your useless friends will stay here to watch the other Scot. What's his name? Never mind, it doesn't matter. Surely four of you can handle one man."

He has no idea what Munro is like.

Unger pushes me out of the entrance cavern. Frisk and Ashley follow us as we clamber over the slab and trudge down the passageway. Haven't I done this already? It feels like déjà vu. But if Frisk wants to drag us into the catacombs again, I'll play along briefly. But only until I think of a way to contain these men until I can implement the plan Alex and I had discussed. I need my bags for that.

I stop at the first intersection, glancing around as if I'm confused about where to go now.

"Cut the theatrics, Errol," Frisk says. "You know which way to go. There's only one way."

"Are you sure about that? I've had an intuition that there might be more hidden chambers, and we just need to search for seams in the walls to access those rooms."

"Bullshit." He grasps Ashley's bindings and yanks, making her wince. "Take me back to the chamber full of gold artifacts."

"All right. But you might be missing out on something even better." I lift my nose and sniff. "Do you smell that? A musty draft."

"So what?"

"A musty draft indicates a hidden chamber. Do ye trust my skills or not?"

Frisk glares at me. "Your skills, yes. You? Not in the slightest."

A cacophony of shouts and thumping noises originates from the far end of the passage behind us.

"Stop him!" someone shouts.

A splash ensues.

"He's getting away!"

Frisk throws his head back and growls, then whirls around and sprints back down the passageway while dragging Ashley with him. I race after them. Munro must have done something. I hope he didn't try anything barmy. Like something I would do. Munro is too clever for that. Right?

We climb back into the entrance cavern.

Four men hover around the pool, staring down into the murky depths. The water is agitated, as if someone or something had fallen or jumped into it.

I donnae see Munro anywhere.

Frisk glances around, at first seeming confused, but that confusion swiftly mutates into anger. "What kind of morons are you? I left you here to guard one man. *One man*. Against four of you."

"This wasn't our fault," a minion says. "He just…jumped into the water."

"While zip tied."

"Yeah, that's right."

Frisk leans toward the pool and peers down into the water. "If that's true, then he must have drowned. And we should see his body floating to the surface. Do you see that?"

"No, sir."

"Then he's not dead, is he?" Frisk raises his gun, jamming the muzzle into the man's chest. "Jump in there and get him, Olsen, or I'll pull the trigger."

Before Olsen can obey his master's edict, a shape surges up out of the water and seizes the man, hauling him down into the depths.

"What the fuck?" Frisk shouts. "Is your cousin a demon from hell?"

"Oh, aye. Might want to rethink your master plan, Christian."

"That's garbage."

Munro surges out of the pool again, snatching another minion before he sinks under the murky water for the second time.

Frisk swivels toward the pool and fires five rounds into the water.

While he's focused on the water, I sidle over to Ashley. "Shove your hand in my trouser pocket and get my switchblade."

She does what I said without even hesitating. The lass brings out my knife and cuts my zip tie, then her own. She knew what I meant to do before I had a chance to say it.

Frisk's four remaining men seem mesmerized by the pool and what might leap out of it next.

My cousin, that's what.

I throw myself at the nearest minion, Milliken, and tackle him to the floor. Then I punch him twice. He passes out.

"Watch out, Errol!" Ashley shouts.

I roll to the side just as Unger tries to grab me, apparently wanting to get me in a choke hold. Ashley straps her arms around Unger's neck and locks her legs around his midsection. She moves her arms up to form a headlock, with her forearms covering his eyes.

And I slug him in the gut. When he staggers backward, Ashley leaps off him, and I punch him in the face three times. Unger drops to the floor. That leaves two minions and Frisk.

I donnae like violence, but tying these bastards up didn't stop them. I had to go further.

Munro springs out of the pool and throws his arms around the ankles of one minion, hauling him downward.

Chapter Thirty-Four

Ashley

Frisk glowers at his only remaining conscious lackey. "Go in there, Sampson, and get that scumbag right now. I command you to do it, or I will fire every last round in my gun into your forehead. So go and get that son of a bitch."

Sampson shakes his head violently. "No way, boss. You can shoot me, because I'm not going in there with that demon."

"He's one Scotsman."

"No, he's a demon." Sampson raises his hands, palms out, and backs away from Frisk. "Sorry, boss, I'm done."

"For pity's sake, he's just one man." Frisk whirls toward me and Errol. "Where did your cousin take my men?"

Errol shrugs. "Ask him yourself."

Munro flies up out of the pool, planting his palms on the ledge, and heaves his body onto the cavern floor. Water sluices off him, dripping from his clothes and hair that have become plastered to his body. Munro's chest heaves, and he aims his searing glare at Frisk.

"Drop the gun," Munro growls. "Last chance. You have three seconds before I drag you into that pool. Three, two—"

Frisk drops his gun. It clatters on the floor.

Wow. Munro is one tough Scot. Based on the look on his face and what he just did, I would've handed over my weapon too—if I had one.

I can't deny he looks damn hot all wet, with his clothes glued to his big muscles.

Errol snatches up Frisk's gun and tucks it inside his waistband. "Get in the corner over there with your mates."

Frisk scuffles to the corner, waving for his men to follow him.

"What did ye do with the henchmen, Munro?" Errol asks. "I'd understand if ye drowned them. One of those bastards nearly killed Ashley, after all."

"Didnae kill them," Munro says. "Go out there and look."

Errol and I walk outside—and see three men lying limp on the ground. Errol checks each man for a pulse. "They're alive. Just unconscious, though I can't see any evidence of how Munro knocked them out. Go back inside while I transport these men."

I do what he said. I go back inside the cavern, where Munro seems to be keeping control of Frisk and his lackeys simply by staring intently at them. I think they honestly believe Munro is a demon. Well, I can't deny his incredible display earlier stunned me. But I've spent enough time with Munro to realize he isn't a demon. He's just one tough Scot.

Errol enters the cavern, carrying an unconscious lackey slung over his shoulders. He sets the man down beside Frisk, then returns for another lackey. By the time Errol has retrieved all three men, Frisk and his lackeys seem to be in shock. They stare blankly at nothing in particular.

"What are we doing now?" Munro asks.

"Time to enact my master plan," Errol tells his cousin. "Shouldn't take long."

I move closer to Errol so I can whisper to him, "Can I help you with your plan?"

His lips twitch upward. "Aye, lass, I'd love the help. You know what's involved. Are ye sure ye want to do this with me?"

"Yes. I'm with you, always."

He finds his backpack and brings out the satellite phone, then we head outside to make our call in private. That means we march across the box canyon and squeeze through the crevice to reach the rocky beach where we had left our raft. I see Frisk's raft too, but it's mostly deflated thanks to what Errol did to it. We stop halfway across the beach.

Errol raises his phone and dials a number.

I resist the urge to chew on my lip. We're about to lie to government officials, but it's for a good reason. Protecting the Grand Canyon treasure requires doing a few things that aren't strictly legal or strictly ethical. If we don't skirt the line, Frisk and his men might steal all those amazing artifacts that have lain hidden inside the caverns for a very long time. We're doing the wrong thing for the right reason.

Nothing we're about to do will make me or Errol rich. We won't become celebrities either. But Frisk and his men will, I'm sure, once their nefarious activities become public knowledge. Being infamous will become their legacy.

"Hello," Errol says into his phone, and he sounds quite casual and relaxed. "I need to report a crime in progress in the Grand Canyon."

I watch Errol's face while he listens to whatever authorities he had contacted.

"Yes, that's right," he says. "I want to report a crime. Antiquities theft. There are some blokes inside a cavern who are trying to run away with ancient artifacts. My wife and I donnae know what to do. They tried to take us hostage, but we managed to run away. Donnae know how long we can hide from them since they slashed our raft." He pauses as he listens to the person on the other end of the call. "Aye, we have a river guide. But he's not a commando. The poor bloke seems to be in shock and unable to speak."

Munro in shock? Yeah, right. Errol is spinning a yarn, for sure. His acting skills impress me, and I have no doubts he can pull off this con. Oddly, his ability to obfuscate the truth makes me want to have sex with him right now.

I've always been a good girl, following every rule, never even violating the speed limit by one mile per hour. What has that gotten me? Nowhere. I told Errol before this expedition started that I will do anything to prove my father had been right about the Grand Canyon treasure, and I've done exactly what I said. I've found the proof. Now, Errol and I need to convince the authorities that Frisk and his men stumbled onto the catacombs, giving them credit only so we won't go to prison.

"Aye, we'll wait here," Errol says into his phone. He nods. "On the beach, aye. We'll hide as best we can, but our river guide has been captured by those lunatics." Errol rattles off a list of numbers that must be coordinates for our location. "Thank you. We'll be watching for you."

Following a bit more listening, he says goodbye and shoves the satellite phone into his hip pocket.

"Who's coming to rescue us?" I ask.

"Law enforcement rangers. It might take a while for them to get here, but we need the time to harass Frisk and his men until they won't be able to cobble together a coherent timeline of what happened."

"You want to brainwash them?"

"No. I want to annoy Frisk. His men are already convinced Munro is a demon. We can leverage that to keep them in line, and we can harass Frisk until he's so enraged that when the rangers get here, they'll believe he's a bampot of the first order." Errol smirks. "They won't doubt he's gone mental. I see a padded cell in his future."

"Frisk deserves it, after what he's done."

"Aye, he does."

We walk back into the entrance cavern hand in hand.

Munro still stands there glaring at Frisk and his men. None of them have moved even an inch, as far as I can tell. They avoid looking at Munro, preferring to study the floor or rest their arms on their knees to brace their foreheads on them. One guy hugs his knees and rocks back and forth while keeping his eyes shut.

Frisk himself glowers at Munro with his lips slanted downward and his nostrils flaring with every breath. "Whatever plan you've dreamed up will fail."

"Donnae think so," Errol says. Then he claps a hand on his cousin's shoulder. "Why don't you show Christian how his men feel about you?"

Munro's mouth kinks up slightly at one corner. "Happy to demonstrate."

He sprints toward the pool and leaps in feet first. Seconds tick by, bleeding into minutes.

Errol moves to stand before the cowering lackeys. He crosses his arms over his chest and nods toward the pool. "Munro is a selkie, ye know. In the Celtic world, selkies are seal-people who can shed their skins to sneak onto the land and seduce humans. The males are known to be incredibly seductive and virile, stronger than any human man. A selkie can sniff out a woman from a continent away, which means Munro could find your wives and girlfriends and have his way with them. Once a woman has enjoyed a selkie's affection, she willnae want a human man ever again."

Damn, Errol really can lie like nobody's business. The stuff he said about selkies doesn't mesh with what I know about the folklore, but I realize he's weaving a whopper of a story for these men, to keep them off guard. No doubt he hopes to neutralize them with fear rather than weapons or brute force. Their fear of Munro, enhanced by the claptrap Errol just spouted, ought to do the trick. That will leave Frisk to fend for himself.

Munro still hasn't emerged from the water.

"Where'd that guy go?" Milliken asks.

Frisk smacks the back of Milliken's head. "He's outside, you moron. The Scottish jackass is sitting outside sunning himself while you're in here quivering like a scared mouse."

Unger raises his hand—while looking at Errol, not his boss.

"What is it?" Errol asks.

"Could I go out there to see if Munro is really sitting outside?"

"I have a better idea." Errol turns sideways to the cavern entrance. "Let's go out there together and see. You can all come with us to learn what the selkie is doing."

Errol tosses Frisk's gun to me.

I catch it and aim the muzzle at Frisk, who puckers his lips.

"Feel free to shoot him," Errol tells me, "if he steps one millimeter out of line. Or if he just annoys you too much."

"Oh, he's done that plenty already." I hold the gun with both hands, one braced under the grip for extra support. "Don't worry, Errol. My dad taught me how to use a gun when I was eight years old. I'd won three sport shooting medals by the time I was fifteen."

And yeah, that's true. My father believed every woman should know how to defend herself.

Errol winks at me, then leads all six of Frisk's lackeys outside. They shuffle along like zombies, but Errol strides out the door with confidence. I guess we really have worn those guys out. They need a nap and a cup of hot cocoa, the poor mercenary babies.

Yeah, I have trouble sympathizing with them.

I keep my eye on Frisk even while I peek out the doorway to see what Errol and the lackeys are doing. When Frisk makes a minute move, I tap my finger on the gun's trigger guard. "Uh-uh-uh, Mr. Frisk. Move one more muscle and I'll shoot your kneecap off. Try it again after that, and you'll be singing soprano."

Wow, when did I turn into a tough chick? I like it.

Frisk slumps against the wall, sitting cross-legged, and glares at the pool.

I peek out the doorway again, where I can see Errol and the lackeys have halted near the pool's edge.

"Any moment now," Errol says in a dramatic stage whisper, "the selkie will appear. Don't get too close. The selkie males are known to be aggressive to human men if they smell a woman nearby."

The lackeys back away from the pool.

I check on Frisk, but he's still sulking, almost pouting. Then I glance out the doorway just in time to witness Munro MacTaggart shooting up out of the pool, spraying water over the lackeys and Errol. Some of it even mists onto me. The lackeys freeze, their eyes wide. Two run back into the cavern and clamber over the slab into the passageway.

Munro slaps his palms down on the pool's edge to heave himself out of the water. Then he shakes himself, spewing more water onto the remaining lackeys. Milliken and Unger stagger backward. One guy tries to escape into the cavern, but he swerves a little too far to his left and slams into the doorway. Eyes wide, he shoves away from the wall and races into the passageway—in pursuit of his buddies, I assume.

"The selkie has arisen," Errol pronounces in a tone reminiscent of a circus showman. "Behold the wonder of the seal-creature."

Okay, he might be going a touch overboard. But Unger and Milliken are lapping it up.

"Don't kill us," Unger says. "You can have the girl, we don't want her."

Munro stalks up to the two men, while water continues to sluice off him. He shakes his head, releasing a shower over the lackeys. In his gruff, growly voice, Munro says, "The Wild Man wants to know what you mean to do with the ancient treasures you've uncovered here. They belong to the ancients, not to you lot."

"We don't want that dirty old crap," Unger says. "Take it. We'll do whatever you say."

"I say go into the catacombs and find your mates. Stay with them. Do not return to the entrance cavern. Do not cross the slab ever again once you've stepped into the passageway. Do you understand?"

The men nod vigorously.

"Go, then," Munro says, flinging an arm out to indicate the cavern entrance.

Unger and Milliken bolt for the cavern. They don't seem to notice me as they hightail it into the passageway and keep running, their footsteps pounding and the sound gradually waning.

Errol and Munro exchange smug looks, then return to the cavern.

Frisk refuses to look at them, keeping his head turned away as he speaks. "That was a childish trick."

"Was it?" I ask. "Errol and Munro managed to scare away all your little toy soldiers."

"How did that outrageous display do you any good? You haven't accomplished anything."

Errol chuckles. "Of course we did. We isolated you from your minions, and we protected the treasure."

"To what end? As soon as you leave, I will take what I want."

"Who said we're leaving?" Errol asks. He strides over to Frisk and crouches an arm's length from the man. "We've got something very special planned for you, mate."

Did Frisk's face just turn a slightly paler shade? I think so.

This will be so much fun.

Chapter Thirty-Five

Errol

Aye, I do have something special in mind for Christian Frisk. Maybe I don't need to kneel in front of him and narrow my gaze on the *cacan*, but I've discovered two things about myself today. One, I cannae stand lying, thieving erseholes like Frisk. And two, I love conning rotten bastards who work for erseholes like Frisk. Those minions deserved to be scared witless. Only eejits would believe that selkies exist and that Munro is one of them. When I stood in front of those men, weaving a barmy tale about Munro the selkie, I experienced a rush that rivals anything I've experienced while solving riddles or hunting for treasure. Only one thing outdoes conning criminals.

Making love to Ashley.

Since I can't do that right now, I'll settle for more conning, just until the law enforcement rangers arrive. I hope more than one ranger comes to help us. They'll need a big raft to hold all these minions.

"I won't confess," Frisk declares. "No matter what you do to me, I will tell the truth—that you three intended to loot these caverns."

"Ye have a strange definition of 'the truth,' Christian." I rise and back up a few paces. "But it won't matter what you say. Six men will testify that you wanted to loot these catacombs, and that neither I, Ashley, or Munro took anything out of these caverns. You've lost, mate. Might as well give up now."

Frisk huffs and turns his gaze away.

"What do we do now?" Ashley asks.

I shrug. "We wait. I don't think we need to worry about those blokes who took off into the caverns. The law enforcement rangers can deal with them. In the meantime, you and I can relax while we let Munro do his wild man voodoo on Frisk."

Ashley sidles up to me and speaks in a voice that's barely a whisper. "What about your raft security system? Don't want the rangers to get hurt."

"I turned it off."

She kisses my cheek, then steps back. "Let's play card games. I know you brought a deck."

"Aye, I did. Might as well play, since we have time to kill before the rangers arrive." I glance at Munro. "Go on, mate. Do that voodoo you do. I expect you'll have Frisk eating out of the palm of your hand in five minutes at most."

"I don't do voodoo," Munro says. "I scare people with my survivalist skills."

"Go on and do that, then."

Frisk scoffs. "Survivalist skills? Oh yes, that's the most terrifying thing I've ever heard of. Threaten me with handmade fishing poles."

What a twat. I'll enjoy watching Munro do his thing.

I find my deck of cards, and Ashley and I sit down a few feet from the pool to play rummy. She suggested sitting here. I would've expected she would prefer to stay well away from the water after what happened earlier. But she seems fine. The lass is resilient. While we begin our game, I keep an eye on the doorway in case Frisk's men come back.

Munro stands near Frisk and just watches the *cacan*.

Frisk fidgets but keeps scowling at Munro.

Oh, aye, that will work. The Wild Man is so bloody easy to intimidate.

Munro checks his watch. "Time for my afternoon snack."

He spins around and leaps into the pool, vanishing into the dark depths. A moment later, he emerges—with a fish in his mouth. He climbs out of the pool while keeping that fish between his teeth and only removes it once he's standing near Frisk's feet. Munro holds the fish by its tail and smacks it into the wall.

"Time to gut it," Munro says. He retrieves a large, wickedly serrated knife from his pack and sits down cross-legged on the floor. "You're about to learn how to gut a fish. I've used this technique on men too."

I assume my cousin is trying to terrify Frisk. He wouldn't actually gut a human being. Well, if someone threatened to kill him or someone he loved, maybe he would do that. I would, for sure. Violence is a last resort, but on those rare occasions, a person learns what they're capable of and how far they'll go to protect a loved one.

Munro starts working on the fish.

Ashley and I play our first round of rummy, and she wins. By the time that happens, Munro has gutted and cleaned the fish. I know he prefers to put the whole fish on a stick and cook it over a campfire, so I think he's putting on a show strictly for Frisk's benefit. Christian Frisk might fancy himself a globe-trotting treasure hunter, but he always left the dirty work to me. He loves to wear designer outdoorswear too. So watching my cousin prepare a fish ought to make Frisk nauseous at the very least.

"Forgot the seasoning," Munro says. He rubs his hands in the dirt on the stone floor, then picks up the fish to rub that dirt all over it. "That's better. Now I need to start the fire. Errol, mind if I steal a wee bit of C-4 from your pack?"

I doubt he really means to start a fire with plastic explosives, but I do know my cousin is having fun harassing Frisk. So I tell him, "Afraid I ran out. Would a grenade do the trick? Might knock a wider hole in the ceiling, and possibly collapse the entrance. But where's the fun in camping out if ye cannae start some trouble too?"

"Ah, well, never mind," Munro says. "I'll eat it raw. My gastrointestinal system has become inured to microbes after decades of eating whatever was on hand."

He peels a slice of dirt-covered meat off the fish, then tosses it to Frisk. "Share and share alike, eh?"

Frisk jerks when the raw fish lands on his lap. He carefully takes hold of the fish using the tips of two fingers, tossing it into the pool. Then he furiously wipes his fingers on his trousers. "You are a heathen. No wonder the British army routed you Scots."

Oh, he really shouldn't have said that to Munro. I donnae appreciate the comment either, but my cousin... Well, there's a good reason they call him the Wild Man.

Munro rises and stares down at Frisk. "Time for dessert."

Ashley and I have paused our second round of rummy, fascinated by whatever my cousin means to do next. Ashley raises her brows at me. I shrug. Her guess is as good as mine.

Munro walks outside.

A moment later, he walks back inside, carrying something in his shirt. He has the hem pulled up to form a sling, and I can see something wriggling inside it. Munro halts right beside Frisk and pulls an item out of his shirt-sling.

My cousin tosses the grasshopper into his mouth and eats it.

Frisk's eyes bulge.

Then Munro plucks up an earthworm and eats that too.

Christian Frisk leaps up, stumbling backward into the wall, his lip curling.

Aye, a man who loves gourmet food wouldn't enjoy the Wild Man's brand of outdoors cuisine.

"You are the most revolting man I've ever met," Frisk says. "Did you grow up in a cesspool?"

"Sit down and haud yer wheesht," Munro growls. "Or I'll go find a rattle-snake for you to play with."

Frisk sits down.

Munro eats another grasshopper, then dumps the rest of his booty onto Frisk's lap. "Eat up, mate. Bugs and worms are full of protein. And since ye didnae like the fish, this is the best option."

Frisk's lip curls again as he watches the grasshoppers and worms move around on his lap. "I'm not hungry."

Munro shrugs and takes up a position along the wall, not far from Frisk.

I walk over to my cousin, because I just have to ask a question. "Do ye get many dates, Munro? Cannae be many lasses who want to eat grasshoppers and worms."

He glances at Frisk, then speaks in a hushed tone. "Do ye think I'm daft? I only do that in the wilderness, when I don't have anything else to eat."

I return to Ashley and our second round of rummy. We've finished two more games after that before the alarm on my satellite phone goes off, alerting me that someone has crossed my perimeter. I'd hidden an infrared motion detector near the rafts.

"The show is about to begin," I say, rising and stretching. Then I help Ashley get up. "The rangers must be arriving soon. You and I should greet them."

"Okay. I'll follow your lead."

"As for you, Munro," I say, "your instructions are simple. Do not speak a word. You're our river guide only, so stay silent."

My cousin lifts one brow.

"I mean it, Munro. You are a mute. Understand?" No, I donnae trust Munro not to say something that will make him sound like a serial killer. I know he isn't like that, but he seems to have no mental filter. He says what he thinks, no matter what. Ordering him not to speak will spare us from an awkward situation.

Munro sighs. "Yes, I'll pretend I'm a mute. Tell the rangers I caught laryngitis from the cold water when I rescued you lot from drowning."

"Whatever. Just *do not speak*."

He rolls his eyes.

I lead Ashley out of the cavern and into the late afternoon sunshine, crossing the box canyon as we make our way back to the rocky beach. The ruined raft still sits there on the shore, not far from our raft.

"What if the rangers want to see our permit?" Ashley asks. "We don't have one."

"You worry too much, *gràidh*." I clasp her hand. "Trust me, I know how to feed people a load of rubbish and make them believe it's the truth."

"I'm aware of that. The way you convinced those morons who work for Frisk that Munro is a selkie, that was amazing. But the rangers are law enforcement professionals, right? They won't be fooled by your incredible skills of persuasion."

"Ye still donnae understand." I kiss her cheek. "But you will soon enough. Now remember what we talked about while we played rummy. Stick to the plan, and everything will work out fine. Are you ready?"

She nods crisply. "I'm ready."

We sit on the rim of our raft, which we have now relabeled as Frisk's raft, and wait for the rangers. We don't need to wait long. Just five minutes after we sat down here, a nondescript raft comes around the bend and into view, drawing up on this side of the river. The men and women inside the raft wear the uniforms of the National Park Service Law Enforcement Rangers. Three men and two women pile out and stash their raft on the rocky beach between our raft and the one Frisk and his men had used.

A woman approaches us and nods to me, then to Ashley. "I'm Park Ranger Sharon Williams. You spoke to my colleague earlier and reported a possible crime in progress. Correct?"

"Aye, that's right," I say. "I'm John McLintock, and this is my wife Maureen. We were taken hostage by those terrible men, and one of them nearly drowned my wife when he threw her into the pool inside the cavern. We were lucky that our river guide knows about self-defense. He saved our lives."

"They sound like very dangerous men, Mr. McLintock. Let us handle it from here."

"Happy to, Ranger Williams. But our river guide is still inside the cavern with those men. Maybe we should go with you just long enough to tell our guide what's happening. He became ill after we landed on this beach and developed laryngitis. He's feeling well now, but he still can't speak, and he might feel better about the situation if we're there too."

"You can come along," Ranger Williams says. "But stay behind us when we enter the cavern. You said on the phone that only one of these men is armed. Is that right?"

"Aye, but our guide managed to get the gun away from that man."

The five rangers follow our instructions about how to reach the box canyon. Ashley and I follow behind them until we reach the outside of the cavern. Then we move to the front to explain to Ranger Williams what she and her coworkers can expect once they go inside. I haven't needed to use my conning skills as much as I'd thought I would, but I donnae mind. As long as the next bit goes according to plan...

While two rangers stay outside to guard the perimeter, Ranger Williams and two others file into the cavern with their weapons at the ready. Ashley and I enter behind them.

Ranger Williams freezes near Munro. And she grins. "Munro MacTaggart, as I live and breathe. I thought you moved to Montana or someplace."

They know each other? I suppose I shouldn't be surprised since Munro had worked as a river guide in the canyon for years. I hadn't anticipated that one of the rangers would recognize him.

Munro raises his brows at me.

I assume he wants to know if he should still pretend to have laryngitis. So I shrug.

He claps a hand on Ranger Williams's forearm and shakes her hand. "It's good to see you, Sharon. Excuse my hoarse voice. I took a wee tumble into the river and got laryngitis."

"Your clients told me you still couldn't speak."

"That bloke exaggerates," Munro says, as he looks at me. "He's a hypochondriac and thinks everyone else must be too. But you know me, I only speak when it's useful, not for the sake of hearing my own voice."

"Oh, I remember that for sure." Ranger Williams places her hand over Munro's on her arm. "We should catch up once this situation is resolved."

She winks at him.

No, Munro couldn't have...

"Give me a moment to confer with my clients," Munro says to Ranger Williams. When she nods, he waves for me and Ashley to follow him to the far corner. "Best tell me your fake names."

"John and Maureen McLintock."

"You turned Ashley into a Maureen? That's a travesty, Errol."

"What's wrong with the name? I got it from a movie that starred John Wayne and Maureen O'Hara." I roll my eyes in the direction of Ranger Williams. "Did you shag her, Munro?"

"Aye. Several times, long ago."

Ranger Williams whistles. "Hey, guys, where are the six other suspects? I only see one."

"They're in the catacombs," I say. "They ran away, though I have no idea why. The doorway over there takes you into the passageways."

"All right." She starts for the doorway while gesturing for the other rangers to follow. "Let's go catch us some suspected looters."

Chapter Thirty-Six

Ashley

Munro goes with Ranger Williams and her colleagues as they enter the caverns, because she had asked him to go along. She suggested that Munro could help identify Frisk's men. But I think Williams just wanted to hang out with her former lover for a while. I don't blame her. Munro is a fascinating man.

But no one intrigues me more than Errol Murdoch.

The actual event of watching the rangers handcuff and take away Frisk and his men feels like a bit of a disappointment. The perp walk happens incrementally, two bad guys at a time, and they disappear into the crevice that leads to the beach. Another raft of rangers has arrived by the time the first bad guys reach the rocky shore. Ranger Williams had told us they'd need to transport the men via raft because the terrain here doesn't provide a good landing spot for a helicopter.

After all the lackeys have been taken away, it's Frisk's turn to do the perp walk. Naturally, he can't stop himself from complaining. The idiot knows he can't prove we did anything wrong, but as Ranger Williams drags him out of the entrance cavern, Frisk starts mouthing off about how Errol and I blasted our way into the caverns and planned to steal the artifacts housed inside. He labeled Munro as our "monster sidekick who murders grasshoppers for fun."

Yeah, I think Frisk has lost his marbles. The shock of losing out to Errol pushed him over the edge. He even starts babbling about selkies.

Ranger Williams and her team had already found the bag of explosives long before they took Frisk away. When Errol and I had moved our backpacks out of the cavern, he had wiped down every item inside his special bag, then left it in the cavern with all those hard plastic boxes Frisk's men had carried inside. It turns out those boxes were designed to protect the artifacts Frisk intended to steal, so they would survive the journey out of the Grand Canyon.

He will go to prison, for sure. Looting an ancient treasure is a serious crime in the United States of America.

Ranger Williams wants to take a photo of me, Errol, and Munro so we can get credit for stopping the biggest antiquities theft scheme in history. But Errol talks his way out of that, saying that we prefer to remain anonymous. Williams understands, and she doesn't try to change our minds. We watch from the rocky shore as Williams and three of her coworkers climb into their raft, heading down the river with Frisk in their custody.

Williams waves goodbye to us. But before she had gotten into the raft, the tough ranger kissed Munro goodbye. On the lips. And she didn't pull away for at least a minute. Then she slapped his ass and walked away.

Now, the last remaining rangers offer to give us a ride to a spot a little further down the river where a helicopter can land to take us back to the Marble Canyon Airport, where our adventure had begun. But first, we need to get through the Tuna Creek Rapid. After everything we've gone through on our epic journey to reveal the truth of the Grand Canyon treasure, a measly class six rapid doesn't bother me at all. I enjoy the bumpy ride.

Then we reach a wide, sandy beach, and the rangers pull the raft onto the shore. They had used Errol's satellite phone to call for a helicopter to meet us at the edge of Willie's Necktie, a class four rapid. Within minutes of reaching the beach, we're in the chopper and on our way back to Marble Canyon.

It's over.

My gaze wanders to Errol, who sits beside me in the backseat with his arm curled around my shoulders. Are we over now too? He came with me on this journey because I paid him to do it. We've shared a lot since then, more than just a desire to uncover a lost treasure, more even than a shared love of history. I've fallen for Errol Murdoch, but I have no idea if he feels the same way.

As we climb out of the helicopter, Munro announces that he's going home to Wyoming. Errol and I will rent a car to get back to Flagstaff. But as Munro turns to walk away, I speak up.

"Don't you want your money?" I ask.

He smirks at me over his shoulder, then saunters back to me. "Aye, lass, give me what I'm owed."

I pull out a single bill and hand it to him.

"That's it?" Errol says. "You're paying him one dollar? I thought the Wild Man demanded twenty thousand dollars. And you mentioned giving him piles of money."

"He asked for a lot more. But we negotiated it down to one buck. I was teasing him when I called it piles of money."

Errol gives his cousin a hard stare. "What's going on here, Munro?"

His cousin shrugs. "Your lass can be very convincing."

Munro turns and walks away.

Errol slings an arm around my shoulders. "I will never understand Munro, but I donnae care. I want to spend the rest of my life learning everything there is to know about you, *mo chridhe*."

I want to ask what he means by that, but the way my heart skipped when he spoke those words distracted me. Now it's too late, because we're heading for the airport terminal to rent a car. We need to hurry, to make sure my dad hears the news from me before it hits the news media. This will become a big story worldwide, I'm sure.

Two hours later, we arrive at the Flagstaff airport and board the jet owned by Errol's cousin Evan. We didn't speak on the drive to Flagstaff. I think we're both still in shock over what happened today. Errol's former partner revealed his true nature as a lying, cheating, thieving scumbag. We fought bad guys. I nearly drowned—twice. We found the treasure, then gave it up. We'll both need considerable time to digest everything that we've experienced.

I'd told Errol from the start that I don't care about the fame and glory. My only goal is to show my dad that he was right and all those people who ridiculed him were wrong. I have the proof now. We're rushing to Ohio so I can show it to my father. Do I feel slightly disappointed that no one will ever know Errol and I discovered the world's greatest hoard? Maybe. But even if we wanted the credit, we could never accept it. Excavating on federal land is illegal. As amateurs who have no PhDs in archaeology, and no experience as avocational archaeologists, we would never have been granted a permit. The US government doesn't give rewards to people who discover ancient artifacts, either, not even when the discovery is legit.

We did the right thing. So what if only four people will ever know what we did? Munro, my dad, Errol, and I will always remember.

Since we want to surprise my dad, we don't call to let him know we're on our way. Our jet lands at the Cincinnati airport, but we need to rent a car to drive to the small town where my father lives—where we used to live together, until I turned eighteen and went away to college. No matter how far we traveled to go on expeditions together, we always came home to Ohio. Even after I got a job in Kentucky, I returned for every major holiday.

My father still has no idea I lost my job and sold my house to pay for a crazy expedition. Maybe I'll leave that part out when I tell him what Errol and I have done.

A rental car gets us to my dad's house. He still lives in the house where I'd grown up, on a quiet street in a quiet neighborhood in a small town. We park along the street and walk up to the front porch. But I hesitate there, with my hand raised to ring the bell. A strange sensation sweeps over me, like a mixture of excitement and fear tinged with a sense of unreality. Is this really happening? Am I about to show my dad the proof that he was always right?

"Want me to ring the bell?" Errol asks.

"No, I can do it." I grasp his hand. "Here goes."

I punch the button and hear the chime going off inside the house.

A moment later, the door opens. My father grins. "Ashley, you're home."

"Yes, Dad, I am. Sorry it's been so long."

He drags me into a hug, squeezing so hard that I have trouble breathing. But I don't care. My dad has never been so happy to see me before, and I still haven't told him the amazing news. Maybe he's hugging me this way because I've stayed away for so long, ashamed to tell him I'd failed in my self-appointed mission to vindicate him.

Well, it's time to share the news.

Dad finally lets go of me and notices Errol. "Who's your friend, Ashley?"

"This is Errol Murdoch," I say. "We've been working together on a special project that I want to tell you about. But can we come inside first?"

"Oh, yes, of course." Dad steps aside. "Sorry to be so rude. Come in, please."

I walk inside, but Errol pauses just past the threshold, where Dad stands. He offers his hand to my father. "It's a pleasure to meet you, Mr. Hartman."

"Call me Isaac. Are you Scottish?"

"Yes, I am."

Dad thumps Errol on the back. "Don't care where you're from as long as you treat my baby right."

"Your daughter is an amazing woman, and I would never do anything to hurt her."

My father glances at me with an amused glint in his eyes. "Glad my daughter finally found the right man."

"Dad, I barely know Errol."

"Really? But you brought him home to meet me. You've never done that before with any of the men you've dated."

My cheeks have started to heat up, so I hurry into the living room and drop onto the sofa. Errol follows me and takes a seat right beside me. All the while, he studies me with a look of faint amusement.

My father settles onto his favorite armchair, the ancient and dilapidated one he's had since I was ten years old. Nobody can wrench that thing away from him. To be fair, it is a super comfortable chair. I get why he loves it, especially since my mom gave it to him as a Christmas present, six months before she passed away.

Errol laces his fingers with mine as he leans in to whisper, "Relax, *mo chridhe*. You're delivering good news."

His words and his touch make my racing pulse calm down just enough that I can tell my father what I came here to say. "We found the Grand Canyon treasure, Dad."

Isaac Hartman freezes. He stares at me without blinking.

"Did you hear me?" I ask. "Errol and I found the Grand Canyon treasure. It's real."

"That can't be."

I expected this kind of reaction. My father was ridiculed into oblivion for believing the treasure might be real. He'll need time to accept that I'm telling the truth. That's why I brought proof. I nod to Errol, and he pulls out his cell phone, flicking his finger over the screen until he's brought up the folder of images we'd taken inside the catacombs.

He hands the phone to my dad. "We took shedloads of pictures. Take your time looking at them. We didn't have time to print them out for you, since we came directly from the Grand Canyon."

Dad flips through the images. From the way he moves his thumb and forefinger, I know he must be zooming in and out to study the pictures. I grip Errol's hand tightly while I wait to hear what my father thinks of our evidence.

"This is…" Dad shakes his head. "I can't believe it. This definitely looks like the hoard Kincaid described."

"It is the hoard," I say. "Soon, the news will spread around the world."

"But how did you find it? The treasure has been missing for more than a century, longer if you count the thousands of years before that, when it had lain hidden and forgotten."

"We found it because nobody else had the secret weapon." I bump my shoulder into Errol. "I found the only treasure hunter in the world who's also a genius at solving riddles and cracking codes. Errol Murdoch made this possible."

"Not true," Errol says. "I didn't believe the treasure existed. If your daughter hadn't mercilessly hounded me for months, never giving up until she convinced me, that hoard would still be hidden underground and lost to history."

Dad's mouth stretches into a closed-mouth smile. "That's my girl. I knew you'd realize your true potential one day, Ashley. Your mom and I saw the fire inside you, even when you didn't recognize it."

Tears sting my eyes. My parents knew? I hadn't realized until this week that I had a wild side and the strength to go for what I wanted regardless of the cost. I'd always played it safe. But Errol taught me that unleashing my desires meant more than just having incredible sex with him. It also meant that I needed to accept who I am and what I want out of life. A crappy day job? No, that's not for me. I crave adventure.

Errol nudges me in the side. "Should we give him the gift yet?"

"Yes, we should."

My father's brows scrunch up. "Gift? I didn't find the hoard, you two did. The world should be lavishing you with awards and praise."

"That can't happen, Dad. I'll explain in a minute. But first, Errol and I did something kind of naughty." I reach into my purse and bring out a small figurine that fits in my hand. I hold it out to Dad. "Look at this. It's a genuine ancient Egyptian *ushabti* figurine."

He leans across the coffee table to take the figurine, cradling it in both hands. "My God, Ashley. It is genuine, isn't it? This is a real *ushabti* from the New Kingdom."

"Yes, it is. And we found it in the Grand Canyon."

My father stares down at the figurine, his eyes wide and his jaw slack.

Suddenly, he leaps out of his chair and pumps his fists in the air. "The treasure is real! Take that, you arrogant bastards! My daughter is smarter than all of you combined."

Then he pulls me into a bear hug.

And we both start to cry.

Chapter Thirty-Seven

Errol

I sit here and watch while Ashley and her father cry, laugh, hug, and even dance around, expressing their joy in every way they can. After years of being a laughingstock, Isaac has been vindicated. While we can't claim credit for the discovery, Isaac can and should take a victory lap and crow about the fact that he'd been right all along. I can tell Ashley's joy represents more than just the success of our expedition. She's glowing because she finally accomplished her goal and made her father proud. Of course, he was clearly proud of her before we shared the big news. Aye, anyone could tell Isaac Hartman loves his daughter and always believed she could do incredible things.

Maybe I hadn't realized that until recently. But I had the privilege of watching her blossom and grow into her true self. The lass was born to be a treasure hunter and to experience adventure. I've never met another woman like her, and I never will.

Once Isaac and Ashley calm down, we explain to him why we can't take credit for the discovery. No one would have ever found the hoard if they followed all the rules. We discovered it because Ashley and I are risk-takers who believe protecting the past and letting the world experience the greatest treasure on earth means more than following the letter of the law. Though I had never bent the law this far before, I donnae regret it.

"I understand why you had to fly under the radar," Isaac says. "And I'm glad the Grand Canyon treasure has finally been found, so the world will get to see it. But you two should get some kind of reward for that, even if it's under the table."

"We can't tell the government what we did," I say. "Donnae care about myself. But I will do anything to protect Ashley."

Isaac gazes at me with a thoughtful expression. "You mean that, don't you?"

"Aye, I do."

"Glad to hear it." He looks at his daughter and winks. "I approve, Ashley."

She blinks quickly several times. "You approve of what?"

"Errol. I'd be happy to have him as a son-in-law."

I'm glad he likes me, but we aren't getting married. I don't even know how Ashley feels about me, or whether she wants to deal with my barmy lifestyle till death do us part. It's a lot to ask of a lass. But she did revel in the adventure we just shared together, and even almost falling into a raging rapid didn't slow her down. Neither did getting tossed into the cavern pool. She came too close to dying then, so maybe she's lost her taste for danger.

Ashley and Isaac move into his office down the hall to discuss the hoard, so they can copy all the pictures we took onto his computer. Though I follow them into the office, my mobile rings a few minutes later.

"It's my cousin Kirsty," I tell Ashley. "I should take this."

"Go on, it's okay. Dad and I could spend days poring over these photos."

To keep from disturbing Ashley and Isaac, I head into the living room to take the call. "Kirsty, how are ye, lass?"

"Very well, thank you. How was your big adventure?"

"I'll tell you when I get home. But I don't think ye rang me to ask how I'm doing."

"No, I didn't." She hesitates. "I've been wanting to ask for your help. Luke and I haven't had any luck finding more information about Kieran, and we hoped the great treasure hunter and puzzle-solver might be able to help."

"I'm in America right now. Not sure when I'll be back."

"This isn't urgent." Her tone suggests that, aye, to her it is urgent. "We can talk about it when you come home. I shouldn't have bothered you."

"You are never a bother, *gràidh*. Let me see what I can do about getting home sooner."

"Are you sure? Donnae cut your trip short for me."

I can't help smiling. Kirsty is one of the sweetest lasses I've ever met, and of course I want to do whatever I can to assist her in the search for information about our medieval ancestor. But finding the Grand Canyon treasure is nothing like searching for a man who died hundreds of years ago and whose grave is empty. Aye, that tidbit does intrigue me. Is hunting for a missing ancestor really so different from tracking down a treasure? I've also employed my talent for solving puzzles in other ways, including when I tracked Royce Hammond's cryptocurrency transactions, which ultimately led to the discovery that he was running an illegal antiquities trade.

So aye, finding Kieran MacTaggart is exactly my sort of mystery. An empty grave? The more I think about that, the more I need to dive into that mystery.

"Let me finish what I've been doing here," I say. "Then I'll be home as quickly as possible."

"Thank you, Errol. You are such a sweetheart."

We say goodbye, and I march into the office.

Ashley and Isaac both turn to look at me.

I clear my throat. "Would you two like to come home to Scotland with me? My cousin Kirsty needs my help, and it's a mystery I cannae resist solving. Our ancestor, Kieran MacTaggart, seems to have vanished from his grave. I'll tell you all the details on the jet."

"Jet?" Isaac says. "Are you rich?"

"No. But my cousin Evan is. He lent us his jet so we could get to America faster."

"Who came with you from Scotland?"

"Ashley."

Isaac stares at me for a moment, then he swerves his attention to his daughter. "When were you in Scotland?"

She winces. "Quite a few times over the past several months. I was trying to convince Errol to search for the Grand Canyon treasure with me. Then this past week, I rented a house across the street from him. I think that's what finally broke his resolve not to go with me."

"I see," Isaac says, though he doesn't look like he understands.

"We can talk about all of that later, Dad. Would you come with us?"

"Ashley, you can stay here," I say.

"No, I'm going with you. We're a team, remember?"

Isaac rolls his chair back and stands up. "Let's all go. I've never been to Scotland."

"You'll love the Highlands," I say. "And you'll get to meet my family, including all my cousins, aunts, uncles, grandparents—"

"Let's not overwhelm Dad," Ashley says. "Your family can be a lot to handle."

"We'll start slow."

Seven hours later, we land at the Inverness airport. A three-hour drive in the limousine my cousin Rory had hired for us takes us directly to Loch Fairbairn—and my house. I don't have a spare room, so I offer to sleep on the sofa. Isaac won't hear of it. He insists on taking the sofa instead. The issue of who sleeps where becomes moot when Magnus and Piper show up on my doorstep.

"We have orders to take you three to Dùndubhan," Magnus announces. "Your mother is waiting for you there, and you're all welcome to stay for as long as you like."

"That's a generous offer," I say. "But it's up to Ashley and Isaac."

"I'd love to stay at the castle," Ashley says.

Her father lifts his brows. "Castle? Yeah, I'd love to go there too.'"

"Would you rather drive yourselves?" Magnus asks. "We would be happy to take you in our car."

"Donnae think we'll all fit, Magnus," I say. "You're very large."

"Then drive yourselves. We'll meet you there in a wee bit."

And that's how we wind up piling into my car for the drive to Dùndubhan. Isaac and Ashley ask me to point out landmarks or anything I think might be of interest, as we roll down the road. I enjoy telling them about my homeland and its history, and Ashley gets excited about all of it. Every time she acts this way, I want to kiss her. But not with her da in the backseat.

I temper my driving style for Isaac's benefit. I'll let him get used to me before I show him my wild side.

By the time we reach Dùndubhan, Kirsty and Luke are already waiting for us.

"I tried to stop her," Luke tells us. "But holding a MacTaggart woman back is like trying to stop a tidal wave by throwing water at it."

"We donnae mind," I say. "Ashley and Isaac would love to meet you, I'm sure. Let's do the introductions, then we can talk about what has Kirsty so excited."

Ashley and Kirsty become instant best mates, laughing and sharing stories while we all head for the dining room. Luke informs us that the family is bringing food for dinner, and it will be a feast of "epic proportions." My mother and Ailpean are waiting for us in the dining room. I introduce them to Ashley as "my ma, Finella Murdoch, and her boyfriend, Ailpean Boyd." No, I can't make myself refer to him as Ma's lover. "Boyfriend" is as close as I can get.

The meal my family arranged for us meets Luke's description perfectly. It's a feast. The desserts have been set up in the dining room, but the meal itself takes place in the great hall upstairs. Naturally, the feast also involves plenty of laughter and bawdy jokes, many of them at my expense. I expected that. MacTaggarts express their affection for each other via insults and naughty humor. Isaac seems a wee bit confused by my family at first, but he quickly acclimates and shares tales of his days in the field. Ashley is having a wonderful time, I can tell. She looks so bloody beautiful when she laughs, and I cannae wait to take her upstairs so I can shag her.

But after dinner, I have a promise to keep. I'd sworn to Kirsty that we could talk about Kieran after the feast. I never renege on a promise. So Ashley, Kirsty, Luke, and I make our way to the sitting room. Kirsty wants me to find out what happened to our ancestor, and she gives me the journal written by Efrica, Kieran's aunt. He had three aunts, and I can't help noticing a coincidence there.

"Were these aunts also witches?" I ask. "You and your sisters are Wiccans, and you're direct descendants of Kieran."

"Donnae know if Efrica and her sisters were witches," Kirsty says. "If they were, I'm sure they only used white magics. No matter what Simidh Gunn said about Kieran, I will never believe my ancestor was a black witch. No one knows if he was a witch at all. That's why I need your unique skills, Errol. Will you take the journal and study it for clues?"

"Aye, I will. Cannae promise anything, though."

"Just give it a go. That's all I ask." She leans across the coffee table to touch my hand. "Remember, you are also a direct descendant of Kieran. Maybe that's why you were born with the sort of mind that can unravel riddles."

I have trouble believing that, but I can't say for sure it's not true.

For the next three days, we stay at Dùndubhan so Isaac and Ashley can get to know my extended family without needing to drive to their homes. Everyone stops by at some point. It's become a revolving door of MacTaggarts and Murdochs, with my ma in residence with us and Great Uncle Torcall stopping by twice.

I spend several hours a day studying Efrica's diary. Ashley offers to help me, but I want her to spend time with her father, and my mother too. I make sure I don't lock myself away in the sitting room all day and all night, like an obsessed man who would starve just to solve a mystery. I need food—and sex. Ashley is more than happy to remind me to do both. I eat breakfast with the family, then work through lunch. But in the mid afternoon, I need a break. Ashley and I go for walks in the woods to relax and discuss the mystery of Kieran MacTaggart.

Kieran was, according to Efrica, a practicing witch who only helped people and never hurt a soul. Despite that, someone managed to frame him for stealing from other members of the family. Kieran was banished from his own clan. He went to live with his three aunts in an abandoned castle. But when Kieran's father died, Simidh Gunn tried to seize control of the Mac-Taggart clan by marrying a MacTaggart woman. She did not consent to the marriage, but Gunn didn't care.

Later on, though nothing in the diary says precisely when, Kieran was accused of witchcraft, tried for the crime, convicted, and executed.

I haven't figured out yet what happened between Kieran's banishment and his witch trial. The diary leaves many pages empty, like a black hole swallowed up the information that had been written on them. Then, six months after Kieran's execution, Efrica writes in her diary that Kieran's daughter has been born, and that Kieran himself is not dead.

His grave is empty, we know that much. Kirsty and Luke asked my cousin Ian to help them determine what, if anything, lies inside that grave. Iain used ground-penetrating radar to prove that Kieran's supposed final resting place contains no human remains.

What happened to Kieran's remains? Who was the mother of his child? If he did indeed survive his execution, somehow, might he have moved far away to escape persecution? With his wife and child?

On our third night at Dùndubhan, Ashley and I sit in bed, side by side, so we can peruse the diary yet again. She leans her head against my shoulder. I absently stroke her thigh. The one section of the diary that confounds me and arouses my puzzle-solving senses is the empty pages near the end. The final ten pages contain a genealogy of the MacTaggart clan.

Those blank pages…

Ashley stares down at them, then glances up at me. "Empty pages fascinate you. Must be a reason why."

"There is. But it might sound barmy."

"You know your insanity is one of the many reasons I love you."

It takes me several seconds before I realize what she just said. "You love me?"

She laughs gently. "Yes, Errol, I love you."

"Well, I love you too."

The bonnie lass kisses me. "I'm glad you feel the way I do. But I'm dying to know what you think you see on those blank pages."

"It's not what I see, but what I don't see."

She studies me for a moment. Then a sly smile curves her sexy lips. "Invisible ink."

"How did you know what I was thinking? Maybe you're the one descended from witches."

"Doubtful. But I've gotten to know the way you think, and the faces you make when you're onto something."

"But how did you get from facial expressions to invisible ink?"

She taps my temple with one finger. "I know your brain. And I was there when you figured out the Ellsworth map had invisible ink on the backside."

"Hmm. Not sure how I feel about marrying a woman who can read my mind."

"Not sure how I feel about a man who needs to think about whether he wants to marry me."

"Let's talk about that later." I hold the diary closer to my face. "I think I see some faint lines on the paper. I wonder if the app on my phone could bring them out."

"How about we take a break for tonight?" She climbs onto my lap and removes her dressing gown. "Give your brain a rest. Let me stimulate the rest of you."

I set the diary on the nightstand and make love to Ashley.

Chapter Thirty-Eight

Ashley

Two days after we realized Efrica's diary might contain text written in invisible ink, we decide to move in together—at Errol's house, since my rental has virtually no furniture. My boyfriend suggests I can "make the place girlie" if I want. Well, I do love pastel colors. Errol might regret giving me free rein to redecorate his home. But I will not go overboard.

Painting every wall pink isn't going overboard, right?

No, I won't really do that. But my first act as Errol's live-in girlfriend is to buy some pretty vases and some pretty flowers to put inside those vases. When Errol tells me he likes what I've done, I can tell he means it.

We haven't given up on Efrica's diary. Errol has tried various non-destructive methods to bring out any text hidden in the paper, but we haven't found anything yet. Trying to bring out hidden text proves to be a painstaking process that takes hours per page, for the simple reason that Errol refuses to give up until he has studied every millimeter of each page. After watching him toil over eight of the ten blank pages, I suggest maybe we should give up on the diary. Maybe there are no invisible messages hidden on its pages.

"No, I can find it," he insists. "I still have two pages to go. Why don't you go shopping with Ma while I work on this?"

"I'm not leaving you to suffer alone."

"Aye, it's much better that we suffer together."

"That's what being a couple means. We do everything together, even going cross-eyed over medieval books."

I lean my head against his shoulder and gaze down at the antique diary on the desk. We've been studying the diary in his cousin Rory's office, where we can get good light and a flat surface to rest the book on. I've wondered since the first time I saw this diary why Efrica would leave so many blank pages. Since she and her sisters lived in an abandoned castle, they must not have had much money. Wasting paper on blank pages doesn't seem like something they would do.

"What if there is no invisible ink?" I say. "Maybe the blank sheets are there to hide something, like one page that does contain an important message."

"We'll find out soon enough. One page to go."

Errol uses all his techniques for bringing out invisible ink, but he still gets nothing. He sighs and sinks back in his chair.

I'm sitting right beside him in my own chair, so I clasp his hand. "No luck, huh?"

"None at all. If it's not invisible ink, I have no idea what sort of encryption it could be."

"You'll figure it out. Is it possible the encryption isn't on the diary page, but hidden somewhere else?" It's my turn to sink into my chair and sigh. "That's dumb, though. If it's not in the diary, we can't find it."

Errol goes perfectly still. His gaze rolls downward, fixating on the final blank page. "You might be on to something."

"Really? I don't remember saying anything brilliant."

"But you might have done." He picks up the diary and carefully holds the final blank page away from the spine so he can see only the front and back of that sheet. Then he swivels his chair toward the windows on the other side of the room. The sunshine beams into the office—and onto the page. "Do you see unusual patterns in the paper?"

I lean forward to study the page. "Yeah, there does seem to be a faded pattern. Could it be a natural effect of the paper-making process? We did find out the diary is made with medieval linen paper, not parchment."

"No, I doubt it's an artifact of paper production." He walks over to the windows to hold the sheet up to the brighter sunlight. "It's definitely a specific pattern. I'm wondering if the page is one half of an encryption code."

"Did medieval people do stuff like that?"

He gives me a sly smile. "Of course they did, love. Medieval people were just as naughty as we are today."

"So, how do we find the other half of the code?"

Errol stares out the window, his lips compressed and his gaze distant. After a moment, he shuts the book and turns toward me. "Kieran's grave."

"What about that?"

"It's empty. Why would anyone go to the trouble and expense of digging a grave and placing a coffin inside it when no one was buried there?"

"To hide something?"

"Exactly." Errol holds the diary to his chest. "We need to visit Kieran's grave."

"To dig it up?"

"No, I doubt that will be necessary."

We drive to the cemetery just outside Loch Fairbairn, where MacTaggarts had been laid to rest for hundreds of years, until the graveyard got filled up. Errol tells me that for the past several decades, MacTaggarts have been buried in a new cemetery on the opposite side of town. But we've come here to see the medieval grave of Errol's ancestor.

The gravestone is simple: "Kieran Aulay MacTaggart. Died 1598."

No birthdate. Only his death was recorded.

Errol kneels in front of the headstone and carefully holds the last blank page of the diary up to the cold stone. He twists his mouth into a frustrated slant. "Can your mobile work as a torch too?"

"If you mean a flashlight, yes. It has that feature."

"Get out your mobile and shine the light on the headstone, where I'm holding the diary."

I get out my phone and kneel beside Errol to shine the flashlight on the headstone. As he slowly moves the diary page down, I keep the flashlight in alignment with the paper. At first, I don't see anything. But then Errol stops moving the page and points at something.

"See this?" he says.

"Looks like writing, but I can't read it."

"Because it's in Gaelic. The markings on the paper and the ones on the headstone, when combined, form words." Errol runs his finger along the line of text as he translates. "Death shall not destroy my spirit. I live on. We live on. Do not grieve for that which is not lost. Seek us out when the time has come."

"What does that mean? 'Seek us out when the time has come'?"

"Ahmno an expert on medieval Gaelic. We should consult someone who is to get a reliable translation. Give me your mobile so I can take pictures of the message."

I hand him my phone and hold up the diary while he snaps pictures of Kieran's message. "We live on" must refer to Kieran and his aunts, as well as his wife and daughter. How did Kieran survive his execution? Did the witchfinder lie and say Kieran was executed when he really wasn't? I thought witches were publicly murdered, but I don't know enough about medieval witch trials to say for sure.

The next day, we contact an expert on medieval Scots Gaelic, who confirms Errol read the message correctly. But knowing it's genuine only deepens the mystery.

We have more important things to worry about, though. Things in the present. The news of the discovery of the Grand Canyon treasure has finally hit the world media. Everyone knows that Christian Frisk and his men illegally searched for ancient artifacts on federal land, and they've been charged with the appropriate felonies.

To make sure my father gets his due, we contacted a reporter in America, one who is an old friend of my dad's and who works for a major newspaper. That reporter wrote an article about the discovery that included two paragraphs about my father's longtime quest for the hoard.

Maybe the whole world won't know about that. But at least my dad will get some of the credit he deserves. He assures us that he doesn't care about that. The only thing he wants right now is for me and Errol to get married.

It's way too soon for that. Isn't it? But if Errol proposed to me today, I think I'd say yes.

A month after we returned to Scotland, Errol and I both realize we haven't heard from Munro. No one has. Errol assures me that his cousin likes to be in the woods, away from people, but I still worry about him. He seems lonely, though I doubt Munro would ever admit to that.

"Donnae worry about the Wild Man," Errol says. "He'll come round eventually and rejoin the family. Besides, I doubt he's completely alone. Munro never has trouble finding female companionship."

"But maybe we should—"

"Hush, love." Errol drops to one knee. We're in the backyard of our house with the sun shining down on us. Errol pulls out a ring box and flips it open. "I know we haven't been together for very long, but I'm certain of what I feel for you. I love you, Ashley. Want to spend the rest of my life with you. Will ye marry me, *mo chridhe*?"

"Yes, I will. If you tell me what that word means."

"It's Gaelic for 'my heart.' And that's what you are."

He slips the ring onto my finger, then picks me up and spins us around. I start whooping. He starts whooping. The way he keeps spinning might make me nauseous soon, but I don't care. Exhilaration rushes through me, warm and tingly, stealing my breath away. When he finally sets me down, we kiss. Then we wind up on the ground, struggling to undress each other. By the time we're naked, and Errol is thrusting into me, I've forgotten the rest of the world exists.

Afterward, we go to his mom's house to share the news. My dad is there too, and so is Ailpean. Our announcement makes everyone's day. And yes, there will be a party for us at Dùndubhan. Errol says it's inevitable that the whole family will get involved and turn a simple ceilidh into a giant bash.

Lying in bed with Errol that night, I know two things for certain. We will live happily ever after, and many more adventures await us.

But I can't help wondering about Kieran's message.

Well, we have the rest of our lives to figure that out.

Epilogue

Munro
Two Weeks Later

I wander down the trail carved out by wildlife, heading to the river, where I will find no other human beings. That's exactly how I like it. People are…troublesome. I love my family, but they've all gone barmy over the past six years, since the last time I saw any of them. Well, except for the trip through the Grand Canyon with Errol and Ashley. Aye, that had been exciting. But I prefer my solitude.

Once I reach the river, I strip off my clothes and wade into the water until it's knee deep. Then I throw my body backward into the river. Ah, this is the life. No one to harass me. No one to complain about how I behave. Just me, the cool water, and the wildlife. I kneel in the river to wash myself and gaze up at the blue sky. The wide watercourse flows toward the mountains in the distance, while more peaks pierce the heavens on either side and trees populate the valley that hugs the river. This landscape always imbues me with a sense of serenity that I've never experienced anywhere else on earth. Wyoming has become my home, or maybe my self-created prison.

No, I love the solitude.

I've just finished washing my beard, so I swim toward the riverbank. My morning routine isn't over yet. I approach a large, flat boulder that hunkers a dozen yards from the shore and set my palms on it, then hoist myself onto the rock. I lie atop it, still completely nude, and let the sun warm my body and dry me off. Aye, drying my hair this way takes a while, but I donnae care. I have all the time I want.

A scream echoes through the forest.

That was not the cry of an eagle or a deer.

I leap to my feet, still perched on the boulder, and scan the surroundings for any sign of what might have produced that scream. I tilt my head slightly to the side and listen.

"Help!" someone shouts. "Please, help! I'm trapped!"

What the bloody hell?

I dive into the river and swim as fast as I can, rounding the gentle bend in the river. There, I pause to search the vicinity.

A kayak rests half on the shore. Nearby, a figure lies prone on the ground, trapped beneath a fallen branch.

"I'm coming!" I shout.

Then I swim to the shore and surge up out of the river. Water sluices off my body as I stalk toward the person—the woman. A bonnie brunette lies crushed under the tree branch, though I doubt it was heavy enough to break any bones. I lift the branch and toss it away.

"Oh God, thank you," the American woman says. "You saved my life."

"Are you injured?"

"Don't think so." She starts to sit up, and I offer her my hands to help. Once she's sitting up, she palpates her legs and abdomen. "Everything feels okay."

"Good. What were ye doing here?"

"Kayaking. This looked like a pretty spot to take a break."

I rise to my feet. "Since you're all right, I'll be on my way."

The lass gawps at me. At my body. My cock, actually. Her eyes widen, and she veers her gaze away. But she keeps glancing at my *slat* like she cannae stop herself. At last, she clambers to her feet and dusts herself off. Without looking at me, she asks, "Um, why are you…naked?"

"Does it matter? My lifestyle choices are my business."

"Uh-huh." She bites her lip as she studiously avoids looking at my body. The lass has beautiful green eyes and the sort of figure any man would love to see naked. "Well, thank you. For helping me. Think I'd better get going."

She starts to walk away but trips over a small rock on her way to the kayak. Hissing a curse under her breath, she tries to climb into the kayak. But she slips again, her foot kicking the thing. It slides off the shore, gets picked up by the current, and swiftly floats away.

"No, no, no!" she cries.

Then the lass tries to reach for the ruddy kayak, which makes her slip yet again, about to tumble into the river.

I catch the lass and hug her to me. Her breasts are crushed to my chest.

She wriggles. "You can let me go now."

Why haven't I released her yet? I take a step backward, no longer hugging the lass to my body. I point over my shoulder. "Follow the game trail until you reach the hollowed-out tree. Then turn east—"

"I don't know which way is east. Can't you take me where I need to go?"

"Which is where?"

"The campground."

I know of only one campground within twenty miles of this place. She expects me to escort her there? "It's too far to walk."

"Don't you have a car?"

"The transmission is shot. I'm waiting for a friend to bring me a new one."

Her brows crinkle. "You're way out here alone with no car? What about a phone? Can you take me to one of those?"

"The only phone anywhere nearby is at my house."

"Okay. Please take me there so I can call someone to pick me up."

Strangers coming to my home? I donnae like that at all. But I can't leave the lass to fend for herself when she clearly knows nothing about wilderness survival. City folk love the idea of the outdoors, but they donnae bother to find out what it's like before they kayak down a mountain river.

A growl rumbles in my throat. "Come with me. But you will wait outside after you make your call."

"Where are you from? You sound Irish or something."

Irish or something? I can't stop my hands from fisting. "I am Scottish, not Irish. Now haud yer wheesht and follow me."

"Um, what does that mean? Hide my wish?"

"Haud her wheesht. It means—Never mind. Just be quiet."

Escorting this woman to my home will require following trails that don't take the most direct route. That means the hike will take longer. Then who knows how long it will be before someone arrives to pick her up.

"Do you live out here alone?" she asks.

"Stop talking."

The lass hustles to catch up to me, and now that we walk side by side, I accidentally notice she's not wearing a wedding ring. Not that I care.

But *bod an Donais*, I'd love to shag her. I've gone too long without a woman.

"Where exactly are we?" she asks. "I mean, I know what river that was. But the mountains must have a name too. Are there grizzly bears here? Maybe that's only in Alaska. No, wait, that's Kodiak bears. Right? Probably are grizzlies in Wyoming."

Bloody hell, she's a talker. So much for my solitude.

Munro MacTaggart returns in
Wild in a Kilt **(Hot Scots, Book Thirteen).**

Love the

Hot Scots

series?

Visit
AnnaDurand.com

to subscribe to her newsletter
for updates on forthcoming books in the series
&
to receive free gifts for signing up!

Anna Durand is a bestselling, multi-award-winning author of contemporary and paranormal romance. Her books have earned bestseller status on every major retailer and wonderful reviews from readers around the world. But that's the boring spiel. Here are the really cool things you want to know about Anna!

Born on Lackland Air Force Base in Texas, Anna grew up moving here, there, and everywhere thanks to her dad's job as an instructor pilot. She's lived in Texas (twice), Mississippi, California (twice), Michigan (twice), and Alaska—and now Ohio.

As for her writing, Anna has always made up stories in her head, but she didn't write them down until her teen years. Those first awful books went into the trash can a few years later, though she learned a lot from those stories. Eventually, she would pen her first romance novel, the paranormal romance *Willpower*, and she's never looked back since.

Want even more details about Anna? Get access to her extended bio when you subscribe to her newsletter and download the free bonus ebook, *Hot Scots Confidential*. You'll also get hot deleted scenes, character interviews, fun facts, and more! Plus you'll receive audio bonus content narrated by Shane East, Vanessa Edwin, and Ava Lucas.

Visit AnnaDurand.com to sign up.

www.ingramcontent.com/pod-product-compliance
Lightning Source LLC
Chambersburg PA
CBHW061240210726
48293CB00003B/837